6/67 Wells

ABSOLUTE FEAR

**Center Point
Large Print**

**This Large Print Book carries the
Seal of Approval of N.A.V.H.**

ABSOLUTE FEAR

LISA JACKSON

CENTER POINT PUBLISHING
THORNDIKE, MAINE

This Center Point Large Print edition
is published in the year 2007 by arrangement with
Kensington Publishing Corp.

Copyright © 2007 by Lisa Jackson.

The text of this Large Print edition is unabridged. In other
aspects, this book may vary from the original edition.
Printed in the United States of America.
Set in 16-point Times New Roman type.

ISBN-10: 1-58547-978-0
ISBN-13: 978-1-58547-978-8

Library of Congress Cataloging-in-Publication Data

Jackson, Lisa.
    Absolute fear / Lisa Jackson.--Center Point large print ed.
    p. cm.
    ISBN-13: 978-1-58547-978-8 (lib. bdg. : alk. paper)
    1. Serial murders--Fiction. 2. New Orleans (La.)--Fiction. 3. Large type books. I. Title.

PS3560.A223A64 2007
813'.54--dc22

2007000963

To Dad.
You were, are, and always
will be the best.

Acknowledgments

There were many people involved in getting this book to print, all of whom were integral. I want to thank my editor, John Scognamiglio, for his insight, vision, input, support, and ultimate patience. Man, did he work hard on this one. As did my sister, Nancy Bush, who was not only my cheerleader and personal editor, she picked up the other balls of my life and juggled them effectively, never once losing her cool. Thanks, Nan.

Also, I have to thank my incredible agent, Robin Rue, and everyone at Kensington Books, especially Laurie Parkin, who also worked very hard on this one.

In addition, I would like to mention all the people here who helped me: Ken Bush, Kelley Foster, Matthew Crose, Michael Crose, Alexis Harrington, Danielle Katcher, Marilyn Katcher, Ken Melum, Roz Noonan, Kathy Okano, Samantha Santistevan, Mike Sidel, and Larry Sparks.

If I've forgotten anyone, my apologies. You've all been wonderful.

Author's Note

For the purposes of the story, I've bent some of the rules of police procedure and have also created my own fictitious police department.

This book was written pre–Hurricane Katrina, before the incredible city of New Orleans and the surrounding Gulf Coast were decimated by the storm. I hope I've captured the unique essence of New Orleans, what it once was and what it will be again.

PROLOGUE

Near New Orleans, Louisiana
Three months earlier

The Voice of God pounded through his brain.
Kill.
Kill them both.
The man and the woman.
Sacrifice them.
Tonight.
This is your penance.
He lay on the sweat-stained sheets of his bed while neon light pulsed blood red through the slats of blinds that didn't quite close over the windows. The Voice thundered in his ears. Reverberated through his head. Echoed so loudly, it drowned out the others—the little, screechy, irritating, fingernails-on-chalkboard voices that he thought of as belonging to bothersome insects. They too issued orders. They too disturbed his sleep, but they were small, annoying, and not as powerful as the Voice, the one he was certain was from God Himself.

A niggling doubt wormed through his mind, suggesting that the Voice was evil, that It might be speaking the words of Lucifer, the Lord of Darkness.

But no. . . . He couldn't think this way. He had to have faith. Faith in the Voice, in what It told him, in Its ultimate wisdom.

Quickly he rolled off the cot and onto his knees. Deftly, from years of practice and sacrifice, he sketched the sign of the cross over his naked chest. Beads of perspiration collected on his scalp as he prayed for guidance, begged to be His messenger, felt a thrum from anticipating that it was he who had been sought out. He was God's disciple. "Show me the way," he whispered urgently, licking his lips. "Tell me what I must do."

Kill.

The Voice was clear.

Slay them both.

Sacrifice the man and woman.

He frowned as he prayed, not completely understanding. The woman, Eve, he understood. Oh, how long he'd waited to do just what the Voice commanded. He envisioned her. Heart-shaped face with a strong, impertinent chin. The faintest hint of freckles bridging a short, straight nose. Intense eyes as clear and blue as a tropical lagoon. Fiery, storm-tossed hair.

So beautiful.

So headstrong.

And such a whore.

He imagined what she let men do to that athletic body. . . . Oh, he'd seen her before, peeked through the slit between her curtains and seen taut skin stretched over feminine muscles, skin that moved fluidly as she bathed. Her breasts were small, firm, and tipped with rosy-hued nipples that tightened as she stepped into the bathwater.

Yes, he'd watched her, spying upon her as those long legs slipped over the edge of the tub, unknowingly flashing him just a glimpse of the pink folds and red curls at the juncture of her thighs.

Thinking of her, he felt that special tingle that only she could entice from him, the hot run of blood that flushed his skin and caused his cock to thicken in anticipation.

If only he could run his fingers inside her legs, lick those tight little breasts, fuck the hell out of her. She was a whore anyway. In his mind's eye he saw himself mounting her, his toned body taut over hers, his cock driving deep into that hot, wanton wasteland where others had spilled their seed.

He was breathing hard.

Knew what he was thinking was a sin.

But he wanted to ram deep into her just once.

Before the killing.

And he had the opportunity. Hadn't the Voice instructed him to prove what a whore she was?

But what of the man?

As if the Voice had heard his thoughts, It whispered, *You are the Reviver. The One I have chosen for this task to revive the souls of the weak. Do not fail me. It's up to you who will live and who will die. Now, go!*

Realizing he was still on his knees, he made another swift sign of the cross and felt a jab of shame that God might have read his thoughts and learned of his weakness where *she* was concerned. He had to fight the lust. Had to.

And yet, as he stood, stretching his honed muscles,

he felt needles of anticipation piercing his skin, desire causing his groin to tighten almost painfully.

The Reviver. The Voice had given him a name. He rolled it around in his head and decided he liked it, enjoyed the thought that he was the decider, the one who ultimately chose who lived and who died. It was a good sign, wasn't it, that the Voice had decided to name him? Kind of like being anointed, or knighted. *The Reviver.* Yes!

He dressed in the dark, pulling on his camouflage pants and jacket, ski mask and boots, the uniform he hung from a peg near the door. His weapons were already stowed in his truck, hidden in a locked drawer in the false bottom of his toolbox. Knives, pistols, silencers, plastic explosives, even a peashooter and darts with poisoned tips. . . .

And something special, just for her.

He slid out of his dark room and stepped into the deep, mist-laden night.

He was ready.

Eve checked her watch.

Ten forty-five.

"Great," she muttered between clenched teeth.

She was running late.

Despite the fact that the night outside the windshield of her Camry was thick with fog, she stepped on the gas. Her dented Toyota had nearly a hundred and twenty thousand miles on the engine but still leapt forward, ever reliable.

So she wouldn't be on time. So what? A few minutes one way or the other wouldn't hurt.

She took a corner a little too fast, cut into the inside lane, and nearly hit an oncoming pickup. The driver blasted his horn and she jerked on the wheel, slowing a little, her heart jack-hammering.

She forced herself to relax her grip on the wheel and take a deep breath. Roy could wait, she decided, thinking of the frantic phone call she'd received less than half an hour earlier.

"Eve, you've got to come," he'd said in a rush, his voice tense. "To the cabin—you know the one. Where we used to go in the summer as kids. My uncle's place. But hurry. I'll . . . I'll uh, meet you at eleven."

"It's late," she protested. "I'm not going to—"

"I've got evidence."

"Evidence of what?"

"I'll tell you when you get here. Just come. Alone."

"Hell, Roy, you don't have to go all cloak and dagger on me. Just tell me what's going on!"

Her answer was several clicks and dead air. He'd hung up.

"No, wait! Roy! Oh for God's sake," she growled, poking a few buttons on her phone, hoping to capture his number on caller ID and return the call. But her screen had come up with the phrase "Unknown Caller," and she was left gnashing her teeth in frustration, her heart pounding with a case of nerves. What "evidence" had Roy found? What was he talking about? Half a dozen possibilities, none of them good, had run through her mind as she'd hurried to meet him.

Maybe she shouldn't have come at all. Cole hadn't wanted her to. In fact he'd practically barred the door, completely infuriating her. In her mind's eye she still envisioned his taut, worried face, and she recalled every angry word. He'd wanted to come with her, but she'd insisted on going alone. She'd hurried out the door into the cold, foggy night before he could bully his way into her decision making.

This was something she had to do by herself.

So now she was driving, in the middle of a moonless Louisiana night, toward the swampland where Roy's uncle, Vernon, owned an old fishing cabin. If it still existed. The last time she'd been there, over ten years earlier, the place had already been going to seed. She couldn't imagine what it might be like now.

Glancing in the rearview mirror, she saw the worry in her eyes. What the hell was going on?

She hadn't spoken to Roy in over a year.

Why would he call now?

He's in trouble again, of course. You know Roy. He's a prime example of borderline paranoia. The man's got his own special brand of neurosis.

So why do you always come running when he calls, huh?

What kind of pull does he have over you?

What's your own special brand of neurosis that you have to bail him out over and over again?

"Oh shut up," she muttered tightly. The problem

16

with being part of a post-grad psychology program was that she was always psychoanalyzing herself.

It got old.

She snapped on the radio. Notes from the tail end of some country ballad about a love triangle trailed into a commercial for the latest weight-loss program. Not much help. Switching stations and listening with half an ear, she peered through the rising mist. Vernon's place was nearby, she thought. Squinting, she spotted a faded No Hunting sign that had been nailed to the trunk of a tall pine tree and blasted with a shotgun several times over, the letters nearly obliterated by buckshot.

Only one other vehicle passed by her as the road wound through the swampland. She shivered, though the night was far from cool. Finally her headlight beams splashed upon a burned-out snag of a cottonwood tree, and just beyond was the entrance to Vernon Kajak's property. A rusted gate hung drunkenly on one hinge; the old cattle guard was still intact, causing her tires to rumble and quake as she entered the private acres.

The drive was little more than twin ruts. Where there once had been gravel, there was now only scattered stones and mud. Weeds scraped the Camry's undercarriage. The car shuddered and bounced over the potholes and protruding rocks, and she was forced to slow to a creep as she picked her way through the bleached trunks of the cypress trees and brush.

God, it was dark. Eerie. The stuff from which horror films are made.

Eve had never been faint of heart, nor was she a coward, but she wasn't an idiot either, and driving around in the middle of the Louisiana swamp on a gloomy night seemed like a bad idea. Years of practicing tae kwon do and a small canister of pepper spray tucked inside her purse didn't seem like enough firepower to fight whatever evil might lie in the dense undergrowth. "Oh, get over yourself," she said aloud.

She clicked off the radio and picked up her cell phone, only to note that it was receiving no service.

"Of course," she said beneath her breath. "Wouldn't you know . . ."

Her car edged forward, and she narrowed her eyes, straining to see the cabin.

Everything that had happened today was out of sync, just not quite right, and it had culminated in that fight with Cole.

How had that happened? Okay, so she'd been prickly after a visit from her father, but had that warranted the kind of cold fury that had been unleashed upon her by the man she planned to marry?

The call from Roy had sent her out here . . . into this seeping, clinging fog. Everything about this day and night felt a little out of kilter, and Eve gave herself a shake, trying to dispel the heebie-jeebies.

She checked her watch again.

In a few minutes it would be over.

The cabin was less than a quarter of a mile ahead.

• • •

The Reviver waited.

Trembling.

Anticipating.

Ears straining.

Every nerve ending stretched to the breaking point.

But the Voice was silent.

There was no praise for his act; no recriminations for not completing the job.

His heart raced, and he turned his face skyward as a cold spring wind rattled through this part of the bayou. The moon, nearly obscured by the rising fog, offered only a chilling slice of illumination in the night.

Senses heightened, he smelled the metallic odor of blood as it dripped from the fingertips of his gloves.

Talk to me, he silently begged the Voice. *I have done Your bidding as best I could. She wasn't there, not where you said she'd be. I couldn't kill her. Should I track her down? Hunt her?*

His breath quickened at the thought of stalking her, cornering her, witnessing her fear, then taking her.

But the night was deathly quiet.

No frogs croaked.

No cicadas hummed.

No crickets chirped.

There was nothing but silence and the sound of his short, rapid breaths—visible breaths that mingled with the fog in the still air.

The Voice of God, it seemed, had grown mute.

Because he'd erred.

Horribly.

And now he was being punished.

He tried to concentrate. Had he been mistaken? Hadn't the Voice told him there would be two inside? Two to sacrifice? Yes, he was certain of it. A man and the woman, Eve, were both supposed to be inside, and yet he'd found only the man.

"Forgive me," he whispered in agony. What would his penance be this time? He thought of the scars upon his back from flagellation, the burns on his palms from hot coals. He shuddered to think what was to come.

And yet . . .

His heart was still beating erratically, his blood still singing in his veins from the kill. Oh, how exquisite had been that first slice of his blade as it separated the soft tissue of the throat. And the thin, pulsing seam of red as the blood began to flow. . . . He closed his eyes and felt the rush all over again.

Nervously, he chewed on the inside of his cheek.

Disappointment gnawed at his guts.

Still he waited.

The Voice had never been wrong before.

And who was he to doubt God's instructions?

Sometimes he became confused. Often the other voices screamed at him—screechy, irritating little things that would hiss, whine, and yell at him, clouding his judgment, causing his head to pound, making him wonder about his own sanity. But tonight they too were silent.

"Help me," he mouthed. "Talk to me. Please assure me that I am doing your bidding."

There was no response, only the sound of a short gust of wind rattling leaves as it whipped through the cypresses and live oaks in this part of the swamp.

He would wait.

Quickly, pleadingly, he made a desperate, deft sign of the cross over his chest, and as he did, he heard the soft rumble of a car's engine approaching.

YES!!!

His eyes flew open.

Tires crunched on the sparse gravel.

He didn't have to see the car to know it was a Toyota. Eve's vehicle. Anticipation gave him a rush of heat through his blood as he spied her headlights, mist swirling in their weak golden beams. His gloved hand tightened over the hilt of the knife, the razor-thin blade scarcely visible in the darkness.

Crouching, he began to steal silently through the undergrowth and stopped near the cabin garage, behind a rotting tree stump, close enough that he could reach her in three steps when she walked to the door.

Her headlights washed over the grayed walls of the tiny cabin, and the engine died. The car door opened, and he caught a glimpse of her, red curls scraped away from her face, jaw set, eyes darting quickly. She cast a glance at Roy's truck, parked beneath the overhang of a carport. Then, using a small flashlight, she walked swiftly toward the cabin's door, tested it, and found it locked.

"Roy?" she called, knocking loudly, a hint of her perfume wafting his way. "Hey . . . what's going on?" Then, more softly, "If this is some kind of sick joke, I swear, you'll pay. . . ."

Oh, it's no joke, he thought, every nerve stretched to the breaking point. She was so close. If he leaped out, he could tackle her.

She shined the flashlight's beam over the dilapidated siding and onto a sagging, battered shutter. "What're the chances?" she asked herself. She reached behind the broken slats, extracted a key, and looked at it a long moment. "I can't believe I'm doing this," she muttered, inserting the key into the dead bolt.

With a click, the old lock gave way.

As she stepped into the house, he moved swiftly. He had his knife gripped tightly in his hand, and he desperately wanted to use it, to watch as it slit her soft, white flesh. But, just in case, there was always the pistol, a small-caliber one but deadly enough.

A light snapped on inside the cabin.

Through the dusty glass of the kitchen window, he saw her, her hair pulled away from the long column of her throat. His heart kicked into overdrive, and he drew a shivery breath, envisioning the act.

She'd hear his footsteps, turn, gasp when their eyes met. Then he would move quickly, slashing that perfectly arched throat, slicing her jugular, crimson blood spraying.

He drew in a swift breath.

His cock hardened.
He could almost taste her.
Eve.
The original sinner.
Time to pay.

"Roy, are you here?" Eve called into the watery light
of the cabin. She didn't know whether to be scared or
pissed as hell as she stepped through the kitchen,
where a thin layer of dust covered everything. "You
know," she said, sweat beading in her hair as she spied
a half-drunk bottle of beer left on the scarred drop-
leafed table, "this is creeping me out. I mean, if this is
one of your games, I think I'll just have to kill you."

She heard a scrape, turned. Her heart jumped as a
small black body scampered across the yellowed
linoleum to hide beneath an ancient refrigerator. She
bit back a scream with all she had, watching the
mouse's tail slide from sight. "Oh Jesus." Her pulse
pounded in her ears. She shouldn't have come here,
and she'd known it from the get-go. When Roy called,
she should have insisted he come to her or that they
meet somewhere in public. Being here was creeping
her out.

Where the hell was he? "Roy?" He had to be here.
His truck was parked in the carport. "Roy? This isn't
funny. Where are you?"

The door to the bathroom gaped open, but it was
dark inside. She tried the switch, but the bulb had
burned out, and when she raked her flashlight beam

across the sink and toilet, she saw only rust, stains, and dirt. Something was definitely wrong here.

She walked three steps to the living room, where a lamp on an old end table was burning bright. Obviously Roy had been here. . . . no, not really. Obviously *someone* had been here, though the room itself looked as if no one had inhabited it for a decade. Dust and cobwebs covered the floor, pinewood walls, and ceiling. Even the ashes and chunks of burned wood in the grate seemed ancient. There was a yellowed fishing magazine, its pages curled and tattered. It was as if time had stopped for this dilapidated cabin on the bayou.

So what the hell was she doing here?

To see Roy? To find out what he meant by "evidence"?

What the hell kind of evidence could he mean?

Something to do with Dad, she thought. *That's what Roy meant. You know it. You can feel it in your bones. Roy knows whether dear old Dad is innocent . . . or guilty as sin.*

Swallowing, she pulled her cell phone from her purse. Still no service.

"Royal Kajak, you've got about two minutes, and then I'm outta here," she called to the shadowed corners of the cabin. "I don't give a damn about whatever 'evidence' you think you've got. E-mail me, okay?"

Irritated, she took one last look around. Just past the open stairway was a short hall leading to the one bedroom on the main floor. The door to it yawned open.

Steeling herself, she walked toward it.

• • •

Shit! She had a cell phone! He hadn't thought of that. The Voice hadn't warned him about the phone. The Reviver stared through the window, watched her walking carefully through the house. He knew she'd call 911. The number was probably on speed dial.

He had to stop her. Fast!

Without a sound, he sheathed his knife, flicked open his ankle holster, and pulled out his pistol.

Time to finish this.

Nerves on edge, Eve pushed open the bedroom door. It creaked on old hinges. "Roy?"

She heard the faintest of moans.

The hairs on the back of her neck were raised as she fumbled for the light switch. With a click, the room was instantly awash in light from an ancient ceiling fixture.

She screamed.

Roy lay on the floor by the old metal bedframe. His entire face was covered in blood, and there was a huge gash on his neck spreading a dark stain across the floor.

She stumbled forward. All she could see was blood. Dark. Black. Sticky. *Everywhere.*

His chest moved ever so slightly as he struggled to breathe. Eve moaned with hope. He was still alive!

"Hang on!" she cried, terror clawing through her, bile rising in her throat. "Who did this? Oh sweet Jesus . . ." She tried to staunch the flow of blood with one hand while dialing with the trembling fingers of the other. The phone slipped from her hand, sliding through a thick smear of blood. Pressing against the gash in Roy's throat, she retrieved the bloody cell with her free hand and punched out 911 with sticky, shaking fingers. "Help," she pleaded, but the screen silently mocked her: NO SERVICE.

Panic welled up inside her. She was frantic.

Calm down, Eve. You can't help Roy without a clear head. Don't lose it. Think! Does the cabin have a phone? A landline? The electricity's working. Maybe Vernon keeps phone service for emergencies. . . . Her gaze swept the room and skated over the pinewood walls. No phone outlet, but near Roy's head, upon the yellowed pinewood walls, was a number written in blood:

212

She recoiled in horror.

What the hell did that mean?

Had Roy written it?

Or someone else? . . . Oh God, was Roy's assailant still here? Maybe in the house? She thought of the can of pepper spray buried in her purse.

She didn't have time to waste. She had to get help. The blood seeping against her fingers at Roy's neck had eased to nothing. Oh God . . .

Another low moan, and it was over. Roy took one last shallow wet breath.

"No! Oh God, no . . . Roy! Roy!" But the hand on his neck found no pulse. "You can't die, oh please—"

A floorboard creaked.

She froze.

The killer was still here!

Either inside the house or on the porch.

Heart thundering in her ears, she tried her damned phone again. *Come on, come on,* she silently pleaded, listening for any sound, her gaze moving quickly around the room and to the doorway. If only there were a back door, a way to escape.

Another soft footstep. Leather sliding over wood.

Her insides turned to water.

She carefully reached into the purse, bloody fingers scrabbling for the pepper spray as she kept her gaze moving from the doorway to the two windows, to the mirror, to the reflection there of her own panicked face. She risked glancing down, found the spray and had the canister out of her purse when she heard the footsteps again. Louder. Coming at her!

He knew where she was.

Get out, Eve, get out now!

She shot to her feet, adrenalin fueled by horror pushing her. She reached for the light switch, slapped it off. Darkness blinded.

She turned quickly, her shoes sliding in Roy's blood. She fell noisily, biting back a scream, holding fast to the canister. Her leg scraped down the iron bedframe. Her head thudded against the wall. Pain exploded behind her eyes.

More footsteps!

Don't pass out. For God's sake, don't lose consciousness!

She flung herself toward a window.

Pitched forward.

She saw him.

In the glass.

He was holding something in his hand. Pointing it at her.

She recognized him in a heartbeat.

Cole?

The man she loved?

Cole Dennis was going to *shoot* her?

NO!

Bam!

The noise slammed like a blow.

The muzzle blazed fire!

Glass shattered.

White-hot pain exploded in her head.

Her knees buckled. She crumpled to the floor. The dark room swirled around her, and Cole Dennis's angry face was the last image burned into Eve's brain.

CHAPTER 1

Three months later

"This is a big mistake, Eve. *Big!* You can't leave yet; you're not ready." Anna Maria, in a bathrobe, fuzzy slippers, and no makeup, was chasing Eve down the driveway of her home.

"Watch me." Eve wasn't going to get into it with Anna again. Not now. It was morning, barely light, the street lamps still offering some bit of illumination as dawn crept down the manicured street of this suburb tucked between Marietta and Atlanta. Time to leave.

Holding a cigarette in one hand and a cup of sloshing coffee in the other, Anna somehow managed to keep up with her sister-in-law. "You're not through with physical therapy, you can't remember jackshit about the night you were attacked, and for God's sake, there's a rumor, probably a good one, that Cole Dennis is going to be released. Did you hear me? The man you think tried to kill you is going to walk!"

At the mention of Cole's name, Eve's heart clutched. Just as it always did. And she ignored it. Just like she always did.

"We've had this argument a kazillion times. I need to get home." Lugging a cat carrier, Eve made her way to her Camry as Samson, her long-haired stray, howled from within. "No matter what you think, you're not dying," she assured the unhappy animal as she scrounged in her purse for her keys with her free hand. The carrier bobbed wildly, and Samson, freaked out of his mind, hissed loudly. She placed the plastic crate on the driveway near the back tire of her car as she kept searching for the damned keys.

"Eve—"

"Don't start." Glancing up at her sister-in-law, Eve shook her head, short strands of hair brushing the back of her neck. "You know I have to leave." She managed to slide her key ring from a side pocket, but as she did, her cell phone, tangled in the keys, popped out of the purse and dropped onto the concrete, landing with a sickening smack. "Oh great!" Just what she needed; another reason for Anna, supposedly a devout Roman Catholic but as superstitious as anyone Eve had ever met, to find an excuse for Eve to linger. It amazed Eve how Anna was forever seeing "curses," "signs," or "omens" in everyday life—so much so that Samson, being a black cat, was nearly banished from Anna and Kyle's home.

"I saw that!" Anna announced. "God is trying to tell you something."

"Yeah, like I need a new cell-phone carrier," Eve muttered through clenched teeth.

"Not funny, Eve."

"You're wrong. It was really funny." She managed a smile and looked up at her sister-in-law as dark clouds, heavy with the promise of rain, moved slowly across a low Georgia sky. Only the slightest breath of wind rattled the spreading branches of a magnolia tree growing close to the drive, but it was enough to cool the sweat that was already sprouting on Eve's neck and spine. Picking up the phone, she saw that the screen was still illuminated. Hitting the speakerphone button, she heard the familiar hum of a dial tone. "Still working. Guess I won't have to switch networks." She tucked the phone more securely into a pocket of her purse, unlocked the door, and slid the cat carrier onto the backseat.

"For the record, I'm against this," Anna said, her arms crossed beneath her large breasts.

"For the record, I know."

"You could at least wait until Kyle gets home. He just ran out for milk and cigarettes. He'll be back any minute."

All the more reason to leave. Eve and her oldest brother had never gotten along. Having her camp out at his house while recovering from a gunshot wound and trauma-induced amnesia hadn't improved their relationship.

"You're not talking me out of this, so don't even try. Nita says I'm eighty-five percent of normal, whatever that is."

"Nita's an idiot." Anna Maria took a long drag on her cigarette and shot smoke out of the side of her mouth.

"Nita's a board-certified physical therapist."

"What does your shrink say?"

Eve paused. "Low blow, Anna." She'd quit going to the psychiatrist after just three sessions. She hadn't

31

"clicked" with him and knew enough about psychiatry to realize a patient had to trust in her doctor completely. She didn't. Dr. Calvin Byrd was too guarded, too quiet, too studious. The way he'd leaned back in his chair, pen in hand, as she'd confided in him had given her a bad feeling. She'd felt as if he were more interested in judging her than healing or helping her. So she'd quit the sessions. She'd been around enough shrinks in her lifetime to know the good from the bad. Wasn't her own father proof enough of that? Not to mention that she herself had been working on her PhD in psychology before her life had been shattered at that cabin in the woods. Bottom line: no doctor should make a patient nervous.

"He might be able to help you with your memory," Anna argued.

"I told you, I don't like him. End of story."

"He's well respected. One of the best psychiatrists in Atlanta."

"I know." Eve had seen all the degrees, awards, and letters of commendation so proudly displayed in Dr. Byrd's office. "It's personal—just a gut feeling." She was already walking back to the house, to the breezeway, where her luggage was stacked. Eve passed by her brother's work van—a dirty paneled truck with the predictable words WASH ME scribbled into the dust on the back windows. Obviously he'd taken his Porsche for his morning run to the store. "Look, Anna, I'm not arguing about this anymore. You can either help me load up the car or stand there and rant and rave to no good end. So what's it going to be?"

"This is nuts, Eve."

Eve smiled gently. "Oh, come on. Things aren't that bad."

"Not that bad? For the love of God! When did you become such a Pollyanna? You were shot. *Shot!* The bullet hit your shoulder and ricocheted to your temple, and your brain was bruised. *Bruised.* You didn't end up dead or paralyzed or God only knows what else, but *pul-eeze* don't tell me things aren't bad. I know better." Anna took a long drag on her cigarette and glared at her sister-in-law over the glowing tip. "You were almost killed. By that son of a bitch you thought you might marry! C'mon, Eve. Things are definitely 'that bad' and probably a helluva lot worse. The problem is, you just can't remember."

Done with arguing, Eve picked up a duffel bag and her computer case, then started hauling them back to the Camry, where Samson was crying loud enough to wake the dead. Yes, she had big holes in her memory. But her amnesia wasn't complete. She did recall bits from that night. Painful little shards that cut through her brain. She remembered being late. She remembered seeing Roy lying on the floor, bleeding out, barely hanging on to life. She remembered the bloody number 212 scrawled on the wall. She remembered reaching for her cell phone, hesitating, her fingers shaking too badly to dial, dropping the damned thing, seeing NO SERVICE in bold letters against a glowing

LCD. She remembered seeing the gun leveled through the window before it went off. And she remembered blood. Everywhere. Splattered on the wall, pooling on the floor, making the touch pad of her cell phone sticky, oozing from Roy's neck and forehead . . .

She closed her eyes for a second and drew a long breath. Guilt, ever lurking, loomed again. Deep, dark and deadly. It ate at her at night. Cut through her dreams. If only she'd been at the cabin earlier as she'd promised, if only she hadn't hesitated or dropped her phone before dialing 911, her friend Roy might still be alive. . . . Shaking inside, she opened her eyes to the somber morning. The clouds overhead seemed even more ominous.

"The doctors think my memory will return," Eve said as she reached her car and tossed the duffel onto the floor of the backseat. She slid her computer next to the cat carrier. She noticed Samson, pupils dilated, glaring through the tiny windows of the crate.

"Maybe getting your memory back isn't a good thing."

Boy, was Anna on a tear this morning. First one side of the argument, then the other. Eve tossed her purse onto the front passenger seat then turned to find her sister-in-law standing within inches of her.

"Aren't you the one who told me that the brain shuts down because of trauma, to protect itself?" Anna pushed her long hair from her eyes. She was close enough that Eve smelled the smoke and coffee on her breath, the hint of perfume clinging to her skin.

"Maybe you don't want to know what happened."

"I want to know," Eve responded evenly.

Across the street, a door opened. In a striped terry robe and slippers, a balding man pushing eighty stepped onto his porch and shot a glance their way from behind thick glasses. He sketched out a wave then bent to retrieve his newspaper.

"Morning, Mr. Watters," Anna said, waving back as her neighbor scanned the headlines and disappeared inside. She lowered her voice and moved closer to Eve. "I'm just asking you to wait. A week. Maybe two. 'Til you're stronger, and maybe by then we'll know what Cole is up to. Stay here until we're certain you're safe."

"I am."

"He's dangerous."

Eve had already started up the drive again. "Besides, I'm thinking of getting a dog . . . a puppy."

Anna Maria took a final hit on her Virginia Slim and sent it to the concrete of the driveway, where she stomped the butt out with her pink mule. "A puppy? Like that'll keep the bad guys at bay!"

"I'm talking about a really, really tough puppy."

There wasn't the slightest hint of humor in Anna's worried eyes. "Look, Eve, you can laugh and make light about this all you want, but the bottom line is: someone tried to kill you."

"I was at the wrong place at the wrong time."

Anna tossed her an exasperated look. "You think it was Cole. You were going to testify that he shot you.

And now . . . now they expect him to be released from prison. The whole case against him has fallen apart. But that doesn't mean he won't come after you. He did before, didn't he? When he was out on bail? He called. Planned to meet with you, and you, being some kind of idealistic numbskull, were actually going to see him! What the hell were you thinking?"

Eve's stomach knotted. The headache that never seemed to quite go away began to beat slowly inside her skull. She didn't want to think about all this again.

"Cole thought you were having an affair. Probably with Roy."

Anxiety clamped over Eve's lungs. The truth of the matter was that she couldn't remember. Her headache thundered. "Damn it all." She found her purse in the car, scrounged through a zippered pocket, came up with a nearly empty bottle of ibuprofen, and tossed two pills into her mouth. "I told you, I don't want to rehash this. I'm done arguing." She grabbed Anna's cup and washed down the tablets with a swallow of tepid, milky coffee. "God, this is awful."

Anna snagged her cup.

Feeling a tic develop beneath her eye, Eve sensed another panic attack in the making. Her heart was racing, and she felt as if her lungs were strapped by steel bands.

Not now. Not here. A full-blown anxiety attack will only add fuel to Anna Maria's you-aren't-ready-to-leave fire. . . . One . . . *Breathe!* . . . Two . . . *Think calm thoughts. . . .* Three . . . *Slow your heartbeat. . . .* Four . . .

By the time she reached ten, she was taking normal breaths again, but Anna was watching her closely. "I gotta go." Eve grabbed her makeup kit, not that it would do much good. Her face was still a bit puffy, the plastic surgery around her right eye not quite healed. She placed the makeup bag beside the cat carrier, then turned to reach for her large roller-bag.

"Okay, fine. Hey! No! Stop! For God's sake, don't lift that. Just wait a sec, will ya?" Anna set her cup down then grabbed Eve's roller-bag. "Jesus, this weighs a ton. What've you got in here, lead weights?"

Eve smiled faintly. "At least you didn't say a dead body."

"I thought about it."

"I know you did."

From within the interior of the car came the pitiful sound of a cat who thought he was being tortured. "Won't that drive you nuts?" Anna asked.

"Probably." Eve flipped up the lid of the trunk. "But I'll survive."

"You know you're impossible, don't you? As stubborn as your brothers." Anna refused Eve's help as she hoisted the bag into the trunk. "And don't give me any of that crap about you not being from the same genetic pool as Kyle and Van. It doesn't matter. You were all raised under the same roof, and that's why you're all so bullheaded."

Eve had given up arguing. There was just no point to it. Not when Anna Maria got going. Logic didn't count, and the fact that Eve's older brothers were from their mother's first marriage, that they were twelve and ten years old when Eve, as an infant, was adopted by Melody and Terrence Renner, wasn't going to change Anna's mind. Eve suspected that the only reason she'd ended up living with Kyle and Anna after being released from the hospital was that Anna Maria had insisted upon it. It hadn't been any bit of brotherly love, or nobility, or even guilt on Kyle's part.

Anna picked up her cup, took a swallow, and scowled. "You're right. This is really bad." She tossed the dregs into the dirt beneath the magnolia tree.

"Told you."

"So, if you're going to go," Anna said, glancing up at the menacing sky, "go already. And Eve?"

"Yeah?"

"Avoid Cole. He's just plain bad news."

"I know."

"That's not the answer I want to hear." Anna wrapped her arms around Eve and held her tight, as if she didn't want to let go, and Eve wondered if it was because she was worried for Eve or because she didn't want to be left alone with her husband. Eve knew only too well what a brooding, moody tyrant her oldest brother could be. The fact that Anna had never bent to Kyle's will or had let him break her spirit was testament to her strength.

"Take care of yourself, Anna," Eve whispered emotionally. "Thanks for everything. I owe you!"

"I'll try. You too." Before the whole scene got any more difficult, Eve extracted herself from Anna's embrace, slid behind the wheel of her car, ignored the yowling cat, and fired up the engine. "Bye!"

Anna was already reaching into her pocket for her pack of cigarettes. She shook out the last one before crumpling the empty pack.

As Eve headed out the drive, drops of rain began to pepper the ground. Just what she needed. She had over four hundred miles of asphalt between here and New Orleans.

And once you get there, then what?

"God only knows." She flipped on the wipers and pressed her toe to the accelerator. To drown out Samson's mournful cries, she turned on the radio, found a country station, and wondered which was worse, the wailing guitar or the unhappy cat.

The rest of her life, whatever that was going to be, was waiting.

"Get me the hell out of here!" Cole Dennis paced from one end of the small holding cell to the other. He was tense. Agitated. This tiny room, with its scarred cinder-block walls and steel bars, smelled of must, dirt, and broken dreams. Worse yet, beneath the strong odor of some pine-scented cleaner was the whiff of ammonia and urine, as if the someone who'd been here last had been scared enough to lose control of his bladder. Or maybe he'd pissed on purpose to mark his territory or just make a defiant, in-your-face point to the cops.

Cole's attorney, Sam Deeds, was seated at the

simple table that was bolted to the floor. Impeccable in an Armani suit, a silk tie, and a haircut that cost what some men made in a month, Deeds looked the part of the slick attorney: clean shaven and hawkeyed, his expression serious, his dark eyes missing nothing as Cole paced from one end of the cell to the other.

How many times had Cole himself sat in that very chair, dressed like Deeds, telling his client not to sweat, never once noticing the odor of desperation that clung to these chipped walls?

"We're just waiting for all the paperwork. You know the drill," Deeds said.

"Like hell. They're stalling. And why am I locked in here? I'm supposed to be getting out. This is an interrogation room, for God's sake."

"Your case is high profile."

"So this is for my protection? So that I'm hidden from the press?" Cole snorted his contempt. "Bullshit!"

"Cool it." Deeds tossed a look to the large mirror on one side of the room as if in silent reminder about the two-way glass.

Cole shut up. He knew all about the mirror and about the pricks standing on the other side watching him squirm, hoping against hope that there was some way to nail his hide for the Royal Kajak murder. Jesus, what a mess. He shoved one hand through his hair and felt warm drops of sweat on his scalp. Just like he'd seen hundreds of times on the poor sons of bitches that he'd represented.

He cast a hard glance at the reflective glass, wondering if Montoya, that useless piece of crap, was on the other side, or maybe Bentz, the older, heavier, quieter guy, Montoya's partner. Or Brinkman . . . Christ, now that guy was a piece of work. How he held on to a job was beyond Cole. Then there was the DA, Melinda Jaskiel. She was probably eating this up. Cole couldn't count how many times he'd sat on the opposite side of the courtroom from Jaskiel or one of her assistants, working against them. He'd been surprised Jaskiel herself hadn't handled his case, that she'd handed it off to an underling.

No wonder they were doing everything in their power to nail his ass.

What was it Bentz had said when they'd booked him? *What goes around, comes around.* Yeah, that was it. Well, that worked two ways. He narrowed his eyes and hoped that pompous son of a bitch was watching him now, that Bentz was feeling the frustration of losing what he considered a "good collar." *Bastard.* And that Montoya, what a cocky, self-serving ass.

The police didn't have enough to hold him. Their case against him had been thin to begin with, then had fallen apart completely because Deeds had found some problem with the evidence chain—someone in the department had screwed up, leaving key evidence against him unsupervised and possibly contaminated. Then there was Eve. Beautiful, deadly, *cheating* Eve. She'd been ready to testify against him, claimed he'd shot her, for God's sake! But then her memory of that

41

night was faulty, Cole reminded himself with repressed fury.

Deeds had been prepared to tear into Eve, making her look like a fool, a liar, a woman without morals or conscience, one who had "convenient" memory loss. Yes, he'd inwardly cringed when he'd heard Deeds talk about cross-examining her, but had girded himself with the knowledge that she'd betrayed him.

Fortunately, the case never made it to court, though Cole had been detained on trumped-up charges.

Morons!

Cole walked over to the mirror, glaring through the glass and seeing only his own reflection: harsh blue eyes; thick brows drawn down in simmering anger; high, flat cheekbones and a razor-thin mouth compressed to the point that white showed around his lips. The crow's-feet at the corners of his eyes and bits of gray in his dark hair seemed more pronounced than they had three months earlier. He'd aged a lifetime in the hellhole of a cell where he'd been locked away. His clothes were a mess: the pair of faded jeans and T-shirt were wrinkled and still smelled of perspiration, his own nervous sweat from the quick ride in the patrol car the night he'd been taken in. He'd been barefoot at the time; thankfully Deeds had brought him a pair of battered Nikes, even if they were a size too small and pinched.

In the reflection, he noticed a muscle working on one side of his jaw.

So did Deeds. "Sit down, Cole."

"I can't."

"Do it." Sam Deeds's voice was calm. Firm. Insistent.

Just as Cole's had been with all of his own clients. That is, when he still had clients, still had a law practice, still had a house, a membership in a country club, a Jaguar, a goddamned life. Things had taken a turn for the worse. A real bad turn. Now he knew what it was like to have zero freedom, to have to do what he was told, to feel the cold grip of steel around his wrists and ankles.

Turning away from the mirror, he rubbed the back of his arm, where the handcuffs had cut into his flesh. There was still the hint of a scar. A reminder of the night the police had shown up at his house, read him his rights, and hauled him to jail. He'd just stepped out of the shower, was wearing nothing but a pair of worn jeans and was pulling on a shirt when the banging had started. He'd opened the door, seen blue and red lights strobing the night sky as his neighbors and the press had watched the circus. Cameras had flashed, his bare feet had sunk into the loam of his yard, and despite his immediate request for a lawyer, he'd been pushed into a cruiser and driven to the station, where, after being booked and Mirandized again, he'd had to wait three hours for Deeds. In that time he hadn't said a word but, from the questions put to him, had surmised that he was being held in a murder investigation involving Eve Renner and Roy Kajak.

His jaw slid to one side as he thought about it.

Eve. Jesus, he'd loved her.

Passionately.

Wildly.

Without regard to consequences.

That was the problem: he'd loved her too damned much.

His ardor for her had been unhealthy.

And she'd used it against him.

Now, not only had he lost her, he'd lost everything.

From this day forward, he would have to start over. From scratch.

Well, it wouldn't be the first time.

He clenched a fist then straightened his fingers, stretching them, only to do it all over again.

Catching another harsh glance from Deeds, he decided not to fight it. He could pound on the damned two-way, scream that he was innocent, rail to the gods, and threaten all kinds of suits against the parish for false arrest.

But that would only make things worse.

And he'd already done a fine job of that, screwing up his bail as he had. Hell, he couldn't win for losing.

The whole damned case against him reeked of a setup. One he planned to prove, once he was out.

But it wouldn't be easy. The damned dicks were determined to lock him away, to prove that he'd been there the night Roy Kajak died, to find a way to show that he had indeed pulled the trigger of the gun that had nearly killed Eve Renner.

He couldn't risk another screwup.

Even if he were completely innocent.

Which, of course, he wasn't.

CHAPTER 2

"**H**e's guilty." Montoya glared through the two-way window into the room where Cole and his attorney were waiting. He jabbed a finger in Cole Dennis's direction. "Guilty as goddamned sin."

Bentz grunted but gave a quick nod of assent. They stood in a darkened room that smelled vaguely of ancient cigarette smoke.

Montoya would have killed for a drag about now, but he'd given up the habit, his beloved Marlboros replaced first by the patch and then, in the past few months, by tasteless gum that was supposed to give him a nicotine hit but, in reality, was nothing more than a useless oral substitute. It was times like this, when he wanted to concentrate, when he missed his smokes the most. He scratched his goatee and tamped down the urge to go flying into the next room, to slam Cole Dennis up against the wall and force the truth from the self-serving jerk.

"Can't hold him any longer. The DA's dropping the homicide case." Bentz too was disappointed. And angry. His jaw was set, the corners of his mouth pinched, his lips flat against his teeth.

"Hell." Montoya wanted Cole Dennis so bad he could taste it. He tugged at the diamond stud in his ear. Though he felt a bit of satisfaction that Dennis had been cuffed and shackled, then spent nearly ninety days in lockup, had been forced to wear the stiff cotton of jail attire long enough to wipe the cocksure grin from his face, it wasn't enough. The bastard had spent most of his adult life wearing designer-label suits, hanging out at all the right golf and tennis clubs, and managed to get some of the biggest, wealthiest scumbags off on crimes ranging from tax evasion to assault. It was well past his time to pay.

But the damned case had fallen apart.

Even after Dennis had made bail, walked out of the jailhouse then been busted again for failing to adhere to the rules of his bail, the damned case had fallen apart. Montoya shook his head. The guy had lost a cool million, but he was still going to walk. Montoya scratched more vigorously at his goatee then caught Bentz watching him, and scowled. "What?"

"Let it go."

"I can't, damn it. Dennis was there that night at Roy Kajak's cabin. There was a footprint outside the door, size twelve and a half, same as Dennis."

"So where's the shoe or boot?"

"Ditched. Along with the clothes. Had to have been a lot of blood from Kajak, slicing his throat like that. We caught Dennis in the shower, you know."

"And we tore his house up looking for something— the shoes, clothes, blood. Nothing there."

Montoya lifted a shoulder. The forensic team hadn't found any evidence of blood, not even in the pipes. But there had been traces of bleach. . . . The bastard had known enough to cover his tracks. And fast.

Bentz, always playing devil's advocate, said,

"Maybe Cole didn't kill Roy. Just shot Eve Renner."

"Then who slit Roy's throat?" Montoya asked for the hundredth time. He and Bentz had been over this same conversation daily. They got nowhere each time. Every once in a while they'd come up with a new idea, only to run headlong into a dead end. And what the hell did the number 212 mean? Written in blood, for God's sake, with the index finger of the victim's right hand.

And tattooed into his forehead. The same numerals. When they'd cleaned up the victim, they'd found that chilling surprise. Was it some kind of code? A number for a post office box? An area code? A password on a computer? A birthday? The police had come up with nothing.

Same as with Faith Chastain. She had been murdered years before at Our Lady of Virtues Mental Hospital. And a tattoo had been discovered beneath her hair. . . . Coincidence? Hell! He could use a smoke about now. Maybe a drink too.

Who would go to the trouble and time of tattooing a victim? The thought of someone inking dead flesh . . . weird. Just the idea made his skin crawl.

Montoya glanced again at Bentz. The older cop's flinty gaze was trained through the glass. His lips were pulled into a thoughtful frown, creases sliding across his brow, and he was chewing a wad of gum. He might show a calmer exterior than Montoya, but he was aggravated. Big time.

For now, they had to release the son of a bitch.

Through the glass, Montoya watched as the release officer entered the interrogation room to literally hand Cole Dennis his walking papers.

Hell.

His stomach clamped. This was wrong. So damned wrong.

A few strokes of a pen and that was that.

Cole Dennis was once again a free man in his wrinkled T-shirt and faded jeans. He might be a million dollars poorer, his license to practice law in question, but he couldn't be locked up any longer.

Shit!

Montoya, his eyes still trained on the glass, hooked his leather jacket from the back of an unused chair.

As he walked through the door, Dennis had the balls to look over his shoulder at the two-way mirror, but he didn't smile. No, his eyes narrowed, his lips compressed, and the skin over his cheekbones stretched tight. He was pissed as hell.

Good.

Montoya only hoped the bastard was angry enough to make another mistake.

When he did, Montoya intended to slam his ass into jail for the rest of Cole Dennis's miserable life.

Hands curled around the steering wheel in a death grip, Eve rolled the kinks out of her neck and tried to ignore the headache that had only intensified as she'd driven south toward New Orleans. The rain had come and gone, spitting from the dark sky in some spots, pouring in sheets a few times, and then disappearing altogether when she'd driven through Montgomery and the sun had broken through the clouds to bask the hills, skyscrapers, and the Alabama River in a shimmering golden glow.

At that point poor Samson had given up his hoarse cries and, if not sleeping, had grown silent.

The good weather and Samson's silence had been fleeting, however. Now, a few miles outside of Mobile, the clouds had opened up again, drenching the Camry in a loud torrent. The wipers struggled with the wash of water, Eve's stomach rumbled, and Samson whimpered pathetically.

Nerves stretched raw, Eve noticed a road sign for a diner at the next exit and decided, since her progress had slowed with the storm, to grab a quick sandwich and wait out the deluge. She pulled into a pockmarked asphalt lot littered haphazardly with only a few vehicles. Using the umbrella she always kept in the car, she skirted rain puddles, her nostrils picking up the acrid scent of cigarette smoke. A couple of teenagers who obviously worked at the place had lit up and were puffing away under an overhang near the back door, and one lone guy was seated in a dark pickup, the tip of his cigarette glowing red in the dark, smoky interior.

Eve didn't pay much attention, just shouldered her way past a thick glass door into the horseshoe-shaped restaurant, where an air conditioner wheezed and fryers sizzled above the strains of a Johnny Cash

49

classic. The smells of frying onions and sizzling meat assailed her as she slipped into one of the faux-leather booths that flanked the windows.

A waitress carrying a large tray whipped past, muttering, "I'll be with y'all in a sec," before flying to another table. Eve fingered a plastic-encased menu, scanning the items before the same waitress, a breathless, rail-thin woman with her hair pulled into a banana clip, returned to take her drink order. A *U*-shaped counter, circa the sixties, swept around an area housing the cash register, milk-shake machine, revolving pie case, and soda fountain. "Now, darlin', what can I getcha?" the woman asked, not bothering with pen or paper. "Coffee? Sweet tea? Soda? I gotta tell ya, our chef's meatloaf, that's the special today, is ta die for. And I'm not kiddin'!"

"I'll have sweet tea and a fried shrimp po'boy."

"You got it, darlin'." The waitress left in a rush, only to deposit the tea seconds later. Eve shook out the last three ibuprofen from the bottle in her purse then washed down the pills with a long swallow of tea and prayed they'd take effect soon. She wondered fleetingly if Anna Maria had been right, if she wasn't ready for this trip.

Don't go there. You'll be fine. Just as soon as you get home.

She closed her eyes. *Home.* It seemed like forever since she'd walked up the familiar steps of the old Victorian house in the Garden District. She envisioned its steep gables, paned, watery-glassed windows, del-

50

icate gingerbread décor, and the turret . . . Oh Lord, the turret she loved, the tower room Nana had dubbed "Eve's little Eden." From that high tower, looking over the other rooftops and trees, she felt as if she could see all of the world.

Crash! A tray of glassware hit the floor, glass splintering. "Oh no!"

Eve nearly leapt from the booth. Her heart pounded erratically as flashes of memory cut through her mind. Blinking rapidly, she was once again standing in that darkened cabin, the muzzle of a gun spewing fire, glass shattering loudly, and Cole's harsh face glaring at her. She glanced down, saw that both her fists were curled. Her breathing was thin and ragged. Slowly she unclenched her fingers, counting to ten. It was only an accident. Eve could see a busboy already rounding the corner with a broom and dustpan as a girl no older than sixteen, flushed and embarrassed, apologized all over herself for losing control of the tray.

Quit jumping at shadows, Eve silently scolded herself as she turned her attention out the window. The storm was really going at it. Rain slanted across the parking lot, blurring her view of the freeway ramp and traffic. Her cell phone rang, startling her, and she banged her knee against the table.

"Damn."

Dr. Byrd's right: you're a head case.

She answered the phone on the second ring, carrying it to the foyer, where she might have a chance at privacy. Caller ID displayed Anna Maria's number, and her sister-in-law's picture flashed onto the small screen. "Hey there," Eve answered, her heart rate finally slowing a bit.

"Where are you?" Anna demanded.

"Not far from Mobile."

"So you haven't heard?"

"I guess not. Heard what?"

"Cole was released today. Just like I told you. All charges dropped."

Eve's stomach clenched. "We knew this was going to happen."

"But on the same day you decide to return to New Orleans? What're the chances of that? It's a bad sign, Eve, I swear. I know you don't believe in it, but I'm tellin' ya, there are forces at work that we just don't understand. Unless you knew about this and that's why you were so hell-bent to leave today."

Eve heard the hint of accusation in Anna Maria's voice. "I had no idea," she said, which was the God's honest truth.

"Then it's a coincidence."

Better than a sign from God.

"It's all over the news," Anna went on, "but I figured if you didn't have the radio on, you wouldn't have heard, and you know what they say, 'Forewarned is forearmed.' "

"Thanks for the forearming."

"That man is dangerous to you, Eve. We both know it. If not physically, then emotionally."

"I'm *over* him, Anna. I thought we were clear on that."

"Yeah, right."

"I mean it. When someone points a gun at you, you kinda lose all that warm, touchy-feely feeling you had for him."

"Good," Anna said, though she didn't sound all that convinced. "Keep those thoughts and watch your back. If you need to, you can always turn around and come back here."

"Thanks, I'll keep it in mind." But she was lying. She was going home, period. She hung up, refusing to let the thought of bumping into Cole again intimidate her. However, as she reentered the restaurant, she turned in the opposite direction from her booth, down a darkened hallway and past a cigarette machine to the bar, where a couple of men hanging out at the counter were sipping beers. Another twenty-something guy with tattoos covering his forearms was sharpening his skills by playing pool solo, and the televisions over the bar were turned to sports stations. No image of Cole Dennis leaving a police station in the company of his high-powered lawyer, saying "No comment" as he avoided a gauntlet of reporters with microphones and ducked into a waiting car, played on any of the screens.

Get over it, she told herself as she returned to her table, where an oval plate held her steaming po'boy, a slice of corn bread, and a cup of coleslaw. Butter oozed and melted across the corn bread while the cabbage nearly drowned in the dressing. Eve's appetite had all but disappeared with Anna Maria's phone call, but she slid into her seat and bit into the sandwich. *Nourishment,* she reminded herself, barely tasting the spicy fried shrimp as she chewed.

What would she say if she ran into Cole? What would *he* say? Would he avoid her? Or try to find her? She swallowed another tasteless bite of the sandwich and tried not to remember his penetrating blue eyes, thick, dark hair, and severe jaw. But that proved impossible, and as she stared out at the gloom, her mind's eye saw him as he'd been when they first met.

It had been on the wide porch of her father's house. Cole had been sitting on a stool, leaning forward, tanned arms resting on his jean-covered knees, dark hair badly in need of a haircut, a day's worth of beard shadow darkening that defined jaw.

She'd mistaken him for a farmhand as she'd parked her old Volkswagen bug and hauled her suitcase out of the backseat. The dust the VW's tires kicked up had slowly settled onto the sparse gravel on that sweltering summer day. She'd been sweating from the drive—the VW's air-conditioning unit had long since given out—and her T-shirt was sticking to her back, her clothes damp and uncomfortable as she walked up the path. Cole stood, stretching to his six-foot-two-inch height, as her father's old Jack Russell terrier mix scrambled to his feet and bounded down the worn steps to greet her excitedly.

"Let me help you with those," Cole offered. His

voice held the hint of a west Texas drawl. She almost expected a "ma'am" or "miss" to be added.

"No need. Got it. I'm fine. Hi, Rufus," she said, bending down to pet the wiggling, whining dog.

Her father, pale, looking as if he'd aged twenty years in the few months since spring break, rose stiffly to his feet, his knees popping loudly. "Hi, baby," he said as she walked up the flagstone path and steps, Rufus at her heels. Terrence hugged her fiercely even though she was still holding on to her duffel bag. He pressed a kiss to her temple, and she smelled it then, the faint scent of whiskey that had been with him more and more often in the past few years. She felt awkward and gangly and foolish as her father released her, and she found the stranger staring at her with eyes so intense, her heart did a foolish hiccup. "Eve, this is Cole Dennis. Cole, my daughter."

"Glad to meet ya," Cole said, extending his hand.

"Hi." She hiked her bag to her shoulder and shot out her arm.

His calloused fingers folded over hers, and he gave her palm a swift, quick shake before he let go.

"Cole is my attorney," her father added, sitting down again. She noticed the small glass on the table, ice cubes melting in the heat while overhead a wasp worked diligently on a small mud nest tucked under the eaves.

"Your attorney?" she repeated, taken aback. "A lawyer?" She tried not to stare at the disreputable state of his clothes—the worn jeans, rumpled, sweat-stained shirt, and battered running shoes that looked ready for a dumpster. Nor did she turn her attention back to the gravel lot in front of the garage and the unfamiliar, dented, and dusty pickup that was parked beneath the leafy branches of a pecan tree.

A slow smile spread across Cole's jaw, as if he were reading her thoughts. "That's right, ma'am," he drawled, and there was that Southern deference she'd expected, along with a tiny glint of amusement in eyes that hovered somewhere between blue and gray.

"What kind of lawyer?"

"Defense," her father said, settling into his chair heavily. "I'm being sued. Malpractice." He made a wave with the fingers of his right hand as if to dismiss a bothersome fly as he picked up his drink with his other. "It's . . . a headache. It'll go away." But the bits of melting ice cubes in his glass clinked, and she noticed that his right hand shook a bit. And the beads of sweat clustered in the thinning strands of his straight hair were unusual for him, even on a hot day.

"So everything's okay. Or gonna be?"

"Of course." Her father smiled tightly. Falsely.

She glanced back at Cole. All signs of amusement had faded from his angular features and deep-set eyes, and in an instant he seemed to transform from a laid-back ranch hand to something else, something keener and sharp edged, something honed. She didn't ask the question, but it hung there.

"Your father's innocent," he assured her. "Don't worry."

"Innocent of what?"

"It's just a little malpractice thing," Terrence Renner muttered again, taking a sip from his glass.

"I don't understand."

The two men exchanged swift glances. Her father gave a quick nod to Cole and then, carrying his now-empty glass, walked to a glass-topped cart where a bottle of Crown Royal Whiskey sat near an ice bucket.

"Civil suit. Wrongful death," Cole explained.

Enlightenment followed. "This is about Tracy Aliota again, isn't it? I thought the police said you weren't responsible, that you couldn't have predicted her suicide, that releasing her from the hospital was normal procedure." She stared at her father's back, watching his shoulders slump beneath the fine silk of his shirt as he added a "splash" of amber liquor to his glass.

Cole cut in. "This is different. It's a lawsuit instigated by the family. It's not about homicide or—"

"I *know* the difference!" she rounded on him. Her face was hot, flushed. The anger and fear she'd been dealing with ever since first hearing that one of her father's patients had swallowed so many pills that no amount of stomach pumping and resuscitation had been able to save her life, came back full force. Tracy Aliota had been under Dr. Terrence Renner's care ever since her first attempt at suicide at thirteen.

"But how . . . I mean, can *they* do this? Legally?"

"If they find a lawyer willing to take the case . . . then they're in business," Cole said.

Eve closed her eyes, hearing the mosquitoes buzzing

over the sounds of a tractor chugging in a nearby field. The trill of a whippoorwill sounded. Everything seemed so perfect, so easy and somnolent. She wanted it to be that way, but it wasn't. "Damn it," she whispered.

Finally she opened her eyes again, only to find Cole staring at her.

"You okay?"

Of course I'm not okay! "Just dandy," she responded tightly.

"It'll be all right." Her father was swirling his drink, ice cubes dancing in the late afternoon sunlight. His voice lacked enthusiasm. And conviction.

"Is that true?" Eve asked Cole, who had rested a hip against the porch railing as Terrence lifted the bottle of Crown Royal, his glance a silent offering to his guest.

Cole shook his head. "No, thanks."

"I asked if everything will be all right," Eve reminded.

"I'll do my best." Again that hint of Texas flavored Cole's words.

"And you're good?"

A ghost of a smile tugged at the corner of his mouth. Beneath the worn Levis, ratty T-shirt, and "Aw-shucks, ma'am" attitude, he was a cocky son of a bitch.

"He's the best money can buy," her father said.

She stared straight at Cole. "Is that right?"

"I'd like to think so." Was there just the suggestion of a twinkle in those deep-set eyes? Almost as if he were flirting with her . . . or even baiting her.

Whistling to the dog, she picked up her duffel bag and opened the screen door. "I guess we'll find out."

And she had. Inside a dark-paneled Louisiana courtroom where ceiling fans battled the heat and Judge Remmy Mathias, a huge African-American man with a slick, balding head and glasses perched on the end of his nose, fought a summer cold, the trial had played out. Cole Dennis, the scruffy would-be attorney, had morphed into a slick, sharp lawyer. Dressed in tailored suits, crisp shirts, expensive ties, and a serious countenance that often showed just a glimmer of humor, Cole was charming enough to woo even the most reticent jurors into believing that Dr. Terrence Renner had done everything in his power to preserve and keep Tracy Aliota's sanity and well-being. Cole Dennis indeed proved himself to be worth every shiny penny of his fee.

And over that summer, Eve had fallen hopelessly in love with Cole, a man as comfortable astride a stubborn quarter horse as he was while pleading a case in a courtroom. A private, guarded individual who, when called upon, could play to judge and jury as well as to the cameras.

He'd been amused that Eve initially thought him unworthy in his disreputable jeans and running shoes, and it was weeks before he explained to Eve that her father had called him and told him to "drop everything" to meet with him at the old man's house. Cole had been helping a friend move at the time and on the way home had stopped by the old farm to do Renner's bidding.

In the end, after days of testimony in that small hundred-year-old courtroom, her father had been acquitted of any wrongdoing.

And Eve, watching from the back of the room, had grown to wonder if justice truly had been served.

CHAPTER 3

Sam Deeds nosed his BMW to the cracked curb of the street surrounding Cole's new home—a hundred-and-fifty-year-old bungalow that was the kind of place described as a "handyman's dream" in a real estate ad. The front porch sagged, the gutters were rusted, the roof had been patched with a faded rainbow of shingles, and several of the original wood-encased windows had been replaced sometime in the past half century with aluminum frames. Cars were parked on both sides of the narrow, bumpy concrete of the street, crowding each other.

"Home, sweet home," Cole muttered under his breath as he climbed out of the passenger side of Deeds's BMW 760.

"Hey, I said you could crash with me for a while."

"You mean with you and Lynne and your two kids. And Lynne's pregnant again, right? Thanks, but I think I'll pass."

Deeds had the good grace not to look too relieved that his friend hadn't taken him up on his offer. No doubt Lynne and Sam's daughters might not have been so eager to have a near-miss felon sharing their roof.

"Fine. But if you change your mind, the offer stands."

"I'll be okay here." He noticed a faded red Jeep parked before a sagging garage. "Is that mine?"

"Not until you fill out the paperwork, but, yeah, essentially it's yours. I bought it from a cousin. Runs great, drinks a bit of oil, and has a little over two hundred thousand on the engine."

"Just broken in."

"That's what I thought. The tires are decent, and I figured you might want a set of wheels."

"Seein' how you had to sell the Jag."

"Seein' how."

Cole eyed the beaten Jeep and gave a quick nod of approval. "I like it."

"Fill out the papers. The title's in the glove box, locked with a second set of keys, a copy of the bill of sale, and the registration."

Deeds popped the trunk of his 760, and Cole pulled out a slim black briefcase and fatter laptop bag. Deeds had managed to retrieve the two small cases from the police. No doubt the hard drive on the computer had been compromised and all of the information on Cole's cell phone, Palm Pilot, and personal files was no longer private. After all, he'd been considered a criminal. Probably still was, in some circles. At least Deeds had gotten his stuff back; that was all that really mattered.

He grabbed his things and glanced again at his new home, if you could call it that. The ramshackle cottage was a far cry from his last house, an Italianate two-story manor whose exterior still boasted its original cast-iron grillwork and wide porticos cooled by slow-turning ceiling fans and shaded by centuries-old live oaks. The interior had been renovated to its original charm with gleaming hardwood and marble floors, smooth granite and marble countertops, shiny white baseboards and doors, built-in pine and glass book-cases in the library, and a wrought-iron and wooden staircase that swept from the grand foyer to the library and bedrooms located above. Outside, behind thickets of crepe myrtle hedges, cut into the smooth stones of the backyard, was a lap pool that he used each morning before the sun had come up, before he drove his Jaguar into the private parking lot of the offices of O'Black, Sullivan and Kravitz, Attorneys at Law.

What was it his pa had said not long before he'd taken off? "The higher they climb, the harder they fall." His old man had been a bastard, a part-time preacher, part-time grifter, and full-time loser, but he'd left his only son with a dog-eared Bible and a few pearls of wisdom.

Maybe old Isaac Dennis had been right. Cole certainly had experienced his own personal tumble. Nearly to hell. This pathetic little cottage only served to remind him of that.

As if reading his thoughts, Deeds said, "It was the best I could do."

"This place is just my style," Cole lied, managing the kind of conspiratorial smile he'd been known to flash a jury when cross-examining a witness and closing in for the kill. He'd never looked smug or self-righteous, just not surprised when the prosecution's star witness was led down the garden path, trapped into admitting things he or she had tried to hide.

"Give me a break," Deeds said. "Think of it as temporary."

"Now you give *me* a break." He and Deeds both knew that not only his credit but his reputation had been destroyed in the past quarter of a year. His once-sizable bank account had withered to a few thousand bucks. His house, Jaguar, and job had disappeared. But he was still good with his hands, able to fix about anything broken, so Deeds had somehow convinced the owner of this shack to rent to him despite his current lack of employment.

"I need a job." Cole rubbed a hand around the back of his neck. Jesus, he hated asking for anything from anyone.

"We're working on that."

By "we," Deeds meant the partners at the law firm, where Cole had once been their brightest star. Now his license to practice law had been suspended and was currently "under review."

"You can still clerk at the firm."

Cole nodded. He'd swallow his pride if it meant getting a paycheck, but it still stuck in his craw that the very interns and law students he'd mentored would now be higher on the food chain than he'd be. Well, so be it. He'd been in tight spots before and had always landed on his feet.

He'd do it again.

Besides, he had a plan. One he couldn't tell Deeds about. A plan that was his personal secret.

A gust of wind swept down the street, trailing after a rumbling, converted bus spewing exhaust. The driver ground the gears as he reached the intersection, and somewhere, a few houses down, a dog barked. Lights began to glow in some of the neighboring windows though night was still far off. A few kids played on skateboards and bikes, and rap music blared from a beat-up garage two doors down, where a couple of twenty-something men were working on the engine of an older Pontiac.

"I had a moving company put your stuff inside. Still in boxes, I'm afraid." Deeds handed him a small ring with two keys, one for the house, the other for the Jeep.

Cole managed another wry smile. "It's not as if I don't have some time on my hands."

Deeds snorted. It was almost a laugh. Almost. "So, I'll be talkin' to ya."

"Yeah." Cole stuck out his hand. "Thanks, Sam."

Deeds grabbed Cole's palm. Squeezed hard. "Stay out of trouble."

"I will."

"I mean it." Deeds didn't let go of Cole's hand. "And for God's sake, don't go looking up Eve or anyone associated with Roy's death, okay? It's a closed chapter."

"Of course it is," he said, forcing conviction into his tone as Deeds finally dropped his hand. He had to play this carefully. No one could suspect what he intended to do.

Deeds's eyes narrowed as if he weren't buying Cole's new attitude. Thin lines of frustration were etched on the lawyer's high forehead. "Just so we're on the same page. Whoever killed Kajak has either left the vicinity or is laying low."

"Or is dead."

Deeds held up a hand, silently warning Cole not to say anything else. "Maybe. Doesn't matter. You keep your nose clean. You and I both know that you're not the New Orleans PD's favorite son, so don't give them anything to work with. We've still got that small charge to deal with."

Cole's jaw tightened when he thought about the misdemeanor that was still smudging his record. "I was set up," he muttered through lips that didn't move. "I haven't smoked dope since I was an undergrad."

"Even if I believe you, the weed was found in your glove box while you were out on bail."

The muscles in Cole's jaw tightened even more, and his fingers were clenched so tightly over the handle of his briefcase that he knew his knuckles had blanched. "Someone yanked the taillight fuse of my Jag to make certain I'd be pulled over. When I reached for my registration, the bag of marijuana fell out. If the stuff was mine, would I have been so stupid? So careless?"

"Hey, you don't have to convince me. But I still have to clean it up. Get it off your record."

Cole swore under his breath.

Deeds touched him on the arm. "So the pot wasn't yours. So someone set you up. Okay. I believe you. But you're the one who broke bail. You knew the terms, that you weren't supposed to talk to anyone involved in the case, and you couldn't help yourself."

Cole couldn't argue that one. He'd tried to contact Eve and had paid the price.

"Stay away from her, man," Deeds advised, lowering his voice as if the kid jumping the curb on his skateboard could hear or care about their conversation. "She's bad news." Deeds's cell phone rang, and he slipped it out of the clip on his belt. "Deeds." A pause. "Oh hell . . . Look, I'm on my way." He checked his watch, mouthed, "I've got to go," and when Cole nodded, he sketched a wave, folded himself into his BMW, found his earbud, and switched to the hands-free mode of his cell as he turned the ignition.

As the sleek car roared away from the curb, Cole headed inside, but he knew he wasn't going to take Deeds's advice. One of his first acts as a free man would be to confront Eve.

Hang the consequences.

She had to keep moving.

Couldn't waste time.

Eve headed to the cash register, pulling out bills.

She didn't want to think about her father's culpability or innocence or anything else about the trial. It was all water under the bridge, and the fact that she'd wondered if Roy Kajak's reference to "evidence" had something to do with Tracy Aliota's death was just her own way of admitting she didn't completely trust the father she'd thought she loved.

She finished paying her bill and walked outside to a day that was even gloomier than before. Purple clouds scraped the tops of the spindly pines in the perimeter of the lot. Raindrops pounded and splashed on the cracked asphalt, forcing Eve to make a mad dash to her car.

Samson howled in his cage, and as she shushed him she spied water on the passenger seat. Swearing under her breath, she grabbed the towel she kept in the car for just such emergencies. In the past few weeks the window had begun to slip a bit, refusing to seal. Kyle had looked at it a couple of times but hadn't been able to repair the damned thing. She mopped up the small puddle then leaned across the bucket seat, pressed on the button to raise the window, and heard the electric motor whine to no avail. The glass didn't budge. She'd just have to live with it and call a mechanic once she got home.

If she ever made it.

Her headache had dulled, the edges softening, and she wasn't going to let something as inconsequential as the broken window bother her. She could even put up with Samson's now-intermittent mewling.

She drove out of the lot and onto a side street before locating the ramp to the freeway again. Nosing her Toyota into the flow of traffic heading toward the gulf, she tried to relax. So Cole was a free man. So what? She wondered if he would return to New Orleans. Her sister-in-law was right about one thing: it was damned ironic that he had regained his freedom on the very day she decided to take the reins of her life again.

Fate?

Coincidence?

Or just bad luck?

Not that it mattered.

Because she wanted to see him again. Intended to face the bastard.

She had a hell of a lot of questions for him.

Within a few miles, the rain let up then stopped completely. Her wipers were suddenly scraping and screeching against the glass, and sunlight, so long filtered by the clouds, bounced off the pavement in bright, blinding shafts. Maybe things were getting better. Even the cat had stopped crying. Eve switched off the wipers just as her cell phone jangled. With one eye on the road, she pulled the phone from a side pocket of her purse and flipped it open.

She put the phone to her ear. "Hello?"

"He's free," a raspy voice hissed.

"Excuse me?"

The phone went instantly dead.

"Hello . . . ?"

A tingle of fear plucked at her spine.

She wanted to think that someone had dialed her incorrectly, that the call had been a mistake, but she knew differently. The message was meant for her, to tell her that Cole had been released from prison.

"No shit, Sherlock," she muttered, scowling as she tried to read the display on the small screen. Caller ID failed her: *Unknown Number* was all she learned for her efforts.

She dropped the phone into the pocket of her purse again and fought a tiny drip of panic. So some idiot had called to . . . what? Inform her? Warn her? Scare her? So what?

It was no big deal.

Then why did whoever called hang up?

Why not finish the conversation?

The gravelly, almost hissing timbre of the voice in those two small words, *He's free*, caused latent goose bumps to rise on her forearms.

She glanced in the rearview mirror and felt the spit dry in her mouth. A dark pickup was following her. Surely it wasn't the same shadowy truck she'd seen in the parking lot of the restaurant nearly an hour before? The one with tinted windows where a man had been smoking . . . ?

Don't go there, Eve. Don't panic. You, of all people, know how dangerous that can be.

But her heart rate jumped and her palms began to sweat.

Don't do this. . . . It was nothing. NOTHING! A phone call. Nothing more.

Her gaze flicked to the rearview mirror. Had the pickup closed the gap? Was he hanging on her bumper? She knew all about incidents where someone would intentionally rear-end a victim on the pretense of an accident, but when the victim pulled over, the assailant would get the upper hand, pull a gun or a knife or . . .

Her heart was pounding crazily now.

She stepped on the accelerator and switched lanes, speeding past an eighteen-wheeler carrying gasoline. The pickup followed, and her heart thumped even more wildly, and she considered calling 911.

Get a grip, she told herself. *The guy's just passing the semi. It happens all the time.*

She was breathing shallowly again, and the cat, damn the cat, as if he were infected with her own fear, started yowling again. She checked the mirror as she shot past a minivan and two cars, the needle of her speedometer twenty miles over the speed limit. Fine. Let her get a ticket. Be pulled over by the police. That would solve the problem!

But as she flew past the last vehicle, the dark truck she'd thought was so malevolent lagged far behind, soon disappearing from view.

He hadn't been following her.

It probably wasn't even the same truck that she'd seen at the rest stop.

She'd overreacted.

Again.

"No reason to borrow trouble," she told herself,

remembering one of her grandmother's favorite phrases: *Why borrow what you know is already coming your way?* "Oh Nana," she whispered, instantly missing the woman who had helped raise her once her mother had died fifteen years earlier.

Her sudden anxiety attack melted away, and she slowly let out her breath. For the next fifteen minutes she tried to concentrate on the radio, talking nonsense to the cat, obsessively checking her rearview mirror every few seconds. The menacing dark truck failed to reappear.

Maybe Anna Maria was right. She was still far from a hundred percent of being herself. Then again, would she ever be the woman she was before she'd been shot?

Of course not.

No one could ever be.

Not when she knew that the man she loved, the man she had trusted above all others, had tried to kill her.

His breath came in short gasps.

His heart was thundering so loudly that the freeway noise, usually crushing, couldn't be heard. He snapped the stolen cell phone shut and licked his lips. Though he stared straight ahead, driving by instinct, his mind was full of her, recalling, relishing the sound of her voice as she'd answered.

Hello.

Innocent.

Trusting.

One little word, and it caused so many emotions to roil deep within him. His fingers gripped the steering wheel more tightly, and he smiled. A tingle swept through his blood, causing his groin to tighten just as the sunlight broke through the clouds. He stepped on the accelerator. The truck nosed up a small rise. Through the bug-spattered windshield, he spied her car again as she switched lanes, the Camry half a mile ahead, gliding easily around another eighteen-wheeler.

His heart thumped in his chest.

Behind his sunglasses, his eyes squinted as if he could focus sharply enough to see her. His fingers stretched over the steering wheel.

Come on, baby. One glimpse . . . that's all I want.

Then her car disappeared around a long, sweeping curve. But he knew she was close, could *feel* her. He knew where she was going, but he couldn't let her get too far ahead, out of sight, just in case she took a detour.

No, he had to remain within view.

Without checking his mirrors, he floored the pickup and sped around an ancient Mercedes burning too much oil, black smoke pluming from the exhaust pipes.

More speed!

He was losing her!

He pushed down on the gas. His truck roared past a newer Ford Focus with heavy-metal music throbbing loud enough that he could feel the thrum of the bass through his closed windows.

Still his eyes remained straight ahead, his gaze focused on the little red Toyota with Eve at the wheel.

He'd blown it the first time at the cabin.

She'd lived.

He wouldn't make the same mistake twice.

CHAPTER 4

Eve couldn't make it all the way to New Orleans. The needle on the gas gauge was hovering near empty, while her bladder was stretched to full. With less than eighty miles to the city, she was resigned that she'd have to stop, so she pulled into a gas station/minimart that shared a parking lot with a coffee hut. Across a small access road was a McDonald's where cars and trucks were stacking up at the drive-up window and vying for spots near the doors.

Eve eased her car to a pump and waited for the minivan in front of her to drive off. Finally she filled her tank, pulled around to a parking spot, took Samson out of his cage for a couple of strokes of his long fur, then offered him water from her bottle. He clung to her like crazy, rubbed the top of his head against her chin as she told him what a good boy he was. He meowed pitifully when she returned him to the crate. "Just a little longer," she promised, leaving him in the car and wending her way through the vehicles parked in front of the market. The convenience store was doing a banner business. Inside, there were people standing in line to buy their gas, sodas, nachos, cigarettes, and beer. At the restroom she waited for nearly five minutes before it was her turn. After using the facilities and washing, she eyed her reflection in the small mirror, scowled, but didn't bother to repair the damage. Who cared that her hair was a mess and her lipstick had faded hours earlier? She walked out of the restroom and through the crowded little store, where she grabbed a pack of M&Ms, a small container of aspirin, and a bottle of Dr. Pepper.

As she waited in line, she noticed a mirror mounted high overhead. Convex, the reflective glass gave the cashier a distorted but panoramic view of the interior of the market. In the reflection she saw several customers searching through the shelves, eyeing products, selecting their purchases, but one man was standing alone, not shopping, just looking at the entrance of the store through dark wraparound sunglasses . . . or . . . was he looking at her?

Don't be silly, she told herself and glanced over her shoulder. She couldn't see past the products stacked on the highest shelf and told herself she was imagining things. No one was lurking, ogling her behind the rolls of paper towels and boxes of cold cereal, for God's sake!

No—this was all in her head. She'd been edgy ever since she'd gotten that weird phone call.

"Get over it," she muttered to herself. Then, when the girl behind the counter peered at her oddly, Eve offered an embarrassed smile and quickly paid for her purchases and tank of unleaded.

Outside, beyond the overhang covering the gas pumps, the clouds had lifted to a high, thin haze that was rapidly burning off. The sun hung low in the sky, promising darkness within the hour, but for now it was bright enough to be bothersome, reflecting harshly against glass and metal, creating tiny rainbows on the oil swimming on the surface of puddles caught in the uneven asphalt.

Eve rotated her neck, heard it crack, then slid into the driver's seat, where she tore open the bag of candy and unscrewed her bottle of soda. After popping a couple of M&Ms and aspirin and washing them down with the Dr. Pepper, she set the bottle into one cup holder and the open bag of candy into the other.

As she turned the key and her car started, she noticed a dark pickup parked near the coffee hut. A ripple of fear slid through her. Was it the same truck that she'd thought was following her earlier?

There are thousands of trucks like that, she reminded herself. She couldn't make out the smudged plates from this distance, but they were definitely from Louisiana. The bed of the truck wasn't empty. A toolbox positioned near the back window had been bolted into the truck's bed.

Probably a construction worker or handyman or farmer . . . no big deal. Right?

But as she pulled out of the lot, she glanced in her rearview mirror and saw a tall man in wraparound shades slip through the glass door of the mini-mart to stand and stare at her. "Sweet Jesus," she whispered. She told herself she was overreacting, that the guy was probably just looking across the street at the drive-in lane at McDonald's, where a vanload of kids were yelling at the speaker box.

BEEP!!

Eve gasped and stood on her brakes.

Her car rolled just short of the access road as a red, low-riding sports car, hip-hop music blaring, jetted by, just inches from her front bumper. The three teenaged boys inside yelled obscenities and flipped her off.

She sucked in a breath, her heart knocking wildly. She'd been so caught up in her own personal paranoia, she'd neither seen the car approaching nor heard it roaring down the road. Had there been an accident, it probably would have been her fault regardless of the other vehicle's speed.

"Stupid, stupid, stupid."

Glancing backward, she saw no one. The man in the doorway had moved. Probably to get into a car and go about his business. It had nothing to do with her. "Get a grip," she growled to herself as she eased onto the narrow road and squinted against the lowering sun. At a red light near the ramp leading to the freeway, she leaned over the passenger seat and opened the glove box, where she'd stashed her dark glasses.

A manila envelope that had been crammed into the small compartment fell to the floor. Dozens of scraps of paper, that looked like jaggedly cut clippings and articles, spewed onto the floor mats and between the seats.

"What the devil?" she whispered as the light turned green.

The driver of the SUV behind her laid on the horn, and Eve stepped on it, somehow accelerating onto the entrance ramp and merging with southbound traffic.

But her heart was thudding, her eyes darting from the road ahead to the scattered pieces of paper. She grabbed one off the passenger seat. It had sharp, jagged edges, and Eve realized the article had been clipped with pinking shears. Her heart was thudding as she held the piece of paper against the steering wheel and scanned the headline:

TWENTY-YEAR-OLD MYSTERY SOLVED.
WOMAN'S DEATH RULED A HOMICIDE.

"What?" Driving nearly sixty miles an hour, she didn't dare read the article as she drove, but several phrases leapt out at her.

Faith Chastain, murder victim.

Our Lady of Virtues Mental Hospital.

Detective Reuben Montoya of the New Orleans Police Department.

Eve's confusion and anxiety increased. "My God," she whispered, dropping the clipping. Montoya was one of the cops who had been integral in Cole's arrest, and the mental hospital was a place Eve knew all too

well. Her father had worked there, been the chief psychiatrist, and she had played on the grounds as a child.
Faith Chastain. Why did that poor woman's name ring
a distant bell in her head?

Her throat turned to sand. She glanced at another
article. It, like the first, had been cut with pinking
shears.

SUSPECT IN TWENTY-YEAR-OLD KILLING ACCUSED OF RECENT MURDERS

"Dear Lord, what . . . ?" Eve eased off the gas as she
skimmed the article about a recent serial killer in New
Orleans, a sick man who had killed at least half a
dozen people.

She didn't bother reaching for another. She got the
idea. Biting her lower lip, she tried to concentrate on
the road stretching out before her.

Who had left the packet in her car?

Who would know that she'd grown up at the old
mental hospital?

Why all the interest in Faith Chastain, a woman long
dead?

Her heart was hammering, her lungs tight. If she let
herself, she could easily slip into a full-blown anxiety
attack. "Hang in there," she told herself and began
counting silently in her head once again. *One . . . Two
. . . Three . . .*

Whoever had put these articles in her car had done
it deliberately . . . to make a point.

Why? When?

WHO?

All the clippings were about the mystery shrouding Faith Chastain's death, and they hadn't been torn or cut carelessly. Whoever had taken the time to cut out the articles had indeed done so with pinking shears. It was as if each of the little printed stories was surrounded by razor-sharp, even teeth.

Eve's skin crawled.

She'd heard about the scandal surrounding the old, abandoned hospital and the more recent murders. The story had been all over the news a few months earlier.

Before Roy's death.

Before a bullet had grazed her skull.

Who had left the envelope in her *locked* car? She checked her mirrors, saw no dark, ominous truck trailing after her. How had someone put the envelope in the glove box? She always locked her car. . . .

Except at the gas station.

You thought you would just run in for a second.

You were distracted by the cat. By your headache. By the fact that you needed to pee.

Even so, she usually hit the remote lock on her key chain. It was automatic, part of her routine, and on this trip security was even more important. She was driving with most of her belongings in her Toyota. Would she have been so careless as to leave the doors unlocked?

She thought hard. She remembered locking the doors at the restaurant, but . . . maybe not at the gas station? A chill whispered through her as she remembered the phone call and the raspy voice:

He's free.

What the hell was that all about?

And the truck she'd thought had been following her, was that somehow also connected . . . to the old asylum?

Don't jump to conclusions.

"I'm not!" she said aloud, and from the backseat Samson growled.

Cold sweat broke out on her skin as she glanced in her mirrors again then floored it. She needed to get to New Orleans as fast as humanly possible. Once she was home, inside the house, with the doors locked, the dead bolts thrown, and the chains secured, she would read all of the articles that had been left for her and try to figure out what it all meant.

She knew this for certain: someone had followed her. The thick envelope hadn't been in the car this morning when she'd shoved her sunglasses in the compartment that held her registration and maps.

Panic pulled at the edges of her mind. What else could the guy have left? A homing device? A bomb? A tiny camera?

Stop it. You've seen too many stupid murder movies lately.

But her breathing was erratic, her pulse jumping.

He's free. The message from the anonymous caller was somehow connected to Cole Dennis's release from prison. Was it also connected to Our Lady of

Virtues Hospital? Had her mysterious caller left her the clippings? Was there some *message* she was meant to understand?

Or was she making up a plot when there was none? Searching for answers that simply did not exist?

Reaction sent a shiver through her, and Eve pressed her foot to the accelerator.

She found the envelope!

He knew it.

Could sense her fear, her panic.

Behind his dark glasses, the Reviver stared through his windshield to the road ahead. She was within striking distance. She was having trouble concentrating, breathing hard, trying to keep her fear at bay.

And failing.

Hidden behind a pickup and an SUV, he forced himself to lag nearly half a mile behind her Toyota. From this distance, he was able to catch glimpses of her car and noted how her Camry hugged the shoulder, never going over the speed limit, even slowing, until suddenly she took off, the Toyota picking up speed as she tore past two semis going sixty.

Perfect.

Finally she understood.

He licked his lips and imagined her as he, too, passed a few cars. But he always kept his distance, tucking into the right lane between the semis, ever following her, knowing where she was heading.

He imagined her face. The terror in her eyes. The

rounding of her mouth as she realized she was being targeted. He knew her fingers were tight and sweaty upon the steering wheel, her heart trip-hammering wildly, her fright nearly a living, breathing beast.

Oh *yes*.

His own pulse was beating a quick, blood-heating tattoo.

I see you. Do you see me? Do you feel *me, Eve? Are you scared? I'm here. I'll always be here. You can't run away. Not ever. You and I . . . we're destined to be together . . . to die together.*

Smiling, he pressed his boot more heavily on the accelerator, his dark truck picking up speed. The bright sun was settling into the western horizon.

Darkness soon to follow.

He felt that sweet torture of adrenaline spurt through his bloodstream.

Because he knew what was to come.

Dusk suited Cole just fine.

He'd waited for it, his nerves strung tight, Sam Deeds's warning playing and replaying like a broken record through his brain: *Stay away from her. . . . She's bad news.*

Yeah, well, he'd known that from the get-go.

But he figured that at this point he didn't have much to lose. After four hours of cleaning and organizing the rental house, he needed a break. And he had business to take care of. He'd already loaded a small tool kit and flashlight into the Jeep. Now he walked outside to the front porch. Though it was dark, the streetlight gave off more than enough illumination for him to see some kids still outside on skateboards and bikes, weaving through the parked cars and trucks. One old guy sat on his stoop, puffing on a cigar, and a gray cat slunk along the chain-link fence guarding an alley. The twenty-somethings were still at work on their old car, the music still cranked loud. He leaned on the porch rail, and the dank scent of New Orleans reached his nostrils, an odor that permeated the smell of burning tobacco, exhaust, and dirt, a reminder that the slow-rolling Mississippi River wasn't too far away.

As far as he could tell, his house wasn't being watched by the police, but he wasn't certain, and he knew for a fact that Detectives Bentz and Montoya wouldn't give up; they'd be gunning for him. So he had to be doubly careful.

He climbed into the old Jeep and backed slowly out of the cracked concrete drive. No other car on the street pulled out, no engine caught, no headlights followed.

Yet he couldn't be certain.

With one eye on the rearview mirror, he spent the next hour driving through the city streets, filling the Jeep with gas, stopping at a market for a few groceries, then easing through the warehouse district and the French Quarter. No one seemed to tail him. No car followed, only to disappear and have another one tag-team. Obeying the speed limit, he drove on and off the Pontchartrain Expressway and across the river twice, all the while checking the cars surrounding him, watching his mirrors, ever vigilant for a tail. The police would be good, probably using two or three different vehicles, but after a final stop at a convenience store a few blocks away from Bayou St. John, and seeing no one pull out after him, he felt he was safe from being followed.

At least for now.

So he let himself think about Eve.

Damn her beautiful, lying face. She'd pulled a fast one on him, betraying him, using him, and setting him up. How had he been so blind?

He'd asked himself the same question for three months and had come up with no answers. Not one lousy explanation. But then, he hadn't been able to see her, to talk to her, to shake some sense into her.

All that was about to change.

As soon as he settled a few things down here, he planned on driving to Atlanta and having it out with her.

Damn but he'd loved her, thought they'd spend the rest of their lives together, and she'd turned on him. Big time.

He'd believed she was sleeping with Roy and still wasn't certain about that. The truth was murky. But he knew there was someone else in her life, a man she'd never named, a man she'd protected.

He ground his back teeth together. Remembering was a form of torture—masochistic maybe, but necessary all the same.

His fingers clenched over the wheel as he recalled their last fight, how she, all rosy in sexual afterglow, teasing, nipping at his neck and chest, playing with his nipples as she lay beside him in the sweat-soaked sheets, had fooled him completely. His heart had barely stopped pounding wildly, his breath was still short, and there she was touching him again, hot fingertips toying, a small purr of delight slipping past pink lips when she'd felt him grow hard against her leg.

"Look at you," she'd whispered, those blue-green eyes glinting wickedly. "All ready again."

"Aren't you?" he'd asked against her ear.

"I suppose I might be persuaded."

He laughed at her sudden coyness.

"If you tried hard enough." Her breath had been warm seduction, rolling over his skin.

"This is a test?" He'd kissed that sensitive spot at the juncture of her neck and shoulder.

"Mmmm."

"Am I passing?"

"Barely," she'd murmured, though her hands were already running their magic along the muscles of his back, and her nipples had tightened. He had run his tongue over one, and she'd arched up.

"Barely, my ass." His breath had blown over the wet tip of her breast.

"And what a great ass it is." One of her hands had cupped his buttock, the tip of her fingers brushing his cleft.

Lust had gushed through his blood, and he was suddenly white-hot with wanting her, feeling her touching him intimately as he swept her legs apart with his knees and . . .

"Shit!" he said aloud to the empty Jeep. He was driving ten miles over the speed limit, taking the risk of being pulled over when he didn't dare have any run-ins with the cops. Not tonight.

He sucked in his breath, his hands sweaty over the wheel. The image of Eve lying upon her back, naked and wanting, her lips parted, cheeks flushed and eyes glazed with wet, hot desire, still pounded through his skull.

Yet on that night, within seconds of further lovemaking, her cell phone had rung and she'd nearly leapt from the bed. It was as if the caller, Royal Kajak, had yanked her to her feet with an invisible string.

"You're leaving now?" Cole hadn't hidden his surprise and growing anger as he watched her pull on a pair of tight jeans.

"Yes."

"Why?"

"He needs me."

"He's a nutcase."

"Doesn't change the fact that he needs to talk."

"About what?"

She'd hesitated then, and he'd sensed she was lying when she said, "I don't know."

"Sure you do."

"I won't until I talk to him."

"At this time of night? It can't wait?" He'd glanced at the clock. Already after ten. But his argument had fallen on deaf ears.

"I won't be gone long. I know it's late but . . . that's Roy for you." She'd slid her arms through her little scrap of a bra then pulled her long-sleeved T-shirt over her head.

"Where are you meeting him? Can't he come here?"

"No . . . he's . . . he's at his uncle's cabin, the one I told you about . . . where he and I used to go when we were kids."

"The fishing cabin?"

"That very one." She'd searched the bedroom, found one shoe, and slid it on.

"Call him back. Tell him to meet you here. Or . . . or at your house. Or in the morning, for God's sake." Cole had rolled to a sitting position. "You don't need to drive out to some decrepit cabin in the swamp. I grew up out there. It's not safe."

"He's already there. Waiting."

"So what? His car won't start? You can't call him back, change the plan?"

"I'm going, Cole." Her voice had brooked no argument. "Oh." She discovered her other shoe near the window and stepped into it. "This isn't open for debate. Roy is critical to some of my research, you know that."

Cole knew in his gut that whatever Roy told Eve over the phone, it had nothing to do with her studies of aberrant psychological behavior. "If it's just about research, then it can wait until morning."

She'd shrugged into her jacket and headed toward the bedroom door. A woman determined. A woman with a secret.

Cole had thrown back the covers. "Hell, if you're so goddamned stubborn, I'll come with you."

"No!" She'd spun on a heel to face him. "He has something he wants to talk to me about. Obviously something important. He won't like it if I don't come alone. He'll clam up. Be embarrassed and self-conscious."

"Eve, listen to—"

"How many times have you left me? Just up and went to meet a client without a word of explanation?"

He was surprised when she suddenly took the offensive. "That's different."

She had snorted and pulled open the bedroom door.

Quick as lightning, suddenly realizing she wasn't going to listen to reason, Cole had shot out of the bed, grabbing his own crumpled Levis. "There's lawyer-client privilege and—" he'd started to rationalize as he stepped into one leg of his jeans and hopped toward the door.

"Yeah, yeah, I know," she'd cut him off.

On the landing overlooking the foyer, still struggling with the damned Levis, he'd called, "I don't like this, Eve."

She was heading down the sweeping staircase of his home, moving quickly, one hand trailing along the polished banister. She didn't so much as glance back at him.

"It's not safe." He had then managed to jerk the denim up his legs and over his bare butt as she reached the floor below.

"I'm a big girl, Cole."

"Wait! Eve, this is nuts!"

She was at the door, purse slung over her shoulder, as he hurried down the stairs, still fiddling with his damned button fly.

"You can't—"

"I can and I will." She'd grabbed for the door handle, but Cole threw himself in front of it, barring her exit.

"Just . . . wait," he'd demanded.

That had really infuriated her.

"You're barricading me in?" she'd asked in disbelief. "These aren't the Middle Ages! Get out of the way!"

"I've never trusted Roy."

"You don't trust anyone," she'd shot back. "Even me, it seems. So cut out all this Machiavellian, macho, backwoods crap!"

That's when he had made his biggest mistake: he grabbed her hard, his fingers circling her upper arms, holding her still.

"I'll come with you."

She had looked down at his taut fingers. "Let go of me, Cole," she'd said in a curiously controlled voice. "So help me God, don't you ever try to restrain me again." When she met his gaze again, her eyes were filled with cold fury.

"What is it, Eve?" he'd asked, loosening his grip. He was at a loss to understand her. What kind of pull did Roy Kajak have over her? Childhood friend? Research subject? Or something more? Something deeper. Darker. Vastly more intimate.

"You're way out of line here." Her voice was low, threatening. "Way out. I'm leaving. You're staying, and if you don't let go of me this instant, I'm calling the police."

He'd dropped her arms as if she'd stung him, watching as she snagged her cell phone from the side pocket of her purse.

"You'd call the cops on me?"

She didn't answer, just had shouldered past him, cell phone still in hand, as she yanked open the door and hurried to her car.

Even now, months later, he could still hear the thud of her car door slamming shut, the cough and catch of her Toyota's engine, and the angry squeal of her tires as she'd reversed out of the drive.

He'd stood stunned for about two seconds before closing the door, taking the steps back upstairs, two at a time. He'd then strode across his bedroom carpet, entered the closet, and hurriedly twisted the combination lock on the safe embedded in the back wall. His hand had closed over a handgun, and he hurried to his car, filled with confusion and fear for her safety. Whatever was happening wasn't right. Eve was hiding something big.

And he knew a shortcut to the cabin.

CHAPTER 5

Streetlights glowed an eerie blue as Eve pulled up to the house she'd inherited from her grandmother. Her shoulders ached and her head throbbed, but at last she had arrived at the one place she could call home.

She parked in the drive in front of the old single-car garage. Nana's old house stood alone, a covered porch leading from a door on its side to the main house, a three-story Victorian complete with the high turret her grandmother had used as an artist's studio for as long as she could mount the spiral staircase. Even as a kid Eve had claimed the room as her own, and whenever she spent weekends or summers with Nana, she slept in the turret with its three-hundred-and-sixty-degree view and easy access to the roof. In the summers, Eve had often sat outside on the old shingles, staring across other roofs and trees, imagining she could see across St. Charles Avenue, Magazine Street, and the area known as the Irish Channel, to view the Mississippi River—which, of course, was impossible.

Now she eyed the old house and smiled with relief. "We made it," she said to Samson as she turned off the engine. First things first: let the damned cat out! Well, if not out, at least free of the cage and in the house. She would keep him inside for a few days, just to make certain he was reacquainted with the house, and only then would he have some freedom outside.

Glancing down at the clippings still littering the passenger seat and floor, she decided to leave them where they were for the time being. She wasn't as panicked about them now. *Later,* she said to herself, hauling her purse and the cat carrier up the back steps to the porch and back door.

As much as she'd always loved this house, with its high ceilings, narrow halls, and smells of pecan pies, rich coffee, and dried flower sachets, she'd been as shocked as anyone that Nana had left the house to her, bypassing her own son and Eve's half brothers as well.

Eve unlocked the back door and walked through a small mudroom before entering the kitchen. She switched on a few lights and wrinkled her nose at the smells of dust and mold that had settled into the old timbers in the time she'd been gone. There was also the pervasive smell of rot, and she had only to look under the kitchen sink to find garbage that had needed to be taken out months ago.

"Great," she muttered, unlocking the cat carrier and watching Samson streak through the cage door. She spent the next fifteen minutes hauling out the trash, refilling the litter box, and setting out food and water for Samson then carrying in her things. After she'd hauled in her luggage and stacked it near the foot of the stairs, she returned to the car one last time and picked up the envelope and all the scattered clippings from the floor of the passenger seat. Just touching them made her feel dirty. Whoever had gone to all the trouble to cut these out, stuff them in an envelope, and wait for the right moment to plant them in her car had done so with a purpose.

He'd intended to scare her.

Why else break into the car and leave the envelope anonymously? Had it been at the gas station, where she'd perhaps forgotten to lock the car? That's where she'd seen the man staring at her from behind dark glasses.

No doubt about it: she'd been followed.

He could be here right now. Watching.

Her head snapped up quickly, and she studied the empty street, the shadowy bushes skirting her house, the alley behind the garage. Her eyes and ears strained, but she saw no one, heard no scrape of shoes against pavement, felt no whisper of air movement, smelled nothing but the rainwater dripping from the broad leaves of the mountain laurel tree planted near the drive.

She shivered as she gathered all the papers and pressed the lock button on her remote. The car chirped, and its parking lights flashed as the Camry locked down. No more break-ins. She glanced over her shoulder and felt the hairs on the back of her neck lift. Who had done this? Had they followed her?

Everything looked safe. The houses flanking hers had warm lights glowing through their shaded windows. The night was quiet, few cars passing, just the soft sough of the wind whispering through the pecan, pine, and live oak trees in the yard. Still, looks could be deceiving. She was wary, nerves strung taut as she hurried inside and slid the dead bolt behind her with a satisfying *thunk*.

She placed the envelope and all of the pieces of paper onto the kitchen table, examining them from a distance, almost afraid to touch them. There were nearly thirty articles, all neatly trimmed with pinking shears, all pertaining to Faith Chastain's tragic death.

Who had sent them to her?

Why?

What did a woman who'd been dead over twenty years have to do with her?

Struggling to make sense of it, Eve considered what she knew. *Faith Chastain died at Our Lady of Virtues. The mental hospital where Eve's father practiced. That massive brick building where she had played as a child, hiding from the nuns, spying on the patients.*

Now Eve rubbed her hands together, tamping down a niggling anxiety. She asked herself: *Don't you intend to go back there, to wander through the hallways and rooms where you witnessed so much cruel abuse once called "treatment"? Haven't you been fascinated with the old asylum? Isn't it integral to your research? Don't you plan to compare the use of physical restraints, so common at Our Lady of Virtues, to some of the antipsychotic drugs used today? The question is, Who else knows? Why does he care? What is he trying to tell you?*

Swallowing hard, Eve felt a little dizzy as she stared at the articles. If her theory was correct and someone wanted to either scare her from her research or . . .

what? Warn her? Then why focus on Faith Chastain? A woman she didn't remember.

Or did she?

Had Faith Chastain been one of the patients Eve had spied on as a child? Eve's heart pounded a little faster and shame washed over her as she remembered lying to her father, telling him she was going to play outside on the swings, or take a walk through the woods, or go to the stables where a few horses were kept, when she'd really been intent on slipping through the hospital itself like a ghost, creeping through rooms and hallways that were supposed to be off-limits, ignoring all the rules.

It had been horrifying but fascinating to her as she witnessed patients in straitjackets or other restraints. She knew it wasn't right, but at times the patients had frightened her. Some of them, perhaps, who had been given lobotomies years before; others who were the victims of electroshock treatment.

Her childish fears still had the power to embarrass her, and now her cheeks flushed. The patients she'd found so captivating, those she'd avoided, or those who had frightened her, had been ill, battling unseen demons. Of course she hadn't understood their maladies or psychoses.

She'd been so uninformed. If not uncaring, then at least more concerned about herself than anyone else. The truth was, some of the more serious patients just plain creeped her out. They had been intriguing, but in a frightening way. Her interest in psychiatry was more than a career choice; it was a means to atone. With her injury and Roy's death, she'd missed the spring semester but hoped to return to the university in the fall.

Shaking the thoughts aside, she turned her attention to the clippings. Someone obviously knew about her connection to the old hospital. But why would they care?

With a determined sigh, she walked to the table again, picking up the clippings one by one, scanning them and trying to put them in some sort of order. There were no dates on the articles and the best she could do was separate them by type of print—newspaper or magazine. She could search the articles on the Internet and planned to do so as soon as she had her modem hooked up again.

But not tonight. Not when her headache was building again after the long trip. She needed to sleep on this, maybe figure out what it meant. Rubbing her temples, she walked to the sink, where she let the water run for a couple of minutes while she scrounged in the cupboard for a reasonably clean glass. She swallowed two more tablets of aspirin, chased them down with cool water from the tap, then leaned over the sink and splashed more water onto her face.

Twisting off the tap, she found a terry-cloth towel in a drawer and dabbed at her face. Everything she'd gone through this day faded a bit as she glanced around the room where she'd spent hours with her grandmother. Pink tile, floral wallpaper in tones of green, gray, and pink, once-white cabinets, scratched hardwood floors—the kitchen hadn't changed since she was a toddler who had needed to stand on a chair at the sink to play with a piece of pie dough as her grandmother created the sweetest pecan and peach pies Eve had ever tasted.

She smiled faintly as she remembered her hands and tiny apron covered in flour while her brothers—"the ruffians," Nana had called them—played outside no matter what the weather. Even then there had been a distinction. Kyle and Van hadn't been allowed to wear shoes past the mudroom or to "roughhouse" inside, whereas Eve had been given carte blanche to do nearly anything she wanted. She was Nana's favorite and had been from the get-go. Even though Eve was adopted, Nana had still considered her special, solidifying the union between Terrence Renner and his wife, a woman who had come to the marriage with two sons sired by a man who had spent more years in prison than out. Though Eve's father had adopted Kyle and Van, they had been surly preteens with attitudes at the time of the marriage—"Troublemakers and hooligans," Nana snorted—while Eve had come into the family as a tiny infant.

It didn't take a rocket scientist to understand why Kyle and Van had so little use for her. Kyle had grown into a brooding, unhappy man, while Van had spent his adult years thinking only of himself, a narcissist to the nth degree.

Eve knew now that the grandmother she'd wor-

shiped was in reality a bigoted old woman who relished playing favorites. And it had only been exacerbated with Dorothy Gilles Renner's death—when
Eve's grandmother spelled out in her last will and testament that the lion's share of her estate would go to
Eve. Token bequests had been left to Kyle and Van,
while Eve's father, Dorothy's only child, had wound
up with an abandoned farm surrounded by swampland
and his father's World War II memorabilia.

A bitter pill to swallow for all of the men in the
family.

At the time of the bequests, Eve had wrestled with
her conscience about the unfairness of it all and had
finally decided that when she ever sold the old house,
she'd make it up to her brothers.

But not tonight.

Now she was beat. She walked through the house,
turning on table lamps. At the base of the stairs, she
grabbed her largest suitcase and lugged it up the
creaking wooden steps. The once-colorful runner
leading upward was worn, just like the rest of the
house, and sometimes Eve wondered if her grandmother had bequeathed her a golden goose or an
albatross. Bringing the old house up to date while
preserving its historic charm would cost a fortune, so
for now the fraying runner, chipped pink tiles and
fading wallpaper would remain.

On the second floor she paused, caught her breath,
and frowned when she realized how weak she still
was. All because of a would-be assassin's bullet.

Cole.

Her lover.

Her confidant.

Her assailant.

Her stomach tightened into a hard knot as she envisioned his handsome, angry face glaring at her as he raised the gun and, in a flash of light and a splintering of glass, nearly killed her.

That's how it was.

Wasn't it?

Cole had tried to kill her. . . .

"Bastard," she whispered, shuttering her mind. She couldn't go there tonight.

Walking into the master bedroom, she tossed her dirty clothes into a basket and hung the others up, wrinkles and all. She took one last trip downstairs, found Samson and held him close, listening to his deep purr rumbling against her body, feeling his long tail wrap around her torso.

"I'm sorry for that horrible, long drive," she said. "You're such a good, good boy. Forgive me?" The cat looked at her with wide gold eyes then rubbed his head beneath her chin and purred loudly. "So, here we are Samson. Now what're we going to do? Hmm? Start over, I guess."

And face Cole. No matter what.

The cat slid from her arms and hopped onto a window ledge near the kitchen table to peer into the night.

"Don't get on the counters," Eve said as she always did. "Or the table."

After double-checking that all the doors were locked and bolted, she headed for the bathroom. Once inside, she locked the door, swabbed out the old claw-footed tub, filled it, stripped off her clothes, then climbed into the warm water.

Heaven, she thought, lowering herself to her chin, feeling the water caress her skin, soaking out the knots of tension in her neck and back. She closed her eyes. The water enveloped her, and over the sound of her own breathing she heard the sigh of the wind rustling the leaves of the magnolia trees in the backyard and the creaks and groans of the old house.

Cole's image floated through her mind. A rugged if not handsome face, startling blue eyes that shifted color with the daylight, a blade-thin mouth that could flatten in silent anger or lift at the corners in amusement. She'd thought he was "the one," if there really was such a thing—and she'd been wrong, she realized now as she reached for a cracked bar of soap.

Dead wrong.

"Son of a bitch," Cole swore as he drove out of the city. Thinking of Eve was getting him nowhere.

With a wary eye on the other traffic, he maneuvered his Jeep across the bridge spanning Lake Pontchartrain and was only vaguely aware of the miles of black water stretching in all directions. He tapped his fingers nervously on the steering wheel and, once he was across the wide stretch of water, drove through several small towns to a wooded spot where one of his few cousins still owned a mobile home. They'd played here as kids, but he suspected that Jim, long married and living near Philly with his wife and son, hadn't been back in half a decade. He parked in the drive and waited.

Five minutes.

Ten.

No one appeared.

It was now or never.

Grabbing the tool kit, he pulled out a flashlight and locked the Jeep behind him. The night was cool, a fine mist rising through the trees and undergrowth of this bayou retreat. Cole pulled on a pair of thick gloves then vaulted the fence and walked toward the old house. It stood long and low, a once-white behemoth in the otherwise dark woods. Chancing the flashlight, he ran the beam over the aging aluminum and glass. The curtains were drawn, stains visible in the lining, spiderwebs tucked along the dirty glass where moss seemed to have somehow taken root.

No one had been here in a long time.

Aside from hunters or fishermen who had trespassed, he was probably the last one to walk around the old single-wide. There wasn't even a sign of a campfire or broken lock to suggest that squatters had found the remote trailer.

Which was all the better.

Feeling as if time were chasing him, Cole hurried along an old deer trail until he came to a fork in the path. He turned unerringly toward the south and ended up at a dock where once his cousin had moored a dinghy. There was no longer a boat, and the pier was rotting, some of the boards missing. Cole shined his light across the dark water and heard a splash that was probably an alligator sliding from the bank.

Sweeping his flashlight's beam over the shore, he located a solitary cypress tree with a split trunk. Bleached white, it stood a ghostly sentinel, and Cole sent up a silent prayer that it hadn't been disturbed in the last year. Making his way to the far side, near the water, he found a hole between the bare, exposed roots. First he pulled on a pair of thick gloves. Then he tested the hollow by shining a light inside. He saw nothing, but it was dark, the slit in the roots barely larger than a man's hand. He couldn't be certain. Squatting closer to the bole of the tree, he withdrew a long-handled screwdriver from his tool kit and used it to poke and prod whatever might have taken refuge there. He didn't want to surprise a sleeping water moccasin or other creature.

No animal hissed, barked, screamed, or flew from the opening, but his heart was pounding double-time all the same. He reached inside carefully and gently scraped at the dirt he'd piled inside until the tips of his gloves encountered something foreign. He smiled in the darkness. "Bingo," he whispered, digging swiftly until he extracted a nylon fanny pack.

Slipping the unopened pack into his tool kit, Cole retraced his steps quickly, half running through the low brush and trees. He heard nothing save the sound of his own short breaths and thudding heartbeat. If anyone found him now, he'd have a lot of explaining to do.

Near the fence, he clicked off the flashlight, climbed over the old chain-link, and landed softly about twenty yards from his Jeep. Where he froze. Waiting. Catching his breath and watching for any hint that he'd been followed or that someone was nearby.

The seconds clicked by.

Nervous sweat trickled beneath his collar.

Somewhere to the east, an owl hooted softly, but he could see no figure in the darkness, detected no scent that shouldn't be in the night air, heard no snaps of twigs or shuffling of feet.

Get moving. It's now or never.

Ever alert, he started forward, and when no one jumped out at him, he walked quickly and surely until he reached his vehicle. He unlocked it, yanked open the door, and tossed his tool kit and dirty fanny pack inside.

He backed out of the lane carefully. No flashing red and blue lights were waiting for him, no burly cops with handguns or clubs. At the county road, he threw the Jeep into first and took off, eyeing the bag on the seat next to him. Only after he'd put five miles between himself and the single-wide and was heading through a small town on his way back to the city did he pull open the fanny pack zipper and reach inside. Plastic met his fingertips. He flicked on the interior light and caught a glimpse of the money. Fifteen tight rolls, each totaling a thousand dollars, banded and wrapped in a ziplock bag. Fifteen grand. Not exactly a king's ransom, but enough to start him rolling again.

Blood money, he thought but didn't really give a damn.

Montoya glared at his badge and flung it on the table. Sometimes the job just wasn't worth it. In the kitchen, he opened the refrigerator, grabbed a beer, and popped the top. The room was chaos, as he was in the middle of a major remodeling job. Some of the plumbing worked, some didn't, and the common wall that had separated his shotgun-style rowhouse from the neighbor's had been torn down. Now, to keep the heat in, Visqueen sheeting separated the two identical halves that would soon merge into one living area. The kitchen would be double its current size; they would have two baths and a second bedroom.

Eventually.

After two swallows of his Lone Star, he sat in a caned-back chair and absently patted the big dog's head. Hershey, his girlfriend's chocolate lab, licked Montoya's palm. Montoya grunted, "Good girl," but he wasn't really paying attention to Hershey as he looked over a copy of the file he'd made of the Royal Kajak homicide.

There had to be something they'd missed, some piece of evidence to tie Cole Dennis to the crime. Correction: some piece of evidence that they hadn't fouled up—or lost. They'd had, in their possession, a torn piece of black fleece that had matched a rip in one of Dennis's pullovers, but the scrap had been lost before it had been tested for blood splatter or epithelials or as a fit into the sleeve of a sweater they'd discovered in Dennis's hamper. Trouble was, the pullover itself had no blood spatter on it, just a hole, so they had nothing concrete. And even if the missing piece were to suddenly turn up, it would be the *only* part of the shirt with incriminating evidence, so what were the chances of that? Still, it was a departmental screwup they couldn't afford, especially with a man like Cole Dennis.

Which meant, apart from Eve Renner's word, there was no proof Dennis had even been at the cabin.

"Damn," Montoya muttered, shaking his head. They hadn't had enough to hold the bastard, and their prime witness had come up with a severe case of amnesia.

So now Dennis was free.

Montoya wondered if Eve Renner had intentionally sabotaged their case. She and Cole Dennis had been lovers. But then why finger him in the first place?

Shoving stiff fingers through his short-cropped hair, he scowled so hard his face hurt. The thought of that slime-bag of an attorney walking on the homicide caused the stomach acid in Montoya's gut to start roiling.

Hershey gave a short, high-pitched bark and lunged for the front door. Her tail was already pounding against the side of a chair, kicking up dust.

Abby was home.

Montoya's bad mood eased a bit.

The front door rattled, opened, and Abby Chastain paused on the porch to shake out her umbrella then folded it and dropped it into the stand near the door. The dog went nuts, wiggling like crazy. As she stripped out of her raincoat and hung it on the curved arm of a hall tree, Abby caught Montoya's eye. She flashed him a sexy grin that caused an immediate shot of lusty adrenaline to spurt through his blood. "Hi."

"Back atcha."

"Sorry I'm late, but I stopped for takeout. Just a sec . . . Hey, you. Miss me?" she asked her squirming dog, kneeling down to scratch the lab behind her ears. Hershey whined and pushed her head into her chest. "Yeah, me too." If possible, Hershey's tail thumped even harder. "Hey, slow down," Abby commanded, nearly falling over and laughing.

Montoya couldn't help but smile. His bad mood disappeared as she straightened and dusted her hands. "Now, that"—she motioned to Hershey—"is the kind of homecoming I expect, Detective." She reached through the open door and pulled a white plastic sack and her portfolio from the porch swing, where she'd left them so that she could open the door.

"You want me to wiggle my fanny and whine at you?" Montoya scraped back his chair.

"For starters, yeah. And then, oh, I don't know, you could nuzzle my face and lick me all over."

She smiled at him. God, she was beautiful. Though she'd tied her hair back, some of the tousled red-blond curls had sprung free to frame her face. With a small mouth that was often in a thoughtful pout and eyes the color of aged whiskey, she got to him the way no other woman ever had. Now those eyes glinted naughtily. "And don't forget to kiss my feet and tell me you're crazy about me and that you can't live without me."

"And what would I get back?"

"Hmm. Let me think."

In three short strides, he crossed the distance between them.

"What would you want?" she questioned softly.

"Careful," he warned, "you're wading in dangerous waters."

One eyebrow lifted in wicked defiance. "My specialty."

"Oh lady." He barked out a laugh and shook his head. Wrapping his arms around her, he said, "Let's forget dinner and go straight to bed."

"No way. Not after I searched for a parking place for ten minutes, parked in a loading zone in desperation, and stood in line for the last order of pad Thai. Sorry, but we eat first. But afterward . . . who knows?"

"You are *so* much trouble." He kissed her hard on the lips. Felt her melt against him. When he lifted his head, she sighed. "Okay, so you're persuasive, but, really, let's eat first. I see no contractor showed up today."

"Tomorrow. He promised."

"Uh-huh," she said, disbelieving as she eyed the wall of plastic behind the big-screen TV. Where there had been built-in shelves, there was now just a murky plastic barrier separating Montoya's living space from the gutted living room that had once belonged to Selma Alexander. "Hey, what's this?" She looked at the table where the files on Dennis were strewn around his badge. "Uh-oh, I heard about this. It was all over the news that Cole Dennis was released." She walked into the kitchen, the dog at her heels, and untied the plastic bag she'd been carrying, then opened each individual container of food. As she scooped steaming noodles, vegetables, and chicken onto two plates, she added, "I know this goes against everything you believe in, but maybe you should just let this one go."

Montoya shook his head. "I can't. Cole Dennis is dirty, I know it."

"But you can't prove it."

"Not yet." He rubbed at his goatee as he followed her to the kitchen, where he rested his jean-clad hips against the counter.

"Sounds like a vendetta to me."

"Call it what you want." He took a swig from his long-necked bottle of Lone Star. "There's got to be a way to nail the son of a bitch, and I intend to find it."

Handing him a plate, she said, "Clear a spot on the table, and I'll get the forks. Unless you want chopsticks . . ."

"Forks'll do."

"So, where's Ansel?"

Montoya lifted a shoulder. "Beats me."

She skewered him with a glare of pure gold. "Was he in when you got home?"

"Don't know. I'm tellin' ya, the cat hates me."

"Honestly!" she said with more than a little exasperation in her tone. "You don't try to be friends with him."

"It takes two to tangle."

"That's 'tango.'"

"Is it?" He grinned widely, and Abby sent him a scathing look, handed him the forks, and instructed him to set the table before heading off in search of the miserable gray tabby. Montoya wasn't big on cats to begin with, and this one was a royal pain, but he tolerated it as Abby seemed bewitched by the damned thing.

A few seconds later she returned, the gray tabby in her arms. The cat was purring loudly as she rubbed his pale belly and made little loving sounds into Ansel's flicking ears. The cat rotated his head and stared at Montoya with wide gold eyes and such a smug look that Montoya could almost believe the feline understood every word and was using it to his advantage. "Safe and sound, I see."

"Cowering under the bed."

"I'm telling ya, I didn't do anything but walk in the door."

"Sure, Detective," she teased as the cat squirmed out of her arms and dropped to the floor, only to hide under the couch.

"Hate at first sight."

"Don't worry about it. Eat," she said and pulled a couple of place mats from a nearby cupboard before slapping them onto the table.

Montoya grabbed a second beer from the fridge, and when thoughts of Cole Dennis regaining his freedom surfaced, he forced his mind from the case. Maybe he needed a break. He opened the bottle and handed it to Abby, added napkins and a bottle of soy sauce, along with knives, then settled into his chair across from her.

Their living arrangement was new enough to feel a little awkward at times. They'd gotten engaged and she'd moved in, and though they'd known each other only a short time, he was certain he wanted to live the rest of his days with her, a divorced woman whose life had been in chaos from the first minute he'd set eyes on her.

"Zoey called today," she said, winding noodles over her fork.

Zoey was Abby's older sister, who lived in Seattle. "How is she?"

"I asked her, and she said, and I quote, 'More beautiful by the day.'"

"No problem with her self-esteem," he said, but they both knew Zoey was referring to the plastic surgery that had helped erase the scars from a vicious attack that had left her nearly dead. Montoya didn't doubt that Zoey's face would heal, but he wondered about her psyche, if the terror of being held by a madman, her life in dire jeopardy, would ever be completely erased.

"She wanted to know if there had been any progress on finding out about our mother's other child." Abby set her fork down and stared straight at Montoya. "I told her I hadn't found anything." Tiny lines of frustration crawled across her forehead, and Montoya understood her agitation. Abby had grown up believing that she and Zoey were the only children of Faith Chastain, a tormented woman who had spent much of her adult life at Our Lady of Virtues Hospital, a mental asylum that had been closed for nearly two decades. Only recently had the mystery surrounding Faith's death been solved and another revealed: Faith Chastain had borne another child. The autopsy report from the time of Faith's death revealed a cesarean scar, one that hadn't been there when Abby, as a young child, had caught a glimpse of her mother's naked body.

So what had happened to the baby?

So far, no one had a clue.

Abby frowned. She pushed her plate aside and folded her arms over the table. "I've searched all the birth and adoption records for the fifteen years between my birth and my mother's death. If she had a baby, it would have had to have been in those years. I came up with zip. What about you?"

"Nothing." The department, of course, had nothing. No crime had ever been reported, so Montoya had phoned an old poker buddy, an ex-cop who was now a private detective. "I talked to Graziano last week, and he hadn't found anything. But he's still looking."

"The only way we'll find out anything is to go through all the hospital records."

"Our Lady of Virtues was a private institution."

"So? There have to be records. Somewhere." She picked up her plate and carried it to the sink. Hershey was only a step behind. "And someone knows about them."

He knew where this was heading, and he didn't like it. "The church."

"Bingo."

He picked up his plate and set it on the counter next to the sink, where she was running water. "You want me to talk to the nuns out there?"

"You don't have to do it. I will."

"Abby," he said softly, touching her arm so that she glanced up at him. "Maybe it's time to let this go."

"You want me to just forget that I have a brother or sister that I've never met?"

"The baby might not have made it." They'd been over this ground before, but as always, she was stubborn as hell.

"Then let's find out, okay?" She wiped her hands on a dishtowel and tossed it at him. He caught it with one hand as she pointed a long finger at his nose. "Look, Detective, I'm getting to the bottom of this. I can't go on living the rest of my life not knowing. So either you help me or I go it alone. Your choice."

"Okay, okay. I know. I'm with you."

"Good."

"I'm just telling you we might not find anything, or, if we do, you might not like it."

"So what else is new?" She let out her breath and held up both hands. "Hey, sorry. I didn't mean to pick a fight."

"You didn't."

She smothered a smile. "I tried."

"And failed miserably," he teased.

"You're impossible."

"At least." He snapped the towel at her rear. "Besides, I'll get even with you later."

"What? In the bedroom?" she asked, eyes widening in mock horror. Splaying the fingers of one hand over her chest, she added, "Whatever do you have in mind?"

"You'll see . . ."

To his surprise, she reached around him, unclipped the small case attached to his belt, and in one swift motion dangled the metal cuffs in front of his face as she kissed the lobe of his ear. Her teeth scraped the diamond stud he always wore. "And so will you, Detective. . . ."

CHAPTER 6

The Reviver was agitated. Ready. Every nerve screaming through his body.

It was time.

At last.

He couldn't wait.

Anticipation propelled him. Bloodlust snaked through his veins.

On silent footsteps, he crept through the undergrowth and followed a sagging, dilapidated fence line. Dressed for battle, his weapons belted to his body, he edged ever closer to his prey. A fine mist rose, adding another layer of camouflage to the already dark night.

In the distance, across a lonely field, he spied the farmhouse, windows glowing faintly. His pulse quickened. He told himself to be careful, to tread lightly; he didn't want to make a mistake and suffer the wrath of the Voice.

Not this time.

God had spoken to him, and His instructions were clear.

Stealthily he slipped around a spindly pine tree.

A sharp hiss cut through the night.

His hand went to the knife at his belt before his eyes adjusted and he spied the thick, furry body of a raccoon. It had reared up on its hind legs, its nasty little teeth bared, its masked eyes glaring at him defiantly.

Stupid animal. It would serve the fucker right if he

sliced its throat, killed the damned creature out of spite and left it for vultures and crows.

But he couldn't risk anything that wasn't planned. He had to remain focused. His orders had been succinct. The Voice of God had been specific and strong, telling him exactly what to do while the other irritating, whining voices had buzzed like white noise. The killing would begin soon enough.

Eyes glittering, the raccoon lowered itself onto all fours and lumbered awkwardly deeper into the underbrush and brambles, as if it hadn't known how close it had come to death. His lips curled, and his fingers itched to grab his hunting knife.

Good riddance.

As the vermin disappeared from sight, he focused his attention to the house where his victim was waiting.

Unknowing.

With renewed purpose, he stretched the sagging barbed wire, slid through the opening, then took off at an easy jog across the open field. The night was cool for May. Rising clouds of mist swirled from the damp ground, and the air was fresh and clean from the recent rain, filling his nostrils with the smell of moist earth.

It had been a long, rewarding day.

And he'd caught glimpses of her.

Eve.
Beautiful.
Seductive.

Deadly.

Oh, to want her, to feel her pliant, soft body beneath his. To smell her. Taste her. Feel the heat of her skin rubbing anxiously, eagerly against him. He would love to hear her moan, see her writhe in fear and ecstasy as he mounted her, claimed her, thrust so deep into her she'd gasp and the cords of her beautiful neck would stand out . . . inviting. He would do anything he wanted to her beautiful body, and she would accept him, understand their destiny. She would kneel before him, licking her already wet lips . . . ready to take him in.

He felt his cock twitch, threatening to harden, and he clamped his jaw tight.

There was no time for this kind of fantasy, not yet.

Later . . . Oh, yes, later . . .

For now, he had to concentrate.

He had work to do.

She would wait.

He knew where she was.

Earlier, he'd followed her. After assuring himself that she had indeed driven into the city and not to this remote farmhouse, he'd turned off the freeway on the outskirts of New Orleans, doubling back a bit and driving unerringly to a spot where he could park his truck. His pickup was now hidden behind a dilapidated old barn on a forgotten piece of soggy farmland near the swamp.

From the truck's hiding place, he'd walked nearly two miles through thickets, woods, and open pasture.

He'd seen the massive dark shapes of dozing cattle, startled a flock of sheep into bleating for a few seconds before he'd slipped from their pasture, and crossed two streams, ever intent upon his mission.

The Voice had warned him that there might be a dog guarding the premises. If so, he would take care of the mutt as easily as he would kill his victim. The Reviver would have to be wary. He slipped his bowie knife from its leather sheath then held it in his mouth.

Through the thin veil of fog, he loped up a small rise to the far side of the pastureland and spied an aluminum gate. Too noisy to open or climb over. Again he stretched the wire between the fence posts and slipped noiselessly to the other side.

He paused.

Listened.

Stared into the darkness.

He sensed no one outside, heard only the sound of his own heartbeat and the soft sigh of the wind rustling the branches of a willow tree and causing an ancient windmill to creak as the wooden blades slowly turned.

The house was only thirty feet away.

The porch light was off, but there was no dark shape lying near the door, no sound of a dog padding in the darkness, no smell of canine feces or urine or hair.

Ever wary, his hand on the hilt of his knife, the Reviver walked noiselessly through the weeds then hurried across parallel ruts of a gravel and dirt drive. At the garage he paused, every muscle tense. Slowly he swept his gaze over the unlit floorboards and stairs of the back porch. Still no mutt was visible.

Good. He pulled on a pair of thin black gloves and stretched his fingers. Then the waiting was over.

On the balls of his feet, he silently crept up the stairs to the back door. Paused. Checked the windows, peering through the glass. The kitchen itself was dark, but enough light spilled into the room from the hall. The room was neat. Uncluttered. Except for the bottle of whiskey, uncapped and sitting on the counter. Good. Just as expected. The Reviver moved his gaze slowly over the rest of the neat expanse and located the tiny light glowing on an area that was obviously used for a desk. Plugged into an outlet and next to an open notebook that was either a calendar or day planner or the like was a cell-phone charger with the phone inserted, the tiny red light glowing like a beacon.

He moved to the door.

Above the thin doorjamb he found a hidden key.

Just as the Voice had told him.

Barely breathing, the Reviver inserted the key.

With only the tiniest click of metal against metal, the lock gave way and the door swung open on well-oiled hinges.

Perfect.

He pocketed the key and took his knife from his mouth, holding it ready. Barely breathing, he stepped over the threshold and into the dark kitchen.

He was inside.

• • •

Eve made the call.

Dressed in her cotton nightgown and robe, she stood in the kitchen, warming one hand on a cup of green tea and holding her cell phone to her ear with the other. She'd promised Anna Maria she'd phone, and even though it was closing in on eleven, she was going to make good.

"Hello?" Anna's voice was clear and chipper. Of course. She was a night owl, always had been, and didn't understand people who rose before dawn.

"Hey, it's me. I made it back. Safe and sound."

"I was beginning to wonder," Anna said.

"Tell Kyle."

"I will, when he gets back."

"He's not there?"

"Uh-uh. He just missed you this morning, ran into the house, took one call, and left not long after you did. Some emergency at work. A breakdown of some computer system he set up for a local bank. They suffered a major crash. Their entire system is down, and with all of the identity fraud and scams out there, the owner of the bank freaked. Insisted all of the computers in every branch have to be up and operational by the time the bank opens tomorrow, so Kyle'll be pulling an all-nighter."

"You'd think they'd have a backup system."

"Probably do, but Kyle's their guy." She sounded totally disgusted with the situation.

"Bummer."

"Don't get me started."

Eve didn't dare. She knew the drill. As much as Anna professed to believe in wedded bliss, her own marriage was a train wreck; she was just too stubborn and too Catholic to do anything about it. "Listen, I'm about ready to call it a day, so I'll talk to you later."

"Have you called your father?"

"No," Eve said quickly then bit her tongue. She and Terrence Renner hadn't been on good terms for a long while. "I'll call him in the morning."

"Right after you get the puppy?"

"What? Oh." Eve smiled at Anna's clever way of calling her a liar. "No, right before."

Anna laughed. "Good. I'll talk to you in a couple of days. Bye."

"Bye," Eve said, but the connection was already severed. Anna had hung up.

Making a face, Eve considered dialing her father and letting him know she was in New Orleans then decided it could wait until morning. Even if he were still awake, Terrence would have already downed a couple of stiff drinks.

She'd prefer to talk to him when he was sober.

Adding a little hot water from the kettle to her cup, Eve sipped at her tea then stared some more at the newspaper articles still scattered over the scarred oak table.

You should go to the police.

She read the clippings over again, taking mental notes. Faith Chastain's obituary, over twenty years

120

old, was included, and within it were the names of the loved ones she'd left behind: her husband, Jacques, and two daughters, Zoey and Abigail. *Abby Chastain.* Why did that name ring a dim bell?

Who had done this? How? There was no evidence that her car had been broken into. No windows smashed, no locks pried or jimmied. It was almost as if someone had used her own key to get inside.

A duplicate?

Her insides turned to ice. If someone had somehow gotten hold of her key ring, then any of her keys could have been copied, including the keys to this house.

She heard a scrape.

The sound of a fingernail sliding against glass.

Her heart clutched before she realized that it was the sound of a branch against a window on the second floor. Still, she dropped her cup onto the counter, and tea slopped over the sides of the rim. She didn't care. She ran up the stairs, stopping at the landing. Sure enough, the wind had picked up, rattling the limbs of the trees outside, causing a small branch to rasp against the glass. That's what she'd heard. No one was trying to get in.

Forcing her pulse to slow and her mind to think clearly, Eve concentrated on the keys.

Don't go there, Eve! Don't think anyone can let himself into your house at will. Your keys were never stolen. They were never missing. Someone slipped into your car when you inadvertently left it unlocked. And they did it today. You know that. Otherwise you would

121

have found the packet earlier, when you put your sun-glasses into the glove box.

She tried to think dispassionately about the guy in the wraparound shades. She'd panicked at the sight of him, imagined him to be the embodiment of evil tracking her down. When she'd calmed down a bit, she'd blown off her fear as the bothersome result of an overactive imagination, but was it really? Could he be the culprit, the one who'd left her the clippings?

If only she'd seen his license plate.

"Get a grip," she said, then nearly tripped on Samson, who was lying on the bottom step. "Careful there, guy." She picked him up and carried him back to the kitchen.

Turn these clippings in to the police.

Eve grimaced. The local detectives already thought she was at least three cards shy of a full deck. Taking in this bundle of news articles would only up the ante on the theory that whatever brains she once had were destroyed when a bullet ricocheted against her skull.

Maybe the police could pull off fingerprints, find out who broke into your car and left the envelope in the glove box.

All too clearly Eve remembered the harsh, no-nonsense visages of Detectives Montoya and Bentz and the skepticism of the Assistant District Attorney who had been chosen to prosecute Cole.

"You're certain about this?" ADA Yolinda Johnson had asked Eve, her dark eyes narrowing. She was a slim, smart African-American woman of about thirty-five who wasn't about to walk into the courtroom without all of her facts straight and her ducks in a row. Eve was seated on one side of a large desk, Yolinda on the other. The office was small and close, no window open, and Eve had been sweating, her pain medication beginning to wear off. "Mr. Dennis shot you."

"Yes." Eve's insides had been in knots, and she'd worried a thumb against the knuckle of her index finger.

"But you don't remember anything before or after the attack, is that right?" Yolinda had clearly been skeptical, her lips pursing as she tapped the eraser end of a pencil on the legal pad lying faceup on the desk.

Eve's stomach tightened. "That's . . . that's right. . . . I mean, I remember being with Cole at his house—"

"In his bed, Ms. Renner. Let's not mince words. The defense attorney certainly won't."

Eve's head snapped up, and she met the other woman's gaze evenly. "That's right. We'd been in bed."

"You were lovers."

"Yes."

"Go on."

"I received a call from Roy . . . Roy Kajak. He was insistent we meet. He said he had some kind of 'evidence,' whatever that meant. But then . . . then it gets kind of blurry."

"Mr. Dennis didn't want you to go."

"That's right."

"He barred the door."

"Yes . . ."

"Did he follow you?"

"I don't know."

"Did you see him leave the house?"

"I . . . I don't think so."

"But you're not sure, are you?" the assistant DA had accused, leaning forward across the desk.

"No."

"So it's all a blur. Until you saw Cole Dennis leveling a gun at you through the window."

"Yes."

"Even though it was dark."

"Yes!" Eve's guts had seemed to shred.

Yolinda frowned, her lips rolling in on each other. Her pencil tapped an unhappy tattoo. She stared at Eve a long minute that had seemed punctuated by the ticking of a clock on the credenza behind her neat desk. "Look, I'm not going to sugarcoat this, okay? The jury will understand why you don't remember anything after the shooting. You were wounded. Passed out. Unconscious. That works. But possessing no memory leading up to that moment in time is a problem."

"I can't lie."

Yolinda held up her hands, stood, then walked to the small window. "The last thing we want you to do is lie, but you're going to be asked some tough questions while you're on the stand." Turning, she rested her hips against the window ledge, her dark gaze boring into Eve's. "The fact is that you've got credibility

124

issues, Ms. Renner. You were taken to the hospital, unconscious, and, along with other medical treatment, you were examined for rape."

Eve had nodded. Braced herself. Felt as if the air in the room had suddenly gone stale. She knew what was coming.

Yolinda's voice softened a bit. "You weren't raped, Eve. We know that. There was no bruising or tearing consistent with rape. But you had semen in your vagina."

Eve met the ADA's hard gaze. She'd been through this before, but it was still difficult to hear. "I'd been with Cole," she said softly.

Yolinda nodded. "Some of the semen belonged to Cole Dennis. But there was other semen as well. Other viable sperm. Definitely not belonging to Mr. Dennis."

The first time she heard that horrifying information, the blood rushed to her head and made her feel like she would pass out, throw up, or both. With an effort, she just stared back at the ADA.

"And it was not from Royal Kajak."

Eve swallowed but still said nothing. What was there to say? What kind of comment could she make? And how could she not remember something so vital? This wasn't right. It couldn't be. True, she had holes in her memory—a dark, blank nothingness surrounding the night of Roy's murder—but she knew herself well enough to understand that she would never sleep with two men within hours of each other. Never.

You weren't raped. We know that.
Then how???

"I only remember being in bed with Cole," she finally managed to get out, sounding as confused and shattered as she felt.

Yolinda shrugged and exhaled a long-suffering sigh. "You see my problem, don't you? If I get you up on the stand, and you 'don't remember this' and you 'don't remember that' and you don't even remember who you slept with, how's that gonna look to the jury? What do you think Cole's attorney, Sam Deeds, is gonna do with that testimony on cross-examination?" Eve shook her head, and Yolinda continued tersely, "I'll tell you what he'll do. He'll go at you, over and over again, get you tongue-tied and angry, so that you look like you're either stupid or a bald-faced liar. Then, when it's already awful, he'll just keep pushing you, so that you get defensive and look like a two-timing bitch."

"It was only Cole!"

"That's not what the evidence says."

They were at an impasse. Eve's paltry excuse of "I can't remember," though the truth, was not going to sit well with the jury.

Yolinda nodded as if they'd come to some kind of agreement. "Even if we can convince the jury that you're telling the truth about your amnesia, the idea that you slept with two men within twenty-four hours will be planted. Add to that, you're trying to pin a murder on a jealous boyfriend. That's how Deeds'll play it. And he'll have clean-cut, smart, innocent-looking Cole Dennis at the table, looking for all the world like the wounded party—the choirboy whose girlfriend was two-timing him with another man she can't, or won't, name." Yolinda pushed herself upright and walked to the desk, found a file in her top basket, and slid it over the polished wood so that it landed, open, in front of Eve. "This will be one of Deeds's exhibits. It's the DNA report. Two different semen samples taken from you. It won't help that the sperm wasn't Kajak's. If anything, that will only make it worse, because you claim you can't remember whose it is."

"Stop." Eve knew she was being goaded, but she couldn't take it a second longer. "I get it. I see your point. But I haven't slept with anyone but Cole in two years."

"Then how?

"I don't know!" Eve shook her head. "It . . . had to have happened . . . after . . . after I got into the cabin."

"But you saw Mr. Dennis at the cabin. Was there someone in between the time you left Mr. Dennis at his home and went to meet Mr. Kajak at the cabin? Before Mr. Dennis arrived?"

"No."

"Was there someone else there?"

"No."

"Who was he, Ms. Renner?"

"No one!"

"Someone after you claim Mr. Dennis shot at you at the cabin?"

"No. I didn't have sex with anyone!"

"How do you know, Ms. Renner? You don't remember."

"Then it . . . it was afterwards. . . ."

"At the crime scene? Or the hospital? When the police were crawling all over the place, or in the ambulance ride when you were still unconscious? Could you pick out the EMT with whom you had sex from a lineup?" Yolinda hammered at her. "You know, those people who saved your life? Which one of them did you have consensual sex with?"

Eve's eyes stung. "I'm telling the truth."

Yolinda nodded. "We can't use your testimony, Eve. You see that, don't you? Not unless I want to completely destroy my case." With a sigh, she said, "We're done here," and that was the end of it.

And Eve had no more answers now than she had then.

The old man was drunk.

So it wouldn't take long.

Hidden in the shadows of the aging trellis in the side yard, the Reviver checked his digital watch. Twenty minutes had passed since he'd slipped into the house, taken care of business, and then noiselessly walked outside again. His victim, who had been in the den and listening to some radio program, was none the wiser that he'd ever had a visitor.

Yet.

That was soon to change.

Everything had gone perfectly, just like clockwork. Just as the Voice of God had instructed.

He watched through the window. The kitchen was now lit, the open bottle of Jack Daniels in the sink, a tray of ice cubes left on the counter, the few remaining in the tray beginning to melt.

Unlike the good doctor to be so messy.

Tsk, tsk, he thought as he retrieved the cell phone from his pocket.

He made the first call. Listened as the man on the other end answered.

"Hello."

The Reviver didn't respond. Not yet. He had to do just as God had told him last night in his dreams.

"Hello?" A pause. "Damn it, who is it? Can you hear me? If you can, I can't hear you." Another pause. "Terry?" he said, a trace of frustration in his voice.

"I have evidence," the Reviver whispered, his voice so low and raspy no one would ever recognize it.

"What did you say?"

There was no need to repeat himself. The message had been heard and understood.

He hung up.

Glancing up at the house, he then swiftly checked the menu on the phone for a list of contacts, scrolled down, and pressed the dial button again.

Within seconds, the phone was connected.

One ring.

Two.

Three.

"Hello?" The old man's voice was brusque, loud over the background noise of the talk radio show he was tuned to. "Wait a minute. Who is this? How did you get my . . . shit!" A beat. "You're calling from *my* cell number . . . but . . . how?"

The Reviver smiled as the man appeared in the kitchen, walking with an uneven gait.

"You have my phone!"

Outrage. And his words were slightly slurred.

The Reviver didn't respond.

"Hello? Are you there? How the hell did you get my damned phone?"

Again, no response.

"Did you find it somewhere? Did I leave it in my car . . . ? No, wait. It was here earlier. I remember plugging it into the charger. . . ." His voice trailed off. "You were in my house? You *stole* it, you punk bastard!"

"I have information," he finally said.

A pause. "Information about what?"

"Information you'll want."

"Hey . . . what is this?"

Another lengthy pause.

"So, what is the information you have for me?" The man's voice was calmer now, but the Reviver spied him walking from room to room, peering out the windows. "Why did you take my phone?"

Checking his watch, the Reviver hung up then flipped the ringer to vibrate and slipped it into his pocket. Within seconds he felt the cell vibrate against his leg, and he smiled inwardly, sensing the man's panic.

Just as he expected.

The vibration stopped as quickly as it had started.

Quietly he walked to the side of the house, careful to stay in the shadows. The cell vibrated again, and he could feel the man's growing unease.

Good. You feel it. It's your turn.

In the window, his victim nervously lifted a short glass filled with whiskey to his lips.

Drink up, moron. Drink it all.

The man visibly swayed, caught himself by pressing a hand to the glass pane.

The Reviver grinned in the darkness. He'd spent so little time in the kitchen, just long enough to steal the phone and slip the small tablets into the open bottle of whiskey.

It had been so easy.

And now those pills were working their magic, making his victim sluggish.

"Bottoms up," he mouthed, feeling a rush steal through his blood as the man stumbled away from the window, heading, no doubt, for his recliner.

No reason to wait.

He hurried to the back of the house and stole up the steps to the back porch.

The door to the kitchen was still unlocked.

Dr. Terrence Renner drained his glass, set it on the table next to his recliner, and tried not to panic. Someone had called him . . . using his own cell phone. Someone had been in the house. Probably the teenagers who lived about a quarter of a mile away; three boys, and hellions every one. Troublemakers.

All that talk about "information" was probably just part of a prank. Right? And yet he'd heard real menace in the caller's voice. Determination.

It took him three attempts to place the portable receiver into its cradle. Then he half collapsed into his recliner and stared at the phone, expecting it to ring again. All the while *Midnight Confessions*, that ridiculous radio show with "Doctor Sam," a pseudo-psychologist, was playing on the radio. The show and woman irritated him, but he hadn't been able to stop tuning in. Pop psychology. Ridiculous.

So who had his damned phone?

"Stupid punks," he muttered and told himself to calm down, enjoy his fire—perhaps the last crackling fire of the season—and the remains of his drink.

He flipped off the radio, couldn't stand to listen to that damned fake shrink another minute.

Had someone been in the house?

When?

Rubbing the back of his neck, he looked at the phone again and considered calling the police but was just too damned dizzy. He'd think more clearly in the morning. Tonight he'd finish his crossword puzzle then go to bed. He pulled the folded newspaper onto his lap and forced himself to concentrate.

From habit, he reached down to pat Rufus's old head then realized his mistake. The dog had been dead over two weeks, and it was amazing how much Renner missed the old terrier, who in his youth had chased rabbits, squirrels, and cars with the same enthusiasm. Fortunately, the stupid dog had never caught anything.

A soft footstep sounded in the back of the house.

What the devil now?

He looked up quickly, knocking the newspaper from his lap as he stared over the top of his reading glasses. The room seemed to rotate slightly, and he blinked a couple of times. His nightcaps had hit him hard. Harder than usual, and as he pushed himself upright, he wobbled slightly, his legs unable to hold him.

"Son of a bitch," he growled as his buttocks landed on the worn cushion of his favorite chair. "Son of a goddamned—"

There it was again. That familiar creak of floorboards in the hallway running from the kitchen, the sound made when someone walked along its length.

But he was alone.

Wasn't he?

The hairs lifted on the back of his skull.

Had the punks who'd stolen his phone returned?

"Hello?" he called, slightly nervous and feeling like a fool. No one was in the house. *No* one.

He strained to listen, to rise from the chair, to push up, but his arms were as weak as his legs, flaccid, useless appendages. Had he had a stroke? Was that possible?

Another footstep. Heavier this time.

His heart froze for an instant.

"Ith thum-one there?" he demanded and heard the slurred panic in his voice. "Inez?" he asked, calling out the housekeeper's name though she wasn't scheduled for another couple of days. "Franco?" But the farmhand who worked for him had left hours earlier, before the sun had gone down. For the first time in his life, he felt isolated out here.

Again he tried to push himself upright, his arms trembling with the effort, his legs wobbly.

Again he fell back.

Don't panic. You're imagining all this. The drinks were stronger than you thought . . . that's all. *Get up, damn it. Get up!*

"Dr. Renner." A deep male voice called to him from the darkened hallway beyond the French doors.

His eyes widened, felt stretched across his face.

He lunged for the phone, throwing himself from the recliner, knocking over the remains of his drink.

Ice cubes skittered over the gleaming hardwood floor.

Pain shuddered through him.

Pushing himself, he was determined to get to the phone, even if he had to crawl. But . . . but his arms wouldn't drag him. His legs were useless. He was facedown on the floor when the light shifted. The glass doors opened, a shadow stretched in front of him, and he found himself looking at a pair of thick army boots.

He nearly lost control of his bladder as he slowly raised his eyes, up, up, up long, powerful-looking legs covered in camouflage, then farther upward past a matching jacket that covered a massive chest. Above the collar was a thick neck and a face concealed by a ski mask.

Startling blue eyes stared down at him.

"Who are you? . . . What do you want? I have money . . . in the safe. . . ." Renner squeaked as panic closed his throat and constricted his lungs.

"Money." The intruder spat the word. Moved his gloved hands.

Renner saw the knife—a long, wicked hunting knife, the blade catching and gleaming, reflecting the fire.

Terror grabbed him. "No," he whispered. "Please . . . I beg you . . ."

"Retribution," the big man whispered in a voice that cut through the air like a whipsaw.

"No . . . please . . . I don't know who you are . . . what you want . . . but you're making a mistake."

"No mistake, Doctor."

Fear blasted through him. He tried to scuttle away, to move anywhere, but his damned body . . . Oh hell, he'd been drugged. He realized that now. It wasn't the booze . . .

His attacker lunged. Was on him in an instant.

A big hand pulled back on his forehead until his

neck bowed back so far he was certain his spine would snap. Pain screamed down his backbone. "No!" he rasped.

In one last terrifying instant, he saw the wicked blade in a strong black-gloved hand.

It moved across his line of vision.

Oh sweet Jesus, this maniac was going to slit his throat!

The tip of the blade pressed against the side of his neck.

"I'm the Reviver," his attacker whispered intimately into his ear. "I decide. Who lives. Who dies. Who will be revived."

Delusional psychopathy with a God complex.

Renner closed his eyes. He knew what was coming.

God have mercy on my soul.

The knife point pricked his skin.

He swallowed hard.

"It's God's will, Doctor, that you go straight to hell," the killer whispered just before he drew his arm backward and the blade slashed in a sharp, clean arc.

CHAPTER 7

Why the hell had Terrence Renner called him? Cole's eyes narrowed on his cell phone's screen as he drove toward the heart of the city.

And how would Renner know that after three months in jail, Cole's cell phone service was restored, courtesy of Sam Deeds?

A bad feeling crawled through him, and he resisted the urge to return Renner's call. In fact, he thought he should probably ditch the phone. The police had confiscated it when he'd been arrested; Deeds had just gotten it back and restored service, but what if someone in the department had put a GPS chip inside the phone? What if the police could tail him without physically tailing him? How would he know?

Shit! He didn't dare use the thing, and the only numbers he needed that were stored in the phone, he had already memorized. He had to be smart . . . couldn't take chances . . . had to ditch the cell and his computer and start over. Brand new. Just to make sure that Montoya and Bentz, or someone higher up, or the damned Feds, weren't listening in.

You're getting paranoid!

But someone had set him up for Royal Kajak's murder. Someone who knew his movements. His reactions. Someone with a hard-on to see him sent away for good.

Who? he wondered for the millionth time over the

137

past three months. Who had set him up? Was Eve involved? And who the hell had she slept with besides him on the day Roy died? His jaw slid to the side, and he squinted against the glare of oncoming headlights.

He would be a fool to think whoever had framed him before would stop now, or that the police would quit thinking he was involved in Roy's death. No, he had to be careful.

So think, Cole, think!

First things first: he had to ditch the cell phone. With that in mind, he stopped the Jeep, placed the phone under its tire then ran over it, hoping to destroy the GPS chip if it had one.

Secondly, he had to hide the money again. Over time he planned to deposit it to his account in small amounts, as if he were being paid for odd jobs. But for now the Jeep was an unsafe bet, as was his new home.

But he knew another place. . . . It would just take some time, once he was back in New Orleans.

For now, he'd take care of this Renner business.

He didn't like the feel of it and would take some precautions, but he wanted—needed—to know what was going on. Why had Renner called him?

Don't step into a trap.

Cole wheeled the Jeep into a one-eighty and headed for the old farmhouse where he'd first met Eve. His jaw clenched, and he felt that same old rush in his bloodstream as whenever he conjured up her image.

The first day they met, she'd had the nerve to question his ability. She stared at him through intelligent eyes half a beat longer than necessary then opened that sexy mouth of hers and started putting him to the test, asking questions, studying him suspiciously, silently suggesting that she didn't think he was up to the job.

"You're really the best money can buy?" Her freckle-dusted nose had wrinkled, and Cole had found her amusing and irritating at the same time.

"I can hold my own."

"Against what?" She'd swatted at a fly that buzzed too close to her loose red-blond curls. Thrusting out her chin, she'd tilted her head and waited, as if she enjoyed putting him in the hot seat.

"I think you mean 'against whom,'" Cole had countered.

"I just want to know that you're up for the job." He had noticed a hint of fear in her eyes, and he realized that beneath her brash exterior was a daughter frightened her father could be sent to jail.

Cole had understood. In his estimation, Terrence Renner was a little off, a doctor with an incredible God complex.

In retrospect, it had been Eve, more than Renner, the psychiatrist, who had persuaded Cole to take the case. Not because she'd asked him to. No. Just the opposite. Because she'd doubted him, eyed his battered jeans and faded T-shirt and made a judgment call: he wasn't good enough.

And he'd been determined to prove to her that he

was everything her father had claimed, the "best money could buy."

What a joke.

The whole situation had spiraled out of control, and look where he was now.

Now, as Cole headed to that same farmhouse where he'd been so hell-bent to prove himself, he found it almost laughable how things had gotten twisted around. Now he was the suspicious one. For instance, why had Eve shown up at Renner's that particular day? Coincidence? Or part of something much bigger than Cole suspected? His jaw slid to the side. And what about Renner's patient, Tracy Aliota? Had Renner been as innocent as he'd proclaimed? Or had he had a tiny bit of hesitation about releasing her? Had he suspected that she might try to injure herself again? It wasn't Renner's fault that the girl committed suicide, but had he borne *some* responsibility for what had happened?

Ethics, he reminded himself. He was thinking about ethics, not legalities. Cole had proven that *legally* Renner had fulfilled his obligation to his patient, but ethically . . . that was another question.

In any event, Renner had been vindicated in the trial, found "not guilty." It had left the prosecuting attorney pissed as hell and Cole Dennis a hero in Eve Renner's eyes. Which had been just what he'd wanted. He'd been so attracted to her, so focused on her, that he'd ignored the warning bells clanging loudly in his mind. He'd all too eagerly broken his own hard-and-fast rule of avoiding any personal contact with a client or any member of a client's family. He had flatly ignored the fact that blending the boundaries between business and pleasure always ended up clouding his clear, razor-sharp viewpoint.

And so it had been.

For over two years.

Now, as he saw the flashing red light in the middle of the small town near Renner's house, he eased on the brakes, and his Jeep rolled to a stop. His was the only vehicle at the junction. The reflection from the stoplight pulsed red against the pavement as he turned, driving down the lonesome street.

The empty town was lifeless, stark, only a few parked cars on the streets where neon lights sizzled and burned in the one tavern and every other shop had been locked for hours. A skinny stray dog wandered across the street a hundred yards in front of him, then, head down, disappeared down a narrow alley. A bad feeling crawled through him. It almost felt as if this part of the world were on a distant planet.

Shaking off the eerie sensation, Cole turned down the main street and headed out of town, past the shop fronts with their security lights, then through a residential area of single-story homes built in the forties and fifties, mostly dark, only a few lamps glowing behind drawn shades.

On the outskirts of town, he stepped on the throttle, pushing the speed limit, suddenly feeling an urgency to talk to Renner. He told himself that it had nothing to do with Eve, this visit to her father. He'd deal with the old man first then decide what to do about the woman who had turned his world inside out, sworn to have loved him only to end up cheating on him and accusing him of murder.

Rage fired through his guts, and he forced his mind away from Eve: beautiful, lying, two-timing, sexy-as-hell Eve. He couldn't think of her now.

He passed familiar landmarks: a narrow bridge, a stone fence, a tilted mailbox only a quarter of a mile from Renner's property. He slowed for the turnoff then cranked hard on the steering wheel, nosing the Jeep into the long, furrowed lane.

The good doctor was apparently still up, as warm light glowed from the windows on the first floor. He had mixed feelings about this place. It was the first place he'd set eyes on Eve. The start of so much that had ended so badly.

Cole parked near the garage. Then, as he had in the months before the trial, he walked up the back steps to the kitchen and rapped on the door. Crickets chirped loudly, and a moth was beating against a kitchen window. "Terrence?" he called, spying an open bottle of booze on the counter along with a tray of melted ice cubes.

No one answered.

He tried again. "Hello? Terry? It's Cole!" He banged so hard on the back door, the glass panes rattled.

Again, nothing.

142

Nor did the old, half-crippled dog appear.

Cole knocked again but knew it was no use.

Well, hell.

Had Renner taken off?

Cole walked to the garage, peered through the side door, and spied the looming dark shape of Renner's truck, a newer model Dodge, parked inside. Which didn't mean he couldn't have taken off with someone. Renner had called from his cell; Cole had recognized the number. So that meant he might not have phoned from the house.

Still . . . the open bottle of booze, the ice tray on the counter? Cole knew a lot of men who wouldn't have bothered capping a bottle or returning the tray to the freezer, but those men weren't the precise and anal Dr. Terrence Renner.

Walking down the cement path again, Cole took the steps to the back porch two at a time and pounded on the door again. "Terry!" he yelled, and when that didn't work, he grabbed the damned door and pushed.

It opened.

Cole stood a moment in surprise. This wasn't Renner's style. He'd been about to search for the spare key he knew Renner kept hidden on the sill above the door, but it hadn't been necessary.

Another oddity.

Renner was a stickler for locking his doors, be it his house, his office, his truck, or his briefcase. Probably from all those years working with the mentally ill. Cole had seen some of Renner's patients. Some were docile, just troubled or depressed. Others were violent. Psychopaths. It was a wonder Renner had never installed an alarm system . . . but then, he'd had the dog. "Terry?" Cole yelled, walking into the kitchen. "Dr. Renner? Rufus?"

No startled response. No surprised bark. No clicking of dog toenails or pad of slippered feet coming down the hallway to investigate. "Dr. Renner!"

Why the hell wasn't he answering? Had he been too drunk to turn off the lights, lock the door, put the booze away, or turn off the radio? Maybe he'd already gone upstairs to bed.

But Cole's gut told him otherwise.

Slowly, he turned down the hallway, his senses on alert.

Maybe Renner had fallen asleep. And the dog had been half deaf. The pop of a crackling ember drew Cole's attention to the adjoining den. He peered inside and noticed a dark stain on the floor.

A drop.

A *red* drop.

And then another.

And another.

"Shit! Terrence!" Cole yelled as he burst into the den.

Every muscle in his body froze.

Renner was lying faceup on the carpet. His eyes stared at the ceiling. Blood covered his neck and face. It pooled thickly on the floor.

"No!" Cole knelt beside him, his fingers clenching

the doctor's wrist to find a pulse, hoping to hear the sound of shallow breathing.

He was too late.

The blood had stopped flowing. There was no heartbeat. Not the shallowest of breaths being drawn.

Renner was dead.

Distantly Cole noticed Renner's right arm lay at an odd angle. His gaze moved upward slowly, and he saw the number scrawled onto the wall in thick red streaks:

101.

Every hair on Cole's scalp was raised. One hundred one? Like 212? The number written with Royal Kajak's blood by his own damned finger?

Cole's heart was a drum.

Renner was dead . . . *dead* . . . and yet he'd called Cole on his cell less than an hour earlier.

Jesus Christ, what the hell was going on?

You're being set up.

Again.

Someone had waited for him. Patiently biding his time until Cole had been set free. And then, within hours of his release, he'd slaughtered Renner—and *called* Cole!

What was it the guy on the phone said?

"I've got evidence."

The same chilling message Eve had received from Roy Kajak before he'd been killed.

The killer could still be in the house.

145

He scanned the room, checking the shadows, searching the darkened hallway where light from the den didn't spill. There was a letter opener on the desk. He grabbed it.

Get out! Get out NOW!

He listened, ears straining for any foreign sound, but all he heard was the tick of an old clock in the foyer, the notes of soft acoustic music playing from a radio on the desk, and the loud, powerful pounding of his heart crashing frantically against his ribs. No running footsteps. No deep breathing. No sound of a knife being slipped from a sheath.

The house seemed still.

Empty.

Not even a whimper, whine, or bark from the dog.

What are you waiting for? Get out!

Full-blown panic ripped through him.

Someone's setting you up, Cole. This is no fucking coincidence. Some sick son of a bitch has it in for you.

Why?

Who?

Someone Terrence Renner had been mixed up with?

Someone who had *killed* Renner.

Cole found the telephone and dialed 911. The dispatch officer answered before the phone rang twice. "Nine-one-one. What's the nature of your—"

"There's been a murder," Cole cut in tersely. "Terrence Renner. Someone killed him. At his house . . ." He had to think for a second before he rattled off the street address.

"Sir? Are you all right?"

"Yes. But Renner. He's dead."

"What's your name?"

He clicked the phone off.

He had to get out of here and fast. Before the cops arrived. He was in enough trouble already. . . . They'd figure out that he'd been here, of course, but for now he needed some time to sort things out.

Spying Renner's laptop sitting on the desk, he snatched it up, yanking the cord from the wall. Face set, mind snapping ahead, he shoved the slim device into the briefcase that lay open on the small love seat that faced the fire.

Taking anything from the house was a crime, but he didn't care. Whoever had killed Renner had purposely called Cole as a means to tempt him here. Maybe there was a clue in Renner's work notes, maybe not, but he'd never have this chance again.

Spurred by fear, fueled by adrenaline, he started a quick cleanup. If he were caught here, or anywhere near here, he'd be taken into custody.

The phone rang, and Cole jumped. He whipped around. It was the cops! The 911 dispatcher calling back!

As rapidly as he could, Cole wiped away any finger-, hand- or shoe-prints he might have left on the desk, the floor, the phone. Distantly he heard sirens screaming, and he flew out of the house, wiping the doorknob on his way out and leaping from the back porch to the patchy grass. Heart thudding, he sprinted to his Jeep, tossing the briefcase inside.

He backed down the driveway as fast as he dared. Then, at the county road, he threw the Jeep into first and stepped on it, rocketing in the opposite direction of the small town, telling himself not to speed, fear knocking deep in his soul. He forced himself to calm down, to step outside the murder, to think as a defense attorney, not one of his clients.

His voice was recorded. The police would eventually figure it out and call him in for questioning. He would have to face them. But not tonight. Not before he had a few answers of his own. In jail he'd vowed he would figure out what really happened the night Roy Kajak died, and that's what he intended to do. He couldn't have Roy's murder forever unsolved, himself the only serious suspect. And now Renner's death would put him at the top of that suspect list as well!

Think, he told himself. *Figure out your next step.*

First things first. He not only had the money, but Renner's laptop. He needed a place to hide them, and he knew a place that should be perfect: Eve's house. It was empty. Had been for months.

And, he decided, his brain clicking systematically, if the police searched her home, they wouldn't think it all that odd that Terrence's computer was there, at his daughter's. Cole would stash the money there too. No one would be able to connect it to him.

He found his way back to the freeway, and as he did he saw the familiar glow of New Orleans in the distance, the city lights visible through a thin, rising fog.

What about Eve? You need to call and tell her about her father. She deserves to know.

His jaw slid to the side as he considered the consequences.

Leave it to the police. If you tell her, she'll lead the cops straight to you.

Son of a bitch, he thought. No matter what he did, he was screwed.

CHAPTER 8

Time is running out.
And there is much to do.
So many rituals . . . so little time.
Yet he couldn't rush things, oh no.

The Reviver was still hyped-up as he parked his truck in a space he'd carved out in a dense thicket of brush and buckthorn. Nerves jangling, his body covered in sweat, he removed his tools from the back of the truck. He worked efficiently, taking anything incriminating from the truck then locking the vehicle securely and dashing up a slight hill to the knoll where his cabin was tucked into a deep copse of trees. The cool night breezes could not quench his heated skin. His pulse was pounding, the scent of blood still tantalizing his nostrils as he headed down the long, overgrown path to the cabin.

He had a place in the city, of course, but here, in the woods, this was where he belonged, where the Voice of God had found him, the only place he was certain to communicate with the Father.

Once inside, he threw the dead bolt, made certain the shutters were completely closed, then stripped himself of all clothing. He dropped all of his clothes into an ancient washer then placed his boots into the stainless steel sink and used a sprayer to wash the blood down the drain. When he was finished, he ran the washer, dumping a quart of bleach into the machine and scrubbing the sink with chlorine bleach as well. Though he felt as if he were doing a good job in covering his tracks, he had to be doubly careful. No plan was fail proof; the cops were far from idiots.

Trust in the Voice. Have faith.

Do not doubt.

Never doubt.

He was still on a high, reliving the kill over and over.

He'd known that Cole Dennis would take the bait.

The bastard had shown up at Renner's house right on cue and discovered the body.

The Reviver hadn't been foolish enough to wait around and watch, much as he'd wanted to. That would have been too risky, and the Voice had been clear about leaving as soon as he was finished. But as he'd driven here he'd turned on the police-band radio mounted in his truck and listened to what the cops were doing.

He didn't need much time to complete the plan. The Voice had been clear that the Reviver's mission was to be finished quickly, in a mere matter of days, culminating with Eve.

He thought about what he would do to her.

How he would punish her for all her sins.

He scratched his palms in anticipation.

He would strip her bare.

Take that body she flaunted and do everything he dreamed . . .

Now, lighting the fire, he spread a plastic sheet in front of the grate before carrying a freestanding full-length mirror from the bedroom and angling it on the edge of the sheeting so that the glass caught the reflection of the fire and of the mirror over the fireplace. He located his "kit" in the bottom drawer of an old cupboard and spread all the implements over the mantle. Once the altar was ready, he hurried into his cranny of a bathroom, turned on the pulsing spray, stepped beneath it. Icy water blasted his skin in a quick, harsh tempo. Thoroughly he washed away all the dirt, all the sweat, all the grime with industrial-strength soap that he used on his hair, his face, his hands, and his genitals. Once the suds were rinsed off, he stepped onto the cold stone floor and, still dripping, his skin dimpling with the cold, padded to the living area, where the fire illuminated the sparse, utilitarian room.

He lit the candles standing ready on the centuries-old mantel. Unscented votives, tapers, and pillars, all pristine white, flickered and burned, their tiny flames reflecting a dozen times over in the angled glass.

Catching the light from the candles' flames, his rosary sparkled as it hung from a hook over the mantel.

Tenderly he removed the glittering strand from its resting place. Letting the cool, blood-red beads run through his hands, closing his eyes as he lowered himself to his knees, he recovered some of his equilibrium. The rosary always comforted him, helped calm him, aided him in keeping the demons and ungodly thoughts at bay. He knew that what he'd done—the killing—was considered a sin, but not, he told himself, when he was on a mission from God, a modern-day crusade, a cleansing of the heathens.

The Voice of God had instructed him.

He was but an instrument; this he believed.

And yet he had unclean thoughts. Lustful thoughts. And he savored the killing. Fantasized about it. Relived it. Which was not God's intention.

How he ached to revel in the taking of Terrence Renner's life, to replay it even more, over and over, in his mind—just as he longed to imagine the violent coupling with Eve before he sacrificed her.

But he had to wait, to calm himself, to ignore the fantasies. In the end surely God would understand, for it was God who had led him to Eve, who had brought them together, as children and now as adults. As a child she'd been intelligent and clever. He remembered seeing her running through the hospital grounds, her tanned legs flashing in the bright sunlight, her coppery hair flying behind her, her blue eyes dancing. Even then, at twelve, her breasts had started to show, little buds that had been visible under her T-shirts until she'd started wearing a bra. She'd been athletic and wild, and he'd watched her grow, feeling heat seep through his bloodstream, causing his groin to tighten, his dick to grow, desire thudding in his brain.

But he hadn't dared mention his want of her to the doctor, her father. Not if he wanted to keep away from the medications that made him feel thick and dull, every movement an effort, as if he were trudging through water.

God had shown him Eve as a child.

God had allowed him to see her develop into a woman.

Then God had taken her away, probably because he'd sinned. Hadn't Sister Vivian told him so when she'd caught him in the closet, alone, touching himself, a picture of Eve taped to the back of the door? He could still see the nun's shock, the horror on her face.

She'd punished him then, threatened to tell the doctor. But his tears of repentance had stopped her from speaking of his sins to anyone but Sister Rebecca, who had pursed her lips and condemned him with her harsh gaze. It was she who had insisted he confess to the priest. To God. While the priest heard his confession, his prayers, and meted out his penance of prayers, good deeds, and clean thoughts, Sister Rebecca had come up with her own punishment. He'd been isolated from the other patients his age, those who had only "clean thoughts." He also was at Sister Rebecca's beck and call, her personal slave.

He'd felt as if he'd been chained to the voluminous

153

skirts of her dark habit and by the dark beads of her ever-present rosary. If he ever complained about his serfdom, Sister Rebecca threatened to tell Eve and Dr. Renner his dark secret, that he found pleasure in fondling himself while watching her.

"Just think what will happen then," Sister Rebecca had warned him in a conspiratorial whisper. "Everyone here will soon know just what kind of a sinner you are. . . ."

Sister Vivian, an underling of Sister Rebecca's, had avoided and abandoned him. While Sister Rebecca had relished punishing him, the younger nun had wanted nothing to do with such a sinner.

But then, they had been impure themselves, had they not?

Hadn't the Voice said as much?

Hadn't God Himself led the Reviver to Eve, who was no longer a girl but a woman?

And a sinner.

A whore.

And as unclean as she was, he ached for her.

His mouth dried of spit, and he began to tremble inside as he thought of her, remembered standing in the closet, staring at her picture. . . .

He needed to pray now, to beg forgiveness for his unclean thoughts and then finish with his own penance, his own private ritual.

Only then could he hope for the Voice to reach him again, to seek him out, to drown out the other tinny, aggravating voices that beleaguered him.

Gently holding the crucifix within the rosary between his thumb and forefinger, lightly touching the tiny image of Christ's body upon the cross, his voice barely audible over the hiss of the fire, he began to pray.

"I believe in God, the Father almighty, Creator of heaven and earth, and in Jesus Christ, His only son, our Lord . . ."

His blood began flowing more slowly, his heartbeat finding a regular cadence again, the beads of water upon his skin drying. As he had since he was a child, he touched each bead, murmured each prayer, until he was finished. "O loving. O sweet Virgin Mary. Pray for us. O holy mother of God, that we may be made worthy of the promises of Christ. Amen."

Slowly he rose, his naked body cleansed, his soul washed free, for he considered this his confession and communion. He didn't need a priest, an intermediary between himself and the holy Father.

God talked to him.

At night.

When he was alone.

And He told him to mark himself to remind himself of his mission. He opened his small case and looked at the gleaming instruments inside.

He took out the needle, filled the syringe with blue ink, plugged in the machine. Staring at the image of his naked, shaved, and waxed body in the tall mirror, he began. With careful strokes, he inscribed the number 101 upon his skin, the tiny, sharp needle moving with rapid, stinging strokes as he worked a foot pedal. He was precise, adding the tattoo to a clean space where he could read it easily among the others that he'd drawn on his body. For his victims, of course, he had to use a smaller, battery-powered needle. His work on the bodies was quick and rough. But on himself, he had the luxury of time to make each letter and number perfect. Exquisite.

The pain was exciting, a turn-on. While he worked his needle, he had to concentrate intensely to keep his cock from coming to attention, to keep his mind free of images of sex and pain, to ensure the quality of his artwork. Over and over the numbers he worked, coloring them in, making certain the scab would form and the impression would be forever.

The number 101 tattooed onto his flesh . . . along with the others, including names and the number 212.

It was over all too quickly. The sensual pain suddenly banished as his job was completed.

Blowing out the candles, he doused the fire with water, cleaned the needles and the tubes, wound the cord around the compact machine, and tucked it all into its case. After replacing the tattoo machine inside the desk, he folded the plastic tarp and stowed it away. Then he examined his artwork, tended to it and lay down on his bed, no sheets covering him.

He was done for this night.

But there would be others.

As there had been before.

Some he'd killed quickly. Others more slowly.

Releasing their souls to heaven. There had even been one who had been revived, but only one, and that was a long time ago . . . so long. Tears came to run in hot streaks from the corners of his eyes.

Now, though, that the killing had started once again, it would continue.

That thought pleased him.

The waiting was over.

He closed his eyes and soon the voices came, little chattering, irritating, and garbled pieces of conversation that whirred like bats' wings in his head.

Go away, he thought. *Leave me be. . . . Let me hear only God. . . . Let the Voice of the Father find me. . . .*

But it was not to be.

By the time sleep found him, the other hissing, crying, wailing voices had eaten away at his peacefulness, had made his muscles tense, his nostrils flare, and his fists clench. The tears that now welled in his eyes were not tears of sorrow but of frustration, and he bit his lip so hard that blood flowed. He nearly screamed aloud. He knew this would be one of those nights. Long, terrible nights. Nights where, when slumber finally did find him, it would be not with peace but with a raging storm of razor-edged nightmares.

Eve's cell phone shrilled loudly.

Her eyes flew open.

Where am I? What . . . what is the ringing? . . . The phone? Where is it?

For a second, Eve was disoriented, the room unfamiliar. She sat up in bed.

"Ssssss!" Startled, Samson hissed, arched his back, then hopped quickly off the coverlet and scrambled to hide under the dresser. Fumbling for the cell, Eve flipped on the night-table lamp. The room was suddenly bright. She blinked, her heart beating triple-time.

She managed to pick up the phone. "Hello?"

"*He's free*," warned the same low, raspy voice she'd heard before.

Eve sucked in a strangled breath. "Who is this?"

No answer. But he was still on the line. She knew it. Could feel him.

"Listen," she said, trying to keep the fear from her voice, "whoever you are, I know that he's free, okay? So you can quit calling me!"

"*Heeee'ssss freeeeeee . . .*" The caller's voice was so low, so ophidian a hiss, she barely heard it.

Click.

The phone went dead.

"Son of a—" she whispered, pushing her hair out of her face and trying to calm down. Who the hell was harassing her? Phoning her in the middle of the night now, for God's sake. She stared at the face of her phone, silently praying for a number or name. Of course the call was restricted, and no combination of punching numbers and reading screens and scrolling down menus gave her a clue as to the caller's identity. Whoever the bastard was, he wanted to remain anonymous while scaring the tar out of her.

Turning out the light, she flopped against the headboard and glanced at her alarm clock where the time was illuminated in glowing red numbers.

Two thirty-six.

Who the hell in his right mind would be calling at . . . Her own question taunted her. That was the problem. There was no "right mind" about it. Whoever was doing this had one serious screw loose. Probably two or three.

"Hell."

She lay in the dark, waiting for her pulse to slow. Who was he? Where was he calling from? Why did he feel the need to tell her that Cole was a free man? It was all over the news. And these calls weren't friendly warnings. No, these were sinister. Evil. Meant to intimidate.

Someone's trying to terrorize you.

"And doing a damned good job of it," she admitted as the cat hopped back onto the bed and curled up against her. She petted him absently, glad that she was forgiven.

Why would anyone—

Rap! Rap! Rap!

Her heart nearly stopped. She bit her tongue to keep from screaming. Someone was knocking on the door! Samson lifted his head and stared at the closed door to the bedroom.

Eve hardly dared breathe, but the knocking downstairs continued, a pounding that sounded as if it were coming from the back door. She thought of the bastard who'd just called. Maybe he was checking to see if she were home.

But no one knew she was here!

"Don't freak out," she whispered but was already in a near panic. She thought about calling the police but discarded the idea . . . for now. This was her neighborhood, not some deserted bayou.

Don't think about the night Roy was killed.

Stay calm. . . . Be rational. . . .

Without turning on a light, she threw on her robe and hurried to the room her grandfather had used as a den, an extra bedroom on the second floor that, twenty years after his death, still held some of his possessions: pictures of him and his wife, his medical degrees, his favorite old recliner, and his revolver. Thin light from the nearest streetlamp gave her enough illumination to find the gun in the bottom drawer of his desk. The gun wasn't loaded, and there were no bullets anywhere in the house that she knew of, but she would carry the weapon, along with her cell phone, downstairs just the same.

If she encountered an intruder, he wouldn't know that the revolver was useless.

Think, she told herself as she eased down the stairs, her eyes accustomed to the darkness. She'd walked down these hallways in the dark hundreds of times as a child and did so now rather than throwing her silhouette in relief and making herself an easy target by turning on a light.

Bam! Bam! Bam!

Whoever it was, was banging hard enough on the back door to rattle the window set into the thick oak panels. Certainly no sneak thief would want to call attention to himself. But a crazy person, one hopped up on drugs, someone desperate, just might.

Her fingers tightened over the revolver's handle as she headed down the long hallway separating the parlor from the dining room, past the bath to the kitchen. Her heart was beating crazily, anxiety firing her blood.

Don't panic, she told herself, but as she stepped into the mudroom, where she could see through the window cut into the back door, she spied a man on the porch—a tall man, his face hidden in darkness. A little cry escaped her taut throat.

"Who's there?" she demanded in a strained voice, her fingers gripped around the butt of the gun, her pulse pounding. She aimed the revolver at the window as if she intended to shoot then flipped on the switch for the porch light with her free hand.

The lamp lit weakly, the dim bulb casting the porch in a watery blue light that only seemed to accentuate the shadows as it flickered, threatening to die and leave the stoop in total darkness.

Nonetheless she recognized the man on the other side of the door.

Cole Dennis, big as life, stood on her porch.

CHAPTER 9

E ve didn't flinch.

She aimed the gun squarely at his chest. As if she intended to blow him and his black heart away.

Cole took one look at her through the glass and froze. Slowly he lifted his arms until both his palms were in the air, his fingers spread wide. "Eve, it's me!" he shouted through the door.

"What the hell do you want?" she asked, hating how scared she sounded.

"I didn't know you were here."

"Then why were you pounding on the door in the middle of the damned night?" She was furious with him, her heart rattling, her mind screaming at her to call the police. *Remember what he did to you! Remember looking through another window, at Roy's cabin, and seeing the gun go off! He was aiming at you, Eve. YOU. He intended to kill you!*

A light went on in the neighbor's upstairs window.

Damn, they were causing a scene. The last thing she needed was the whole neighborhood privy to her personal life. She'd had enough scandal to last her a lifetime.

But this was *Cole.*

"I need to talk to you," he said.

A second light shone in Mrs. Endicott's house, and Eve swore under her breath. If she didn't want the police and everyone on the block to know what was going on, she'd have to let him inside.

Reluctantly she unlocked the door and let it swing open, leaving the thin barrier of the screen door between them. "You can stop shouting. Say what you need to say, then leave."

Cole lowered his voice. "I didn't know you were here when I came by. I just got out of—"

"I know about that. It's all over the news."

"—but I saw your car."

"So you decided to wake me up at two-damned-thirty in the morning?" she mocked, trying to whisper. What the hell was he doing here? *Nothing good.*

He hesitated, his hands lowered a bit, and he nodded.

"Why?"

"I think you'd better let me inside."

"No way." She was shaking her head violently, the short strands brushing the back of her neck.

"Eve, please. This is serious."

"You bet it is!" Trembling inside, her emotions nearly strangling her, she couldn't help staring at him. Three months earlier, she'd seen him aim a gun at her, viewed it with her own eyes. Witnessed the blast. Felt the bullet. Suffered the aftereffects.

He lowered his voice even more. "No, I mean it. I need to talk to you."

"I'll be damned if you'll set one foot inside my house. It's over, Cole. Got it? Over!" She felt in the pocket of her robe with her left hand, found her cell phone, and held it up, all the while training her grandfather's handgun on his chest. Good Lord, she'd been a fool to love this man so fervently. How blind she'd been. "I'm calling the police."

"Great." He frowned, his lips twisting in that familiar thin line of frustration she'd witnessed dozens of times. He muttered something to himself then said, "Go ahead."

"You don't think I will? You think I'm bluffing?" She began pressing buttons with her thumb and watched as he scowled into the night.

"I don't think you know what you're doing."

"Nice, Cole. Way to score points."

"It beats pointing a gun."

"You should know!"

"Damn it, Eve. I didn't come over here just to kill time!" He stepped closer to the door. Through the mesh, in the weak light, she noticed how tired he looked, how the crow's-feet around his eyes were etched deeply into his skin, how his jaw was dark with a day's growth of beard. "Hear me out."

"So you can lie to me again? So you can kill me?"

"I never tried to harm you," he insisted angrily, his gaze finding hers in the darkness. Blue eyes so serious, so sincere, she wanted to cry out, to trust him. But she didn't dare. Couldn't trust herself. "I *never* put your life in jeopardy."

"Liar!"

"You know it, Eve. Deep in your heart, you know I would never do anything to hurt you."

"I saw you, Cole."

"No." He held one hand lower, palm flat as if to stop the tirade he sensed was coming. "You *think* you saw me. But you're not sure. That's why you couldn't testify. Your memory's messed up."

"You were there," she insisted, trying to convince herself. Hadn't this been the problem all along, that she hadn't believed what her eyes, or trusted what her damned faulty memory, had told her had to have happened? And the ADA had known it. Yolinda Johnson had said as much. "I *know* what I saw."

"Do you?"

She waggled the gun. "Don't try any of this BS with me. Got it? All your wow-the-judge-and-jury tactics don't work with me."

"I'm telling you the truth."

"The 'truth.'" She sighed and noticed another light in the neighbor's house switch on. Damn it all to hell! No doubt Mrs. Endicott could hear the argument. "That's the problem, Cole. You're deluded. You wouldn't know the truth if it sat down to dinner with you."

"I'm not the one who's suffering from amnesia."

"That's right. *Your* memory is selective. You *choose* to believe what you want to believe. I don't get that luxury. You know what's sick about this? You actually believe all the crap you're peddling my way."

Some repressed emotion flashed in his eyes, and his lips flattened over his teeth. "Fine." He drew a breath deep into his lungs. "But I think you might want to know about your dad."

"My dad?"

"Terrence."

"I know who he is." Her composure cracked a little. She wanted to think that he was baiting her, but there was something in his serious expression that kept her from arguing. "What about him?" she asked, but as the words passed her lips and he looked at her again, she caught a glimmer of something that squeezed her heart with dread.

"I think it would be better if I came inside."

She paused, her pulse drumming.

Could she trust Cole Dennis?

Not as far as she could throw him.

This was probably some kind of trick.

"We're fine this way."

"I'm serious, Eve."

"So am I."

"It's not good news." He hesitated as if he were trying to decide how to deliver the news.

Her insides turned to ice. He wasn't bluffing. Swallowing back a mounting sense of dread, she dropped her cell phone on the counter, unlocked the screen door, pulled it open, and stepped to one side. "Just don't tell me he's dead," she said.

"Eve . . ." His voice was unsteady.

Her mouth opened in horror. No. It was a trick! It had to be. A way to gain her sympathy. "I–I don't believe you."

But his face was white and stern. "I just came from there. I found him on the floor of his den. Someone killed him, Eve. Just like they killed Roy."

Her legs started to give way, and she backed up into the kitchen, where she leaned against the counter to avoid collapsing. He wouldn't lie about this, would he? Even Cole wouldn't stoop so low.

Don't trust him, don't trust him, do NOT trust him!

Anxiety skittered up her spine. Somehow she managed to flip on the light over the sink. She caught sight of her weak reflection in the window: a thin woman with haunted eyes, pale lips, and short, streaked hair that, in some spots, had barely started to grow out to cover the scars. "You said . . . You, uh, said you didn't think I'd be here. . . . Why were you . . . Oh God!" She gasped as he moved into the room, into the illumination.

Dried blood so dark, it seemed brown had stained the hem of his white T-shirt. "Cole?" she whispered, horrified. What had he done? Terror widened her eyes.

He followed her glance down, noticing the stain. "It's not like that. Eve, you know I had nothing to do with this."

"With . . . ?"

Her body was shaking from the inside out. Her stomach roiled. Nausea climbed up her throat, and she dry-heaved into the sink. The gun nearly fell out of her hand as she clutched the edge of the counter for support. Her father was dead? *Dead?* She retched again, spitting bile, her brain pounding with denial. *No! No! No, no, no, no!* She couldn't, wouldn't believe it. Cole was a practiced actor, a lawyer, for crying out loud. A liar!

"He called me . . . I thought it was him, and I went to see him. When I got there, he didn't answer the door. It was unlocked. I went in and found him in the den."

She looked up, wiped the back of her hand across her lips. "How?" she squeaked, fighting tears and the grasping fear that clawed at her brain.

Cole's arms had fallen to his sides. He looked like hell. His eyes were sunken, his usually tanned face pale. "It was just like Roy, Eve. Just like Roy. Your father's throat was slit. There was blood all over. . . . Oh Christ, Eve, it was—"

"Stop."

"—the same."

"I don't know why you're here, why you're doing this to me. It's unfathomable. . . . It's . . ."

"I tried to revive him and failed. He's dead, Eve."

Blood rushed noisily through her brain. "You just got out of prison. Today. Why would anyone . . . anyone but *you* kill my father?" She drew in a shaky breath and felt sick again. From the corner of her eye, she saw her cat pause in the shadows of the hallway.

"Eve." He looked stricken. "I had no reason to kill him."

"Since when are your actions reasonable, Cole? You tried to kill me, and now my father . . . Why are you here now? To finish me off?" she said, fighting down hysteria.

"Stop it, Eve. For Christ's sake, listen to me. I thought you were in Atlanta."

"Why the hell are you here, Cole? Why did you come here if you thought I was still in Atlanta?"

He hesitated.

"Don't," she whispered. "Don't lie to me." Samson, as if sensing the tension in the air, took off, disappearing into the shadows. Eve straightened, her back stiffening though she felt tears tracking down her face. "The least you can do is tell me the truth."

One hand closed into a fist then opened. "I was going to hide some things here," he admitted.

"What? Here?" She sniffed loudly and shook her head. She didn't believe him. She swiped at her tears with the sleeve of her robe. "What things? Incriminating evidence?"

He shifted his weight from one foot to the other.

"What things?" she demanded.

"Money."

"Money?" she repeated, shaking her head.

"Yes. And a briefcase."

"Yours?"

Another beat.

"Whose briefcase, Cole?"

"Your father's."

Every muscle in her body froze. "You stole my father's money and his briefcase?" she repeated, thunderstruck. This was all so bizarre. So surreal. Unbelievable. And yet, staring at him, seeing his bleak, solemn expression, the pain in his eyes, she was nearly convinced he was telling the truth, or part of it. But her father? Was he really gone?

Killed? A sudden chill, cold as December, slid over her skin.

"The money was mine."

"Yours?"

"I'd hidden it, a long time ago."

"Oh Cole—"

"It's the truth, damn it! Something I learned a long time ago from my old man."

"The con artist?"

"Who would know better about needing an emergency fund?" he asked, walking farther into the kitchen, out of range of the window, keeping one eye on the revolver she still held loosely. "I'd already picked up the cash when I got the call—a weird call—so I went to his place and found him lying on the floor. I tried to revive him, but it was too late. So I called 911. Then, before I took off, I saw his laptop. I stuffed it in the briefcase."

"You stole from a dead man, a murdered man." Eve could scarcely get the words out. She couldn't process what he was saying.

"I thought I might be able to figure out what's going on," Cole said tensely. "Why your father was killed. Who's responsible. Was it because of something he knew, something related to Roy's murder?"

"That's a job for the police."

"Is it? Because they didn't do such a bang-up job with Roy, did they?"

Eve pressed a hand to her forehead. "You'll be arrested for . . . tampering with evidence, leaving the scene, I don't know what all. You're in big trouble."

"That's why I'm here."

"I can't . . . think," Eve murmured, but Cole went on.

"The two murders have got to be connected. Roy Kajak had been a patient of your father's—"

"Years ago."

"Look, Eve, no one's going to try and figure out what really happened. The police aren't going to look any further than me."

"Do you blame them?" she demanded, but her voice had no volume, no power. "You just got out of jail today, and now my father is dead. Look at you. Look at his blood. It's all over you." She was hanging on to the shreds of her sanity for all she was worth.

"I'm being set up, Eve. I'm not a killer. And if I were, I'd be a helluva lot smarter. I wouldn't be here with you now. Someone called me tonight. I thought it was your old man. He said, 'I've got evidence.'"

Eve flashed back to the night Roy had called her, the panic in his voice, his insistence that she come. *I've got evidence.*

"That's right," he said, watching her face. "Just like the call you got from Roy." He glanced down at the gun quivering in Eve's outstretched hand. "Oh for Pete's sake, Eve! Give me that. You're not going to shoot me or anyone else." He wrested the revolver from her nerveless fingers, and she didn't fight him. She was too stunned, too disbelieving, and he was right. She'd never thought him brainless. But he was

171

passionate, that much she knew. If her father had set him off . . .

Cole checked the chamber of the gun and sighed. "I thought so." He tossed the useless weapon onto the counter next to her cell phone.

"You have an alibi?"

"No." He stared at her long and hard, his eyes an intense steel blue that had always caused her heart to pound, though now she was too numb to care. "Someone's behind this, whatever it is, and I think it's a lot bigger than I can imagine. But your father and Roy were killed for a reason. This wasn't random, or coincidence. Someone *waited* until I was released."

"I can't believe it." Anxiety, fear, and disbelief twisted in her brain, calling up the damned headache again. She reached for the kitchen phone.

"What're you doing?" he demanded.

"Calling my father's house."

"Eve, he's gone. I already phoned the police. They've got to be at the farm by now. They'll answer and come directly here."

But the call was connected, already ringing through. No one was picking up. Eve swallowed back her fear. *Come on, Dad, answer!* Her heart was beating a thousand times a minute, nervous sweat rising on her back and palms. When Terrence Renner's voice mail answered, she said, "Dad? This is Eve. I'm sorry to call you so late, but I thought you'd want to know that . . . that I'm back in town. . . . I, um, should have called earlier. Call me back."

172

She hung up, clutching the phone tightly, as if it were a lifeline.

Cole was pale as death.

She said, "No one answered."

Cole took the phone from her hands as fresh tears welled in her eyes. "Oh, darlin'," he whispered, wrapping his arms around her and folding her shivering body against his. "I'm sorry. I'm so sorry."

"He can't be dead. He can't be. . . ."

Strong, steady arms held her firmly and for a second she collapsed against him, accepting the grief that rose like a giant within her. The fingers of one hand curled over his biceps, and she fought the urge to strike out, to flail at him, to scream and rail to the heavens. Instead she held the feelings inside, apart from silent tears.

For just a minute.

Just long enough to catch a glimpse of their reflection in the window, a ghostly image of two lovers entwined. She squeezed her eyes closed. This was a mistake of gargantuan proportions, an irreversible error. She couldn't trust him. Not for a second! Stiffening her spine, she pushed away from him. "Leave."

"What?"

"Get the hell out of here, Cole." Still trembling inside, she crossed her arms under her chest and glared up at him. "I don't need you or want you here. If you're telling the truth, then the police are going to show up here soon, and they'll be all over you. You'll be back behind bars before you can think twice. If you're lying and have come here for some other reason, to get back at me, to play a cruel joke, or whatever, I don't want anything to do with you, and I will call the police. Make no mistake. Either way, you'll spend the rest of your first night as a free man back in jail."

"I'm not lying."

She believed him but steeled herself. "Fine. Go."

"Eve."

"Really, Cole. Get out."

The muscles in the back of his neck tightened. "I don't want to leave you alone."

"I'm fine."

He hesitated. "I don't have a phone. If you want to call—"

"I won't."

He seemed nearly convinced, when his gaze landed on the table where all the scraps of newspaper were spread. "What're these?" he demanded, and before she could say a thing, he switched on the Tiffany lamp suspended over the table. He started to pick up one of the clippings, and she said, "No! Don't touch anything!"

"Why? What're you doing?" He scanned a few of the articles. "Making a scrapbook? About the days you spent at Our Lady of Virtues?"

"No."

"Pinking shears?" He sent her a sideways glance full of questions. "Wait a minute. These are all about Faith Chastain."

"I know."

"She was Abby Chastain's mother."

"So?"

Frowning, he read each of the articles. "Abby Chastain is Montoya's fiancée."

"Reuben Montoya? The detective who . . ."

"Yeah. That one." He looked baffled. "So, why are you interested?"

"I'm not. . . . I mean, these were left in my car."

"*What?* When?"

"Today, I think." She explained quickly, and the muscles in his face tightened.

"Why today? Why now?"

"I don't know . . . but . . ."

"What?" he demanded.

In for a penny, in for a pound, she thought. "I got a couple of weird phone calls today."

"Today?"

She nodded then told him about the calls—the one on the road and the one less than half an hour earlier with its raspy voice that warned her, *"He's free."*

Cole studied her soberly as he listened to her narrative. His eyes narrowed and his lips became a thin crease, but he held his thoughts in check.

Eve finished with a helpless gesture in his direction. "The next thing I know, you're pounding on my back door."

A muscle clenched in his jaw. "I don't like it."

"That makes two of us."

"You need to go back to Atlanta. Or anywhere else. I don't think it's safe here."

175

"Now, wait, this is my home."

He stepped forward. "Two men are dead, Roy and your father. They were killed violently, viciously, and Eve, you were hit by a bullet. The day of your father's murder, you get a packet stuffed into your car and strange phone calls. Eve, you need to leave. Drive to Atlanta, or at least check into a motel tonight. In Lafayette or Baton Rouge or anywhere else, but you really have to leave."

"I'm not leaving. I need to know about my dad."

"Oh hell, Eve!"

Her cell phone jangled, and she nearly jumped out of her skin. Glancing down at the screen, she saw her brother Kyle's number.

"Hello?"

"Eve!" Anna Maria's voice sounded strangled. "Ohmigawd, I'm sorry to call so late, but Kyle's not here and I just got a call from a friend of mine who works for a newspaper in New Orleans. He's always listening to the police band, and he said there was a possible homicide and the victim's name is Renner. He's not supposed to have that information until everything's confirmed and the next of kin is notified, but he thought . . . Oh Mother Mary, is it Dad? The address sounded like the farm and . . . and I don't know what to do and . . ."

"No one's called me," Eve said, refusing to look at Cole, refusing to fully believe.

"I've tried to call Kyle, but he's not picking up," Anna babbled. "He's an idiot when it comes to operating a cell phone. And then I didn't see any reason to call Van, as he lives so far away, and until we know what's happening . . ." She paused, and Eve heard the click of a lighter, then a deep breath.

"Don't call Van."

"Someone should. I tried to call Dad, but no one answered. Just the damned machine."

"I'll drive out there," Eve assured her, and she saw Cole react out of the corner of her eye.

"No . . . you've gone through too much already. Kyle should be handling this!"

"It's all right, Anna. I'll take care of it," Eve insisted, although it almost felt as if she were having an out-of-body experience. Her phone stuttered in her ear. "Look, I've got another call coming in. I'd better take it."

"Call me back!"

"The minute I know anything, I promise."

Cole's eyes found hers. Then Eve glanced down at her phone. She recognized the prefix on her LCD as one for the parish in which her father resided. She snapped the phone closed without answering and gave Cole a twisted smile. "That was Anna Maria."

"And the other call?"

"My guess—the sheriff's department. You said the police would call back, didn't you?"

A muscle worked in Cole's jaw. "Yeah."

The phone rang again, and she glanced at the luminescent screen. "Same number."

Cole gritted his teeth. "They're on their way to inform you of your father's death."

"Then you'd better take off."

He hesitated a fraction, swore under his breath, and stared at her so hard she thought he might kiss her. Instead, he reached for the handle of the door and yanked it open. With one foot over the threshold, he glanced back. "For the record, I'm really sorry about all this, Eve, really sorry."

She swallowed hard.

"It's not over, you know."

She gazed at him. She didn't pretend to misunderstand what he was talking about.

But she knew better than to think there was anything left between them.

She shook her head, but he'd already disappeared into the night.

CHAPTER 10

B entz climbed into the cruiser, and Montoya threw the car into reverse, flooring it.

"Fill me in. What've we got?" Bentz asked, looking pissed as hell. Montoya hadn't explained, had just told him that they had a case and he was on his way, that he would pick Bentz up at the cottage he shared with his wife, Olivia, in the swampland on the outskirts of the little town of Cambrai. Grumbling, Bentz had said he'd be ready, which today meant faded jeans, no socks, slip-on shoes, and a sweatshirt.

"Terrence Renner. Dead. Killed with the same MO as Royal Kajak."

"Shit."

"On the first day that Cole Dennis is out of prison," Montoya added, his headlights cutting into the predawn gloom. "A buddy of mine from the parish where Renner lived called me. Knew about the Kajak case and thought we'd be interested."

"We are," Bentz said with a snort. He was a big man, a guy who had to fight his weight by working out with a punching bag, a man who had to battle his addictions day by day.

"How stupid is Dennis?" Montoya asked, his leather jacket creaking as he reached up to adjust the mirror.

"He's not." Bentz ran a hand around his unshaven face and glared out the windshield. "He's a smart-ass attorney. A street kid who worked the system, kept his nose clean after getting into some trouble as a juvey, and somehow got through college and law school. Graduated third in his class."

"He knows how to work the system." Montoya braked as he rounded a corner, then hit the gas again as they reached the freeway. He punched it, and the Crown Vic shot forward, flying along the pavement. The engine thrummed, the tires whined, and the police band crackled as Bentz, solemn, held onto the door handle with his usual white-knuckled grip. "Dumb prick."

"Dennis isn't dumb," Bentz reiterated.

"He broke the terms of his bail."

"Yeah." Bentz didn't sound convinced.

Montoya was having none of it. He wanted to nail the slime-ball so bad he could taste it. "Look, man, he screwed up. Tried to see Eve Renner while he was out last time."

Bentz grunted.

"And he was found with weed. Pulled over because his taillight was out. Opened his glove box and— looky here!—out falls a baggie of pot."

"My point. Why would Dennis do something so spectacularly stupid?"

"Cuz he's obsessed where Eve Renner is concerned. He can't stay away from her."

"And the taillight and baggie? A fuse was taken out of his car. Missing. Someone removed it. So he'd be pulled over. Then, when he goes to get his registration, the weed falls out."

"What are you tryin' to say?" Montoya demanded, flying around an eighteen-wheeler before cutting across to the off-ramp.

"You think the son of a bitch was set up?"

Bentz shook his head, reached into his pocket then came up with a stick of gum that he unwrapped and popped into his mouth. "Why not hide the weed some-where else?"

"Cuz he's an arrogant SOB who is above the law."

"And the fuse?"

"He could've taken it out to replace something else."

"He was out on bail, knew the terms." He chewed thoughtfully for a few minutes while Montoya negotiated the winding country roads leading to Terrence Renner's farmhouse. "Nah."

"He's our guy!" Montoya couldn't keep the irritation out of his voice. He and Bentz had been working the Roy Kajak murder for months, trying to put the pieces together, always coming up with the same answer: Cole Dennis was the killer. Cut and dried. Now his partner was waffling. Shit! Montoya was tired and cranky and didn't need Bentz pulling a one-eighty on him now.

They drove through a podunk town with a single stoplight blinking red at the main intersection. No one stirred. It was so quiet, it gave Montoya a case of the creeps. He liked the city with its bright lights, open-twenty-four-hours atmosphere, and action. This was way too quiet.

"Just doesn't feel right," Bentz said, his gum popping. "Something's off."

"Everything's off." Montoya stepped on it, heading deep into the Louisiana farmland. While Bentz stewed about the case, silently turning it over in his mind, Montoya tried to fit the pieces together as well. He'd been called by a deputy from this parish, a guy who had worked in the city and recognized the connection between this case and Kajak's. Montoya and Bentz would have to tread gently in case the sheriff decided he didn't want any New Orleans cops messing inside his jurisdiction. But if it turned out this kill matched Roy Kajak's enough that a serial killer was suspected, then the Feds would join the manhunt . . . unless Montoya could collar Dennis and throw his ass in jail first.

He saw the flashing lights before they'd reached the turnoff to Renner's house. A car from the sheriff's department was already parked at the end of the lane, nearly blocking traffic, while two uniformed officers discouraged anyone—from the curious, to neighbors, to the press—from turning in. Other official vehicles were parked nearby, along with a van from a New Orleans television station, two pickups, and a sedan, all of whose passengers stood outside, staring at the farmhouse. Montoya nosed into a spot across the road then climbed outside into the night that smelled of recent rain and turned earth. Frogs were croaking loudly, and he heard a police officer's radio crackle.

The two New Orleans detectives approached the two officers standing guard. Montoya and Bentz introduced themselves and flashed their badges while Montoya explained that they'd been called to the scene.

"You still need to log in," the tall, skinny deputy said. His hat was a size too big, his Adam's apple bobbing, his teeth slightly bucked. His nametag read Deputy Blair Mott.

Both Montoya and Bentz signed the crime-scene logbook.

"Anyone keeping track of these people?" Bentz asked, motioning with his pen to the ragtag group of bystanders who had collected beside their cars.

"Yep. Checked their IDs. Even wrote 'em down."

"Good. Anyone else stop by?"

"Nah. A couple of lookie-loos slowed down then took off, including the paper guy. It's early yet. In an hour or two we'll get more action. People gettin' up and goin' to work or makin' deliveries."

"Thanks."

Careful to disturb as little as possible, Bentz and Montoya walked along the tracks leading to the house. The scene was already crawling with crime-scene investigators, detectives from the sheriff's department, and someone from the coroner's staff. A videographer panned the rooms of the house, where bright lights had been set up. Bonita Washington from the crime lab was giving orders to Inez Santiago, who was measuring blood spatter, and A.J. Tennet, who dusted for prints. Measurements were being taken, the rooms dusted for fingerprints or shoe prints, a vacuum used to suck up any unseen trace evidence. Bags of evidence had already been collected.

They walked into the kitchen where a bottle of booze was being examined and a tray that had once held ice was half filled with water.

Down a hallway and through open French doors they found the crime scene—a den where embers in the fireplace glowed red under white ash. Renner's body lay on the floor in a pool of blood, his forehead marked with a tattoo. A newspaper was on the floor, an overturned glass beside it.

"Jesus," Montoya said and noticed that his partner's complexion had blanched, jaw muscles working as if he were trying to keep whatever was in his stomach down.

On the wall near the top of Renner's head, the number 101 had been scrawled in blood. Probably Renner's. Just like Kajak.

"The number is wrong," Bentz said.

Montoya sniffed loudly. "We don't know that. We only know that it doesn't match the other killing."

"Copycat?" Bentz offered up. A few facts from the Kajak homicide had never been given to the press. The actual number written on the wall of the cabin had been withheld. Just in case some nutcase tried to claim he was the murderer. With a few facts secret, the police were able to sort out the looney tunes from the real players. "Someone with a grudge against Renner who read about Renner's association with Kajak and thought they could pin this on the other doer."

"My money's on Cole Dennis."

"Yeah, I know." Bentz's gaze swept the interior, landing on the officer in charge, Detective Louis Brounier, a burly African-American man with silver hair, fleshy face, and intense eyes that seemed to miss nothing.

"Look familiar?" Brounier asked, and Montoya nodded.

"Who called this in?" Bentz asked.

"The caller didn't ID himself, but the call came from Renner's landline, and it wasn't Renner." Brounier pulled out a small notebook and flipped back a few pages, his big face creasing as he scanned his notes.

"A male phoned 911 at one forty-seven A.M. today. He said, 'There's been a murder. Dr. Terrence Renner. Someone killed him. At his house.' Then there's a two-second pause while he comes up with the address."

"You think it was the murderer?"

"Maybe. Whoever it was didn't stick around. By the time the first officer arrived, the place was empty, back door unlocked." Bushy eyebrows rose in speculation. "By the way, no forced entry."

"Anything missing?"

"Not that we can tell. Yet. We're still looking. But if robbery were the motive, the killer missed out on some expensive art, and Renner's wallet was in his back pocket. All his ID, credit cards, and nearly a hundred bucks. His stereo is here, his television, and he's got one of the new expensive ones, as well as his computer, a desktop in a bedroom upstairs."

"Laptop? Cell phone?"

"Haven't found either."

"Anyone see anything? Any phone messages?"

"Not that we know of. Two phone messages came in just after the first officer arrived. One from Eve Renner, the victim's daughter. Another from Renner's daughter-in-law, Anna Maria Renner. Deputy Mott didn't answer either call. He wanted to hear what kind of messages they would leave." Brounier walked to the answering machine in the kitchen and hit the play button. The breathless, worried voice of Eve Renner filled the room.

"Dad? This is Eve. I'm sorry to call you so late, but I thought you'd want to know that . . . that I'm back in town. . . . I, um, should have called earlier. Call me back."

Brounier clicked off the machine. "That call came in at two fifty-one, according to this machine."

"She knows," Montoya said, his heartbeat quickening, the synapses in his brain moving so quickly he felt agitated, nervous, already ahead of the game. "How could she know unless whoever had done it had called her?"

"You don't know—"

"No one calls their parent at three in the morning unless you want to give them a heart attack. She was worried about him, otherwise she would have waited until the morning."

"Maybe something happened to her, and she needed to talk to him. Maybe she hurt herself, fell, or—"

"Oh shut the hell up, Bentz. You don't need to play fucking devil's advocate. Eve Renner knows because someone told her, and that person is the killer."

Bentz turned to Brounier. "Maybe," he conceded. "So, where did the call originate? Eve Renner's been in Atlanta."

"Caller ID says the call came in from a New Orleans number. I checked already. It's her house. The second one, that's the call from Atlanta." He hit the play button again.

"Dad? This is Anna Maria. Could you call me back? I just want to make sure you're okay. I've, uh, I've got

186

this friend who works for the paper. He called and said there might be some trouble at your place, so I kinda got worried. Kyle's not home right now, but you can probably reach him on his cell. But you can call here. Okay? Please. Just let me know that everything's fine. Love ya."

Click.

"Stupid reporters," Brounier said. "Listening in on our bands. I know they're just doing their jobs, but hell, they're such a pain."

"So Eve Renner's back in New Orleans," Montoya whispered. "Same day that Cole Dennis is released. Same damned day that her father gets himself offed. How much of a coincidence is all that?"

"You know how I feel about coincidences," Bentz muttered.

"Don't believe in 'em." Brounier took off his glasses and rubbed the lenses with the tail of his shirt.

Montoya said, "Someone from the department should go and give Eve the bad news."

"A unit's already been dispatched," Brounier said. He checked his watch and scowled. "They should have reported back to me by now." His mouth pursed in aggravation, and Montoya guessed Louis Brounier suffered no fools, especially if they were underlings.

"Anything else you can tell us?" Bentz asked.

"Not until we gather more evidence and sift through what we've got. It looks like the victim was surprised, attacked, his throat slashed, and then, as he was

187

bleeding out, the killer wrote the number on the wall with a finger."

"The vic's finger," Montoya said, adding, "If it's the same killer."

"Then there's the number tattooed on his forehead. One hundred one, same as on the wall."

"Same MO as the Kajak homicide," Montoya said, "but a different number."

Bentz stared at the body then glanced up at Montoya. "Got to be the same guy."

"Now you're talkin'."

Brounier's cell phone jangled. "Brounier. What? Oh for Christ's sake! Now? No . . . no, I'll be right there." He clicked off and looked at Montoya. "The daughter's here."

Eve saw the police cars, flashing lights, officers, and news crews parked haphazardly on the road running past her father's small farm and felt ill all over again. She found a spot near the neighbor's fence, nosed her Camry into the weeds, and pulled to a stop. Saying a quick prayer, she climbed out of the car and half ran toward the end of the lane, where a skinny officer was standing guard. The night was bone cold, or so it suddenly seemed. She pulled her hastily donned jacket more tightly around her.

"I'm Eve Renner," she said as she reached the deputy. "I need to see my father."

"Sorry, ma'am, no one's allowed. Crime scene."

"But I'm family. Terrence Renner is my father. I

lived part of my life in this house," she said as if the man hadn't heard her correctly.

"If you'll just step to one side, I'll have one of the detectives come and speak with you."

"The police came to my house to tell me. That's why I'm here," she insisted.

"Excuse me." The officer spoke into the radio microphone attached to his uniform. Eve felt all the starch drain out of her and sank against the police cruiser and tried to pull herself together, but all the while images of her father flashed through her mind.

Dad! Oh Dad! I'm so sorry . . . so sorry. Tears again filled her eyes as she remembered Terrence Renner as a young man, over two decades earlier, when she hadn't yet entered kindergarten. She recalled how he'd tossed her into the air, only to catch her again, and how she'd she squealed in glee. "More, Daddy," she'd cried, though her mother had been horrified at the game. "More, more, more!"

Another fleeting image, of her father as a doctor, the tails of his blindingly white lab coat catching in the breeze as he walked briskly across the tended lawns and gardens of Our Lady of Virtues campus. His professional smile had always been in place, though he'd rarely looked side to side at the patients who sat in the shade or pushed walkers or clustered in "outdoor group activities." He'd been self-important then, a brilliant, educated man among the mentally incapacitated, the patients he'd tried to help.

She closed her eyes and turned her face to the night

breeze. Another memory seared through her brain: she'd been older, maybe preteen, and her father had made a daily ritual of returning home to their house just off the campus of the hospital. Eve's mother, lipstick bright, forever in jeans and a colorful T-shirt, had always had a pitcher of drinks waiting for him. Each night Terrence had set his briefcase in the front closet, deposited his keys in a dish on the table in the foyer, and brushed a kiss over his wife's cheekbone. Even so, he was distracted, lines of worry creasing his high forehead, his gaze trained on the living room, where the sanctuary of the television and nightly news waited.

And then there was the most painful memory: Eve and her father standing at the cemetery in the hot sun on an August afternoon without a breath of breeze. Her brothers, red eyed and uncomfortable in their suits and ties, had been a few steps away, part of the family but not too close. Nana, draped in black, had been there as well, as Terrence stood staunchly in the blazing sun, his face pale, no tears visible as his wife was laid to rest.

Now, leaning against the police car, Eve tried to rally.

"I would like to see my father," Eve repeated to the skinny officer with the big hat.

"Sorry, ma'am. I can't let you. Crime scene."

"I heard you the first time. I understand a crime has been committed." Her head was thundering again, pounding mercilessly. "Can you please tell me what's happened to my father?" When she realized the deputy wasn't about to budge, she added, "Or . . . or can I talk to whoever's in charge?"

"Detective Brounier's on his way."

"Brounier?" Eve turned toward the house and saw not one but three men, backlit by the lights of the house and flashlights, striding down the lane. She didn't recognize the big, burly black man, but she knew the others.

Too well.

Her heart nosedived.

Detectives Bentz and Montoya.

More bad news.

Before they spoke, just as the threesome reached the barrier of yellow tape, she said to the approaching black man, "I'm Eve Renner. Dr. Renner's daughter. I want to see him."

"Detective Louis Brounier," he said, extending a big hand, though he didn't smile. He stared at her with surprisingly kind eyes. "You were alerted to the news about your father?"

"It's a homicide?"

"Yes, ma'am. I'm sorry."

He didn't equivocate, and for that she was grateful. She nodded slowly several times. "I would . . . I would like to see him."

"No, you don't," Montoya interjected.

Her temper snapped, white hot. "He's my father, damn it." Who was this guy to tell her what she did or didn't want?

191

Bentz said, "We can't let you do that. Not yet, anyway. In a few hours, after he's been transported to the morgue, then we'll need you to make an identification."

Brounier said, "The sheriff's department is going to work with the state police and the New Orleans Police Department. We just don't have enough resources to handle something like this alone." Eve knew there was more to it. Bentz and Montoya had been called in because her father's death was similar to Roy's. There was a connection. Sooner or later, the police would be knocking on Cole's door again. And she was betting on sooner.

Montoya said, "You called here earlier. For your dad."

She nodded. "I got into town late, and I wanted to call him and let him know I was back. But I got his machine, and then my sister-in-law from Atlanta phoned me. A reporter friend of hers had called her and told her there was trouble at Dad's house, a possible homicide." Eve managed to keep her voice in check. She'd already decided not to mention Cole. Not yet. "Then the police came and alerted me, and then I drove straight here."

"It would have been better if you'd stayed home and let us do our job," Montoya said.

"I couldn't," Eve said simply.

Montoya eyed her. "What time did you call your father?"

"Two-thirty, three . . . Does it matter?" Eve felt herself begin to perspire. Cole had been with her when she'd made that call, and it felt as if the detective knew it.

"It couldn't wait till morning?"

"I really wasn't concerned about what time it was. I was too keyed up and worried to sleep."

A moment passed when no one said anything. Eve broke the uncomfortable silence. "Do you have any idea who would do this? Or why?"

"We thought you might be able to come up with a list of his enemies," Bentz suggested.

"Enemies? I . . . I have no idea. He was retired." She flashed to Tracy Aliota's parents and their accusations that her father had been responsible for their daughter's death. "I'll think about it," she promised, suddenly so tired her bones ached. Her father was dead. There was nothing more she could do for him, and even if she did regret their recent estrangement, it was too late now to make amends. "I think I'd better call my brothers."

"What about Cole Dennis? Has he contacted you?" Montoya asked, the diamond stud in his ear reflecting sharply in the strobing lights.

Eve nearly stopped breathing. "What?"

"He's out of jail, you know."

"Of course I do. It's all over the news."

"So did he call you?"

"I just got into town, Detective, and I have a restraining order against him, and let's just say I'm not exactly his favorite person these days."

"So he *didn't* contact you?"

"He hasn't called me, no. Not in a long, long while," she said, wondering why she felt compelled to protect the man who she'd once thought had tried to kill her. She started for her car, but Montoya stepped in front of her.

"We have a few more questions."

"Can they wait?" she asked. "Until tomorrow?"

"Yes, ma'am. Let us have someone drive you home," Brounier offered.

"No. I'm fine."

"Are you certain? Is there someone I can call?"

"No, thank you. I'll be all right," she said, hoping to appear more collected than she felt. Her head was throbbing, she was dead on her feet, but the last thing she wanted was to be cooped up in some vehicle with a cop. She had to be careful, sort things out.

"We'll call you later," Detective Bentz said, though Montoya studied her as if he didn't trust anything about her.

Brounier nodded his agreement. "Thank you, Ms. Renner. Again, I'm sorry for your loss."

"Thanks," she whispered, walking quickly toward her car. She didn't wait for anyone to change his mind. She just needed some time alone. To think. Tomorrow, after a night's sleep, she would talk to the cops again, and when she did she'd show them the weird clippings about the mental hospital and admit that she thought she'd been followed. If they blew her off as a nutcase, so be it.

And will you tell them about Cole?

One of the news reporters looked her way. Oh God, she didn't want to talk to anyone from the press. Not now. Probably not ever. Averting her face, Eve unlocked her car and quickly slid behind the wheel. Slamming the door closed, she prayed the reporter wouldn't recognize her, wouldn't put two and two together about Royal Kajak and her father. *And Cole. The reporters will make that connection too.*

She rammed her key into the ignition.

Will you tell them? Will you?

She shook her head and bit her lip, wondering what it said about her that, against all reason, she was protecting Cole.

CHAPTER 11

"I think I'm in trouble." Cole held the grimy payphone receiver to his ear while drinking a brutally hot cup of coffee he'd gotten from an espresso hut on Decatur. He'd called Deeds collect. Thankfully his attorney had deigned to take the call.

"Already?" Deeds said, and Cole imagined him leaning back in his desk chair, looking through the panoramic windows of his corner office. "It's barely eight in the morning. You haven't been out of jail twenty-four hours. What took you so long?"

Cole was in no mood for wisecracks. "Terrence Renner's dead."

Silence.

"It's all over the news."

"What happened?" Deeds bit out.

"He was murdered. Throat slit. Just like Roy Kajak."

"This is a joke, right?"

"I'm not in the mood for jokes. Turn on the television. Renner's homicide is nearly identical to the Kajak murder. The only difference that I know is that the numbers scribbled in blood on the wall and tattooed onto his forehead were different: 101 instead of 212."

"All of this information was on the news?" Deeds asked.

"Probably not all of it. Some was held back."

"Then how do you know?"

"I was there. Renner called me."

"Damn it, Cole! I knew it! You can't keep your nose clean for a day!"

"I told you I thought I was in trouble."

"Trouble is a traffic ticket. This isn't trouble. It's a fucking catastrophe!" He paused to draw in a deep breath then continued his rant. "What the hell were you thinking?" He swore again, calling Cole every name in the book before he somehow managed to calm down. "Okay, okay. Let me get this straight. *You* witnessed the crime?"

"No." Cole sipped the hot coffee from his paper cup and kept staring through the smudged glass of the booth, watching people pass by. Some were walking to the bus stop one block away, others whipping by on bicycles, still others strolling or out for a morning jog. No one seemed to be paying any attention to him. A police cruiser stopped at a nearby light but rolled past the booth without either of the officers inside even glancing in his direction.

"I got to the scene just afterward, I think." Talking quietly and rapidly, he sketched most of the details of the events of the night before, only omitting the part about locating his stash of money, stealing Renner's things, and visiting Eve. Those details could come out later.

Maybe.

Deeds listened.

Cole knew the legal wheels were whirling at light speed in his attorney's mind as Deeds tried to come up with a good "spin" on the unwelcome news of his client's escapades. As Cole concluded, Deeds said, "Just tell me you didn't call Eve."

"I didn't call Eve." That, at least, was the truth. He didn't know how much he could confide in his lawyer, and as for Eve, oh hell, he didn't know what to think about that himself. He hadn't intended to meet her last night, but in truth, had he known she was back in town, he might have made a beeline for her door anyway. "Look, I gotta go. I'll call you later, and we'll meet."

"I'm booked until six. Got a squash match after that, but I'll change it. Come in then."

"No, let's meet somewhere else."

A beat.

"Okay. Your place?"

"How about O'Callahan's, on Magazine, a block or two off of Julia?"

Deeds said, "I'll be there around six-thirty. Don't, and I mean do *not,* do anything stupid in the meantime."

"Right. Oh, and Sam, don't call me. I had to ditch the phone."

"Son of a bitch, Cole, what's got into you?"

"I don't want to be traced. If you don't show up at O'Callahan's, I'll call you.

"Jesus H. Christ, what the hell have you done this time?"

Oh man, if you only knew. "I'll explain when I see you," Cole lied then hung up and started walking.

Don't do anything stupid. What Deeds really meant was don't contact Eve. Deeds didn't yet know that Eve was in town and that Cole had already found her.

Taking another scalding sip of coffee, Cole kept walking, over the slight rise that separated the city streets from the waterfront. He needed time to think, to clear his head.

Except his damned thoughts kept tumbling back to Eve. Dressed in a soft robe, her eyes glimmering with tears and emotion, her lips compressed angrily, and her hands pointing a revolver straight at him, she'd been ultimately desirable. He should have been scared, angry, but there was something about that woman that just got to him. Even though she'd obviously been with another man, cheated on him, and despite her admitted memory loss would have willingly testified against him, he still found her the most intriguing woman he'd ever met.

So much for thinking rationally.

He strode toward the Riverwalk Marketplace, watching the sluggish water of the Mississippi roll past. A barge was heading upstream, and a bit of wind, blowing across the water, brought the dank scent of the river to his nostrils.

Who had killed Terrence Renner?

The same psycho who had slit Roy Kajak's throat?

It had to be . . . So what did the numbers mean? 212? 101? Were they clues to the killer's identity or a part of the homicidal maniac's sick sense of justice?

Why, on the very day he was released, had the killer found his next victim?

Maybe it isn't about you. Maybe the killing resumed because Eve returned to New Orleans. Or maybe because of some incident entirely unrelated.

A coincidence.

Oh yeah, like he believed that for even an instant.

Watching a teenager throw a Frisbee to some kind of mixed-breed shepherd wearing a red bandana, Cole downed the rest of his coffee, crumpled the cup, then tossed it into a trash receptacle. He had too much to do to spend time thinking in circles. He headed to the spot he'd parked his Jeep.

In the early morning hours, after leaving Eve's house, Cole had headed back to his place, changed into clean clothes, then driven across town to a laundromat where he'd bleached the hell out of the blood-stained T-shirt and jeans before drying them and dropping them off at a depository for the Salvation Army. He was back home by six, slept three hours, showered in the thin spray of his bathroom, then walked to get his coffee and make the call. Fortunately, the caffeine was doing its job, jolting his system awake. He had a lot of things to do today, the first of which was to buy one of those prepaid, nearly impossible to trace cell phones that, he suspected, were popular with the drug-dealing crowd. Once he'd purchased a new phone, he'd make a few calls and see if he could connect with one of his former clients, a low-life slumlord who might just be able to help him out.

In the meantime he was going to go against his attorney's advice and his own better judgment.

Because he couldn't leave well enough—or Eve Renner—alone.

It was nearly ten when Eve finally forced herself out of bed. Somehow, despite the confrontation with Cole, the drive to her father's house, the further phone calls to Anna Maria and her brother Van's answering machine, she'd slept.

Like a log.

Now, though, she was sluggish, and the events of the past twenty-four hours bogged her down. Scrounging in the freezer, she discovered a bag of opened beans, which she ground, and started the coffeemaker. As she let Samson outside, Mr. Coffee began to gurgle and scent the room with the rich, warm aroma of some dark blend called Mississippi Mud. She didn't remember buying the coffee, but that was pretty much standard these days. Her memory, though recovering, just wasn't reliable.

She walked through the shower. Then, with a towel cinched around her body, swiped at the steamy mirror and nearly cringed at her reflection. Her long hair was cut short and highlighted, compliments of Anna Maria the hairdresser. The "style," if you could call it that, was spiky and uneven due to the large spot over one temple that had been shaved for her surgery. Her hair would grow out, and, for the moment, she decided to "go with" the new "do." It wasn't all that bad, and a hairstyle was the least of her problems.

The face beneath her shaggy bangs was a concern, however; she looked as if she'd aged ten years in the past three months. Her skin was pale, her eyes without their usual sparkle, her cheekbones pronounced with the loss of nearly ten pounds. She hadn't been heavy to start with, and losing the weight hadn't aided in her attempts to appear healthy and athletic.

"In time," her physical therapist had told her, "you'll be a hundred percent, but it will take awhile." So maybe the eighty-five percent motion in her shoulder would improve. She ran a toothbrush around her teeth, added a little lip gloss and minimal mascara, and called it good.

Who really cared anyway?

When she stepped into the jeans she found in her

drawer, they hung lower on her hips than she remembered. The sweater she tossed over her head draped loosely but was comfy, so she went with it. As for the headache that had followed her around all day yesterday, it had abated a bit, and, despite the grief she bore for her father, she felt as if she could tackle the day.

She slid into her favorite pair of slip-ons and clattered down the wooden steps just as the phone jangled. Racing to the kitchen, she snagged the receiver before it rang for the third time. "Hello?"

"Eve Renner?"

She braced herself at the sound of the unfamiliar male voice. "Yes," she responded cautiously.

"This is Miles Weston with WKMF."

Her heart sank. She recognized the name.

"I'd like to talk to you about your father's death."

"No comment," she said.

The reporter continued, "The police are listing it as a homicide."

She hung up. Her anonymity had been short lived. Last night she hadn't been recognized, but today the press was already putting two and two together, having figured out she'd returned to New Orleans. She was Eve Renner, the woman whose lover had been accused of murdering Roy Kajak in a bizarre homicide, and now she was also Eve Renner, the daughter of Terrence Renner, who'd been killed in like fashion.

And Cole Dennis, blast his hide, was a free man.

At least temporarily.

The phone rang again. She saw it was the same number as before, so she let the answering machine take the call. The last thing she needed to deal with today was the damned media. She'd had enough to last her a lifetime.

And she wasn't ready to deal with her father's murder.

Not yet.

The coffee, despite its enticing smell, was a little bitter without any cream, but she sipped it as she read over the articles about Faith Chastain and Our Lady of Virtues again. They seemed less sinister in the morning light, almost childish with their perfectly cut notched edges. Why the pinking shears? Why sent to her? Why, why, why?

She sat at the table and read each clipping carefully. Faith Chastain. She fingered a grainy picture of a beautiful woman with a haunted expression. Had Eve seen her before? She checked the articles closely and determined that Faith Chastain had been in and out of Our Lady of Virtues but that she'd stayed for an extended length of time when Eve was young, . . . She'd been killed twenty years earlier, about the time Eve was fifteen . . . not long before Eve's own mother's death.

Moving the clippings around, Eve tried to put them in some sort of order, and as she did her thoughts returned to Our Lady of Virtues. The hospital was a creepy and fascinating place for a curious child. Though she'd been warned time and time again about keeping to the main hallways or her father's office on the first floor, she had, over the years, explored all of the old brick asylum, from the basement with its cool tile walls and shining equipment to the dusty attic where unused and broken furniture and records had been kept. She'd loved to sneak into that forgotten space under the rafters.

Our Lady of Virtues was where she'd first met Roy. . . . They were both around ten at the time and up to no good. Roy was the son of the caretaker, and they'd instantly connected, two normal kids in a bizarre world of insanity, delusion, and pain. For the most part, they'd played outside, off the grounds of the hospital, in the surrounding woods and fields, but when the weather was bad, they spent time inside the campus of Our Lady of Virtues. Though both the convent and hospital were deemed off limits, they ignored the rules as much as possible.

It had been a game to them both, slipping through the quiet hallways, up the service stairs, and avoiding the ever-rustling skirts and stern glances of Sister Rebecca. How many times had Eve hidden in the laundry cupboard, peering out, seeing the dangling cross from the heavy belt rosary Sister Rebecca wore around her waist? Or viewed the crisp uniform and pinched lips of the nurse, a slim blond woman who seemed to do her job with long-suffering efficiency? What was her name? Nurse . . . Suzanne . . . That was it; there had been an old song by the same name, one she'd heard on her mother's tape player. Roy had always whistled it under his breath, singing only, "You want to travel with her, and you want to travel blind . . . but you know that she's half crazy . . ."

They'd thought they were so funny, so clever, so sly as they'd filched cookies and apples from the kitchen then sneaked them upstairs to the attic to build their own hiding space with the old furniture, drapes, and broken equipment.

She remembered the gloomy day that Roy had led her to the attic and then, making her promise not to tell on pain of death, showed her a series of holes in the floor where light from the rooms below filtered upward. "Spy holes," he had told her, and they'd spent many afternoons looking through them into the patient rooms and hallways below.

Eve had felt a little guilty about it, uncomfortable that she was peering into another person's privacy, but it hadn't stopped her.

Had one of the people she'd observed secretly been Faith Chastain? What was the reason so many articles about this woman had been forced upon her?

Now, as morning sun filtered through the dirty windows and slats of the blinds, she had no answers, just the same feeling of unease that had chased after her so many years ago.

Her stomach rumbled from lack of food. She made a quick mental note to pick up a few essentials before she returned, then scooped up the newspaper articles and slid them into the envelope in which she'd received them.

No doubt the police, if interested, would want everything.

Especially the truth.

What are you going to tell them about Cole, Eve?

Sooner or later, you're going to have to explain that he stopped by, that he was covered in blood, that he'd been at your father's house but you, the woman who'd accused him of trying to kill her, had believed his story when he told you he hadn't slit your father's throat.

"Later," she told herself as her cell phone indicated she had a text message. She checked, saw that it was Anna. All it said was, *Hope you're okay. Call later.* What was it with Anna and the texting?

She stuffed the envelope into her purse then headed outside, locking the door behind her. The air was warmer than the day before, and sunlight was filtered through high, drifting clouds. Samson, pressed flat on the floorboards of the porch, was peeking between the rails, his body frozen, only the tip of his tail twitching as he stared at a bird flitting between the budding, twisting stalk of a clematis winding its way up the rain gutter.

"In your dreams," she told the cat, smiling to herself.

She unlocked the car, slid inside the already warm interior, and was about to start the engine when she saw the glove box. Closed. No evidence that anyone had opened it. Yet her heart kicked into a quick tempo and she couldn't help but open the small compartment.

It was empty except for her sunglasses case and owner's instruction manual for the Camry. "Good," she told herself as she backed onto the street. She noticed Mrs. Endicott busily weeding her flowerbed and as the older woman waved, Eve raised her hand then drove toward St. Charles Avenue. She hated to imagine what her neighbor had overheard last night but decided not to dwell on it. If she were lucky, it would never come up.

"Yeah, right," she said with more than a trace of sarcasm as she braked for a red light.

Her cell phone rang before the light changed and she pulled it out of her bag. Caller ID told her that *Renner, Kyle* was calling, but Eve was laying odds that Anna Maria was on the other end of the wireless connection.

"Eve?" Anna asked when Eve answered. She didn't wait for a response. "You didn't call me!"

"Just got your text message a few minutes ago. Sorry."

"It's okay. Did you get hold of Van?"

"Yeah. I left him a message."

"Me too, and he hasn't called back." She sounded worried, but that was nothing new. "I just don't get him. Do you know anything else? I mean, we've got to plan a funeral. Kyle hates these things; I think he's in denial, and . . . Oh damn, I didn't mean to go on like this. How're you?"

"I'm okay."

"You sure?"

"Yeah. What about you?"

"Fine, I guess. The news reporters have started to call and, well, that's kind of weird. You know, unnerving."

"I hear you," Eve said. "They've started with me too."

"I'm glad Kyle's not around, or he'd be having a fit. Has he phoned you?"

"No. Where's Kyle?"

"Still at that damned job I told you about."

"When he gets home, have him give me a call and we'll figure out funeral arrangements once the police release the body. I just don't know when that will be."

"Okay. . . . Listen, I hate to bring this up, but what about his will?"

Someone behind Eve honked, and she saw the light was now green. Easing into the intersection, she said, "I don't know. He never talked about one."

"I suppose we'll find it when we clean out his house or safe-deposit box."

"If he has one."

"I know it's kind of uncomfortable to be talking about it so soon, but it's just that Kyle thought you might know something about it."

Her stomach soured. Their father had been murdered, and her eldest brother's first thought was the estate? It was just so like Kyle. To this day, she didn't understand what Anna saw in him. Slowing for another amber light, Eve decided to end the call.

"Look, let me call you back later, Anna. I am no good at multitasking when one of the tasks is driving."

In the business district, she found a small storefront that advertised all kinds of copying and mailing services. She parked then walked inside past a bevy of mailboxes to a wide room lined with different sizes of copiers and counters. One wall held boxes of all sizes and shelves holding envelopes, tape, and various office supplies. Behind a counter, clerks were busily helping customers with faxes, shipping, and mailing services.

Eve tossed her purse onto an unused counter near a vacant copy machine then made photocopies of each of the clippings that had been left in her car. She planned to go to the police with a complaint and expected they would want the originals. She would keep the copies for herself, to pore over, to try and figure out why the specific, jagged clippings had been left for her.

When she was finished xeroxing, she picked out a large envelope and paid for it along with the copies then shoved the door open and stepped onto the street.

Where she came face-to-face with Cole Dennis.

"What are you doing here?" they asked in unison.

CHAPTER 12

Leaning against the side of the building, wearing jeans, a T-shirt, and shades, Cole looked as sexy, irreverent, and outwardly cool as he always had. Gone was any trace of a man on the run, a man worried about being questioned by the police for a second murder, a man in near panic. In fact, she saw no indication of stress whatsoever in the sharp angles of his face.

He'd changed and taken the time to shower and shave since she'd last seen him. An improvement. A vast improvement. But, she told herself, she was impervious to any of his charm. "Im-freaking-pervious!"

"You knew I was going to be here. No need to lie about it. You're following me," Eve said as he pushed away from the brick wall of the bistro situated next to the UPS store. When she saw Cole wasn't going to deny it, she added dryly, "Or you just happened to be in the neighborhood."

The sun was bright and intense enough that rays spangled the street, catching in bits of glass on the sidewalk. Eve concentrated on her surroundings, anything but Cole.

"I just happened to be in the neighborhood."

"Uh-huh." She shot him a sideways glance. Was that a smile tugging at the corner of his mouth? Sometimes he was difficult to read. "So, you've recovered from last night?"

"I don't think I ever will." The smile faded, and creases appeared on his forehead above the rims of his sunglasses.

Neither would she. "So, why are you following me?"

"Unfinished business."

Eve sighed. "You're just making me feel tired."

"Am I?" Again with the smile. As if he were calling all the shots, still playing the role of Hollywood's interpretation of a rebellious hero.

She slipped her sunglasses onto the bridge of her nose and ignored him.

His smile grew at her irritation, became that insufferable and damnably sexy grin that showed off white, straight teeth and a bad-boy charm that he seemed to cultivate. Well, it wasn't working. Not on her. "Quit following me, Cole." She started toward her car and noticed that the meter had run out, so she quickened her steps across the sidewalk and was only vaguely aware of the notes from a plaintive saxophone over the rumble and whine of traffic.

He walked a step behind her then stood by as she scrounged in her purse and came up with her key ring. She unlocked the driver's side door, asking, "Have you gone to the police?"

"Not yet."

She sighed and shook her head, felt the noonday heat slide through her hair. "Look, I can't cover for you forever. I lied last night, though God only knows why. I'm on my way to the station now, and if they start asking questions about you, I'm going to have to be straight. They already think I'm a lunatic."

"I just need a little time."

She pulled her door open. "Sorry. All out."

Before she could slide into the car, he slammed the door shut, nearly pinning her with his body.

"Hey!"

He was so close to her, she saw the pores in his skin, noticed the tiniest of dark hairs on his chin, smelled that same musky aftershave she'd come to think of as pure Cole. "I'm not asking you to lie. Just to give me a little more time."

"Wait a minute. You stole Dad's computer. From a crime scene. I'm sure that's a felony. And I know about it. So if I lie, I'll be aiding and abetting or . . . Wait a minute, why am I explaining all of this to you? You're the hotshot defense lawyer. You already know what laws I'm breaking."

"You're going to the police now?"

She lifted the envelope with the clippings. "I was, yeah, but . . ." Oh God, why on earth did she consider giving into his request? She tried to step away from him, away from the edge of the curb, but he reached forward, and his fingers tightened around her arm.

"I'm only asking for a couple of hours." Behind his wraparound shades, his gaze locked with hers, and she felt the warmth of his fingertips on her bare skin. Which was ridiculous. This was a man who was, if not her enemy, still dangerous. At least as far as her emotions were concerned.

"If you go to the station now, we both know what will happen," he said. His cool exterior had cracked. Anger was evident in the set of his jaw.

She jerked her arm from his grasp. "I won't lie for you, Cole."

"Just to me."

She recognized the silent fury in the corners of his mouth and knew exactly what he was talking about, what he was insinuating. "Low blow, Cole. And not very smart. You follow me, chase me down, ask a huge favor, and then insult me? It takes a lot of nerve to practically beg me not to tell the police what I know, then make some disparaging crack about me. Careful, Counselor."

"I'm just trying to get to the truth."

She couldn't believe the nerve of the guy. "So here, in broad daylight, on the day after my father was murdered, you accuse me of lying to you . . . about my sex life, right?" She was steamed. Beyond steamed. "You're unbelievable."

He held up a hand, and the sharp edge of his jaw slackened a bit. "You're right. I was out of line."

"Waaay out of line! Leave me alone. Okay? Just leave me the hell alone." Before he could say another word, she climbed into her car, twisted on the ignition, then nearly clipped a bicyclist who rounded a corner on the fly as she was pulling out. She stood on the brakes, the biker shot her a dirty glare, and then, adrenaline flooding her bloodstream, she slowly nosed the little car away from the curb.

Visible in her side-view mirror, Cole stood where she'd left him—arms crossed over his chest, gaze following her car. "Bastard," she muttered, furious with herself for caring the least little bit about him. It would serve the jerk right if she drove to the police station this very second and explained everything he'd done. No doubt Detective Montoya would take great satisfaction in tossing Cole's ass back in prison.

And what about you? What then? Maybe you overreacted a bit. Maybe guilt got the better of your temper. All Cole wanted to know about is, who you were sleeping with, what other man was in your life. Her hands were sweating over the wheel, anger radiating from her cheeks. Damn the man. She slowed for an amber light and rolled down the windows to cool off.

The trouble was, he'd hit a nerve.

A sensitive nerve.

Why couldn't she remember another man in her life, a man she'd known so intimately as to have gone to bed with him? When had it happened? *Before* she'd been with Cole on that night, or after? Certainly not on her way over to Roy's. She'd been late as it was; she remembered that much. Her fingers tapped nervously on the wheel.

If there had been another man in her life, one she'd slept with, wouldn't she remember? His face? His touch? His smell? While she recalled being with Cole that night, looking upward into his stormy gray eyes, raking her fingers down his chest, feeling him sweat as he pushed into her . . .

In her mind's eye she again witnessed how the cords on his neck stood out, how the sweat shone on the sinewy muscles of his shoulders and arms as he propped himself above her. She could hear the exertion of his rapid breathing over her own gasping breaths and moans again, feel the tingle of lips that tasted slightly of whiskey. . . . And yet not one image of this other supposed lover. Not a glimmer of who he was.

A horn blasted, and she was instantly brought back to the present. She looked up, saw the green light. Instinctively she pushed on the accelerator then glanced into the rearview mirror at the angry, impatient motorist in the car behind her.

Her heart nearly stopped.

A dark pickup with tinted windows loomed just beyond her back bumper. "Oh God," she whispered and nearly floored it as she took a corner and headed northeast along St. Charles Avenue. Could it be the same truck from yesterday? No way. . . . And yet . . . and yet . . .

She kept one eye on the rearview mirror as she drove. Another car came between them, but even as the pickup lagged back, two, maybe three cars behind, he stayed the same course as she did. At Poydras Street, she angled toward the freeway and, four cars behind, so did the truck.

"You sick bastard," she said, her voice shaking.

Enough was enough.

At the next cross street, she timed her speed so that the light turned from amber to red just as she sped through the intersection. The silver car behind her stopped abruptly, tires screeching a little, and the dark truck, trapped behind a minivan, was forced to an abrupt stop. Eve stepped on the accelerator and drove as fast as she dared to the next light. Braking slightly, she pulled a quick right turn, tearing around the corner, intending to turn the tables on the creep and follow him for a change. She would get his license number and as much information about the truck and the driver as she could. Maybe she would even recognize the prick. Still driving over the speed limit, she cut down two narrow streets before she was able to angle back toward Poydras.

"I've got you, you bastard," she said, her fingers tight around the steering wheel.

But at the intersection, she was thwarted by road construction.

A bearded flagger held up a hand and spun his sign from *Slow* to *Stop* as if on cue. She had no option but to slam on her brakes and stew in the resulting dust and dark glare she received from the flagger.

"Damn!" She punched her steering wheel in frustration as a lumbering dump truck loaded with gravel and belching black smoke rumbled slowly into the construction site.

She counted the seconds as the flagger motioned traffic from the opposite direction to move. A short stream of cars bounced around a gaping hole and steel plate in the intersection. After what seemed a lifetime, the flagger twirled his sign to *Slow* then made frenzied hand signals to get her to step on it and drive through the dusty intersection. By the time she reached Poydras Street again, the menacing dark blue pickup was nowhere to be seen. Her chance of getting the make, model, and license plate numbers vanished.

Damn the luck.

Her phone rang, and Eve's gaze jerked to it. Her skin crawled. The creep was onto her! He'd seen her desperate attempt to chase him down and was calling to taunt and laugh at her. Breath quivering, she picked up the phone and flipped it open, carefully guiding her Camry onto Poydras.

"Hello?"

"Hey, Eve!" Her brother Van, always affable, never reliable, was on the other end of the wireless call.

Not some bogeyman. Van. Exhaling in relief, Eve said, "I guess you heard, huh?"

"Anna Maria got hold of me. Bad news about Terrence."

She'd forgotten. Neither of her brothers had ever referred to the man who had adopted them as "Dad" or "Father." "Real bad," she agreed.

"Same guy who did Roy?"

Word was leaking out. "I don't know."

"Cole Dennis?"

Her stomach clenched as she melded into traffic, her gaze scraping every inch of the area. She looked hard at all the surrounding cars, trucks, SUVs, and mini-vans. "I doubt it."

"You said he killed Roy."

"I said I thought he did. Now I'm not so sure."

"Going soft?"

"Just . . . trying to remember and get the facts straight."

"So, I'm in New Orleans," Van said, easily changing subjects.

"What? I thought you were in Arizona."

"I was. Came into New Orleans for a sales confer-ence. I'm selling spas right now. High end. How's that for a coincidence? Just when Terrence checks out."

Eve's blood turned to ice. "Yeah . . ." Almost too much of one.

"So I thought maybe we should get together. Talk things over. Kyle's on his way."

"On his way? Here?"

"Yeah." Van acted as if nothing were odd about their conversation, though she hadn't spoken to him in months. "There are the arrangements, and the will, lots of stuff to deal with. Kyle and I, we know you've been through a lot. Thought we could help out."

"Is that right?" she asked bitterly. The brothers who had never been close to her were now concerned. And she knew in her heart it was because of her father's estate. Great. Just what she needed on top of every-thing else!

"Look, I gotta run. Another call coming in." He

hung up, and she considered turning her phone off. What a loser. Their dad hadn't been dead twenty-four hours and the vultures were already circling.

The phone rang in her hand. Hadn't turned the damn thing off fast enough. She stabbed her thumb on the green talk button, certain Van had ended his other call and come up with a new, great idea concerning the estate. "Hello?"

"He's free!"

Click.

The phone went dead.

He watched from his parking spot. His pickup was next to the curb, hidden behind a moving van. He'd seen her frustration as she'd been forced to sit at the construction site, waiting to drive forward. She was nervous. Antsy. Her eyes searching the side streets because she'd noticed his vehicle—known he was following her.

Stupid! He'd gotten too close again. Been too eager to be near her, had driven up behind her. When she hadn't been quick enough at the red light, some idiot behind him had laid on the horn, startling her, making her check her mirror.

He'd lagged back, but it had been too late.

She'd seen him.

Knew he was tailing her.

Even though he'd let several cars weave between them, she'd been aware of his truck.

He realized immediately she would try something; a

trick to read his license plate or get a better look at him.

Fortunately, he'd figured what would happen. Sure enough, she'd gunned it through a red light and turned quickly at the next corner, her tires squealing a bit. He'd known that she was on the attack. Quickly, across oncoming traffic, he'd wheeled into an alleyway then driven behind two restaurants and back to a tree-lined avenue where the moving van was nearly filling the street. He'd been forced to pull in behind the truck while two burly guys struggled with a refrigerator. From his hiding spot, he could observe the main street, expecting her to wheel onto it again, though he couldn't be certain where her little Toyota would appear. Then he'd spied her car, trapped by a sign-wielding construction worker.

The Reviver had waited.

Now his heart was pounding like crazy, and he licked his lips in anticipation. The Voice had been clear that he was to follow Eve, to observe her, yet there were others to come before.

Frustration burned through him.

She was the one he wanted.

But he would hold back, listen to the instructions, leave his life in God's hands. Hadn't God, through the Voice, told him what would be?

Your patience and your acts will be rewarded. Fear not, Reviver.

He felt thrilled when God called him by his name. Only God would tell him who would die and who would only suffer, to be revived again.

Had that not happened with Eve?

Had she not nearly died, only to be revived?

He wasn't certain that he could really be credited for her return to the living, but he was glad she'd been revived all the same, because he could kill her again, more slowly this time, more intimately.

She would look into his eyes, and she would know.

A shudder of desire snaked through his body, touching his soul, its forked tongue flicking at his genitals, touching both balls, making his palms sweat in anticipation and his cock thicken.

He was breathing shallowly and fast when he saw the flagger wave Eve through the intersection. She turned onto Poydras Street, heading toward the freeway, but he couldn't follow. He had too much to do. As much as he wanted to pursue Eve, there would be time later. For now, he would return to his life on the outside, deal with the idiots who knew nothing about him and thought they understood him. Fools, every one.

He pulled slowly from behind the moving van, waiting as another couple of husky movers eased a recliner down the ramp from the interior of the truck. Once they'd packed the chair out of the way, he drove around the van and stopped at the intersection. Far in the distance, he spied Eve's Camry. He imagined her nervously checking her rearview mirror or glancing anxiously at the passing side streets, the other vehicles.

So how do you feel now, Eve? You, the princess. . . .

Do you sense me watching you? Or do you think you lost me? Do you know I can see you? Do you even suspect that I'm under your skin? Oh pampered, spoiled Eve.

Just you wait.

CHAPTER 13

"This is the best I got." Ivan Petrusky, a penny-ante grifter, unlocked the door to what he optimistically had referred to as a furnished "studio" apartment. In truth, the entire unit was one twelve-by-twelve room that had been narrowed to allow for a minuscule bathroom and a closet that hid a tiny sink, an impossibly short counter, and a microwave/refrigerator.

A sagging sleeper sofa, table, and lamp with its burned shade, where a lightbulb had overheated, were the extent of the furnishings, but the apartment was cheap. Better yet, Petrusky took cash and kept no records.

Cole needed that.

"You off the hook for that murder a while back?" Petrusky asked. A short, wiry man pushing seventy, he had bristly white hair and sported an unlit cigar forever tucked in the corner of his mouth. His glasses were thick, his eyes sharp, his mind as clear as it had ever been. Petrusky had known Cole's father, and then, a few years back when one of his three ex-wives had accused him of battery, he'd hired Cole to fight the charge. It had been a slam dunk as far as Cole was concerned. Belva had set the chump up by having her new boyfriend beat on her, then claiming Ivan had assaulted her. Cole had smelled a scam from the get-go. He hadn't done all that much, as the police were on to Belva, but Ivan, who had experienced his share of run-ins with the law, had decided Cole was his savior. Since that time, as far as Cole knew, Petrusky had sworn off marriage for good. "You know the one I'm talking about," he added. "That one that happened up in the cabin. The Kajak murder."

"I didn't do it."

"That's not what I asked." A bushy eyebrow was raised over the tops of tortoiseshell glasses. "Here ya are, looking for a place . . ."

"And I came to you because you usually don't ask a lot of questions."

The older man shrugged. "Okay. But this is a gem, let me tell you. I could rent it for a lot more, but you . . ."

"You don't have to sell me. I'll take it." He reached into his wallet and peeled off two months' rent then waited until Ivan got the hint and left.

The place wasn't much, but it would have to do. He could set up the computer he'd purchased and pirate into someone else's wireless connection so that he had Internet access. Along with purchasing the new laptop, he'd already copied everything he could from Renner's briefcase. His next step was to download all the information he could from Renner's computer onto discs then find a way to get the information to the police.

But he wasn't going to hand it over himself.

No way.

"I'm telling you he's dirty," Montoya said, resting a shoulder against the filing cabinet in Bentz's office. The door was slightly ajar, and through the crack came the buzz of conversation, click of computer keys, ringing of phones, and every once in a while the protestation of innocence from some scumbag giving his statement. Montoya found a pack of nicotine gum in the pocket of his leather jacket. As he unwrapped a piece, he stared at the computer monitor, where gruesome pictures of the Terrence Renner crime scene were displayed. "Somehow Cole Dennis is involved."

Bentz leaned back in his chair until it creaked in protest. "Give me a for instance."

"I don't know." Montoya frowned darkly, popped the gum into his mouth. Under the fluorescent lights, his black hair gleamed almost blue, and his eyes glittered like obsidian. He was angry and not afraid to show it. "I'd like to say he's our guy, but . . ." He chewed furiously. "You're right. He's not stupid, and I don't make him for a psychopath. A killer maybe, and I can see him offing someone for messing with Eve, but . . . I don't make him for a bloodthirsty psycho."

"So who is?"

"The same guy who did Roy Kajak."

224

"Not Dennis."

Montoya wouldn't answer. Just chewed his nicotine gum.

"Back to square one," Bentz muttered. The Kajak and Renner murders weren't the only unsolved homicides in the department's case file. There had been a stabbing on the waterfront two nights earlier, a drug deal gone bad from the looks of it, an assault in the French Quarter over a woman, and what appeared to be an accidental shooting: a kid had found his old man's gun and hadn't known it was loaded when he'd pointed it at his friend and pulled the trigger.

Sometimes the job got to him. Bentz glanced at the computer screen and felt a little of the same queasiness that always attacked him when he first stepped into a murder scene. "When can we expect the preliminary autopsy report?"

"I think they're putting a rush on it, but it'll be at least another day; the complete by the end of the week. And the lab? Trace evidence? Fingerprints?"

Bentz sighed. "I made the mistake of asking Washington and about got my head snapped off." Bonita Washington was in charge of the crime lab and a force to be reckoned with, a black woman with coffee-colored skin, green eyes, and, Bentz guessed, an IQ pushing the genius level. She also didn't take any crap from anyone, so Bentz had learned to tread lightly. He'd even resorted to bringing her coffee upon occasion. The first time he'd showed up at her office door with a steaming cup in his hand, she, seated behind her desk, had looked over the tops of her reading glasses and nodded to herself. As if something she'd figured out long before had just been proven.

"You catch more flies with honey than vinegar, Detective?"

He'd nodded and handed her the cup. She gave the contents a cursory glance then took a sip. He thought he'd scored major points.

"You know, if you're gonna try to bribe me, I'm partial to diamonds. A caramel macchiato latte with whipped cream and drizzled in chocolate is damned nice, but, really, diamonds would work so much better. Hell, for a measly carat, your case might just miraculously work itself to the top of my in-box." She grinned and took another swallow. "Think what two carats would get you."

"It's just a coffee."

Those intense green eyes had narrowed. "I know your story, Bentz. Heard about what happened in LA, and I realize that you're here because the DA stuck her neck out for you. Without Melinda Jaskiel going to bat for you, you could very well be out of a job. As for this?" She held up the paper cup he'd given her. "It just happens to be my favorite kind of coffee, which means you went to a lot of trouble and used those keen California surfer-dude detective skills to find out exactly what I like."

He felt the muscles in the back of his neck tighten warily and an embarrassed heat crawl up his face. The woman was a barracuda.

"You want something, Bentz, and we both know it. Trouble is, you're just gonna have to wait in line. I'm understaffed and overworked. But you knew that, right? If not, you do now."

After her sharp-tongued tirade in front of her staff, he'd learned his lesson. As she'd turned back to the work on her cluttered desk, she'd muttered something under her breath about "smart-ass, know-it-all dicks" and then added, just loud enough so that he could overhear, "Good thing I like you."

Within three hours, the report he'd wanted had landed on his desk—a good two days before she'd promised it. Since that initial conversation, they'd had an understanding.

Montoya's cell phone beeped, and he took the call. With a nod to Bentz, he walked out of the office and was about to shut the door when Bentz's daughter, Kristi, pushed it open. In a tight denim skirt and a fuchsia tank top, she said, "Hey, Reub" as he passed, then dropped onto a chair in front of her father's desk.

"Hi!" she said a little breathlessly, and he was reminded of her mother, Jennifer, his first wife. Though Jennifer was long dead, she wasn't forgotten. Kristi had recently cut her hair, her coppery curls now in unkempt layers to frame a face that was as intelligent as it was beautiful. Curiosity filled her green eyes, and, at least in his opinion, she was so full of energy and life, she seemed to light up a room when she walked in. Then again, he might not be objective, as she was his kid.

"Hi, yourself."

"I thought you might want to go to lunch or coffee or something." She was grinning at him widely, again reminding him of her mother. Bentz was a little wary of all this enthusiasm.

"Lunch?" He glanced at his watch. "It's almost three."

"Okay, make that a late lunch, or, like I said, coffee. We could even indulge in a beignet at Café Du Monde."

He made a point of checking his watch again. The last thing he wanted in the middle of the afternoon was something sweet, like fried dough dusted with powdered sugar. "Kristi, what's up?"

"What do you mean?" she asked so innocently, he couldn't fight the smile that threatened his lips.

"How long have I worked here at this station?" Before she could answer, he held up a hand. "That was a rhetorical question. Okay? But the point is, I've been here, at this desk for years, and this is the first time you've just popped in and suggested lunch. So as I asked before, 'What's up?' "

"Your detecting skills are amazing," she said as if she meant it.

He knew when she wanted something. "You didn't come down here to flatter me."

"Well . . . no . . ." she admitted. She wasn't quite looking at him. Her gaze had strayed to his computer screen, where the pictures of the Renner homicide were still visible. "Oh wow. That's Dr. Renner, right?"

"Yep." With his mouse, he clicked the file closed, and instead of gruesome shots of Terrence Renner, a rotating screen of his favorite spots in New Orleans came to view. "Level with me. Why're you here?"

At least she didn't throw the can't-a-daughter-come-down-for-lunch-with-her-father line at him. She exhaled a disgusted breath and looked out the window for a second. When her gaze found his again, she was decidedly more serious. "I want to work a case with you."

He shook his head. "You're not a detective. Not even a cop. And you're my kid."

"I don't mean that kind of work," she said, making air quotes around the last word.

"What other kind is there?"

"I want to write about it."

Now she had his full attention. She'd mentioned writing before. English had been her best subject in high school and at All Saints College in Baton Rouge. One of her English professors, a Dr. Northrup, had called her essays "brilliant," and though Kristi had admitted that she thought the guy was a weirdo, she'd basked in his praise nonetheless. So she'd toyed with writing, had inquired to several magazines, even mentioned a book before, but this?

"I'd love to write true crime, and I figure that I've kinda got an inside track, what with you being a detective and all."

"Whoa. I can't let you be a part of an ongoing investigation. You know that. It would be unethical and potentially compromise the case."

"Even if I promised to keep everything confidential until it was solved?"

He stared at her long and hard, this bull-headed, smart-as-a-whip, athletic daughter of his. "No."

"I'll talk to Montoya."

"He won't buy into it either."

"Then Brinkman," she countered, her chin thrusting just a bit, the way it had when she was a child and was determined to get what she wanted, no matter what. "Or Noon."

"You wouldn't last two seconds with Brinkman," Bentz said, thinking of the irritating detective. Though good at his job, Brinkman was misogynist, bigoted, and had a foul mouth. The thought of his daughter being anywhere near the man caused bile to climb up Bentz's throat. "And Noon's a prick. Somethin' not quite right with that guy." Noon was a younger detective and on his own kind of authority trip. "You know, you're right. Let's go to lunch."

"You're trying to change the subject."

"Uh-huh."

"Well, it's not working. I mean it, Dad," she insisted, climbing to her feet and letting him hold the door for her. "I want to do this. Working for Gulf Auto and Life isn't my idea of a career."

"You just started with the insurance company."

"Nine months ago!" They were wending through the cubicles and desks where detectives and clerks were typing, answering phones, taking statements, or finishing up paperwork.

"Not exactly a lifetime."

"But why not do what I really want?" she countered as they started down the stairs. "Why waste any more time?"

"There's the matter of bills. You know, gas, rent, cable, you name it."

"I'm not quitting," she insisted, "at least not right away. Not until I write the book and it sells."

"If it sells."

They were on the first floor, and she shot him a harsh glare. "Way to be supportive, Dad."

"I am supportive. Just being realistic. Come on, cross here," he suggested. He yanked at his collar. Only May, and already the temperature was over eighty. "There's a restaurant up about three blocks, open all afternoon, has great gumbo."

She wrinkled her nose, and again he was reminded of Jennifer, so beautiful but so different from Olivia.

At the thought of his new wife, he couldn't help but shake his head. She was an enigma, that was for sure. Olivia Benchet Bentz was a beautiful woman who was as smart as she was mystical. He still didn't understand the little bit of ESP that seemed to flow through her blood, but she was the best thing that had happened to him. Even if she had brought a feisty mutt named Hairy S and a parrot into the marriage.

"I'm not really into gumbo," Kristi said as they crossed the street against the light.

"Don't worry, they'll have something you'll like."

"You don't even know what I like."

"Last I heard it was tofu and beans."

"Very funny."

He laughed and held the door open for her. The rich smells of hot Cajun cooking wafted from the kitchen and invaded his nostrils. The booths were dark wood with stiff backs and thin cushions.

They split a fried-shrimp-and-crawfish basket complete with curly fries. Over cups of sweet tea, Kristi tried to convince Bentz what a great idea it would be for her to be privy to information on the Renner investigation. He wasn't buying it and told her so.

"Not gonna happen," he said.

"Then how about one that's already been solved?" He dredged a french fry through a pool of catsup as she championed her cause. "What would it hurt? I'd make sure all the facts were correct and that everyone who needed to got credit and—"

"Why?" he cut her off, skewering her with a gaze that had caused more than one would-be assailant to think twice.

"I told you."

"I mean *why*, after what you've gone through, would you want to dwell on this crap?"

"Probably for the same reason you do."

He scowled, pushed the basket aside, and leaned across the table. "What about that nutcase who called himself the Chosen One, huh? Remember him?" When he thought of it now, the black fear that had enveloped him during the hours Kristi and Olivia had been held captive, Bentz still felt chilled inside.

"It's over, Dad," she said, but he didn't believe her. Such a harrowing, mind-twisting ordeal was never over, never completely forgotten.

They finished the basket, and he paid the check.

"This is something I want to do, for me," she said as they headed outside. "I thought you'd be all for it."

He glanced at her skeptically. As she started to step off the curb, distantly he heard the roar of an engine and caught the flash of chrome out of the corner of his eye. Instinctively he grabbed her arm and jerked her back onto the sidewalk. A motorcycle, engine roaring, took the corner fast, skidded through the crosswalk, and nearly wiped out.

"Holy crap!" Kristi cried, her eyes wide.

Bentz glared after the disappearing bike but didn't catch the plate. Every muscle in his body had flexed, taut as bowstrings. He realized he was still holding on to his daughter's arm in a death grip and slowly uncoiled his fingers. "Sorry."

"No . . . it's . . . it's okay," she said, still shaken. "I saw him and I heard him, but I just thought he wasn't turning."

"Neither did I, but I couldn't be certain." He grabbed her arm again and gave it a squeeze. "I couldn't take a chance."

"Okay, Dad. I get it. You've made your point. But I am going to write a book about a real case, one that I find fascinating, and it will probably be one of yours, so"—she flashed him a blinding smile—"you're going to have to find a way to deal with it."

CHAPTER 14

Eve stood on one side of the glass and watched as the sheet was pulled back. Her father, his skin pale, his eyes closed, lay on the slab. She thought of all the things she wanted to say to him, all the things she never could. They'd been close once, long ago when she'd been a little girl and her mother was still alive. After Melody Renner's death, they'd grown more distant rather than closer. And then there was Tracy Aliota, a girl under her father's care, a girl who, like Eve, had rebelled, but had gone further, a girl who had ultimately lost her battle with sanity and her life. Though no criminal charges had been filed against Dr. Terrence Renner or the hospital where Tracy had been treated, the girl's family had taken him to court for wrongful death. Cole Dennis and the high-profile, high-priced law firm of O'Black, Sullivan and Kravitz had convinced the jury that Terrence Renner hadn't failed his patient, that he'd done everything possible, that in no way whatsoever was Tracy Aliota's condition misdiagnosed, nor was Dr. Renner responsible in the least for her death.

The only person who hadn't been convinced in the courtroom, other than Tracy's grieving family, had been Eve.

I'm sorry, Dad, she thought, her throat hot. *Oh God, I'm so sorry. If only I'd talked to you, if only I'd tried. . . . If only . . .*

"Ms. Renner?" Montoya asked, his voice low.

"It's him," she said, nodding, her insides twisting as she stared past the glass. Her father's body had been cleaned. She could see the gash around the base of his neck and the dark, garish tattoo embedded into his forehead.

She imagined the last seconds of his life. The pain. The terror.

What kind of monster would do such a thing?

Who?

Why?

Shaking, she sniffed and ran a finger under her eyes to wipe away her tears.

"Are you okay?"

She nodded, cleared her throat, and stiffened her spine. The headache that was forever her companion threatened to rise again, but she ignored it, didn't have time to deal with it. "Get the bastard who did this," she told Montoya.

"Believe me, I'm trying. But I do have some questions."

"Fire away."

"Maybe we'd better do this at the department."

"Wherever." She didn't care; she just wanted to get through the interview.

"Great." Montoya called Bentz, and they met Bentz in his crammed office. His desk was littered with reports and old coffee cups, and a dying plant was withering in a pot on top of a filing cabinet. The room was stuffy and close despite an open window through which the sounds of the street filtered in. As she took a seat in one of the chairs near the desk, Eve watched two pigeons flutter near the window ledge and listened to the hum of tires and rumble of engines along with some impassioned street preacher begging passersby to "accept Jesus into your hearts."

Montoya didn't bother sitting, just stood near the filing cabinet.

"What is it you want to know?" Eve asked as Bentz pulled out a small pocket recorder, shuffled some papers out of the way, and set the machine on the cleared desk blotter that had seen better days. Rings from ancient coffee cups were visible as he pushed the record button then identified everyone in the room, noting the date, time, and place of the interview.

"Okay, for the record, tell us what you know about the night your father died."

She did, explaining about driving to New Orleans from Atlanta, the panicked calls from Anna Maria, and her own attempt to reach her father. For now she left out any mention of Cole or the fact that she thought she was being followed. Montoya leaned against the file cabinet and didn't say a word, content, it seemed, to let Bentz ask the questions. It took nearly an hour, and finally, just when she thought they were about finished, Montoya pushed himself away from the cabinet and took up a spot in front of Bentz's desk. "Okay, Ms. Renner, so here's the thing. Your story hangs together except for one thing. We've listened to your father's answering machine and are in the process of getting his phone records. Your call came into his house *before* the call from your sister-in-law. I've made a duplicate from the answering machine we found at the scene." He pulled a small tape recorder/player from his pocket and hit the play button.

Eve tried to remain calm, but her fingers curled of their own accord as she heard her panicked voice.

"Dad? This is Eve. I'm sorry to call you so late, but I thought you'd want to know that . . . that I'm back in town. . . . I, um, should have called earlier. Call me back."

"That call, the one you just heard, came in at two fifty-one. Then later, at three oh-two, we get this . . ."

"Dad? This is Anna Maria. . . . I've, uh, I've got this friend who works for the paper. He called and said there might be some trouble at your place. . . . Kyle's not home right now, but you can probably reach him on his cell. . . . Just let me know that everything's fine."

"See the problem?"

"I'm not sure."

"You knew something was wrong before your sister-in-law called."

The detectives were silent, still staring at her. "I just wanted to talk to him." She wasn't going to tell them she'd learned about her father's death from Cole. Not yet.

"The other problem we have is that someone, a man, called in the murder."

"Who?"

"We don't know, but we're going to compare the 911 tape to other voices we've got on record. We thought maybe you might know."

She swallowed hard. "I don't know. But . . . do you think the man who called was the person who killed my father?"

"Could be. Or a witness." Montoya folded his arms over his chest, his black leather jacket creaking with the movement. "We just have a lot of leads to follow."

"Is there anything else you can think of that might help us?" Bentz asked.

"Maybe."

The cops waited.

"I think I'm being stalked. Someone's following me, calling me at all kinds of weird hours, and leaving me the same message."

"Which is?"

" 'He's free.' The voice is male, I think, low and rough, as if he's whispering to disguise it, and I have no idea who it could be."

"He's referring to Cole Dennis? Or someone else?"

"Cole, I think. The calls started about the time he was released."

Bentz's expression darkened.

Montoya shot him a look that Eve couldn't decipher.

She reached for her purse and pulled out the manila envelope she'd tucked inside. "I don't know if this is connected or what it means, but there have been some strange things happening to me too. I think I was fol-

238

lowed from Atlanta, and someone put these in my car."

Using a handkerchief, Montoya picked up the envelope then slowly spilled its contents onto the desk near Bentz's recorder. The jagged-edged clippings, looking like snowflakes from a kindergartener's art project, scattered over the ink blotter. "What is this all about?"

"I don't know. My dad was the chief psychiatrist at Our Lady of Virtues Hospital for some time, and that woman, Faith Chastain, was one of his patients, I think."

Montoya's head snapped up. "Faith Chastain?"

"All of the articles are about her, not just the hospital. I'm sure there have been dozens of stories written about the hospital itself, or the staff, or its closing, or whatever, but these stories are all about Faith Chastain. You two are mentioned too, in a couple of them. . . . Oh, there's one." She pointed to one of the clippings in which both detectives were quoted.

"You don't know where these came from or why?" Montoya demanded tersely.

Eve shook her head. "Someone broke into my car and left them in the glove box, but as to why, I don't have a clue."

If possible, Montoya grew even more serious. Patiently he asked her to go over her story a couple of times. She explained about the dark pickup but could provide them no concrete information, no license number, not even the make or model of the truck, just

239

that it was full-sized, very dark blue or black, and that the windows were tinted. "If I were to guess, I'd say it was a domestic pickup, but I really can't be sure."

"But you think it's in New Orleans."

"I think, but I can't be certain. I thought someone was following me earlier today, but I could be wrong."

"Can we keep these?" Bentz asked, motioning toward but not touching the clippings.

"Sure."

"Has anyone else touched them?"

She thought of Cole and how he'd read the articles, nearly picked one up, but hadn't when she'd told him not to. "Not since I received them."

"Have you shown them to anyone else?"

"No, Detective. I just received them yesterday." Oh, how easy it would be for them to catch her in another lie. All they had to do was talk to Mrs. Endicott, who no doubt had heard enough of her conversation with Cole while he'd been on the porch to point the police in the right direction.

"Can you tell me about your relationship with your father?" Montoya asked as the tape continued to record and Bentz took a few notes on a small spiral pad.

"It was pretty good when I was a child, but then, as I hit adolescence, we grew apart. We, uh, we weren't that close in the last few months. Not quite estranged, but . . . but just not as close as we once were."

"Because of the Kajak murder?"

"No—it was before that."

"Because of your relationship with Cole Dennis?"

"No, not really."

"Not really?"

"Dad and I really drifted apart after he was accused of being responsible for the suicide of one of his patients."

She didn't elaborate, and Montoya asked suddenly, "Your mother's deceased?"

"Yes."

"How?"

"Heart failure. When I was sixteen, about fifteen years ago. Why? What does that have to do with anything?"

"Just filling in case history. You have a brother living in Atlanta and one in. . . ?"

"Phoenix . . . well, Mesa, really. But I think they're currently both in New Orleans. Van, he's . . . well, the middle child, the younger of the two. He just called me and said he's here for a convention of spa dealers, and he told me Kyle was on his way here, though I haven't talked to him."

"Will they be staying with you?"

"I doubt it. Van didn't say anything about it, and Kyle doesn't like to spend the night at other people's homes. He'd rather live in a hotel. He doesn't like to play by anyone else's house rules."

"Is that so?" Bentz asked.

Eve shrugged. "It's not like we were all one big happy family, okay? My dad adopted Kyle and Van when he married my mom. The boys were half grown when my parents adopted me."

Montoya's eyes turned dark as night. "So Terrence Renner isn't your biological father?"

"Right."

"Who is?" Bentz asked, leaning forward, his pencil unmoving.

"I don't know either of my biological parents. I asked a few times, got no answers, was told mine was a closed adoption, which I guess means my birth parents don't want to hear from me." Eve's mouth twisted. "It was a private thing, arranged by an attorney, and, well, Mom died before I got any real information from her, and Dad was always so vague. I always figured I'd try to locate my biological parents someday. What's the worst that could happen? I'd get a door slammed in my face?" She sighed. "I never got around to it."

Montoya scratched at his goatee as Bentz said, "We'll need the phone numbers of your brothers."

She gave them Kyle's house number in Atlanta, then said, "Just a sec" as she found her cell phone in her purse. Scrolling down the menu on the phone, she found the cell numbers for Kyle, Anna Maria, and Van. "I don't have Van's home number anymore. He moved to Mesa not long before I was injured, and I always just call his cell and leave messages."

"That's all right." Bentz was writing on his notepad. "What about enemies? Did your father have anyone who would want to harm him?"

In her mind's eye she saw Tracy Aliota's grieving parents and brother as they'd sat in the courtroom, hearing the verdict of "not guilty" ringing to the rafters. They'd fallen apart, Tracy's mother, Leona, nearly crumpling. If not for her husband's strong arm, she might have fallen to the floor. Tracy's older brother, J.D., had been red faced and seething, his eyes burning with the certainty that a dark injustice had been done. "I suppose," she said, giving the detectives a quick review of the Aliotas' grievances. "They were probably not the only patients who were unhappy, though none that I know of had gone so far as to sue him. But he did deal with people who were mentally ill."

"Psychotics?"

She nodded.

"What about personally?" Montoya asked.

She thought hard. "My brothers' father—their biological father, Ed Stern—didn't like him much. Blamed him for the divorce, as I understand it, but he ducked out of the picture early. When the boys were very young, he gave up all parental rights. I've never met him, and as far as I know, my brothers haven't seen him since he took off."

Bentz was still taking notes.

"Anyone else?"

She shook her head. "I think my father got into some legal thing about use of an access road that cut across the farm . . . with the neighbor, Hugh Something-or-other. . . . Hugh . . . Hugh Capp, I think, but I only heard Dad say something about it a couple of times, and that was five or six years ago. As far as I know they resolved whatever it was."

"What about professionally? Any enemies?" Bentz asked.

"I really don't know."

"Or patients or staff at Our Lady of Virtues—that's the last hospital where he was on staff. Afterward, while he was in private practice, he worked alone, right? And was just associated with a small, private hospital"—Bentz flipped back a few pages in his notebook—"St. Andrews, not far from Slidell."

"That's right," she said, remembering the small hospital across Lake Pontchartrain.

"Do you know anyone who held a grudge against your father at either of the hospitals?"

"No. You'd have to ask someone who worked there," she said, feeling her headache toying with the edges of her brain again. "There must be records."

The detectives asked a few more questions before the interview wound down, and by that time Eve's headache was back in full force. Montoya escorted her through the department and down the stairs. When she was outside again, she finally felt like she could breathe.

Clouds had gathered in the sky, and shadows had lengthened over the city. The air was thick. Muggy. It pressed her clothes against her skin.

She walked to her Camry and looked over her shoulder. Once again she experienced the eerie feeling that someone was watching her, someone inherently evil. Unease crawled up her neck, breathing on her scalp, and she turned to slowly search the sidewalks and streets.

A woman pushed a stroller. Two teenagers were walking, holding hands and almost yelling at each other, each plugged into an iPod. An elderly man was walking his little dog, a terrier of some kind, and several people waited for a city bus. One guy in a silver sedan was studying a map and scowling as if he were horribly lost. A couple of twenty-something kids with spiked hair were skateboarding recklessly through the crowds, and a panhandler claiming to be a homeless vet was waiting for someone to drop money into his open guitar case as he strummed a tune from the eighties.

She saw no one hiding malevolently in the umbra of an awning, no one smoking a cigarette in a large, dark pickup with tinted windows, no one paying her the least bit of attention. The street preacher was still in full force, handing out literature, still pleading with anyone who would listen to accept Jesus as his or her savior.

But no luminous eyes stared at her from the shadowy alleyways, and the only dark truck that passed by had a sign advertising a florist's shop and was driven by a girl who looked barely sixteen.

It's all in your mind, she told herself but couldn't shake the feeling that someone nearby was observing her every move.

• • •

"I know what you're thinking," Bentz said when Montoya returned. "That Eve Renner is Faith Chastain's missing daughter. But you're jumping the gun. Just because she's about the right age, was adopted, and someone stuffed a bunch of articles about the hospital and Faith Chastain in her car doesn't mean she's the missing kid."

"It's something to check out."

"Agreed." Bentz tapped the eraser end of his pencil on the desk.

"We could tell her about it. Ask for a DNA sample."

Bentz glanced out the window at the pigeons that had taken roost. "It isn't really a police matter," he said. "Not a crime if a woman has a baby and doesn't tell anyone."

"What about a woman who has a tattoo hidden in her hairline? A tattoo she probably got while she was a patient, for crying out loud?"

"Again, no crime that we know of. And the woman's dead. We know how she died and how she was abused. The tattoo happened more than twenty years ago. And we don't even know if it was forced upon her."

"A tattoo on her head, a head that had to be shaved . . . You think she wanted it?"

"She wasn't exactly stable."

"Oh come *on*. The woman was brutalized. We know that." Bentz scowled but couldn't argue. They'd found proof that Faith had endured unspeakable crimes while a patient at the hospital.

"I know, but face it, this is a personal issue with you. Any crime that was committed is long over."

"Then what the hell are these all about?" Montoya pointed to the clippings littering Bentz's desk. "Don't you think it's strange—one helluva coincidence—that someone wants Eve Renner to know about Faith Chastain at the same time people who know Eve are being slaughtered?"

"Damned strange." Bentz glowered at the newspaper clippings. All neatly clipped, with jagged, precise edges. All about Faith Chastain. Could it be that easy? That Faith Chastain's unknown child had just waltzed into the department carrying evidence linking her to the dead woman? Who would know about the adoption? Why bring it to the fore now, after thirty years? And how would Eve, being Faith's daughter, have anything to do with the murders?

Roy Kajak spent time at Our Lady of Virtues, not only as the son of one of the caretakers, but later, as a patient.

Terrence Renner was the head psychiatrist at the mental hospital before it closed.

Faith Chastain died at the old asylum.

Once again there were homicides and a mystery linked to the once-grand brick buildings now in decay.

"You're the one who doesn't believe in coincidence," Montoya reminded him.

"So what do you want to do?"

"Check it out. If Eve agrees. DNA test. Compare it

247

to Abby's. If Eve is Faith's daughter, she should have enough matching markers to Abby."

"Don't need Abby's. We've got Faith's DNA on file, the lab took it when her body was exhumed. All we need is Eve's, if she goes for it," Bentz said. "She may not want to help us."

Montoya snorted. "She's holding back." He reached into his shirt pocket for a nonexistent pack of cigarettes then stuffed both fists into the pockets of his leather jacket.

"I think so too."

"Remember, she's still recovering from her attack, still has memory problems." Montoya made the statement as if he didn't believe it. "If you ask me, she's a nutcase."

"No argument there, but even so, someone's playing a head game with her." He reached into the drawer of his desk, found a bottle of antacids, and tossed a couple into his mouth. He wouldn't necessarily think the two incidents were related; a woman getting weird notes and two murders, but they all revolved around Eve Renner.

Why?

And how the hell was Faith Chastain, a woman dead over twenty years, the mother of Montoya's fiancée, involved?

Montoya was restless, pacing in front of the desk, nervously rubbing the diamond stud in one ear. "Remember last fall and the siege at the old hospital, when we nailed the son of a bitch who was terrorizing Abby?"

Bentz knew where this was going. In the last case involving Our Lady of Virtues, the killer had warned Montoya, *No matter what else happens, tonight is just the beginning.*

Over half a year had slipped by. Montoya had started to believe that the killer had been rambling, shouting a dire prophecy that was little more than a bluff, but now he wasn't so certain.

Because of these clippings with their saw-toothed edges, left in Eve Renner's car. If they could believe her story.

"Let's not jump the gun," Bentz said. "We'll send these down to the lab, have them fingerprinted and checked for any kind of trace, and go from there."

"I've got to tell Abby." Montoya was already out the door. He spun on the other side of the threshold. "Be sure that I get copies of those."

Bentz nodded. "You got it." Through the open door, he watched as Montoya cut through the desks to the stairway then disappeared from sight. Bentz was left with the strange newspaper articles.

What was the connection?

He made a note to find out about Eve's brothers, her dead mother, and, if possible, her birth parents. Like it or not, he knew he'd have to make a visit to the convent at Our Lady of Virtues and talk to the Mother Superior.

Bentz turned to his computer, clicked open an old file, and found a clear photograph of Faith Chastain, noting her haunted beauty, the high cheekbones, straight nose, gold eyes, and wild mass of untamed dark curls. Abby Chastain was nearly a carbon copy of her mother, but Eve Renner? There could be a slight resemblance, but certainly not enough to make that kind of call.

He tapped his pencil on the desk again, then, using gloves, placed the clippings back into their envelope to take them to the lab. He didn't understand what was going on yet, but he knew, whatever it was, he didn't like it.

CHAPTER 15

D eeds was late.
He was also pissed as hell.

"Tell me you're not screwing up," he insisted as he ordered a beer from the bartender. O'Callahan's was dark and cool, filled with timeworn mahogany and leather, smelling of cigars, aged whiskey, and Cajun spices.

"I'm not screwing up."

Deeds didn't accuse him of the lie, just accepted the frosty mug of beer and took a long sip, then glanced toward a couple of guys hanging out at the bar, where they watched a television mounted near the ceiling. Only a few patrons were seated around the scattered tables. Smooth jazz filtered from hidden speakers. One guy was shooting darts near the back by the restrooms. All in all, the place was quiet. Low-key.

"So you're minding your p's and q's?" Deeds was

skeptical as he reached for some of the mixed nuts the bartender had placed between them.

"Yep."

"Then tell me Eve Renner's not back in town and you haven't seen her." He popped a couple of peanuts into his mouth.

"Can't do it."

"I knew it! Cole, are you out of your fucking mind?"

"Probably."

"This is no time for jokes," Deeds said furiously. He took a long pull from his glass, glanced at his reflection over the mirror, and said tightly, "So tell me what's going on."

Cole did.

For the most part anyway. He explained about Terrence Renner calling him and about visiting the farm, finishing with, "Renner was dead when I got there, but he hadn't been for long. I checked for a pulse. None. Nor was he breathing." Cole's voice lowered as he remembered the crime scene. "There were numbers written in blood on the wall and tattooed on his forehead."

"Like Kajak." Deeds tossed another couple of nuts into his mouth.

"Except instead of 212, the number was 101."

"You think it was the same killer?"

"Had to be."

"Then why change the numbers?"

"I don't know." Cole shook his head then took a long swallow from his draft. "Maybe the guy messed up, or maybe they were meant to be different. Who knows?"

"Just our killer."

"I've been wracking my brain, but I can't come up with a thing."

"You have to make a statement to the police."

"They'll try to pin this on me."

"Why would you kill Renner? And on the first day you're free? It doesn't make any sense." Deeds dusted his hands then drained his beer. "So, you haven't exactly been keeping your nose clean since you got out."

"Renner called *me*. Or at least some guy claiming to be him."

"Okay, and what about Eve? You've seen her. And I suppose you're planning to see her again."

Cole stared at his beer, didn't answer.

Deeds shook his head woefully. "You're making a big mistake there. You know, I've already warned you about her, so I'll shut up. But use your head, Cole. The big one. You'd better tread very carefully. Someone's trying to frame you, my friend. Someone made certain you were at Renner's house last night." He set his empty mug on the table. "Just like before."

Cole didn't respond. Decided there was no reason to. He'd never admitted to a soul that he had been at Royal Kajak's cabin on the night Roy was killed, that Eve's memory wasn't completely faulty.

He figured he wouldn't start spilling his guts now.

• • •

". . . So you see, Ms. Renner, if you wouldn't mind, we'd like to check your DNA, just a mouth swab to begin with," said Detective Bentz through her cell phone as she pulled into her driveway. She rammed the car into park and let it idle as she digested what Detective Bentz had just told her about Faith Chastain's mysterious C-section, a birth that had most likely occurred when she was a patient at Our Lady of Virtues, a birth that Eve's father no doubt knew about. Bentz was still making his pitch. "We should have asked you about this when you were in, but we hadn't really quite connected the dots at that point."

"Let me get this straight," she said. "You think I could be Faith Chastain's daughter, one no one knew about?"

"That's right."

"And you think that somehow whoever put the clippings in my car knows this."

"Could be."

"So why not just call me up and tell me?"

"Unfortunately, I don't have an answer for that yet. We're still investigating."

"Dear Lord," she whispered, looking through her windshield, where the old wipers had streaked the glass.

"We'll subpoena the hospital records, of course, but that will take time; the hospital has been closed for years. Fortunately we already have samples of Faith Chastain's DNA on file. We'd like to compare it to yours."

"Of course," she said. "When?"

"As soon as possible. Unlike the labs you see on television, our testing will take weeks, even though I can put a rush on it."

"Can I come in now?"

"If it's not too much trouble."

To find out my biological parents? Are you kidding? She was already backing up. "I'm on my way." He gave her instructions and promised to meet her at the lab. She turned onto the road and headed into the heart of the city again.

Eve's head was spinning. Was it possible? Could she really be Faith Chastain's long-lost daughter? Sister, or at least half sister, to Abby Chastain, who was now involved with Detective Montoya? How was that for a bolt of lightning? The whole six-degrees-of-separation thing seemed to be working double- or triple-time.

"Weirder and weirder," she muttered as she worked her way through traffic.

A few drops of rain began to pepper her windshield as she found a parking spot and met Bentz in the lab. Her mouth was swabbed by an efficient tech who smiled at her, took her information, then assured Bentz he'd explain that the tests needed to be done ASAP so that Bentz could get the information he required.

It was all over in minutes.

And soon she'd find out if she was, indeed, Faith Chastain's missing child.

"You think that Eve Renner might be my half sister?" Abby said, thunderstruck. She had just finished her last photography session; her clients had walked out of her studio at the same moment that Montoya had walked in. He'd locked the door behind them, grabbed her, and twirled her off her feet before kissing her as if he'd never stop.

"Hey! What's gotten into you?" she'd asked, breathless, as he'd set her back on her feet.

Then he'd dropped the bombshell. "I think Eve Renner might be your long-lost half sister."

She stared at him. "What? Back up. Explain what's going on." Abby couldn't help feeling a little thrill of excitement to think that finally, after learning her mother had most likely had another child, she would finally get to meet the mysterious sibling . . . if it all panned out. But Eve Renner? How was it all connected?

Montoya sketched out the story as quickly and concisely as he could. Abby listened, frowning as he finished with the unsettling news that Eve thought someone was following her. "But who knows?" he added. "The woman's got trauma-induced amnesia and God knows what else. She's not exactly reliable."

Abby tamped down her own expectations as she turned off the lights and set the security alarm. "But you seriously think she could be my half sister? Because she was adopted and her father worked at the hospital? That's kinda slim, isn't it?"

"I'm just saying it's possible."

"Hmmm." They walked outside, where dusk was stretching in long, lavender fingers through the city streets and alleys and the air was thick with the threat of rain. Montoya slung his arm around her shoulders and guided her toward his car, a gleaming black Mustang parked illegally in a tow-away zone. "Someday you're going to come out here and your car's going to be gone," she predicted.

"Nah. Not with my luck." His teeth flashed white, and his hair, longer than he usually kept it, gleamed blue-black in the watery glow from the streetlamps. The scent of cologne mixed with cigarette smoke reached her nostrils, and she figured the case was getting to him, and, against all sound advice, he'd broken down and started smoking again. She decided not to call him on it as she settled into the passenger seat even though she noticed the open pack of Marlboros on the dash.

"We have your mother's DNA. We're hoping Eve will give us a sample for comparison, but even if she does, getting the results will take time."

"I won't hold my breath," she said as he flicked on the ignition, rammed the Mustang into reverse, then swung the car around. He skimmed through the city streets as if he were a NASCAR driver, and, as always, Abby clung to the passenger door's armrest for dear life.

"I'm still going to contact the convent and find out what they know," she said as Montoya turned onto Chatres. "Are we going somewhere?"

"How about out to dinner?"

"Don't tell me, a quick bite and then you're back on the job?"

"Yeah, that's what I was thinkin'."

"Then it better be takeout," she said, checking her watch. "Hershey hasn't been out since this morning, and neither has Ansel."

"Worse than kids," Montoya grumbled.

"You think?" She laughed as he negotiated the next turn, heading toward their house with its half-done renovations. "Wanna put some money where your mouth is?" she asked and glanced down at the diamond ring she wore, his gift to her last Christmas when he'd proposed. She'd said "Yes" and moved most of her things to his shotgun house in the city before New Year's Eve.

"A wager on whether kids are worse than pets?" he suggested.

"Hmm. Payoff after you have two kids."

"You're not trying to tell me something, are you?"

She caught his drift and laughed. "I'm *not* pregnant. But once I am and you're the father of a couple little hellion Montoyas, then we'll compare notes and see if you think being up all night with bottles and diapers is as tough as a litter box for the cat and Hershey's two walks a day."

"You're on," he said. Then one dark eyebrow raised in invitation. "Let's get the research going."

"What? You mean have a baby?" She smiled as he shifted down. "You're out of your mind, Montoya."

"Well, I'm thinking, you know, it might not be such a bad idea if we . . . you know . . ." His voice lowered suggestively.

"You want to go to bed when we get home?"

He slowed for a light and flashed her another heart-stopping grin.

"I thought you were going back to work tonight."

His dark eyes sparkled devilishly. "I am, but I might be able to be persuaded to stay an extra fifteen minutes."

"Oh wow," she said laughing. "A quickie. Be still, my heart."

He wheeled the Mustang around a final corner and onto the street they'd called home together for over four months. At their house, he eased his car into the short driveway. "We'll order pizza."

"So much for romance."

He parked the Mustang and winked at her in the soft light from the dash. "We can make it as romantic as you like."

"Promises, promises, Detective," she said, reaching for the door handle. His cell phone jangled, and he, as ever, took the call. Obviously the pizza would have to wait.

He answered as she climbed out of the car. Fingers scrabbling through her purse as she searched for her keys, she stepped around a discarded sink and cabinet the contractor had ripped out of Mrs. Alexander's side of the building and had yet to take away.

Pulling out her key ring, she started walking up

the broken cement walk toward the front door, where through the glass panes and backlit by a single lamp, Hershey was going nuts. Jumping wildly, tail thumping, letting out sharp, excited barks.

"I'm coming! I'm coming! Hold your horses!"

"Stop!" Montoya's voice was raw with panic. "Abby! *No!*"

She froze.

Turning, she saw him vault over the hood of the Mustang, touch down, then leap over the sink as he dashed across the small patch of grass that was their yard. His expression was as hard as she'd ever seen it. "Move away from the house! Get the hell away!" He didn't waste time, just grabbed her arm and pulled her away from the cottage, propelling her backward, toward the street. She dropped her keys and nearly tripped at the curb.

"Are you crazy?" she shouted.

Montoya just moved faster, urging her across the street. Abby lost her purse. "Wait!"

He twisted his head to view the house. His dark eyes focused on the door. "Some son of a bitch just called. Said he left me some 'evidence' on my front porch, and goddamn it, there it is."

"What?"

"Next to the damned door!"

Abby followed his gaze. Her heart nearly stopped. Propped against the siding, next to the old porch swing, were two small cases.

"Shit!" Montoya swivelled his head, his eyes searching the street.

"I don't understand," she said, an unspoken terror scraping down her spine.

Montoya didn't usually give in to fear. Right now he was frantic.

"It could be a bomb, Abby. Some nutcase with a grudge who has my cell number and my address. Maybe someone I sent away who is on parole. Who knows?"

"But Hershey—"

He held her tight with one arm while pulling his phone from his pocket and punching out 911.

"No one put a bomb on our porch," she said, trying to convince herself. She had to get the dog and cat out! Now!

But Montoya didn't release her. "The animals will be okay," he insisted, holding on to her for dear life.

Abby heard the operator answer.

Montoya identified himself and demanded officers from the bomb squad be sent to his house immediately.

Once the operator took the information, he hung up, his gaze searching the neighborhood.

"Ansel and Hershey are inside," Abby whispered, her nerves shredding one by one. So this was what it was like to be involved with a cop.

"They'll be okay," he said, but his voice was sober, and Abby wondered if her life would ever be the same.

Eve slept like the dead.

No phone calls interrupted her dreams.

No one pounded on her back door in the dead of the night.

She woke up refreshed, the headache that had been plaguing her for months having retreated. At least for the time being. She made the bed, showered, messed with a bit of makeup, added a touch of gel to her short hair, then called it good.

Who cared?

She and Samson had even eaten breakfast, kitty bits for him and a bagel with cream cheese and coffee for her. Not exactly gourmet, but not half bad.

She was beginning to feel almost like a normal person when she spied Cole Dennis big as life walking through the back gate and up the steps. "Now what?" she said but couldn't help the tiny rush of adrenaline that sped through her bloodstream whenever she saw him. "Masochist," she muttered under her breath.

This time she opened the door before he knocked.

"What? No revolver?" he asked, one dark eyebrow lifting.

"It's early, Cole. You could still get lucky."

A sexy grin stole over his lips, and she regretted her words. "That's not what I meant, and you know it."

"Tease."

"Yeah, that's me," she said, rolling her eyes, then realized that his cocky grin had faded. "There is, I assume, a reason you're here?"

He walked into the kitchen, and, as he passed, she closed the door, trying to ignore the scent of after-shave that lingered in the air. Though she couldn't remember the details of the night Roy was killed, she could recall in an instant the electricity she felt whenever Cole's lips brushed across her cheekbones, or touched the underside of her chin, or pressed against the back of her neck. Oh yes, those intimate, sizzling memories still found their way back to her consciousness.

"I thought you'd like to know that your father's belongings are safely with the police."

"You turned them in?" she asked suspiciously.

"I made sure they got into the right hands."

She narrowed her eyes. "Evasive, Counselor." Walking to the counter where the coffeepot sat warming, she watched as he made himself comfortable in a chair at the table. "Coffee? Or what's left of it?" She lifted the glass pot, where the dregs of the morning's brew sloshed darkly.

"That would be great. Thanks."

"So you talked to the detectives?" she asked, reaching for a cup, checking it, then rinsing it with hot water before dumping in the coffee and sticking the cup into the microwave.

"Not yet, but I will. Deeds is paving the way."

She set the microwave for a minute. "I don't trust Sam Deeds."

"You don't trust anyone."

She considered. He wasn't too far off the truth, but

she hadn't always been so cynical or jaded. Although she'd never been one of those upbeat, innocent Pollyanna types, there was a time, a time before she'd gotten involved with Cole Dennis, when trust had come much more easily. Bits of her memory might be foggy or missing, but she hadn't forgotten that.

"Deeds is a good guy."

"If you say so." She wasn't convinced. The defense lawyer was just too damned slick in his tailor-made suits and expensive shoes. And then there was all that talk from ADA Johnson about how Deeds would, if given the chance, tear Eve's testimony to ribbons. Nope, she didn't like him.

The timer dinged, and, using an old oven mitt, Eve extracted the steaming cup from the small oven then handed the mug and mitt to Cole. "Sorry. It's hot."

"Thanks." He blew across the cup. "What did the police say about the newspaper clippings?"

"They think whoever planted them in my car might have been trying to tell me that I could be Faith Chastain's long-lost child."

"What?" He held his cup in midair. "What long-lost child?"

She explained. He already knew that she was adopted but hadn't heard the latest speculation. "Isn't that a bit of a leap?" he asked. "From clippings to missing daughter?" He took a sip from his cup. "That . . . that's too out there. Who would know that information? No, I think this has to do with

263

your dad's murder and the fact that Faith was a patient at the hospital when he was on staff."

"There're only two ways to find out."

"Two ways?" he asked.

"Well, I could sit around and wait for the DNA test results, or I could go out to the campus of Our Lady and see if there's anyone there who might know something."

"The hospital's been closed for years."

"But the convent's still open, and I'm willing to bet some of the nuns who worked at the hospital might still be alive and living there." She walked to the drawer where she'd put the envelope holding the photocopies of the clippings. As he sipped his coffee, she sorted through them. "Let's see. . . . Okay, here we go. This one"—she handed the sheet to Cole—"quotes Sister Rebecca Renault, who is now the Reverend Mother. I remember her from the hospital."

Cole's eyebrows drew together as he scanned the article.

"I think I'm going to try and talk to her," Eve said slowly.

"You believe she'll remember something?"

"I don't know, but it's worth a shot."

To prove her point, she picked up her cell phone, called information, and was connected to the convent, where a secretary told her that the Reverend Mother's schedule was full for the next several days but that if she called back at the first of the following week, something might be arranged.

"Can you have the Reverend Mother call me back?" Eve asked, not about to be put off.

"Of course. She usually returns calls before Vespers, but today she has appointments all afternoon. I'll see if she can get back to you tomorrow."

"That would be great," Eve said and gave the secretary her phone number. She hung up, feeling disappointed.

"Struck out?"

"Not yet." Tapping her fingers on the counter, she added, "But close."

"Join the club."

"Meaning?"

"I didn't find anything on your father's computer. No information."

"So much for us playing Nancy Drew."

He drained his cup, stood, and set it in the sink. "Speak for yourself. I'm not giving up."

"Fine, Nancy, what's your next move?"

"My next move? After you call me Nancy?" Cole smiled at her in surprise.

Eve felt the change in atmosphere between them and suddenly wished she hadn't been so open and teasing. "I just meant, what do you plan to do next?"

"I don't know. Give me a minute."

They stared at each other. Eve drew a breath. Oh, she was in big trouble.

He took a step forward and she said, "Don't."

"It's still there, isn't it, Eve?"

"No. I don't remember."

"Sure you do."

She held her hands up. "No . . . no . . ."

Cole crowded into her space. She told herself not to lift her eyes, not to look at him, NOT TO DO ANY-THING, but she slowly raised her gaze.

"Yes," he said. Then he pulled her against him and before she could utter another word of protest, pressed coffee-laced lips to hers.

CHAPTER 16

Kissing Eve was a mistake. He knew it instantly. He knew it before it happened, but he hadn't been able to stop. Touching her, holding her tight against him, hearing her heart beating so close to his own, feeling her breasts crushed against his chest, tasting her, for God's sake—all of it was a colossal error in judgment.

Colossal!

But it had been such a long time since he'd felt her bones melt as they kissed, and when he slowly, steadily walked her backward so that her spine was pressed against the wall and her arms surrounded his neck, he couldn't breathe.

"This is . . . this is wrong," she whispered when he finally lifted his head.

"Yep."

"We shouldn't. I mean . . . we just can't."

"Uh-huh." He kissed her again and lost himself in the feel of her. She closed her eyes and moaned almost imperceptibly. Through her T-shirt, he felt the soft, pliant muscles of her back, the indentation of her spine. His fingers dipped lower, into that smooth curve and just below the waistband of her jeans.

Heat sizzled through his blood.

Desire pounded in his ears.

He remembered making love to her. The power. The passion. Sometimes teasing and laughing, almost girlish, other times all feminine, nearly feline seduction, Eve had always been passionate.

He remembered the time he'd come home and found her waiting for him in the bed, and when he'd stripped his clothes off to join her, she'd laughed and run to the shower, already warm and steaming when he'd caught her and had lifted her up to make love to her with her shoulders pressed to the tile. . . . And the time they'd been hiking, cresting a mountain ridge, and all she'd had to do was turn, her hair catching in the sunlight, her eyes squinting up at him, her breasts heaving from the exertion of the climb, her lips curving upward in invitation . . .

But now, here, in her grandmother's kitchen, he kissed her hard and felt her response. Familiar. Tempting. Oh so arousing.

One hand tangled in her short curls, pulling her head back, bowing her neck as he kissed her at the base of her throat.

Desire thundered through him.

He found the button of her faded Levis, popped it open. The zipper hissed downward with the slightest of pressure. And then he was cupping her, fingers brushing silky panties.

"Oh God!" Her eyes flew open. She blinked, and the arms surrounding his neck stiffened. "Cole. No . . . oh no." She pushed away from him and stared at him in horror. "We can *not* go there! Oh my God, what was I thinking?"

"You weren't."

"And neither were you." Stepping away from him, she rezipped her pants, buttoned them, and straightened the hem of her T-shirt. "No way. I can't do this. I just . . . can't!"

He raked a hand through his hair and willed his half-masted erection to relax. "If you expect me to apologize . . ."

She looked up at him, her aquamarine eyes dark with desire, her cheeks still flushed. "Apologize? No. I'm not blaming you. For God's sake, Cole, I'm not some whimpering virgin going to point a finger at you. You know that. You felt my response." She drew a breath and said in self-condemnation, "I wanted to go to bed with you, to lose myself, to just end this nightmare for a while too, but considering everything . . ." She threw up a hand, then finger-combed her short hair.

"Considering everything." He had to agree with her, but damn, he wanted her. His stupid cock wasn't taking the hint, and he turned his back on her and forced his mind to a different place. A darker and more dangerous place. The reason he was here.

"I spent last night thinking," he said. "Whatever is going on, it's dangerous and we're both involved. Someone, and I'll be damned if I know who, is making certain we're in this together."

She nodded and, as the cat wandered into the room, picked him up and stroked his long fur.

"So it only makes sense to me that we should fight it together."

"How?" she asked, lines appearing between her eyebrows.

"I'm not sure yet. But someone sent you clippings about Faith Chastain. Someone followed you from Atlanta to do it. Someone killed your father and made damned sure that I'd show up there." She nodded again, pensive. "What made you leave Atlanta when you did, Eve?"

"It was time to go. I'd really worn out my welcome. Kyle and Anna Maria weren't getting along, and I felt that I was exacerbating an already bad situation."

"It had nothing to do with my release?"

"Not directly, no. I knew you were supposed to be getting out, yes, but wasn't certain as to the day."

"Did you call your father and tell him you were on your way home?"

"Not that day, but I'd called him sometime the week before, I think. I can't remember the exact date." The cat wriggled in her hands, and she let him hop to the floor. Samson shot like a streak to the door, pacing and meowing.

"So only you, your brother, and your sister-in-law

269

knew for certain that you were leaving?" Cole asked.

"Even Kyle wasn't sure, I don't think. I'd been talking about it and had one bag packed, but the morning I woke up and thought 'I'm outta here,' he wasn't around. Anna said he ran to the store."

"What about friends or neighbors? Did you phone anyone and tell them you were coming back?"

"No, but my physical therapist, Nita, she was aware that I was moving." Eve walked to the door of the mudroom and opened it. Samson shot outside.

Cole looked away, didn't want to concentrate on the way the denim of her jeans fit around her ass. He grabbed a chair at the kitchen table, twirled it, and straddled the back. "Anyone else?"

She shut the door then returned to the kitchen, where she started making more coffee. "Probably my shrink, a guy named Calvin Byrd." Glancing over her shoulder at him, she rolled her eyes. "I got his name from Anna Maria. A mistake. I saw him a couple of times then stopped. I told him I'd locate someone down here if I thought I needed a session. He wasn't all that cool about it. Thought I was in major denial, which maybe I was." She rinsed out the pot, filled it, then poured the water into the reservoir of the machine. "That's about it, I think. Anna could have told her friends, I suppose."

"Whoever left you the clippings was ready for you. Waiting. Have you seen that truck again?"

She found her bag of coffee beans. "I think so, but I'm not sure," she admitted. "Yesterday, after I left the police station, but . . . I tried to double back and get behind him for a better look and maybe get the numbers of his license plate, but it didn't happen. I lost him." She cast him a rueful smile as she poured beans into the grinder. "I guess it's me who's not cut out to be Nancy Drew."

She pressed a button, and the screaming, whirling sound of coffee beans being pulverized destroyed any chance of conversation.

"I just don't understand what the hell's going on," she said once the grinder was silent again.

"Neither do I." Cole rubbed the back of his neck. "I'm going to talk to the police. Maybe later today. Whenever Deeds can arrange it. I don't know what's going on, Eve. But someone made damned sure that I was at your father's house the other night. I think it's time I came clean."

"Good." She was relieved. "And in the meantime?"

"As I said, let's pool our resources." He walked over to her as she lined the coffeemaker with a paper filter and poured in the dark powder. "I don't like it that someone's following you, breaking into your car."

"That makes two of us."

"So I think I should camp out here."

"No!" She spun so quickly she knocked into the coffeemaker, and water sloshed onto the counter. "You're kidding, right?" When he didn't respond, she laughed, grabbed a paper towel from a roll sitting on the counter, and began blotting up the spill. "You can't 'camp out' here, for God's sake! What do you think

271

you can do, protect me? Oh, Cole, think about it. I was the one who said you tried to kill me."

"But you don't believe that, do you?"

"I don't know what to believe!"

"Eve . . ."

"All right. Yes, I don't think you would want to hurt me. I don't think I ever really thought that, but when I go back to that night and concentrate . . . I see your face and a gun that fires." She finished wiping the counter and tossed the soggy towel into the trash. "But you still can't stay here. That's out of the question."

"We're going to have to have a little faith in each other if we're going to do this."

"That works two ways, Counselor." As Mr. Coffee gurgled and spat, she folded her arms under her breasts. "I wasn't involved with anyone other than you," she said positively. "But the police say I wasn't raped during my blackout period, so . . ." She shuddered. "I don't know. I can't explain it. But I don't remember anyone but you, Cole. I was in love with you. I hoped to marry you and . . ." Her eyebrows slammed together as she studied a coffee stain on the tile. "I never cheated on you." She rubbed at the stain then lifted her gaze to meet his. "I would know if I had, wouldn't I?"

It killed Cole to see her indecision. Looking past his own anger and betrayal, he suddenly understood how truly devastating her memory loss was for her.

But Eve, hearing her own confusion, seemed to shut down, cut herself away emotionally. "If this is going

272

to work, we both have to start over," she said briskly.

He nodded. Resisted the urge to pull her close to him again. "I know."

"It'll take trust, and that's a pretty tall order for each of us."

"The way I figure it, we don't have much choice."

She handed him a cup of coffee. "Okay then."

"Okay."

Cole gazed at her over the rim of his mug. A tenuous pact had been formed between them, an alliance, whether Eve realized it completely or not.

They were together!

Eve and her lover.

From his vantage point on the property of the vacant house whose yard abutted the grand Renner home, he had a perfect view of the kitchen. He rarely dared come this close, but he'd taken a chance, been drawn to stop as he drove past when he noticed the battered old Jeep: Cole Dennis's rig.

Through the watery glass he saw him kiss her, force himself upon her, and she, of course, did little to resist.

His nostrils flared. He chewed nervously on a fingernail. He swore that, even from this distance, he could smell them together, the stink of their rutting, the reek of their sex. His skin wrinkled in revulsion, and the stench of it burned his airways.

Eve the princess.

Now Eve the whore.

Sensual, flirting, and dangerously cunning.

How she used her feminine wiles so indiscrimi-
nately!

And yet he wanted her.

Desperately.

Achingly.

A bad girl. The kind his mother had warned him
against.

If he closed his eyes, he could hear his mother's
voice as clearly as if she were standing next to him
beneath the protective branches of this willow tree.

*"You mustn't want her! She's unclean! A whore!
Spawned by Satan!"*

Though Mama had been dead for years, he still
heard her recriminations, her dire warnings, her heart-
felt prayers, her quiet sobs . . .

Hers had been a low, soft voice, one that on the surface seemed kind and caring. But beneath the warm,
dulcet tones there had always lurked a warning. Strict.
Insistent. But sugarcoated with a false Southern gen-
tility. A voice that had permeated his days and nights
and scraped through his brain.

"Oh, sweetie, don't you ever go near those girls,"
she'd admonished him time and time again. At school,
where the nuns had still worn voluminous habits, on the
playground where other children were laughing and running and screaming in delight, in the car as they drove.
An image from his youth flashed behind his eyes.

He'd been eight years old, and she was dragging
him through the city to mass at St. Louis Cathedral in
the French Quarter.

He remembered standing in front of the old church, feeling small as the three whitewashed spires knifed upward against a cloudless summer sky. Horse-drawn carriages creaked by, big wheels turning, horseshoes ringing on the cobblestones. People were bustling around the Cathedral and Jackson Square.

His mother caught him looking at a curlyhaired girl who had been about his age. The girl, wearing a yellow sundress and matching ribbons in her hair, was walking with her mother across Jackson Square, pausing at the statue of Andrew Jackson upon his rearing horse to look back over her shoulder and smile at him, her brown tresses bouncing.

His mother had intercepted the glance and recognized pure evil in the girl's innocent brown eyes.

"Stay away from her," his mother had said, spinning him around to face her tall, trembling, furious form. "She's one of them." She hissed this into his ear, and he'd smelled the scent of the same perfume she always wore, a cloying scent he could remember decades later.

"Do you hear me, Son? That girl will make you want to do vile, nasty things that will take you down a path that leads straight to the depths of hell. They're all sinners. Oh, I know they look pretty and innocent. Believe me, I know. But they are all the same. Never, Son, do you hear me, *never* trust them. They are all like Eve with the apple in the Garden of Eden. Born of original sin. You understand, don't you? You must never, never touch them." Mama had shifted, placing her body directly in his line of vision, casting a cool shadow over him. Bending slightly so that she was peering through the black lace of her hat, she had glared hard then, her eyes wide and unblinking, her pupils mere pinpoints in pale blue irises. "Girls like that one are heathens, honey. Daughters of Lucifer. Do you hear me?" Her glossy red lips pulled into a tight smile. Her fingers dug into his arm so deeply, the sharp, polished nails had pinched his skin, painfully etching tiny white crescents on his flesh, nearly drawing blood.

"Y–yes, Mama," he'd said, shamed.

"Good." She pushed him in the opposite direction, toward the whitewashed towering walls of St. Louis Cathedral. The girl turned away. Bells were tolling, people bustling and talking, a saxophone wailing from a street corner two blocks down. The August sun was high in the sky, shining down in hot, blistering rays that bounced against the pavement.

"Don't ever forget." Mama straightened then adjusted her hat with one hand, making certain the partial veil covered her eyes before shepherding him through the yawning doors of the cathedral.

Now, years later, he felt that same hot shame burning through him. Because of Eve. Always Eve.

He itched to call her again, to warn her . . . to remind her . . . to let her feel that icy drip of terror that would chill her wanton soul.

All in good time, he told himself as he headed back to the nondescript silver sedan he'd parked three blocks away. All in good time.

Everything had to go according to plan.

Eve was forbidden. A sick sin and yet he couldn't help his lust. Yet, as much as he wanted to feel her writhing beneath him, hot for him, her legs strapped over his ribs, it might never happen. But, he thought, biting off the tip of another fingernail and spitting it out into the street drain, he knew with infinite certainty, he and Eve would die together.

He would make it so.

It was their destiny.

Montoya lit up, took a long drag, then crumpled the pack of Marlboros in his fist and tossed it into the trash can on his way into the station. He'd bought the pack at a convenience store the night before and smoked three cigarettes, counting this one. His last.

At least for a while.

But the Renner case had gotten under his skin in a way that only nicotine could salve.

He paused at the steps and inhaled again.

"Hey, I thought you quit." Brinkman, the biggest dick alive, was lumbering toward the station from a nearby parking lot. A smart enough detective, Brinkman was a royal pain in the ass, always pointing out flaws or making crude remarks or being a general social misfit. Now he motioned to the filter tip smoldering between Montoya's fingers.

"I did." Montoya flipped the rest of his cigarette onto the pavement and crushed it with his boot as he started up the stairs.

Brinkman was right on his heels. He wore his hair long on the sides, just brushing his ears, to make up for the fact that there was nothing on top, just a freckled pate. He was always fighting his weight and was wheezing as they reached the top step.

"I heard there was a bomb scare at your place."

Montoya didn't respond as he yanked open the door.

"But it turned out to be nothin', huh?"

"It was evidence from the Renner case. His laptop computer."

"Just dropped it off on your porch?"

"The guy called me and told me what he'd left, but I didn't trust him." Montoya figured he didn't owe Brinkman more of an explanation as he headed toward the stairs.

"Who was he?"

"Don't know. Probably the same prick who called in the murder."

"The doer?"

"Maybe."

Brinkman paused at the elevator, but Montoya kept walking, taking the steps two at a time, glad to be rid of the other detective. On the second floor, he headed toward the kitchen, poured himself a cup of coffee, and watched as Lynn Zaroster, a smart, cute junior detective, slapped a packet of artificial sweetener against the counter. She'd been with the division a little over two years, and already some of her idealism was starting to wash away. She ripped open the packet and dumped a minuscule amount of fake sugar into her cup, where coffee steamed.

"That stuff'll kill ya," Montoya said.

"Oh yeah?" She cocked a dark eyebrow and seemed amused as she blew across her cup. "Is that before or after you die of lung cancer?"

"He quit smoking," Brinkman said as he angled into the room and tried to hide a smirk.

Bastard. Jesus, would the guy never transfer? Why not Kansas City or Sacramento or effing New York City, anywhere but here?

"I'll believe it when I see it." Zaroster headed back toward her desk.

Muttering under his breath, Brinkman lifted the glass pot from its warming tray. Only a swill of black gunk swam around the bottom of the carafe. "You know how to work this thing?" Brinkman asked Montoya, though his gaze followed after Zaroster and her tight little ass, which, Montoya suspected, she swung a little more sexily just to bug Brinkman.

"Yeah, but so do you," Montoya said. The I'm-incapable-of-doing-this-woman's-job act didn't wash with him. He opened a cupboard where the premeasured packs of coffee were kept and tossed one to the other detective. "Knock yourself out."

Quicker than he looked, Brinkman caught the packet. "Great."

Before the balding detective could grumble, complain, or whine any further, Montoya headed down a short hallway toward Bentz's office.

He found his partner poring over an open file that

was labeled Royal Kajak. Pictures of the crime scene were scattered over his desk, along with notes and lab reports. His computer monitor, too, displayed pictures of the deceased along with interior and exterior shots of the cabin and woods.

Bentz looked up as Montoya arrived. "Heard you thought a bomb was left on your porch."

"Good news travels fast."

"Renner's laptop?"

"Yep. I didn't get a chance to look at it. Once the crime techs have done their thing, I'll see what I can find." He kicked out one of the chairs in front of Bentz's desk and sat.

"Who left it?"

"The guy who called me and told me that the briefcase and laptop were on the porch didn't ID himself, but I'm thinking the items were at Renner's house, and whoever called in the murder lifted them then got the hell out."

"Why?" Bentz raked fingers through hair that was still damp from his morning shower.

"Don't know."

"A witness?"

"Maybe, but why not come forward?"

"Could be this guy's the doer."

"The number on the screen said pay phone, and I'm pretty sure we'll get nothing when we figure out which pay phone it was."

"But it could have been the doer."

They banged that theory around awhile, but neither

one of them bought it. Why would the killer bother to return evidence?

"Take a look at this." Bentz picked up a couple of sheets of paper that had been lying on his desk then handed them to Montoya.

"Tox report. On Renner. Not complete, but interesting."

"His blood alcohol level is high," Montoya said, his gaze scanning the document. "Drugs? Alprazolam? A sedative?"

"Hmm. Brand name Xanax."

"He took it with booze?"

"Not a good combo."

"He was a psychiatrist, could have prescribed it himself."

Bentz nodded. "But we didn't find any bottles of the med at the house. I double-checked. No samples either."

"Could've used 'em all."

"Packets should have been found in the trash. Again, no dice."

Montoya scratched at his chin thoughtfully, scraping the bristles of his goatee. "So the doctor was out of it when he was attacked?"

"Uh-huh. The lab is all over it. They tested the bottle and, sure enough, plenty of Xanax mixed in with the Jack Daniels."

"So you're thinking the killer did this to him on purpose to sedate him, make him more malleable, easier to attack?"

"Looks like it to me."

"And no forced entry."

"Yes."

"He was visiting?"

"Only one glass at the scene. No evidence that Renner was entertaining."

Montoya pointed to the older file. "Kajak's tox screen came back clean, right? No booze. No drugs."

Bentz tossed the file to the younger detective. "Not even a trace of an antidepressant, and the guy had been under a psychiatrist's care for years."

"So you think our killer is evolving?"

Bentz shook his head. "Maybe." He stared at the grisly pictures of Roy Kajak. "I don't know." Frowning, he added, "I've already got a call from the Feds. They think there might be a link, a serial killer on the loose."

"So now we get to deal with the FBI."

"Looks like," Bentz nodded.

"Task force?"

"Probably. I've already got a partial list of everyone who knew Renner. Of course the neighbors heard nothing."

"The nearest one's pretty far away."

"Yeah, I know, but you'd think someone might notice a car parked in the drive, hear an argument, something, but no. I'm trying to chase down his sons. So far no one's returning my phone calls."

"Really?" Montoya said, surprised. "I did reach Kyle Renner's wife, Anna Maria. She's upset but couldn't tell me where her husband was. 'At work on a job out of town,' was her explanation."

"Thin."

"Very. As for the last person to see Renner alive, it might be the clerk at the liquor store where he bought a bottle of Jack Daniels."

"New bottle?"

Bentz nodded. "That's right. Purchased around four-thirty in the afternoon. Doctored after that."

"And no fingerprints?"

"None that shouldn't be there."

"Just like Royal Kajak's cabin."

"Yeah."

Montoya frowned. "You know, Eve Renner's right in the middle of this."

"Tell me something I don't know." Bentz stretched his arms over his head and rotated the kinks from his neck.

"Wish I could." Drinking from his cup, eyeing the bloody numbers smeared onto the walls and tattooed on the victims at both crime scenes, Montoya tried to figure out what the damned numbers meant. 212. 101.

Significant?

Or just a nutcase's idea of a joke, something to throw them off?

Time, he figured, would tell.

CHAPTER 17

Eve locked the door then watched through the window as Cole walked across the overgrown yard to his Jeep. She couldn't help but notice the way his shirt pulled across his shoulders and the casual manner in which his ragged, faded jeans hung low on his hips. In her mind's eye she remembered his body, naked and hard, firm butt muscles, legs so strong the skin stretched taut over his thighs and calves. And then there was his back. . . . Oh Lord, how she'd loved to trace a finger down his spine and experience his reaction. One slow, twisting movement of her index finger and his eyes would darken, his pupils wide. Eagerly his mouth would find hers, and he'd wrap those sinewy arms around her and pin her to the mattress, pushing her knees apart in one smooth motion . . . unless he rolled her onto her stomach first and, cupping her breasts, pushed into her from behind. She touched her lips and quivered inside at the memory.

What that man could do to her!

She watched as he opened the Jeep's door and found his sunglasses, sliding them onto the bridge of his nose.

She thought of the kiss here in the kitchen and how easily it could have turned into more. Her mouth turned to sand at the thought of the sex they could have had and might be having still.

Watching him slide into his rig, she called herself

seven kinds of fool. What was she thinking, letting him kiss her?

Not smart, Eve, she thought, though she'd convinced herself that her memory of the night that Roy had died wasn't just faulty, it was flat-out wrong.

Cole wouldn't have tried to kill her. Of course not. She was missing something. The image in her mind was off somehow; that had to be it.

Her gaze was still on him as he yanked the door closed, then rolled down the driver's side window of the battered Jeep and, as if sensing her stare, looked up suddenly, catching her. Damn the man, if one side of his mouth didn't lift into a knowing, amused grin. Her silly heart fluttered, and she couldn't believe her reaction to him. "He's just a man," she told Samson as he hopped from a chair to the counter, then sat, tail twitching, defying her to scold him and shoo him off his perch.

However, she knew she was lying to herself.

Cole Dennis was not just another man. Which was just plain bad news.

Disgusted with herself, she tried to pluck Samson from his spot by the sink and only succeeded in brushing his back as he leapt from the counter. After landing softly on the battered linoleum, he slunk, ears backward, belly nearly sweeping the floor, down the hallway. Eve looked back to see the taillights of Cole's Jeep as he braked at the corner. She was a damned fool where he was concerned. Her feelings for him were, and always had been, a problem.

285

"One among many," she said as she hurried to the stairs and raced upward, not bothering to stop on the second floor. Tennis shoes pounding the steps, she climbed to the turret and headed straight for the old secretary desk her grandmother had used eons before.

Her grandmother had given the secretary to her, and Eve, delighted, had promptly stored all her precious nothings in the locked section. After all these years, she still had the key, and now she fished it off her key ring.

With a click, the lock sprang and the top of the secretary folded downward to become a writing desk. Inside were tiny drawers and cubbyholes meant for stamps and writing paper, sealing wax and pens. Behind the slots for envelopes was a false back and a small drawer that, if you pressed just right, sprang open. As a girl, Eve had hidden her most secret treasures in the tiny cache, but now the space was empty save for a small leather key holder and the three keys inside, keys her father had given her long ago. Keys, she now hoped, that would open some very old doors.

What were the chances?

She palmed the smooth, worn leather and slipped the keys into her pocket. She couldn't sit around and do nothing.

When Sister Rebecca hadn't returned her call by early afternoon, Eve decided to seek the Reverend Mother out. Of course she was busy, of course she had a schedule, but damn it, two people close to Eve were dead, two people who had connections to Our Lady of

Virtues. Then there was the matter of Faith Chastain's pregnancy. If she gave birth at Our Lady of Virtues, wouldn't there be a record of it? Eve had already called the state offices and gotten nowhere, so she'd tried the Internet. Again to no end. If Faith Chastain had borne a third child, there seemed to be no record of it.

As for her own birth certificate, her biological mother and father were listed as "unknown." The story she'd heard was that she, as a newborn, had been left at an orphanage associated with the order of nuns at Our Lady of Virtues. Word had gotten back to the mental hospital, and Dr. Renner had examined the baby. Since he and his wife had been thinking seriously of adoption, they'd made the necessary arrangements through a local lawyer, who, when Eve had checked, had died nearly twenty years earlier, the records of his business locked away in some storage unit that his only heir, a nephew living out of state, saw no reason to disturb. Short of a court order, those records were lost to her.

So it was time to do some digging on her own.

No telling what she'd find, she thought as she pocketed the small leather key case and returned downstairs to the kitchen, where, digging through a drawer next to the mudroom, she found a heavy flashlight. She clicked it on and, surprisingly, the beam, though weak, was visible. "Good enough."

Lastly she found an ancient, dusty backpack and loaded it with a few of her grandfather's forgotten

287

tools: the flashlight, a roll of duct tape, a pair of gloves, and a small hand towel.

Half a second later, she was out the door.

The interview with the police was going to hell in short order.

Deeds had set it up, and Cole had done his part. He'd admitted that he'd been at Terrence Renner's house on the night of his murder, had discovered the body and called in the homicide. He believed phone records would bear out his story and admitted he was wrong in not waiting for the police to arrive or in identifying himself. He also admitted to taking the briefcase with the laptop inside. The cops wanted to cuff him right then and there, but Deeds calmed them down, pointing out that Cole had come clean when it might have served his purposes to keep his mouth shut.

Montoya had been incensed, blistering in his condemnation that Cole had tampered with evidence. Deeds had suggested the department's computer techies check it out. He assured them that if the techs were any good, they would see nothing had been changed or deleted.

In the end, though deeply suspicious of his motives, the cops apparently believed that Cole hadn't killed Renner. Either that, or they didn't have enough to hold him. More than likely, they didn't want to arrest the wrong guy again and end up looking like idiots in the press.

Cole was nervous throughout the ordeal but tried not to show it. He sat in the straight-backed chair in the small, stuffy room with Montoya's near-black eyes glittering with suspicion and Rick Bentz pencil-tapping as he asked questions. Montoya, that prick with his signature leather jacket and ridiculous diamond stud, was itching for a fight; it was written all over him. His expression was tense, his skin stretched tight over his face, his lips flat against his teeth as he spat out question after question around a wad of gum that he chewed furiously, as if his life depended on it. Cords showed on the sides of his neck above his collar, and one of his hands kept curling into a fist.

Cool, he was not.

As for Bentz, the older cop was methodical, slower, more even keeled, but, Cole sensed, as eager to pin the murder on Cole Dennis as his hothead of a partner. There was no game playing, none of the good-cop/bad-cop crap you saw on TV, just two damned determined detectives.

"You broke the terms of your bail," Montoya pointed out, stuffing his fist into his pocket.

Deeds shook his head. "The charge was dropped. There is no bail to worry about."

"But there's still the matter of the marijuana found in his possession," Bentz said.

Deeds looked over the tops of his reading glasses. Disappointment was written all over his face. "We all know what that was about," he said, "and we're dealing with it. Someone set him up." Montoya opened his mouth to argue, and Deeds held up a hand. "Another time, another place, Detective. My client came in here voluntarily. He's committed no crime, and so, if there aren't any other questions, we're leaving."

"Theft is a crime," Montoya said, taking a step forward, but the accusation was without teeth, considering the laptop was now in the authorities' possession. Catching a glance from Bentz, Montoya checked himself but said tightly, "We may have more questions, Dennis. You're not off the hook on this."

Deeds got to his feet. "When you have enough to charge him, call me."

Cole scraped back his chair. The metal legs screamed against the old tile floor. He'd answered all their questions, told his story, and it was all he could do. Being in the small, airless room, pent up with detectives who were looking to trip him up, knowing that his every word and movement were being taped and that other cops were standing on the other side of the two-way glass, waiting for him to mess up, had nearly been more than he could bear.

Kristi Bentz thought she might puke if she had to take another phone call from one more cretin-client for one more insurance claim. How many dented bumpers, broken windshields, bent axles, and smashed quarter panels was she supposed to hear about and pretend like she cared while the client raved on and on about the "idiot" who'd been "driving up my ass" and rear-ended them, or the "moron" who stupidly had backed into the client at his local grocery, or the "ass" who had been driving like a bat out of hell while the client decided to switch lanes?

Now, seated at the small desk in her cubicle, her computer monitor showing off all of the "products" Gulf Auto and Life had to offer, she was talking to the mother of a fifteen-year-old who, despite the fact he had no driver's license, had taken the family's minivan out for a spin and ended up in the ditch. Now the woman was wondering if Gulf Auto would pay for the damages on the near-totaled vehicle.

Kristi had referred the woman to her agent and told her that she'd call an adjuster, but that wasn't good enough. Client/Mother-of-an-Imbecile wanted Kristi's promise that she was covered.

Holy Mother of God.

"I'll have Ms. Osgoode call you," Kristi said and finally was able to hang up.

She had a few more hours of paperwork before she could go home.

Home.

A studio apartment in the University District that was furnished with hand-me-downs and pieces she'd picked up at the local thrift stores. It was cozy enough, she decided, but not exactly where she'd thought she'd be now that she'd graduated from college. Nor was this dead-end job the height of her aspirations.

No way.

Not when there were true-crime cases to write about

and she had an insider's view on some of the most interesting homicides in this town. And the most interesting one at the moment was right under her nose, the victim being Dr. Terrence Renner, the suspects all connected to that spooky old mental hospital located not too far out of town. What could be more perfect?

Who cared if her father didn't want her involved?

She could do a little digging on her own, start her own file. From writing for crime magazines and being cheap, cheap, cheap with herself, she'd already managed to save enough money that she could quit this job. She could work nights as a waitress or bartender to survive while researching and writing her book during the day.

So her social life was a big fat zero.

Big deal.

She'd kind of struck out with the boyfriend thing long ago.

The dork she'd dated in high school, the guy who'd planned to be a farmer and had wanted to marry her, had ended up going to school, getting not only a BS but a damned PhD in criminology, and now worked in the state crime lab. Go figure. The guy she'd been nuts about in college had been a two-timing jerk who had ended up dead. Since that time she'd only dated casually and hung out with her friends some weekends.

The phone rang, and she groaned.

This just wasn't working. The tiny cubicle was stifling. She had nothing in common with most of her coworkers. Her degree in English Literature wasn't being used. At all. She could have gotten this job without stepping one foot over the threshold of All Saints College in Baton Rouge.

She was going to give it up.

Soon.

Like maybe this afternoon as soon as her boss decided to roll back in.

Terrence Renner's murder had all the earmarks of a best seller. If she didn't write about it, someone else was sure to, and Kristi decided that just wasn't going to happen. The Renner homicide, especially if it was tied to the Kajak murder, was hers!

The phone blasted again, and she picked it up.

Forcing a smile in her voice that she didn't feel, she answered, "Gulf Auto and Life. This is Kristi. How may I help you?"

"Hey, Diego, looks like you got company," Brinkman said as he passed by Montoya's desk on his way out. "Isn't that the name you use whenever there's a hot woman nearby?"

"Bite me, Brinkman," he said as he looked up and spied Abby hurrying toward his office. Her jaw was set, her face paler than usual, her freckles more visible, her hair clipped away from her face as she zigzagged her way through desks, filing cabinets, and cubicles.

"I have something I thought you might want to see," she said without preamble, fishing in her purse and pulling out an envelope.

Montoya took it carefully, opened the flap, and slid the contents into his palm. Inside was a black-and-white photograph and a negative of Our Lady of Virtues Hospital.

"I took this a while back," she said a little breathlessly. "When . . . well, when we were all trying to figure out what happened to my mother. I'd forgotten that this roll was in the camera, and today I developed it."

He was staring at the photograph, trying to figure out what was important enough to spur her to the station.

"Look there," she said, pointing to a window located on the third floor, the window that her mother had fallen through twenty years earlier. "See that shadow?"

He frowned, sliding the envelope under the shade of his desk lamp. Barely visible was a dark smudge.

"It's a man."

He looked up sharply. "You're certain?"

"Yes. Look at it with a magnifying glass." Again she rummaged in her purse and found an enlarging lens, which she handed to him. He walked around the desk, sat down and, like a jeweler checking for flaws in a diamond, went over the photograph.

"I'll be damned." Sure enough, there was an image of someone standing in the window.

"It's not him," she said, and they both knew she meant the killer who had terrorized New Orleans the previous fall, the murderer who had sought his victims in pairs and had been so closely associated with the hospital.

"Then who is it?"

"Exactly."

"You think this guy might have something to do with what's going on now?"

"I don't know, but it's something." She jabbed at the picture with her finger. "No one was supposed to be in that old hospital. It's nearly condemned, but there, big as life, is a man."

"Maybe the caretaker."

"Sure," she said, mocking him because they both knew that the caretaker for Our Lady of Virtues at the time had been a man named Lawrence Du Loc, and despite the lack of clarity in the photo, when Montoya stared at the image with the magnifying glass, he had to agree. The man in the window was not Du Loc.

But Terrence Renner's killer?

Maybe. Or someone who knew something.

Montoya grimaced, wondering if they were chasing shadows. But since they had no real leads in the case, he couldn't afford to overlook anything, no matter now insignificant or far-fetched it might appear. "I'll check it out. See if the guys in the lab can increase the clarity. Do you know the date you took this picture?"

"Not exactly, but a few days before you caught the guy."

"Close enough. For now."

She leaned her hip against his desk. "I talked with Zoey. About Eve."

"Yeah?"

"I'd like to meet her. Actually, Zoey would too, but she's stuck in Seattle a while. Can't get away, and it's really pissing her off. So it's up to me."

Montoya found it incredibly hard to say no to Abby, except when it was police business. "The woman in question's involved in an ongoing investigation. It might be better if you waited until we know what's going on and have a suspect in custody."

She angled her head up at him, and, by the set of her chin, he knew he was in trouble. "Look, Detective, not that I don't have faith in you, but it could be weeks or months or even years before you close this case. I'd like to meet 'the woman in question' now."

He was about to protest, but she whipped her hand into the air to stop him from arguing.

"I know you could wrap things up in a matter of days. I do. But just on the off chance this takes a while, or, God forbid, the killer is never found and brought to justice, I think it's only fair that I meet someone who could very well be my half sister."

"You could wait until the DNA results are in."

"And when will that be? This afternoon? Tomorrow? Or maybe weeks away. And it doesn't matter anyway. I'm not going to compromise your case. I just want to meet her." She pushed herself away from the desk. "Instead of looking at this negatively, you might turn your thinking around. This could be a good thing. I'm guessing Eve could use a sister about now."

"She's got two brothers."

"Sisters are different."

He shook his head. He didn't have a good feeling about Eve's siblings. They were elusive, didn't return calls, not even to the police. Red flags waving at full mast in Montoya's head when he thought about Kyle and Van Renner, both of whom, it appeared at first glance, had money problems. Credit card records showed that the brothers Renner were both maxed out on several cards, and Kyle had three separate mortgages on his house. Van rented, but he'd skipped town a couple of times owing money to various creditors. Collection agents were on his ass.

So maybe Abby was right. It could be that Eve needed a sister to confide in. He sighed. "Okay. I'll set it up."

"I think it would be better if I did it myself. You know, 'No cops.' "

"I'm not sure I like this. People around Eve Renner die."

"I'll be fine, Detective," she said. "Besides, I have a big, macho fiancé whom I'll call if I get into any kind of trouble."

"You'd better."

"Always." She winked at him and wasn't able to hide the sexy glimmer in her eyes. His pulse immediately elevated. Damn the woman, she knew what she did to him, and she used it.

"You owe me."

"Mmm . . . I'll try to think of some clever way to pay

you back." Then she pressed a warm kiss to his cheek, whispered a naughty invitation in his ear, and sashayed out the door as if she were pure as the driven snow. "Devil woman," he said, just loud enough for her to hear.

"That's me, honey!" she called over her shoulder.

He settled back into his chair and stared at the picture of the hospital. Was it possible? Could the shadowy figure caught in the camera's lens be Terrence Renner's and Roy Kajak's killer, the same person who had sent Eve the jagged-edged clippings?

No way.

Too coincidental.

Or was it?

Hadn't Faith Chastain's killer given him a warning? *Tonight is just the beginning.*

Those words slid like ice through Montoya's veins.

CHAPTER 18

"I'm sorry. I thought I told you," the prim secretary for the convent said, "the Mother Superior is busy all day. I gave her your message, and I'm sure she'll get back to you." The woman, wearing a black skirt, crisp white blouse, wedding ring, and crucifix on a petite gold chain, rained a patient, beatific smile on Eve. Her nameplate identified her as Mrs. Miller, and her blue-tinged gray hair was permed tight above ears that supported tiny gold crosses.

"I thought she might squeeze me in," Eve said. She

felt awkward standing in the vestibule, out of place in her jeans and T-shirt, but she figured she'd try to get what she wanted through the normal, conventional way.

It was getting her nowhere.

Mrs. Miller, it seemed, considered herself a guard dog who appeared as small and mild as a toy poodle but, when backed into a corner, was more protective than an English Mastiff.

"Please tell her it's very important," Eve said, and left her name and phone number again.

She retraced her steps out of the darkened, serene hallway and into the parking lot, where her Camry sat in the late afternoon sun. Sliding behind the wheel, she noticed that someone was watching her from a window on the second floor. Sister Rebecca? Or just one of the nuns stopping at the window to stare out at the manicured grounds? With sunlight refracting on the old glass, it was difficult to make out the person's facial features or even gender, for that matter. Eve assumed anyone in the convent would be a woman who had joined the order, but in the glare, she wasn't sure.

Not that it mattered.

She knew what she had to do.

And it involved breaking into the old mental hospital.

"Great," she muttered to herself. She didn't think too highly of her skills as a cat burglar, and she sure as hell didn't want to be discovered breaking and entering. She couldn't imagine trying to explain her actions to the police.

Just don't get caught.

Driving out of the compound, she headed her Toyota away from the convent. When the access road forked, Eve angled toward the hospital grounds, away from the country road that eventually fed into the freeway and New Orleans.

Though the convent and hospital abutted each other, they were separated by a tall fence that surrounded each separate campus. There were gates linking the two parcels, of course, and Eve, from years of growing up here, knew exactly where those portals were, but she had to be careful. She didn't want anyone to see her flagrantly ignoring the No Trespassing signs that were posted around the property.

Slowing at the entrance to the hospital, she noted that the huge, wrought-iron gates were locked. Beyond those filigreed gates was the long drive leading to the asylum. No longer tended, the grounds were in shambles. The long concrete driveway was buckled and cracked, crumbling away.

A small shiver slid through her as she caught a glimpse of the hospital with its boarded windows and weed-infested lawn. How different it had been all those years ago.

She drove farther along the access road until she came to the cemetery. There was no gate here, just an archway of filigreed wrought iron that spelled out OUR LADY OF VIRTUES CEMETERY. On either side of the archway were statues, once white, now gray from grime and years of neglect. One was of St. Peter, the other of Jesus, and the arch itself was wide enough for a truck to pass beneath it.

Eve drove into the graveyard and parked her Camry in the gravel lot facing a field of headstones as well as several family tombs built above and below the ground. Here, as opposed to New Orleans, the land was stable enough, the water table low enough, to support in-ground burials. She parked beneath a tree then made her way unerringly through the graves, just as she had dozens of times as a kid. She and Roy had spent hours in the cemetery, looking at the old headstones and inscriptions, wondering about those who were interred. Roy had even suggested they dig up one of the graves, just to see a dead, decomposing body, but of course they never had. She was certain he brought it up just to gross her out.

Around the perimeter of the cemetery was a forest of cypress and pine that had been, years before, intersected with deer trails. Who knew if they still existed?

"Time to find out," she said as she grabbed her backpack and locked the car. She headed toward the stretch of fence line that separated the cemetery from the hospital grounds. At the edge of the woods, she ducked into a thicket of pine, still making her way toward the fence and scaring up a rabbit as she passed. Sunlight dappled the ground, but the air turned cooler in the shade, and the forest seemed hushed, oddly quiet, the slightest breeze moving through the trees. Eve didn't pause to think about it. She was on a mission after months of recuperating, of lying idle and useless, a victim. Finally she was doing something, not waiting around for someone else to come up with answers. Brushing aside cobwebs, she found an overgrown path and wandered through thickets and open spaces, never more than three feet from the fence line.

A woodpecker drilled somewhere nearby, and she nearly jumped when she saw a black rat snake sunning itself on a pile of flat stones left near a fence post. The snake flicked its tongue in the air then slithered quickly through the crevices in the stones and disappeared.

Get a grip, she told herself. A rat snake wasn't poisonous, and that one wasn't all that big, yet her anxiety level notched up a bit, and when she found the spot where she and Roy had climbed the fence, she checked the ground and branches of trees for any snakes. Satisfied that she wouldn't startle another serpent, she climbed up the chain link and then grabbed a limb of an overhanging tree to swing over the coiled razor wire atop the fence. As a child she'd been agile and strong; now the feat was more difficult, and she couldn't help but hear the warning voice of Nita, her physical therapist: "Remember, you're only at about eighty-five percent, and that's good, but just keep working out and be careful not to strain anything."

Too late, she thought, her shoulder screaming in agony as she hoisted herself upward then shimmied along the branch. Once she'd cleared the fence with its jagged, vicious wire, she dropped to the other side and felt a splinter of pain in her legs and spine from the impact.

Fortunately the pain dissipated, and she found the old trail that led through the thickets of pine and cypress and around a hedge of arborvitae to the rear of the hospital and a parking lot that had been reserved for employees and deliveries. Her father had been assigned a designated spot for his sporty little Carmengia, and if she looked hard, she could almost see the lines that had been painted on the asphalt.

It had been so long ago, she thought as she viewed the asylum for the first time in over ten years. Built of red brick, the main building rose three full stories. Its roof was steeply pitched, and on either end old fire escapes zigzagged to the highest window. The gutters were rusted and bent, some completely detached, though gargoyles still perched near the eaves. Some of the roof's shingles, torn by wind and rain, had tumbled into the yard of crabgrass and weeds. Once there had been manicured grounds and pools where brightly colored koi swam beneath lily pads. Now overgrowth and brambles prevailed near stained, cracked basins that only held rainwater before it drained away or evaporated.

On the other side of the parking lot, the garages and sheds still existed, though roofs sagged, walls had started to lean, and the few windows that had escaped being boarded over were cracked and broken.

The place was a mess.

And more than that, there was not just a feeling of disrepair that was visible, but something else, something darker, a sense of despair that seemed to cling to the vine-clad walls.

Oh for God's sake, don't get all melodramatic! Just do what it is you have to do.

Nonetheless, Eve fought a sense of foreboding. Not only was she trespassing, but she felt as if whatever it was she would find here might be better left undisturbed.

"Oh get over yourself," she said. It was broad daylight, and she planned to go inside, search around, see if she could find any locked files, then leave. She figured she'd be in and out in less than an hour, long before evening even thought about stretching lavender shadows over this part of the world.

She started with the back door, one that led into the kitchen, but none of the keys worked the lock. "Great." When she couldn't open that door, she headed around the building to the side door, at the bottom of one of the fire escapes.

Once again, none of her father's keys would turn the dead bolt.

"Strike two," she told herself, feeling the heat from the late afternoon sun beat against the back of her neck. She realized she was standing upon a wide veranda once filled with tables and umbrellas, where some of the more infirm patients had been rolled in wheelchairs outside. There had been planters filled with a dazzling display of flowers, and chaise longues for those who wanted to lie in the sunshine. Now there was just cement spiderwebbed with crevices, weeds, and one rusted lawn chair crumpled beneath a tall magnolia.

If she closed her eyes, she could still see the patients in wheelchairs, the nuns hurrying by, the nurses eyeing a group of younger, silent patients whose gaze followed Eve as she and Roy crossed the lawn. What had that boy's name been? Rick or Ralph or Ron . . . God, she couldn't remember, though she would never forget his silent, angry face and the fiery blue eyes that burned a hole in her every time she passed.

The hairs on the back of her neck raised, and she turned back to her task, pushing aside all the disturbing memories this place was certain to evoke.

The wind had kicked up. Hot as Satan's breath, it did little to calm her nerves or cool her skin. She hurried to the front of the hospital, past overgrown crepe myrtles and along a nearly submerged path of flagstones through the tall, uneven grass.

She remembered taking this very walkway with her father, hurrying to keep up with his steady, long strides, trying like crazy to get his attention. To no avail. Not when he was stopping to talk to nurses or the nuns or, now and then, a patient.

Nurses in white,
Sisters in black
All in all
They don't know Jack . . .

305

Roy's voice rang so clearly in her head, she nearly stumbled. How often had he whispered those very words to her? One of his clever little poems about the place. Then there was the "Ode to an Asylum."

Made of mortar, stones, and bricks
Housing retards, nuns, and pricks
Our Lady of Virtues is really of sins
God turns His back while Lucifer grins.

Roy's attempts at poetry had been amateurish and cruel, but even now the crude rhymes ran through her head and she walked faster, rounding the corner of the building leading to the front entrance with its sweeping drive and elaborate fountain, all now in ruin.

She walked up the marble steps to the broad front door.

So, what if all the locks have been changed?
What then?
Are you going to literally *break in?*

She tried to insert the first key.

No good.

The second didn't work either.

"Third time's a charm," she whispered and slid the key into the lock. But it wouldn't turn.

"Great." She pulled the key out of the dead bolt and felt sweat drizzling down her face and back. What had she expected? She should just give up. The interior of the hospital was probably long gutted, and then there had been the police and crime-scene technicians. . . . What could possibly be left?

Nothing. Go home. Forget this. Really, what are you doing? This is just a bad trip down memory lane.

And yet she walked around the building, careful not to disturb a papery wasp's nest as she turned the corner of the far end and stopped dead in her tracks.

The last section of the fire escape had been lowered.

How odd.

Had someone forgotten and left it hanging?

She noticed a piece of yellow plastic on the last rung and realized it was a torn section of crime-scene tape. Slowly she raised her gaze upward. The metal staircase had a landing at each window. The first floor was boarded, but the second was intact.

A possible entry?

Only one way to find out.

Adjusting her pack on her shoulders, she grabbed hold of the lowest rung and swung upward. Pain rippled down her shoulder, but she knew that if she let go, she'd never be able to find the strength to try again. Gritting her teeth, ignoring her weakened muscles, she started climbing, pulling herself up rung by rung until her foot found the lowest bar.

Her heart pounded, and sweat trickled down her back. More than once she asked herself if she was as certifiable as the police had intimated, but she kept at it, one rung at a time. Gritting her teeth, she finally managed to reach the lowest platform on the second floor and pull herself to her feet. She stood gasping for a second.

Glancing around, she half expected someone, a caretaker or one of the nuns, to appear and insist she climb down. Instead, she saw only a whippoorwill flying low to land in the branches of a pine tree.

Aside from the gentle rush of a summer breeze, the grounds were quiet.

Undisturbed.

Almost too silent.

She refused to think about the troubling quietude. She tried the window on the second floor, but it didn't budge.

Undaunted, she climbed up the clanging, rickety steps to the third floor.

The window, though splintered, was half open.

Almost in invitation.

Eve swallowed hard. It was probably just an oversight. Nothing more. She pushed on the casing, expecting it to stick or screech, but instead it slid easily upward, as if the tracks had been oiled.

Don't even think it, she told herself as she crept into the dark, noiseless interior.

Despite the open window, the building smelled musty and dank, the floors dusty and scratched, wallpaper and paint peeling from the walls.

Eve made her way downstairs, past the landing with the stained-glass window of the Madonna still intact, all the while letting her fingers run along the worn banister just as she had as a child. She decided to start her search on the first floor, though she was certain this part of the hospital had been torn apart by the police last autumn when a deranged killer had ended up here.

Because of Faith Chastain, the woman who could very well be your birth mother.

The lower floor was nearly empty and dark. Very little sunlight seeped in through the boarded-over windows and broken shutters. The grandfather clock that had chimed off the hours at the base of the stairs was no longer there. The reception area still possessed its long counter/desk that separated the foyer from the offices behind.

She imagined how it used to be, filled with briskly walking nurses, worried visitors, an office staff that was cheery but firm, and patients whose lives were fraying. Always and ever present were the nuns. Now the foyer was shadowy and gloomy, smelling of dust and disuse. Eve felt nervous, as if she were stepping onto someone's grave.

Stop it. This is just an old building. Nothing sinister about it. Outside, the day is bright. Warm. Get on with it.

Using her flashlight, she walked through the linked offices and short, mazelike hallways, noting the rooms that the hospital secretary, two nurses, the Mother Superior, and the priest had once occupied. Though the names on the doorways had disappeared, a few faded numbers remained, and Eve remembered the whispers that seemed to seep from half-open doors, the discussions and concerns, the odors of antiseptic and pine cleaner that were ever present. The floor creaked as she shined her fragile beam ahead of her. She ended up at room number 1, her father's office, a small interior cubicle without windows, only a transom over the doorway that allowed in natural light from a window in the corridor.

The room was empty, the wooden floor discolored where a desk, file cabinet, and bookcase had once stood. The walls were dark with dirt, showing lighter patches where once pictures and degrees had hung.

Aside from spiders watching from their corner webs near the ceiling, the room was unoccupied.

What had she expected?

She could visualize her father as she'd often seen him, seated at his wide desk, his head bent over some medical journal or patient chart. A banker's light had created a pool of illumination. Upon the smooth plaster walls, his degrees had hung proudly. On the bookcase, a bifold frame held two pictures: one of Eve, one of her mother. Aside from one family portrait, there had been no pictures of Eve's brothers.

And now her father was dead.

Murdered.

Like Faith Chastain.

Like Roy Kajak.

Disfigured with a tattoo.

Goose bumps crawled along her skin as she explored the rest of the main floor quickly, shining her light in the corners of the parlor, dining room, and kitchen, then trying the basement door.

It was locked.

None of her keys worked there either, and she felt a bit of relief. She could do without dark, dank rooms belowground. Ever since her brothers, in an inspired and cruel prank, had locked her in the cellar at their aunt's house in the country and left her there for hours, she'd become slightly claustrophobic. She'd been five at the time, traumatized, and never again felt safe in dark, dank places underground. She'd slept for months afterward with the light on in her room and had often woken up to horrible dreams of trickling water, tiny beady eyes staring at her from dark corners, and spiders with dripping fangs. She'd woken up screaming, and her mother had usually crawled in bed with her, whispering softly and holding her close until she'd finally fallen asleep again.

Yeah, real sweethearts, her brothers, she thought as she returned to the staircase and climbed to the second floor, where she found empty bedrooms, baths, and closets. Like those of the lower level, the floors and walls here were scarred and shaded where artifacts and pictures had hung.

On the third floor, she walked unerringly to room 307, having remembered it had belonged to Faith Chastain. It was different from most of the other rooms in that it had a higher ceiling, fireplace, and a tall, arched window . . . the window through which she'd fallen. On the walls were outlines of pictures and, it seemed, a crucifix.

Was this the home of her mother?

Eve bit her lip and tried to remember Faith Chastain.

311

She only had fleeting images of a haunted, petite woman who in moments of clarity could smile, her amber eyes intriguing and intelligent.

A dark stain discolored the center of the floor, and Eve backed away from what appeared to have once been blood.

You're imagining things, she thought. *You're letting this gloomy, dark place with its history of evil get to you.*

In the hallway, she walked past the other rooms, shining her flashlight into each doorway and seeing nothing other than emptiness. The bathrooms and showers were grimy and forgotten, infested by insects.

At the end of the hall, there was an empty linen closet and across from that doorway another closet with a second door at its back that led upward to the attic. It was locked, but this time one of her father's keys slid easily into the dead bolt and turned. The lock clicked, and the door opened to a steep set of stairs that wound upward around a chimney to a long, narrow garret with exposed rafters and unfinished plank floors.

This had been her hideaway as a child. She and Roy had snuck up these twisting steps and spent hours playing make-believe games or spying on some of the patients and doctors. She cringed now as she thought about the peepholes they'd discovered that allowed them to view into the rooms below.

Including Faith Chastain's bedroom.

Roy had spent hours numbering the tiny slits in the

flooring with the appropriate rooms. Now Eve walked along the floorboards, ducking the cobwebby rafters and crossbeams, shining her weak light until she saw the number 307 written in a felt-tip pen and covered with dust and grime.

The wind whistled through the old rafters, sweeping through this oven of a chamber but not bringing any relief from the heat.

The place was creepier than she remembered it, and, she thought, if she closed her eyes, she could still hear the soft cries, the whimpers, the desperate whispers of some of the most tormented patients.

How many times had she and Roy looked down this very peephole into Faith Chastain's room? Now, of course, she was embarrassed. How could she have been so uncaring, so callous, so ultimately curious?

"Forgive me," she whispered but couldn't resist the opportunity to look down that dime-sized hole once more, one created by the wiring for the overhead lamp in Faith's room. As she did, she found herself staring at that damning crimson stain.

A shadow passed over the discoloration.

She gasped.

Her lungs constricted.

No one was in this decrepit hospital but her.

Right?

Fear splintered through her body. *It's just a shadow, a trick of light. It doesn't mean anyone's inside.*

But she swallowed hard, and the back of her skull

tightened as she strained to listen, not moving a muscle.

She blinked.

The shadow vanished.

As if it had never existed.

Light from the window . . . that was it. . . . There was still some glass in the higher panes, and a tree branch could have swayed in the wind, blocking the sun. . . . She had heard the wind up here, how it swept through the rafters. But there was no wind now. Not a whisper of a breeze skimming over the roof.

She waited.

The shadow didn't appear again.

Nor did she hear the sounds of breathing, or foot-steps, or a voice. . . . Perhaps she'd imagined the dark umbra that had been cast for a few seconds over Faith's room.

But the skin on the back of her arms prickled in warning, and her insides had turned to jelly.

Just do what you have to do and get the hell out of here!

Moving more quickly now, she walked past a junk-yard of old hospital bed parts and dresser drawers and medicine trays and God knew what else until she found a stack of cabinets. Old files. Long forgotten. She withdrew her keys again, found the smallest, and unlocked a tall cabinet.

Inside were old charts and records, dusty, some cov-ered in mildew, all smelling like they were a hundred years old. Not quite a century, she realized, but old enough that the information was all handwritten or typed, no computer printouts.

She wondered if Roy's records were here. He had eventually wound up here as a patient, at least for a few months before the facility closed forever. She'd always thought it was pure irony that perhaps Roy had been spied on himself once he'd had his own break-down.

These files, though, were older, and she found a folder marked *Chastain, Faith.* "Oh God," she whis-pered and opened the dusty manila file. It was thick, filled with notes and charts and evaluations, too much information to sift through here. She tucked the file inside her backpack and tamped down the feeling that she was not only trespassing but stealing as well.

Too bad.

This was information that she, if she were Faith's daughter, deserved to know. If it turned out she wasn't related to Faith Chastain, then at least she might have some insight as to why someone was linking her to the woman and this hospital, why her father and Roy might have been murdered.

She flipped quickly through the other tabs and saw a few names that conjured up faces. Rich Carver . . . Oh, he was the odd boy who was so silent . . . always watching, a tiny smile playing upon his lips until he looked away; then his expression turned demonic. . . . The next name was Enid Walcott, a thin, birdlike woman with wild hair and wide eyes. Merwin Anderson, a big man who had sat and stared for hours at the birdhouse near his window. John Stokes, a sly boy who was always sedated, rumored to have murdered his cousin. Ronnie Le Mars . . . She stopped at the name. That was the name of the boy who'd stared at her with such intensity. Ronnie Le Mars. She shivered as she thought about his hot blue eyes. What had he been in for? Self-mutilation? Or . . . did she have him and John Stokes mixed up? Had Ronnie been the one who had killed a member of his family? She glanced back to the files. The last name she recognized was Neva St. James, a bright, crafty girl whose aunt had committed her because of some form of autism.

Though she would find the files fascinating and could use them for her research, she couldn't take them with her, at least not now, so she quickly closed the cabinet, relocked it, and headed toward the stairs. Walking quickly, she bent to avoid hitting her head, while the beam of her flashlight, offering ever-weaker light in the sweltering attic space, swept side to side.

She saw the doll.

Her doll, one that she hadn't seen in nearly twenty years, caught in the yellow sweep of illumination.

"Sweet Jesus," she gasped, training the fading light onto a corner where an old, faded sleeping bag was pushed near the tiny, dirt-covered window, a little nook where she had come and played for hours as a child. With her impish face and pleading tone, she'd managed to wheedle plates and forks from the kitchen staff, along with some of the cook's key lime pie or pralines, then had dragged her booty up here. She'd nearly forgotten about this little nook, and she hadn't seen the Charlotte doll in so, so long.

Now the doll was lying facedown on the dingy sleeping bag that seemed to be losing some of its filling to mice.

Something didn't feel right about this.

She didn't remember leaving Charlotte here, and she'd been up here long after she'd had any interest in rag dolls. This one had been sewn and stuffed by her grandmother. Nana had even made a blue dress and pinafore, then braided the doll's brown hair and added a hat, as if she were a small girl at the turn of the century.

Now, as she edged closer, Eve noticed that Charlotte's hat was tossed to one side, its ribbon ties askew. The doll's braids had been clipped off and tossed away as well, leaving her plump head practically bald. Worse yet, Charlotte's arms and legs were spread wide, and the hem of her dress was raised over her waist and fixed with a rubber band. Her panties were pulled down to the tops of her felt shoes, and her faded pink butt was sticking upward in the air in some weird pose.

"Sick," Eve said, knowing she had never left Charlotte in such disarray. It was sexual and freaky and, she knew from her studies, the work of a psychopath. Her stomach turned, and a deep, clawing fear curled through her guts. As hot and stifling as it was up here, Eve was suddenly cold to the bone.

317

Who had been playing and had left Charlotte like this? One of the mentally unstable boys who was a patient at the asylum years ago?

Was this just a tormented soul's idea of a joke?

No, Eve, this isn't random!

You know it.

Someone left the doll positioned this way on purpose. And they wanted someone, probably you, to find her.

Her mouth went dry. She swallowed back her fear and inched closer to the sleeping bag then reached down and turned Charlotte over.

As she did, her blood ran cold.

A scream worked its way up her throat and ended in a terrified gasp.

Charlotte's button eyes had been clipped off, her pinafore slashed with jagged cuts made by pinking shears, and she'd been mutilated across her belly, the number 444 scrawled in blood-red ink.

And below the numbers was a single word.

EVE.

CHAPTER 19

Eve dropped the doll as if it had burned her fingers. "Oh God, oh God, oh God," she said, backing toward the top of the staircase. Who would do such a thing? What sick mind would—

Briiing!

Her cell phone shrilled, and her heart nearly stopped. Scrambling for the damned thing, she pulled it out of the backpack and noticed that no number showed on the screen. *Restricted call.*

Oh hell!

It rang again, and she, paralyzed, thought about turning the damned thing off. *Don't answer it.*

She clicked on the button.

Lifted the phone to her ear.

Didn't say a word.

"Heeeee'sssss freeee . . ."

She slammed the phone shut and spun, the fading light from her flashlight splashing on the walls and underside of the roof where tiny nails poked through the ceiling. The person on the other end of the phone had known she was here, had realized she'd found the doll. She was certain of it. She reached into her backpack and withdrew a screwdriver, one of her grandfather's tools. Her fingers wrapped around the grip, and, heart hammering, sweat staining her clothes, she searched all of the dusty corners, the hidden spots of the attic.

He's not up here . . . remember? He's a floor below. You saw his shadow.

She trained her flashlight on the doorway at the top of the stairs, the only entrance to the garret.

Heart in her throat, she waited, inching her way toward the door and the brick chimney. If she could hide to one side of it, when the psycho entered and stepped into the room, she could shoot past him, fly down the stairs, lock the door, and run to the fire escape and safety . . .

Or you could dial 911 now!

Even if the killer didn't appear, you could show the police the doll.

And then what?

So someone messed with an old, forgotten toy.

She was the one who had trespassed.

She was the one who had broken into the hospital.

She was the one who, even now, had a stolen file in her backpack. No, she couldn't let panic overtake her . . . She had to fight the anxiety.

Crouched by the chimney with its rough bricks and crumbling mortar, she turned off her flashlight and waited, hardly daring to breathe. Panic stormed through her. Her head began to pound.

Straining to listen, she silently counted. *One . . . two . . . three . . . four . . .*

Drops of sweat slid down her forehead and nose.

. . . five . . . six . . .

She blinked.

Her breath came in panicked, wild little gasps.

Seven . . .

Creak!

Oh Jesus, was that a footstep?

Her heart began knocking out of control. Someone was in the hospital with her.

She caught her breath.

Strained to listen.

Nearly screamed when she saw a mouse dart across the floorboards.

Another footstep.

Her fingers tightened around the screwdriver. Could she use it? Damned straight!

Give me strength.

More footsteps. Climbing faster now, no more hesitation.

He knew she was trapped!

A looming dark shape appeared in the doorway.

Every muscle bunched, she was ready to spring. *One more step, you son of a bitch, just take one more step.*

"Eve!" a strong male voice echoed through the attic.

She nearly broke down completely. "Cole?" she whispered, and her voice was little more than a whimper.

"Where the hell are you?"

"Here!" She flung herself at him, her arms circling his neck as she collapsed against him.

"Hey!"

A part of her screamed, *The last time you were in a dark, scary place, he raised his gun and . . . No!*

321

She wouldn't believe it and nearly sobbed when she felt his strong arms wrap around her.

"Shh . . . darlin', what?" he said against her hair. "What the hell are you doin' here?"

She nearly laughed. Her nerves were strung to the breaking point, and she needed release . . . laughter, tears . . . any kind of relief. Instead, she kissed him. Hard. Anxiously. Fervently. On the lips.

His response was immediate. His arms tightened, his hands splayed over her back, and his mouth molded to hers eagerly.

Desperately she clung to him and slowly, oh so slowly, her reason began to return. She was holding Cole and kissing him and practically lying down for him on this hard, dirty, vermin-infested attic floor.

Slowly she pulled away, stepping out of his embrace and running a hand through her hair as she caught her breath and grabbed hold of her runaway emotions.

"Change your mind?" he said, his voice a little raspy.

"You were lucky. . . . You, um, you almost ended up with a screwdriver through your neck."

"From whom?" he asked, then guessed, "You? No way."

"I was pretty freaked out," she said shakily.

"If this is the reception I get, maybe you should be freaked out more often."

"No thanks." She flipped on her flashlight and shot the pale beam at his face. "How did you know I was here?"

"I followed you."

"What?"

"Didn't I tell you I thought we should camp out together?"

"I thought you were going to the police station." She drew a breath, collecting her thoughts. "Wait a minute. How did you follow me?"

"You were trying to contact the Mother Superior. This hospital is connected to the case."

"But how would you know? Why now? Why here?"

Cole seemed to come to a decision. "Since I'm trying like hell to make you trust me, I guess I've got to come clean. I put a bug on your car."

"What? You're kidding. Cole, you did *not* put some kind of electronic device on . . ." She could hardly speak. "This is . . . this is like stalking. You can't just go around and . . . and invade my privacy—"

"While you're breaking and entering?"

"Don't turn this around."

He laughed. "Come on, let's get out of here." He slung an arm around her shoulders.

She tried to hang on to her sense of injustice. It was far better than gratitude . . . or fear. . . . "Don't try to talk your way out of this, Counselor," she said. "Um, there's something I think you should see." Using her flashlight to illuminate the way, she led him to the corner with the sleeping bag and Charlotte.

He stared down at the doll. "What the hell is this?"

"A message, I think. I saw it, then started to leave, and my cell rang. He said it again: *He's free*. It was almost as if he knew I was in here looking at Charlotte."

"Charlotte?"

"That's what I called her. My grandmother made her for me years ago, and I thought she was locked in a trunk at the house. Nana insisted I save her for my own daughter if I ever have one. I hadn't seen the doll in forever."

"You're sure it's the same one?"

"Oh yeah. Charlotte's an original."

He bent down on one knee and, using a rag he found near the sleeping bag, picked up the doll gingerly, looking at her and the message slashed across her body. "Your name."

Eve nodded, looking away from the tortured doll.

"Who knew about this place?"

"I . . . I don't know. . . . Some of the kids who lived here, I guess, and I imagine the nuns knew what was going on. My dad even got wind of it and had a fit, which my brothers found particularly vindicating."

"So they knew about it too?"

"Eventually, yes . . . and, well, I left all this stuff up here. Anyone who came up here over the last twenty years could figure out that I'd been here. I think I left some books with my name up here and, oh God, maybe even a diary." She played the beam of the flashlight over the area under the window, where some old comic books and paperbacks were flung. "There's my old English/Spanish dictionary." Cole picked the book up. Inside the flap in girlish hand-writing was the name Eve Renner.

"So, how did he lure you to the attic?"

"I don't know. I didn't even know I was coming here. If Sister Rebecca had seen me this afternoon, I probably would have gone straight home."

Cole's expression hardened, became more grim. "I wonder if he thought he would bring you up here."

"What do you mean?" she asked but felt her skin tighten over her back as she understood.

"As in kidnap you."

"God, no . . . don't even say it."

"Okay, I won't." He stood, a muscle working in his jaw. "But from here on in, I'm not losing sight of you. I'm going to stick to you like a burr."

"You think you're going to protect me?"

"Either me or the police." He was grim.

"Not the police," Eve responded instantly.

"Not the police, then."

"But . . . we'll have to tell them about this."

For once he didn't disagree. "As soon as possible. Let's go."

"Should we take the doll?" she asked.

He hesitated then shook his head. "Let's leave things as they were, let the police come up here and see how it was."

"All right." Plucking Charlotte from his fingers, Eve turned her facedown on the sleeping bag and felt a little queasy to be even remotely associated with anything so perverted. Then she led the way down the rickety stairs that curved around the chimney. "You know, I almost had a heart attack earlier. You scared the liver out of me." She relocked the door to the attic and stepped through the closet. "I was looking through a peephole into Faith's room, and I saw your shadow pass by. I nearly lost it."

"What do you mean?"

"I mean I was creeped out anyway, and this was before I caught a glimpse of Charlotte. Then I saw you in 307."

"In 307?" He motioned toward the closed door of the room in question. "I was never in that room."

"Yes . . . you had to be."

"No." He was dead serious, his brows slammed together, his lips compressed. "I climbed the stairs, heard someone overhead, saw the open closet door, and climbed up to the attic."

"But I saw you," she insisted. "I know it was the right room, because your shadow passed over that horrible stain on the floor . . ."

"Not me, Eve. I swear."

Her insides turned to water, and Cole, the idiot, strode down the hallway toward 307.

"Wait!" she said. She imagined her father's killer behind the door, knife raised, ready to slice Cole's throat. "Don't!"

Ignoring her, he opened the door and stepped inside.

"Cole!" She started after him, but her toe caught on the edge of a baseboard that had come loose. She tripped. The flashlight went flying from her hand. Eve hit hard, the wind knocked out of her, pain splintering through her shoulder. She cried out, and Cole was beside her in an instant.

"Eve! Are you okay?" His gentle hand touched her back.

NO! "I think so," she whispered, but tears sprang to her eyes and fire burned through her shoulder and arm. She tried to push herself upright and winced.

"Here. Let me."

"My flashlight," she said weakly.

Cole located it and stowed it in her backpack. Then, guided by light trickling in through the few intact windows, he carefully picked her up and carried her down two flights of stairs. She had no choice but to sling her good arm around his neck for balance.

"I'm fine," she said.

His face only inches from hers, he sent her a look. "Yeah, right."

She felt like a fool. Yes, her shoulder pained her, but she was perfectly capable of walking on her own. "I take it there was no one in Faith's room?"

"No."

"Well, I was in there earlier, and I didn't close the door on the way out. Unless you closed it, someone else was here."

He muttered an oath under his breath. On the first floor he set her on her feet and twisted open the lock on the front door. Before he could attempt to pick her up again, she held her bad arm with her good and walked outside, where the sun had settled deeper into the horizon and the air had cooled a bit.

She felt as if she could breathe again.

Cole fashioned a sling out of the strap of her back-pack, then helped her as they walked out the way they'd both come in, through the forest and along the fence line to the cemetery.

There was no way she could climb over the fence, but Cole helped her through the spot he'd chosen to enter, a section of weakened chain link that he'd kicked through. Now he bent it back and held it open, straining against the metal to allow Eve to pass through. By this time, her shoulder was throbbing.

"I'll drive," he said, but she shook her head as she spied his Jeep, which was parked near hers at the front gate of the cemetery.

"We'll just have to come back later and pick up your car."

"Not we. Me. I'll get Deeds to bring me out here."

"Oh, he'll love that." She moved her arm and sucked in her breath as pain shot through her shoulder.

"He'll be fine with it."

"Yeah, right."

He took the keys from her, opened the passenger-side door for her, and without further argument she slid into the Camry's sun-baked interior. A few seconds later, Cole climbed behind the wheel, dug through her backpack, and pulled out Faith Chastain's file. "What's this?"

No way to lie her way out of this one. "Something I found."

"Breaking and entering, and now larceny?"

"You should talk," she said, and Cole gave her a quick smile. She nodded toward the file. "That's the reason I came here. I thought I remembered some old files up in the attic."

"More than this one?"

She nodded then leaned back in the seat. Not only was her shoulder throbbing, but her head as well.

He hesitated. Drummed his fingers on the steering wheel.

"What?"

"I want to look at those files."

"They're ancient. Forgotten. At least twenty years old."

"But they might hold a clue to what's going on now," he said.

"Why do you think that?"

He tapped his finger against the folder for Faith Chastain. "Because of her. She was here over twenty years ago. She had the baby no one knows about. Someone's sending you clippings about her death. Why wouldn't you think it might be someone in that file cabinet?"

"But why wait twenty-some years to start all this?"

"I don't know," he said as he started the Toyota's engine. "But it could be that we might find out by searching through those files."

"Let's just start with this one to begin with," she suggested, trying to smile and feeling her lips tremble.

He gave her a look that was hard and tender at the same time. "You need to see a doctor."

"I'll be all right, really."

He touched her near the elbow, and she sucked in a sharp breath. "Sure you will, once you suffer through an emergency room experience, get X-rays, and have some doctor prescribe painkillers as he stitches you up."

"I'm not going to the hospital, Cole."

He flashed her a grin. "I hate to tell ya this, darlin', but right now you're going to go wherever the hell I take you."

"Bastard," she grumbled.

"That's me."

That night, the Voice was clear.

And angry.

Rising above the irritating little squeaks of the others who infiltrated his brain with their wheedling demands.

"There is another you must sacrifice soon," God told him, and he trembled on his bed, sweating, thinking of Eve. Was it her turn? Would she be one of those that God had chosen? Closing his eyes, he conjured up her face. So perfect.

Now, as a woman, she was beautiful.

Then, as a child, she'd been elusive.

She was the one he wanted.

God knew how much he wanted her. Wasn't his lust for her the very reason the Voice had first come to him?

"Who, Father?" he whispered anxiously, his fingers

curling over the edges of his quilt. "Who is to be taken? Tell me, and I will do Your will."

He closed his eyes and concentrated. So soon after the others, he was to do the Lord's bidding again. To take up his knife once more. To slay those who had so obviously infuriated the Almighty. This was his mission, his quest, for hadn't the Voice promised if he did as he was bidden that he too would be deified?

Deified!

He would someday sit next to the Father in heaven. . . . Tears filled his eyes at the thought. He just had to do the Voice's bidding, to follow His instructions, to wash away his own sins . . .

Please, please, may it be Eve's time.

"There are those who sin," the Voice said harshly. "Under the guise of innocence they walk the earth, guiding others, pretending righteousness, feigning faith. They are the worst of sinners, hiding behind their sanctity, and they must be sacrificed, their artifice exposed to all. Sacrifice this one first and take the second . . ."

"Take the second? Take her where?"

There was only silence.

"Father?" he cried and wondered fleetingly if, as his mother had said, he was insane. Hadn't that been what the doctor had diagnosed, the nurses had suggested, the nuns had pitied and prayed about?

And yet the Voice of God was real. It spoke to him. Had It not named him, called him the Reviver? Told him he would be deified? No, he could not doubt. He must believe.

"But Eve," he finally said. "When will it be Eve's time?" He'd seen her today at the hospital, lured there as he'd known she would be. Our Lady of Virtues belonged to her. To him. Soon, he thought, anticipation sliding through him. "Father?" he asked, hoping beyond hope that it was finally her time.

There was no answer, just the tomblike quiet of his room.

God was angry with him.

He knew it.

He'd been too bold.

"Thy will be done," he said aloud.

Trembling with excitement, he rolled off his bed and fell to his knees. Bending his head, folding his hands over his mattress, he eagerly awaited his instructions, anxiously considered what would be his mission.

And God told him.

CHAPTER 20

"Come here," Eve said as Cole tucked her into the bed, her bed, high in the turret of her house.

He smiled down at her and shook his head, his dark hair catching in the light from the bedside lamp. "I don't think that's such a good idea."

"Why not?" She felt so good. Better than she had in a long time, and Cole, damn him, was as handsome as ever. She felt so protected at the hospital with Cole standing beside her, helping her through the admissions process . . . She sighed happily and patted the bed beside her.

He sat on the edge of the bed and kissed her forehead. "Listen, Eve, this is not for lack of wantin', y'know. But I think we should wait until you've got all your faculties."

"You're turning me down."

"Uh . . ." A dimple showed in one cheek. "Let's just say I'm taking a rain check."

"I thought you said you wanted to take care of me . . . to protect me."

"I do and I will."

"But you won't sleep with me? You don't want to make love to me?"

"You're twisting my words. I need to call Montoya and Bentz or Deeds or someone and tell them about what we found at the asylum—"

"But I want you to stay with me," she said.

"Sure you do. You're feeling no pain now, all due to artificial means. But I'd feel a whole lot better about this if you weren't on a cocktail of happy pills."

"Come on, Cole," she said, sticking out her lower lip. A part of her realized she had lost her inhibitions because of the drugs she'd been given; the other part of her didn't care.

"You're no fun."

"Oh, that's where you're wrong."

"Prove it."

"Prove what?"

She lifted an eyebrow and stared up at him. "Just how fun you are."

She let her teeth sink into that lower lip and heard him groan. "You're a bad woman, Eve Renner."

"Am I?"

"And I love ya." With that, he kissed her, his lips fitting against hers so perfectly that she felt as if she were floating. She opened her mouth and felt his tongue play against her teeth before sliding inside.

Her bones melted as his hands skimmed her body, slowly caressing her arms and ribs then touching a breast. "Oooh," she moaned and knew it was his undoing.

All restraint was lost.

His kiss deepened, his breath hot and hungry, his body stretched out next to hers. He was careful. . . . She was aware that he was more tender than she remembered him being. He cradled her as he kicked off his jeans and tore off his shirt and settled the length of his body against hers, bare skin to her nightgown.

"You're sure about this?" he asked one last time as he pushed an errant curl from her forehead then tugged her nightgown down, exposing one breast. With a quicksilver touch, he traced the areola of her breast with one finger until she squirmed.

"Absolutely."

"Really?" He kissed her nipple then breathed across it as she watched him in the lamp's golden glow.

"Mmmmm." Her abdomen collapsed against her spine as his hand traveled downward, bunching up her nightgown, strong fingers exploring the lace of her panties.

"I don't know," he whispered.

"Cole! Please . . ."

"You got it, darlin'." He yanked the panties downward, nearly ripping them as he pulled them over her feet, and then he kissed her in the most intimate of regions, his lips and tongue tasting her, his breath curling hot and wild deep within.

Perspiration sheened her skin, and deep inside she felt an ache that begged to be released. The fingers of her good hand twisted in his hair as the first ripple poured through her, a cascading wave of pleasure that was as warm as it was intense. She bucked upward, wanting more, so much more . . . and Cole didn't disappoint.

He prodded her knees apart then pulled her up to meet him as he thrust inside. She gasped, her good arm holding tight around his neck, her head pressed so tightly against his strong shoulder muscle that she could barely breathe. She kissed the spot where his neck joined with his shoulder, and he groaned, moving faster, deeper, until he leaned back and pulled her atop him, still moving, still thrusting, still touching the most sensitive part of her. Faster and faster, deeper and deeper.

Eve, already floating, felt as if the world were spinning, a world only big enough for the two of them.

"Cole," she whispered, barely able to speak. "Oh God, Cole . . ." The next wave hit her so hard she shuddered and was still shaking when she felt him stiffen beneath her and then, with a hoarse cry, release himself.

She fell against him and, entwined, lay with him in her bed high above the city. It felt so right to be with him, she wouldn't let go, wouldn't let the rest of the world in, wouldn't question what they'd done.

At least until the morning.

Vespers was long over and the moon had risen above the walls of the convent. Stars winked in a vast array. Usually this midnight darkness in the cloister wrapped around Sister Rebecca like Christ's robes. Most often this hour of the night was a time of calm and strength for Sister Rebecca, a moment when she would seek the solitude of the garden, where she could reflect on the day that had passed and pray for the morrow. As Mother Superior, she felt great responsibility and even greater unworthiness.

The air was scented with magnolia and pine, the night quiet aside from the rhythmic hoots of an owl hidden in the darkness. It was here that she'd sat so often on the edge of the fountain, watching the water spray upward only to cascade down upon the statue of an angel, hoping that her own sins would be washed away.

Oh, were it so.

But there were too many secrets.

Too many sins.

And soon all of her perfidy would be exposed.

"Forgive me," she whispered, making the sign of the cross over her bosom, her fingers brushing the chain that held her glasses. She was tired, her life's struggle of over eighty years had exhausted her. It was time for her to be called home. First, of course, there was confession—confession to sins she'd not revealed for, oh, so many years.

She stood, heard her old knees pop, and stiffly walked toward the door that she'd left ajar to let in the night's cooling, fragrant breeze. With some difficulty she walked down the long hallway, where the lights were turned down to a feeble glow, reminiscent of a time when only candles had illuminated these old, hallowed corridors.

The chapel door creaked as she opened it, and she reminded herself to ask the caretaker to oil its hinges. Then she slipped into the nave, moving slowly along the central aisle toward the chancel, her fingers touching each of the backs of the wooden pews as she passed.

This was a small place of worship and, despite its cold stone floors, soaring ceiling, and imperious tracery windows, a cozy chapel where Sister Rebecca had always found solace and repose. The hours she'd spent praying on her knees, her fingers moving easily over the time-smoothed beads of her rosary, had been too many to count, but tonight that feeling of tranquility had given way to restlessness.

She knew why.

Terrence Renner was dead.

Murdered by some poor soul who had wielded a knife, if the newspaper stories were to be believed. Sister Rebecca had known Renner well in the years he'd been employed by the hospital. An arrogant man and not without his own private demons, but to be murdered? Brutally slain?

Staring up at the crucifix, at Jesus' serene face and bloody crown of thorns, she crossed herself again then settled into a pew. Praying, searching her soul, she felt a darkness steal through her. There had been a time when she'd thought all of the evil was behind her, that the old hospital would be sold and razed to be replaced by a modern assisted-living facility. Naively she'd hoped that the scandals and secrets that had swept through the halls of the asylum would be buried deep within its rubble, never to be revealed, never to see the light of day.

But her dreams had been shattered, the police having held up the demolition of the building indefinitely. Because of all the questions about Faith Chastain, though the poor, tormented woman had died twenty years earlier.

"Father, forgive me," she whispered.

Through the quiet of the night she heard the chapel bell toll, sounding off the hours.

Midnight.

There was no reason to tarry. She should leave the chapel and go to her quarters even though she knew sleep would, again, remain elusive.

The product of an impure conscience, she reminded

herself. It had been less than a year since the last spree of killings. That murderer, the serial killer behind those heinous crimes, had stalked through these sacred halls.

Once he had been exposed, it had been Sister Rebecca's hope that, finally, she would find peace again. Freedom from the pain of the past.

Of course, that expectation had proved impossible.

Yes, the police had eventually pulled up stakes, leaving Our Lady of Virtues's reputation besmirched and pieces of crime-scene tape still flapping in the breezes, a reminder of the atrocities that had occurred on the hospital grounds. But it was the memories that truly remained, the memories that haunted.

Sister Rebecca had prayed that the scandal was finally over, but she knew, deep in her heart, it never would be. And now the new murders, not only Dr. Renner's but Royal Kajak's as well, both of whom had been a part of Our Lady of Virtues, only proved her worst fears true.

She shivered in the church, a sudden premonition sliding through her soul. She realized that the reign of terror which had held everyone associated with the decaying hospital fast in its grasp was far from finished. The serene period of the last few months had been only a lull, a short time of peace meant to trick all of those involved; the proverbial calm before the storm.

Shattered by two brutal murders.

No doubt a new evil had been unleashed.

One that was, most likely, worse than the last.

"God be with us," she whispered, the marrow of her bones turning to ice.

Should she go to the police?

Tell them what she knew? The secret she'd borne for three long decades?

God would let her know. She had to pray, to trust in Him.

"Father, please, please guide me," she whispered, genuflecting before leaving the chapel and crossing the cloister again. As she passed beneath the overhang, she heard the sound of a crow cawing and told herself it was *not* an evil omen, *not* the heralding of Lucifer. Besides, she didn't believe in such idiocies; her faith was much too strong.

But as she passed by the fountain, she thought she heard the sound of leather scraping against flagstones. A footstep.

At this hour?

Surely not.

She had to be imagining things. Her worries getting the better of her.

Nonetheless, her heart began to beat irregularly and she cast a glance backward, scanning the shadows not illuminated by the moon's pale light.

Nothing.

Silently scolding herself, she kept walking while she murmured a familiar prayer, her footsteps moving faster than they had in a decade. "Our Father, who art in heaven . . ."

Another telltale scratch of a sole against stone.

Every muscle in her body froze. She gathered her breath. Perhaps she was being tested.

Turning, she saw no one. Nothing. Just the trailing flowers in the hanging baskets swaying in the breeze—

A dark form, lightning quick, flashed by, seen only in the corner of her eye.

"Who is there?" she whispered, her skin crinkling in premonition, her voice wheezing as her lungs grew tight. "Show yourself!" Was it her imagination? A trick of shadow and eerie light? Her peripheral vision deceiving her? Swallowing back her fear, she slid a hand into her pocket and twined her fingers in the beaded strands of her rosary.

Fear not, the Lord is with you.

She turned toward the convent door. She was just imagining things. An old, foolish woman whose guilt was eroding her common sense.

In that instant, he sprang.

Out of the darkness.

A huge, shifting shape that landed against her back.

His weight was impossible to bear, and she started to crumple. Tried to scream, but a big gloved hand covered her mouth.

No!

No, no, no!

She felt her spine crushing as he held her fast from behind.

His other arm arced upward in front of her face. In

341

his gloved hand, a long blade caught in the moonlight.

Help me! Someone, please help me! Oh dear God, please.

Terrified, Sister Rebecca tried to scream, to bite, to fight, but his strength was overpowering.

He struck.

Fast.

The blade sliced downward.

Deep into her chest.

She gasped, gurgled, toppled to her knees. Her mind swirled, pain burning deep in her soul. Who would do this? She tried to see his face, but the darkness hid it. Her voice failed her, and she watched, unable to move, unable to warn anyone of the hideous terror that was to come.

He slipped through the open door of the convent as she felt her lifeblood ooze onto the smooth, timeworn stones.

He wasn't finished.

There would be more killing.

And the secrets she'd tried so desperately to conceal would be exposed.

Father, forgive me, she silently prayed as the fog and darkness pulled at her consciousness, *for I have sinned.*

The sounds of the night, the lapping of a slow-moving stream, the rush of wind through the leaves of the trees, the rattle of a train rumbling on tracks not far away, were obscured by the thrum of blood rushing through his veins and the exhilarated pounding of his heart.

He'd killed the old nun, just as the Voice had said. He'd had to leave her bleeding out while he entered the convent because he thought he'd heard someone approaching, had expected to have to take care of the intrusion, but the hallways of the convent were empty. Quiet. Still.

Assuring himself that he was alone, he returned to the body and, using the old woman's finger, wrote upon the cloister wall in blood then pulled out his portable tattooing machine and quickly embedded a number in her forehead. He hated having to do such a rough job. He needed more time, but time was never a luxury. He could only do his best work, his artist's work, on his own body.

He finished quickly then crept through the undergrowth, following the footpath, his blood still singing through his veins. He wasn't done with his mission; there was still another to deal with, but the head nun, the Mother Superior, had been dispatched.

Her spirit released.

Her body not revived.

Now, for the ritual . . .

Once inside, with the door bolted behind him, he lit the fire despite the warmth of the night, stripped off his clothes, washed his boots and clothes, then spread his plastic tarp in front of the fire. Once he'd arranged his mirror to the right angle, he showered beneath the pulsing spray, cleansing his body and mind. Afterward, naked, he lit the candles slowly, one by one.

Holding his rosary, he prayed long and hard. Then finally, once his soul was as cleansed as his body, he retrieved his kit and began his work.

He chose red ink and worked in an area not far from the scab still formed on one hundred one. Carefully he drew a new number upon his skin, one so similar to the other it was nearly identical. One hundred eleven for Sister Rebecca. Once he was satisfied with the look of the new number, he switched on the machine, watched the red ink flow. He felt the first little sting of the needles and gritted his teeth, his lips curling in a grim smile, for there was always pleasure in pain, tranquility in torment.

As for the Reverend Mother, there had been no reviving her, oh, no. Her black soul was on its way straight to hell.

Where it belonged.

CHAPTER 21

The phone call came at four-thirty. Montoya opened a bleary eye, groaned, and, rolling over, away from the warmth of Abby's naked body, he grabbed his cell. "Montoya," he mumbled, his voice low, nearly guttural with sleep. The damned cat, which had inched onto the bed during the night, hissed and slithered away.

"We got another one." Bentz sounded irritatingly awake.

"Another what?" But he knew. As he sat up in bed, he understood.

Abby groaned, turned over, and rubbed her eyes. "Now what?" Hershey, another late-night visitor who'd found a way to sleep between Abby and the edge of their bed, lifted her head then let it fall between her paws again.

"Another DB, same as the others," Bentz was saying. "Only this time it's a nun."

"A *nun*?"

"Sister Rebecca. The Mother Superior at—"

"Our Lady of Virtues," Montoya finished, all thoughts of slumber, or even morning sex with Abby, pushed from his mind. He'd met with Sister Rebecca Renault more than once and liked the little woman who was in her eighties. God Almighty, who would want to kill her? He threw off the thin sheet and scrounged in the dark for his jeans.

"The officer who responded said her throat was slit and a tattoo inked into her forehead. Different, though. This time it's one hundred eleven."

"A hundred eleven?" Montoya dragged on jeans, not bothering with his boxers.

Abby hit the switch to her bedside lamp and the small bedroom was instantly awash with light. She pushed herself to a sitting position and squinted up at him. Her face had paled, and she looked as if she might break down altogether.

"I think we'd better go check out the scene," Bentz said.

"I'll be ready in five."

345

"I'll be there in three."

Montoya hung up. "It's the Mother Superior. Killed like the others," he said as Abby reached for her rumpled nightgown and tossed it over her head. Her beautiful face was stone-cold sober, her burnished curls falling into her eyes.

"No," she whispered, shaking her head. "I don't believe it. Not Sister Rebecca . . ."

"I'm sorry," he said, and meant it.

She swallowed hard, her eyes filling with tears. She glared up at Montoya, some of her shock and grief morphing into anger. "I don't get it. Why?"

"Yes, why?" he repeated grimly. He looked around. "Where the hell is my wallet?"

"Over there." She pointed to the dresser, and Montoya snapped up his wallet, badge, and keys then threw on a shirt.

"Get this guy," Abby said as he slid into his shoes. "I mean it. Get him."

He met her angry gaze as she rolled out of the bed and walked up to him, all sexy and sleepy and damned irresistible.

He kissed her just hard enough to let her know that no matter what, he thought she was hot.

"I will," he promised. "I'll nail his ass." He slapped her on the butt. "Go back to bed."

"I can't sleep."

"I'll call later."

"Good." She yawned and sat on the edge of the bed, searching for her slippers.

Montoya took off, walking quickly down the short hallway and past the wall of plastic sheeting in the living room. He snagged his jacket from a hook by the door and heard the dog's feet hit the floor as if Hershey intended to shoot past him and out the door. He didn't have time for the dog this morning. Abby could deal with her.

Stepping outside, he pulled the door shut and cut across the lawn. A police cruiser was already in his driveway, Bentz at the wheel. Montoya climbed in the passenger side and found a cup of coffee in the holder.

"How'd you manage this?" he asked, picking up the cup and sipping.

"All-night convenience store." Bentz backed out of the drive, put the car into gear, and flipped on the lights as he stepped on the gas.

"For crying out loud, how long have you been up?" Montoya asked, swallowing some of the hot brew and noticing that Bentz's hair was wet.

"Long enough to have worked out with the punching bag and showered."

"And stopped for coffee." Montoya frowned as dawn began to streak the sky. "You morning people bug the shit out of me." He took another drink as Bentz sped past a delivery van double-parked near a restaurant and headed toward the freeway. "So tell me what happened."

"I got a call from Sister Odine at the convent. She found Sister Rebecca in the cloister."

"Damn." Montoya stared into the coming dawn,

noticing that even at this hour traffic flowing into the city was picking up, the stream of headlights seeming endless. "I suppose the press is on to the story already."

"It wouldn't surprise me." Bentz shot his partner a look. "If not now, then soon."

"Same with the Feds. The FBI will be all over this like stink on shit. At least they can take some of the heat."

Bentz grunted his agreement as he edged over a lane, ready to exit. "I finally connected with Tweedle-Dee and Tweedle-Dum."

"Who?" Montoya said, irritated. It was too damned early for word games.

"The brothers. They're still both in town. I've got a meeting scheduled with them later this morning. I'm interested to hear what they have to say about dear old dad."

"Amen to that." Montoya grimaced. "They both called you? Individually?"

"Within half an hour of each other."

"They're together?"

"Seems like. And the Mrs., Anna Maria, the one married to Kyle? I don't think she likes it much. She's called me a couple of times, asking if he's been in to see me."

"Communication breakdown."

"My guess is they want the body released so they can stuff the old man in the ground and divvy up his estate."

"You haven't even met them yet," Montoya pointed out.

"I'm just saying that's what it feels like to me. The type of questions they asked didn't lead me to believe there was any love lost between Renner and his sons."

"Adopted sons. Have we ever located their old man, the one that gave 'em up?"

Bentz shook his head. "Still MIA. Has been for over twenty years."

"Be interesting to see what became of him."

Bentz angled the cruiser along the fields and forests of the country road leading to Our Lady of Virtues. The police band crackled and the stars faded with the coming day and Montoya tried to wrap his mind around this case. Another person murdered. Not half a mile away from the old hospital. "You have any idea when the DNA on Eve Renner will be processed?"

"I called Jaskiel because I figured the DA had a lot more influence than I did. She told the lab to put a rush on it, whatever that means."

"Yeah," Montoya agreed, frowning to himself. "But it's better than nothing."

The road forked, one stretch angling off toward the abandoned hospital, the other toward the convent. As they passed the split, Montoya looked through the window, unable to see the asylum from the car.

But it was there.

And he knew in his gut that this latest spate of killings revolved around whatever secrets it hid.

• • •

Deified!

The Voice had promised he would be *deified* if he finished his tasks.

He drove through the dark night, his blood thrumming through his veins, his pulse pounding in his brain. He barely saw the headlights of the vehicles heading in the opposite direction. No, in his mind's eye he replayed the sacrifice over and over again. He'd sensed the old nun's fear, saw the terror in her eyes as she'd recognized him, felt her surrender, for she'd known there was no escape from God's will.

Sister Rebecca.

Nun.

Mother Superior.

He held the steering wheel in a death grip, his hands sweating inside his thin gloves. Insects splattered against the windshield of his pickup as he headed northeast along the freeway away from New Orleans.

He was nervous.

Baton Rouge was far afield from his usual hunting grounds, All Saints College unfamiliar. But he knew his next victim, the other liar and false innocent, was there.

He kept his speedometer two miles below the limit, never drawing attention to his dark vehicle but never veering from his path.

God had told him where she would be.

What she would be doing.

How he could abduct her.

He must have faith.

"Never even, never even, never even . . . ," he whispered, calming himself, using the mantra that forced all doubts from his mind. The Father had told him to whisper it whenever he felt as if Satan were luring him from the path of righteousness.

"Never even . . . never even . . . never even . . ."

He spied the turn-off for Baton Rouge and on his portable GPS screen he saw his ultimate destination, the campus. He'd changed in the truck, just so that no one—a late-night jogger, some idiot out walking his dog, or a drunken college kid weaving his way back to his dorm—would notice anything out of the ordinary, such as blood staining his neoprene jogging suit.

As the Voice had directed, he drove past All Saints's main gates, and a chance meeting with a campus security guard, then parked his truck in an alley behind an abandoned service station with boarded windows, dry pumps, and a signboard indicating the price of gasoline at under a dollar a gallon, either someone's idea of a bad joke or the service station had been closed for a long, long while.

Fortunately, the alley backed up to a far edge of the campus and no one paid him any notice as he headed quickly across the lawn. He wore a jogging suit with an oversized jacket covering his backpack, tools and weapons. Anyone who saw him cutting through the live oaks would think he was an overweight man trying to jog off a few pounds before starting his day.

The small convent was on the perimeter of the

campus, far away from the quad, library, and lecture halls. He glanced neither left nor right as he jogged, as if he'd run this particular course a hundred times. At the convent garden, he stopped, leaned over, gloved hands on his knees, as if to catch his breath, and then, glancing around the immediate area and seeing no one nearby, he scaled the fence, an easy job for anyone athletic enough to hoist his own weight upward. The edges of the bricks made perfect finger- and toeholds, and as he reached the top of the wall, where a single row of wrought-iron spikes prevented most people from even entertaining the thought of trying to climb over, he placed his hands on the smooth concrete, arched his body up and over, and did a handspring into the air. He landed as soft as a cat on the interior side of the wall.

Easy as pie.

Now for the hard part.

He only hoped the Voice knew Sister Vivian's routine.

Doubt not, God is with you, he thought, wishing the Voice would speak with him, guide him. Of course, it was not to be. God spoke to him only when He wanted. It seemed always late at night while he was lying in his bed—having trouble falling asleep, the aggravating little voices scraping through his brain—that God would visit and the Voice would offer him counseling and instructions.

The convent was darker than the campus had been, but his eyes adjusted, and, with moonlight as his guide, he followed the map in his head, around one vine-clad building, across a small patio, and through a creaking gate to the lush and fragrant gardens.

He checked his watch. The illuminated dial read four-forty. He would have twenty minutes to wait, then only ten more to execute God's intricate plan. He hid behind a tall pillar and prayed for strength, pleaded for understanding, begged for God's help, and implored the Father to show him the way . . . though all the while he thought of Eve. Surely when he dispensed with this one, God would see fit to—

Bong!

His heart nearly exploded in his chest. Then he realized it was the church bells pealing at the stroke of five.

Bong!

He was ready. Knife, rope, drink, and, if necessary, small pistol, all at hand.

Bong!

He leaned out from behind the pillar, waiting, watching.

Bong!

He saw a dark figure approaching, hurrying forward, head bent. She was small. And frail. This would be easier than he'd anticipated. She found a place on a bench and mumbled softly, her fingers working a rosary as he slid silently up behind her through the tall, shadowy plants.

Bong!

The death knell. He leaped forward, slung his small

garrote over her head and around her throat. She gasped, struggling, her fingers scrabbling desperately at her throat, her tiny body stronger than she looked in her habit. Her rosary dropped to the smooth stones of the garden; her small prayer book, too, fell to the ground. Her spine flexed and bent. She tried to scream, to fling him off her, to save herself as she fought tooth and nail.

But she, this little nun, Sister Vivian—"Viv," as they'd called her—was no match for him. No match whatsoever.

Grimacing, he pulled tighter, his arm muscles flexing as she began to go limp, the fight slipping out of her.

Feeling powerful. Indeed Godlike, he took her to the brink, into the darkness of unconsciousness, then he hauled her swiftly and efficiently in a fireman's carry out of the garden, through the main gate. This was where it was tricky.

If anyone saw him now he would have to use his gun and that, too, would cause complications, the kind that he didn't want to deal with. He moved swiftly through the shadows, away from the security lights, hiding whenever he heard anyone, ducking into an alley when a garbage truck, lights flashing, passed.

He was sweating, frightened, but exhilarated as well.

This, the capture, was a new thrill.

This one would be revived.

But only for a short while.

Then she, too, would die.

Kristi rolled out of bed and groaned. It was just too damned early to get up. It wasn't even light out yet, but she had no choice, not if she wanted to stay fit, keep her body honed. Besides, she needed a release, something to help mentally prepare her for her day ahead of eight hours of calls and complaints to Gulf Auto and Life.

"Yuck," she said aloud as she propelled her body from the bed and walked to her closet where her gym bag was already packed with her swimsuit and workout gear. The club where she exercised was kind of a "rat gym," but it had a clean, Olympic-sized pool, and at this time of the morning she was assured of her own lane. If she changed her routine and swam later in the day, the pool was too crowded, and besides, she needed those hours after work to read, watch cop dramas on television, or work on her own writing projects. She'd just sold two more true-detective stories to a magazine but had resisted her editor's offer to write some kind of funky "real-life Nancy Drew–type series," seeing as how she was the daughter of a New Orleans detective. The editor seemed to still believe she could draw her father into this writing gig and give his insight into the cases she was writing about.

Yeah, right.

She tore off her oversized New Orleans Saints T-shirt and flung on her jogging bra, T-shirt and shorts. That accomplished, she used the toilet, splashed water onto her face, twisted her hair into a tight little knot that she banded in place, then did a quick series of stretches, just to get her blood flowing. After stepping into flip-flops, she slung the strap of her gym bag over her shoulder. The small canvas bag was packed with a fresh set of clothes, tennis shoes, and anything else she would need if she wanted to add to her routine and jog on the treadmill or lift weights.

Grabbing a bottle of water from her small fridge, she threw a glance at the police scanner that sat on her desk as she headed for the door. Her father'd had a fit about her buying the equipment and listening to the radio band, but she didn't care. She figured it was her money, her apartment, her business.

And as for the apartment . . . She looked around and frowned. She had clothes draped over her few pieces of furniture, a floor that should be mopped, a sink filled with glasses and cups that needed to be washed, and the shower—gross! If her stepmother Olivia ever stopped by, she'd probably faint. Housework wasn't exactly "her thing," but even Kristi knew that before she settled in at her desk she'd have to do major cleaning. Fortunately the place was small.

The police-band radio started sputtering out reports as Kristi was opening the door. She heard the words "at Our Lady of Virtues Convent" and froze in the act. Several officers were speaking, and then she recognized her father's voice. It was a homicide. A murder.

Correction, make that *another* murder.

Kristi stepped back into the studio and let the door softly close.

She felt a little tingle. This was *the* story. No matter what her father said. The killings that were swirling around Our Lady of Virtues were perfect for her book. *Perfect!*

She dropped any idea of heading to the gym this morning. Her workout could wait.

And she still had three hours before she would have to even think about getting ready for work. There was plenty of time to run out to the convent and get back in time to hit the shower and fly to the office. Her dad would kill her, of course, be mad as hell that she showed up, but with the crowd of reporters that were no doubt already gathering around, she'd blend right in. He was just no damned help . . . yet. She planned on changing that and soon. In the meantime she already had a leak in the department, a cute guy who, after a few drinks, could be counted on to give up something. True enough, he was just trying to get her into bed, and they both knew it, but still, he would let a few things slip.

If her dad didn't come through, and he wouldn't, she could count on her friend.

For now, though, she needed to get out to the scene and fast, learn what she could firsthand. There would be news crews at the convent and lots of loose chatter. And she was a cop's daughter, trained in the art of observation. Her father had always been overprotective, forcing her to learn to observe her surroundings and be prepared at all times for a potential attack or kidnapping. He'd paid for self-defense classes and had insisted she run with a whistle and can of pepper spray when she was jogging. But most of all he'd taught her to watch everything that was happening around her. He was a damned freak about it, always believing that someone he'd sent away to prison might get out and seek retribution by harming Kristi.

But, as she'd proven before, she knew how to handle herself.

And after that time she'd been abducted, she'd taken her father's advice more seriously and had redoubled her efforts in the martial arts and weaponry. As her computer-geek friend had once told her, "You're one badass dude . . . or is that dudette?"

Whatever.

Digging in her closet again, she came up with a battered Marlins baseball cap then located her sunglasses in her purse. She crammed the cap onto her head, pulled the brim down low. Next she slid the shades onto the bridge of her nose.

Checking out her reflection in the mirror mounted over her bureau, Kristi figured her dad might not even recognize her.

And if he did, so what?

The last she heard, it was still a free country.

The half-dead nun was lying on his bed, stripped of her clothes and moaning softly. Irritating him. She was waking again, and that was a mistake. Hadn't the Voice said to kidnap her, kill her, then dispose of her?

Hadn't God's instructions been precise as to what He wanted?

Yet the Reviver had improvised.

He'd driven her to his little cabin in the woods rather than to the spot God had indicated.

And she was still alive.

Because he'd let his emotions run away with him. While he was still on an incredible high from the first killing, he'd decided that he was able to make his own decisions, that he was the Reviver and could decide who would live and who would die. But that was wrong. God would be very, very angry. Perhaps punish him. Even take away his promise of deification. He had to work quickly. To cover his mistake.

God is all-knowing. And he's furious. That's why he hasn't spoken to you. You are already being punished! Agitated, he stood in front of the fire, the last number—111—gleaming upon his body near the others. He stared at the words he'd spent so many hours inscribing into his flesh, feeling the sting of the needle, the bite of the first little puncture. And now there were so many fresh ones with scabs.

"Oooh," she moaned.

Revived.

Brought back from the brink of death . . . only to sink into oblivion forever. He thought about decorating his body with her information but decided he would have to wait. The ritual was always the same. . . . The engraving was to take place after the killing.

Not always, though. You've broken that rule. . . .

Look into the mirror. At your reflection. What do you see?

He saw *her* name. *Eve.* Etched into his skin, reminding him of her. He traced her name with one finger, rubbing his skin over and over, imagining the needle pressing into her firm flesh, puncturing her, deeper and deeper, faster and faster, the sweat on their bodies mingling as he reverently and indelibly made her his.

His blood thrummed. *Eve. Eve. EVE!*

He'd broken his own rules because of her, but this . . . this inconsequential nun was different.

He turned and saw that she was awake, her eyes round with terror, her voice gurgling in panic behind her gag.

"Viv," he whispered, and she visibly cringed in the firelight, her pale body cast in gold.

She was shaking her head, silently screaming, "No."

In a way, he felt sorry for her—the sinner—and he walked back to his altar, found his rosary, and carefully twined the blood-red beads through her bound fingers. Tears filled her eyes and she blinked, but he knew she was already, in her mind, seeking comfort in the prayers.

Then he went to work.

CHAPTER 22

W*hat had she done?*
Eve opened a bleary eye and rolled over, expecting Cole to be lying beside her. What felt like hours of intense, glorious lovemaking hadn't been a dream. She was sore in all the right places to remind her that last night, while still on medication, she'd practically seduced Cole Dennis!

But the bed was empty, and as she turned to one side, pain ripped down her shoulder.

Oh yeah.

That.

She looked down at herself. All she was wearing was a sling.

"Great," she mumbled, climbing out of bed and catching sight of her reflection in the mirror over the dresser. It was worse than she'd thought. Inwardly groaning, she noticed her bruises, messed hair, and sunken eyes. Either she'd had a really good time last night or a really bad one.

So where was he?

Maybe he'd already taken off.

That would be good. Very good. She couldn't get involved with him again. Not unless she wanted to play emotional suicide.

Face it, Eve. You are already involved.

Cringing at the thought, she heard Cole singing off-key, the atonal melody floating up the stairs along with the warm scent of coffee. Just like old times. As if they'd never experienced a horrid rift where they'd almost ended up in the courtroom, when she'd been certain he'd tried to kill her and he'd thought she was sleeping with another man.

And poor Roy had ended up dead.

"I'm living a soap opera," she said, grabbing her robe, then heading barefoot to the second floor, where she locked herself into the bathroom, showered quickly, tossed back half a dose of pain pills, and towel-dried her hair. A slash of lipstick and the tiniest bit of mascara was all she could manage before she slipped on her robe, tightened the cinch, and nearly tripped over Samson on her way down the stairs.

"Watch out," she warned the cat, then followed him to the kitchen, where bacon was sizzling in a frying pan.

Cole was at the sink.

Having the audacity to look chipper and hale.

Pouring coffee and scrambling eggs while a platter of hash browns steamed on the counter.

"You went shopping?" she asked as her grand-mother's old toaster clicked and two pieces of only slightly burned toast popped up.

"Just to the local market." He cast her a glance and grinned wickedly, reminding her of the night before.

Bastard!

But her stupid heart rate skyrocketed despite herself. Damn the man, he *knew* what he did to her, and he took advantage of it. Even now, in the crummy jeans and T-shirt, facing away from her, slapping butter on the toast, he was sexy as all get out. His jeans hung low, his shirt stretched over his shoulders, and every once in a while she caught a glimpse of his smooth, muscular back as the hem of his shirt shifted.

"Like the view?" he asked, not even turning around.

She flushed. "The view's fine."

"Better than fine."

"Way to be humble."

He looked over his shoulder. "What do you mean? I was talking about the yard," he said, hitching his chin toward the window, where the magnolia tree was visible. But his slow-spreading smile told her differently.

"You are a miserable piece of work, you know that?"

"I've been called worse." He found a cup, rinsed it in the sink then poured coffee into it. "Sleazeball, scumbag, jackass, you name it."

"Lawyer?"

He laughed. "Yeah, I've heard that one too." He added a little cream to the coffee then placed it in front of her.

"You're trying your best to be charming, aren't you?"

"Just doin' what comes natural."

"Yeah, right." She blew across her cup and tried to ignore how comfortable it felt here, in her house, with Cole. She'd been alone these last few nights, had told herself that's what she wanted, but now she wasn't so sure.

"Look, Cole, about last night . . ."

"Hmm?"

"What we did was . . . wrong."

"According to whom? The sex police or the Kama-Sutra squad?"

"Not funny," she said, but her lips twitched a bit.

"Kinda funny."

"Don't derail me here, I have a point."

"Which is?"

"We can't act like horny teenagers."

He turned to face her, his hands braced against the counter, his eyes boring into hers. "Your memory about the events might be a little fuzzy and disjointed, but mine is clear, and basically, I said 'No' and you kept pushing."

She held up a hand, remembering how it all came about.

"You seduced me, not the other way around. I tried to be noble, but you were having none of it."

"Okay, yeah, I know—"

"So just enjoy it. Chalk it up to a great experience."

"But it won't happen again?"

Now he smiled. "That, I can't promise. And, judging from your actions last night, neither can you. Don't even try to tell me it was all the meds, okay, cuz I just don't buy it. I was there, darlin', and in my right mind. I remember it all. Vividly."

She dropped her gaze, felt the back of her neck grow warm.

"Don't worry about it, okay? I think we have much bigger problems."

She couldn't argue that logic. "True. But in the light of things, I guess I need to call my lawyer and have the restraining order against you lifted."

"That might help." He slid a plate of scrambled eggs with cheese, hash-brown potatoes, and crisp bacon under her nose. "Here ya go. Dig in."

"What, no parsley sprig?" she asked, though the food looked so good, her mouth watered.

"They were fresh out at the local market," he quipped then set his plate on the table and handed her a paper towel and utensils. "No napkins either. But apples." He pointed to a basket on the counter.

"You're slipping," she charged, taking the fork, knife, and spoon from his outstretched hand.

"No doubt. Now"—he gestured toward her plate with a finger—"eat. Then we'll discuss who gets to call the police and tell them about the doll and the old hospital."

She bit into a piece of toast. "I don't want to think about it."

"I know. But we have to."

"After breakfast."

"Definitely."

The eggs were delicious, the bacon smoky and crisp, the potatoes divine. Eve had just decided she could get used to Cole pampering her when the phone rang.

"I don't even want to know," she said with a sigh. Then, seeing her brother's number flash on the caller-ID screen, she braced herself. "Hello?"

"Eve? It's Anna." Her sister-in-law was breathless.

"Have you heard from Kyle? He, uh, he hasn't been home, and when I did reach him on his cell, he said he was in New Orleans!" She sounded undone as she took a deep drag on her cigarette. "Can you believe it? He never even asked me if I wanted to come down with him, didn't so much as come home or pack or anything. Just left, apparently, on the same damned day you did!"

"I didn't know," Eve said, and in a heartbeat the warm domesticity of the few minutes before evaporated.

"He said he was going to see you. . . . Remember, I told you that he's interested in the will? Look, if he shows up, have him call me, okay?"

"Of course."

"I'm packing some things, not just my own, but for the big jerk too. I'll leave in a few hours, and I'll be down there sometime tonight, depending on traffic. But please have Kyle call me."

"If I hear from him, I will."

"Thanks." Anna Maria let out a long sigh. "I don't have to tell you we've been having some problems, but, unlike your brother, I think the best way is to face them and talk about them, not run away from them. Look, I've got another call coming in. . . . Have Kyle call me. Love ya, bye!"

She hung up, and Eve was left holding the phone. "My sister-in-law," she said, setting the receiver into its cradle. "My brother's in town. I guess he never went back home after I left Atlanta."

"Why?"

"She didn't say, but, believe me, I quit trying to figure out my family a long time ago."

He snorted. "Join the club. Now, I think we should call the police and tell them about what we found." He grabbed the backpack and pulled out the file on Faith Chastain. "After we look at this."

Eve nodded with more than a little trepidation then scooted her chair back and scrounged in a few drawers with her good arm before coming up with two notepads and pens. "My guess is that the police will want to keep this." She tapped on the file with a finger.

As she sat at the table again and started reading, he refilled their coffee cups then pulled a chair up next to hers.

It was weird, really, reading all the different notes, some typed, others handwritten, all regarding a woman who had suffered several nervous breakdowns, who'd battled depression, and who'd seemed to hallucinate. Nurses, psychiatrists, psychologists, and even some of the clergy had added to the file. Nowhere was there mention of a pregnancy or birth.

"Maybe this is all wrong," Eve said, shaking her head. "I mean, what are the chances that I'm Faith's daughter?"

Before Cole could answer, the doorbell pealed.

"Expecting someone?" Cole was already walking in his stocking feet toward the front of the house.

"At eight-thirty in the morning?" she asked, right

behind him. "I don't think so. . . . No, wait! Anna said that Kyle was on his way."

"I think he's here," Cole said.

She peered around him, and through the narrow window flanking the door, she spied her oldest brother. Big and grim, he stared back at her through eyes that never seemed to smile.

Her heart sank.

"And he's not alone," Cole said, his voice terse and cool.

Eve caught a glimpse of Van standing off to one side, sporting an Arizona tan, smoking a cigarette, and looking nervous as a caged cat.

Both her brothers.

Here.

Now.

The morning just took a turn for the worse.

"No comment," Bentz said, brushing past a reporter as he made his way to the cruiser. The crime scene, roped off and already being processed, was exactly what he'd expected, and as usual he'd nearly lost the contents of his stomach when he'd viewed the body, still lying in the courtyard, bloody number drawn on the wall, an unsightly tattoo scrawled upon her forehead, blood staining the edge of her wimple from white to red.

He'd managed to hold onto his morning's coffee and ask a few questions before he discovered that the batteries in his pocket recorder had died.

The story was that Sister Odine, on her way to the chapel, had discovered the Mother Superior's body. She'd called 911 and then, because she'd met him last fall, phoned Bentz as well. A deputy from the sheriff's department had stopped by, and once he'd called in the homicide, Bentz was notified a second time, just before he'd pulled up to the convent.

Now he found an extra set of batteries in the glove box and headed back inside. The press were too close, and he barked at a couple of deputies to push the reporters, cameramen, bystanders, and vans back farther down the lane leading to the convent. It was light now, the day promising to be sweltering. He was already sweating.

Another reporter approached him, a thirtysomething woman with a toothy smile, salon-streaked hair, and intelligent eyes. "Detective, please, if I could just have a minute. Recently there were three murders, all similar, and all connected to the Our Lady of Virtues campus. Could you comment on any link to the crimes? Do we have another serial killer on the streets?"

Bentz stopped under the glare of the camera's lights. "I have no comment at this time. But I'm certain the public information officer will issue a statement later today. Until then, there's really nothing I can say."

"But the public has the right to know what's going on."

"A statement will be issued." He kept walking, leaving the reporter without any answers. He tried to keep his cool, but the press and the damned bystanders, gawkers who fed on this type of grisly crime scene, aggravated him to no end.

"Keep them back," he said to a deputy as he made a sweeping gesture to the news crews and bystanders. From the corner of his eye, he saw a slim figure of a woman in a baseball cap who looked familiar. He looked more closely and recognized his daughter standing in a crowd of onlookers. She was looking straight at him but now turned away.

What the hell did Kristi think she was doing? If he weren't so damned busy, he'd march over to the crowd and tell her to go home, go to work, go any-where, but *go away*. For now, though, he had a job to do.

Christ, what a mess!

Bentz strode back through the gates and along a path to the convent itself. In the garden area, Bonita Washington moved carefully over the crime scene with gloved hands and booties on her shoes. "We've got a real sweetheart with this one," Washington said as she nodded toward the frail nun's body. "Santiago, make sure you get a shot of the tattoo on her forehead."

Inez Santiago, long red hair wound onto her head, moved closer to the corpse and snapped a photo.

"Don't mess with my scene, Detectives. We're still processing," Washington warned them.

Montoya hadn't shaken his bad mood. "We know the drill. We just want to see what's going on here." He shot her a glare, and Bentz noted that his jaw was tight, his lips thin. He had personal ties to this order of nuns who still wore traditional habits long after Vatican II had loosened the dress code.

"Don't we all?" she said, then motioned to two of her technicians. "Santiago, Tennet, how're we doing?"

Santiago snapped another photo. "I need a few more minutes."

A.J. Tennet, who often worked with the medical examiner, held up his collection case. "Got the blood samples."

"Hold onto them. . . . We don't want anyone accusing us of losing or compromising evidence," Washington said, reminding everyone of the situation with Royal Kajak's murder.

Tennet flashed a smile. "No way."

"Good."

As the technicians continued their work, Montoya and Bentz carefully studied the cloister garden where Sister Rebecca Renault had lost her life. Crickets chirped, a frog croaked, and the fountain gurgled as night slowly gave way to day. Aside from the dead body and blood staining the flagstones, this would be an idyllic place, a peaceful spot, an area of repose and contemplation.

Desecrated forever.

"Sometimes this job is a real bitch," Montoya muttered.

Bentz squinted as sunlight began to pour over the garden walls. "Not just sometimes," he said. "Always."

He spent another couple of minutes eyeing the area, envisioning how the killer got in, how he surprised the little nun, how the killing went down.

She never had a chance, he decided as he headed inside. The dark hallways were quiet, just a few hushed whispers as the nuns sat in a row, waiting their turn to be called into the small room they were using for interrogation. Sister Rebecca's own sparse room and more opulent office were being processed, considered part of the crime scene, as was the area where she was found, in the cloister not far from the chapel door.

Helluva place for a homicide, Bentz thought, refilling his pocket recorder with the batteries and taking a seat across from Sister Odine. She was a frail-looking woman, somewhere in her late sixties or early seventies he guessed, and as sharp as a tack.

She and the other nuns told him essentially the same thing. Sister Rebecca had been at Vespers and then, as was her usual routine, worked later in her office. Several of the sisters had looked through their windows and seen the lights glowing in the Reverend Mother's place of business.

It wasn't all that odd for her to go alone to the cloister gardens or chapel. She'd been a spry woman who existed on few hours of sleep each night. Sister Odine had discovered her body on the way to the chapel early in the morning.

Montoya asked for records of anyone who had visited or called Sister Rebecca over the past two months, and Bentz requested the same of everyone who lived in, or was employed by, Our Lady of Virtues. Some of their questions were deferred to the local parish, others to the Archdiocese, and when they asked for records of employment or admittance to the hospital, Sister Odine opened her mouth, closed it again, then shook her head, her wimple rustling.

"I'm sorry," she said, "but I have no idea where those might be. You could check with the Archdiocese, of course, and go through whatever we have here, but the hospital has been closed for so many years, I'm not certain those records still exist." She blinked several times then anxiously touched the crucifix dangling from her neck. "They must, of course. I'll search for them."

"An officer will be assigned to help you," Bentz said, and the little nun's eyebrows raised over her rimless glasses. Though it was unstated, she knew that Bentz was doggedly pursuing evidence, that he trusted no one, not even a woman who had pledged her life to the Lord forty years earlier.

They questioned everyone and found out little while the crime-scene techs vacuumed, photographed, videographed, and dusted the scene. As Bentz and Montoya left, the techs were still searching the grounds for trace evidence. So far no one had discovered how the killer had breached the walls of the institution. The gates had been locked, as they had been for the past few years, and the perimeter appeared undisturbed.

Bentz glanced up at the walls. They were certainly not impossible to scale, especially with the use of a ladder, but they'd found no impressions in the mud to indicate that a ladder had been used, nor had they yet discovered any boot- or shoe print. But it was still early.

The killer couldn't be so lucky.

Not all the time.

Sooner or later, he'd slip up.

Bentz only hoped it happened before another person was butchered.

"For Christ's sake, Eve! What the hell is he doing here?" Kyle demanded, eyeing Cole as if he were Satan incarnate.

"I was invited," Cole said, though Eve knew that was a bit of a stretch. "What about you?" He'd made it clear to her more than once that he'd never much cared for either of her brothers. Obviously, he didn't see any reason to be polite now.

"We're here because of our father," Van said as he tossed his cigarette over the railing to sizzle in the dewy grass. He was shorter and fairer than Kyle, his hair straight and dirty blond while Kyle's was thick and the color of dark coffee. Both of them had inherited the same icy blue eyes of their father, or so Melody Renner had claimed, though Eve had never so much as seen a photograph of the man.

"But this is the guy you accused of murdering Kajak, and now you're what—?" Kyle ranted.

"Sleeping with him? Are you out of your fuckin' mind?"

"Let's not get into it out here," Eve said calmly, stepping out of the doorway to allow her brothers inside. "And keep it clean, would you, Kyle? I have neighbors."

"For the past three months you claimed that this guy murdered Kajak and tried to kill you!"

"I was wrong." She slammed the door shut and tried counting to calm down.

"Just like that?" Kyle snapped his fingers while Van looked like he wanted to melt into the floor and disappear. "This is fucking unbelievable."

"She said to clean it up," Cole said, bristling, the muscles on the back of his neck rigid.

"So the minute you're out of my sight, you hook up with this . . . this *killer* and lay on your back for him. What kind of weird fantasy are you having now?"

"You'd better leave," Cole bit out, eyes narrowing, the sizzle of a fight in the air.

"Take your own advice," Kyle said, his face red, his nostrils flared. He jabbed a finger at the floor. "This was our grandmother's house, man. You have nothin' going on here!"

"Enough!" Eve stepped between them. "I think we've heard and seen way more testosterone this morning than we want to." She looked from Kyle to Cole. "Both of you, just back off and take it down a notch or two."

Kyle muttered tersely, "Don't be an idiot, Eve. He's playing you."

Every muscle in Cole's body flexed, but his voice was cool, the detached counselor, when he said, "If anyone's playing anyone, Renner, I figure it must be you. Why are you here now? Because of your old man? Don't forget, I represented him. I know how close you were. You two boys just rolled into town to pick over his corpse."

"That's not the way it is!" Van sputtered, but he was nervous, and when Cole focused on him, Van looked away.

"So, let's start over," Eve suggested. "And be civil about it."

No one said a word for a few seconds. Eve's brothers eyed the foyer, parlor, and staircase as if they'd never been inside Nana's old house before. As she shepherded them toward the kitchen, Kyle ran a finger along the top of the hallway wainscoting and Van stared at the pictures, light fixtures, rugs, and furniture as if he were doing a mental tabulation of what it was all worth.

"Nice place," Van observed, clearly trying to defuse the situation.

Grateful that the fight had abated, Eve realized it had been years since either of them had set a foot on the ancient floorboards. "We just finished breakfast, but there's coffee and toast," she offered.

Cole led the way and somehow managed to scoop up Faith Chastain's file and place it under a stack of three-month-old magazines.

"Don't bother," Kyle said as she reached for cups in the cupboard. He wiggled a finger at her arm in its sling, as if he finally noticed she might be hurt. "What happened?"

"I fell."

Van glanced at Cole. "Yeah?"

"Over my own two feet," she said tightly. "A real klutz move, but I can still make and pour coffee."

"I'm okay," Kyle said.

"Me too. Coffeed out." Van nodded. "We're here about Dad. To see if you need any help with the funeral or the estate."

"To be honest, I haven't thought of either yet. The police still haven't released Dad's body."

"How long does that take?"

"Depends. On a lot of things." Cole picked up an apple from the basket, passing it between both hands, a release of tension. "You can request it, but until the police have all the information and tests they need, you'll have to wait." He tossed the apple upward and, without watching it, caught it one-handed. "In a hurry?"

"No need to drag it out." Kyle reached into his pocket for his cigarettes, shook one out, and jabbed it between his lips. He found his lighter in the same pocket and was about to light up when he caught Eve's discouraging gaze.

"Oh for the love of God, Eve, you won't let me smoke? After all the time you stayed at my place?"

"Outside." She tossed him the phone. "And call

377

your wife while you're at it. She's half out of her mind with worry about you."

"Half out of her mind is about right. That woman!" But he took the phone.

"Call her cell. She's on her way down here."

"Oh fu—!" Sending her a dark glance, he hauled the phone and his cigarettes outside.

As the door closed behind him, Van said, "Listen, Eve, I'm sorry I didn't come and see you more often, you know, while you were recuperating, but I was busy and . . . well, I know that isn't much of an excuse, but you know I've never really caught a break." His lips compressed. "Not one damned break. I've just been trying to make ends meet. Hell, I even moved to Arizona because an old army buddy of mine said things were booming out there."

"Not so?" she asked while Cole stood near the window, where he could watch Kyle outside.

"More like a bust. I was about to pull up stakes anyway. I'd already called Kyle."

"He never said anything."

"I don't think he wanted to worry you or Anna."

Bull, Eve thought but held her tongue.

Van ran a hand through his hair. "So the thing of it is, I'm . . ."

"Broke," Cole guessed.

Van nodded, glanced through the window, and frowned. "So the faster we could wrap up Dad's estate, you know, the better it would be for me. For Kyle. Hell, for you too."

"I'm not the executor, Van. At least I don't think so."

"You don't have a copy of the will?"

She shook her head.

"Then it must be at his house." Van brightened at the prospect.

"The farm is a crime scene. I'm not sure the police have released it yet."

"Jesus, how long does it take?"

"A lot longer than on television," Cole said.

"So how do we find out about the money? He was loaded."

"I don't know anything about it," she admitted.

"But someone must," Van insisted. "I could really use the money."

"Who says you're entitled to any?" Cole asked. "Terrence might have left everything to charity, for all you know."

"Nah. He couldn't. He wouldn't." Van seemed almost frantic. He shoved his long hair from his eyes. "Look, Eve, we have to get this settled."

"We will, when we get into his house and find the will."

Cole pushed away from the window. "Check with Guy Perrine at O'Black, Sullivan and Kravitz. I'm not sure, but Terrence might have worked with him. You'll be better off not mentioning my name. I'm still persona non grata down there."

"And if this person, this Guy, doesn't have the will?"

Cole's cool gaze met Van's anxious one. "Then I guess you're shit out of luck."

"Let's not go there," Eve said as Kyle pushed the door open so hard it banged against the wall.

"She's on her way," he said, glowering at Eve as if all his marital problems were her fault. "And she's really freaked out about the nun."

"The nun?" Eve asked blankly.

"The Reverend Mother at Our Lady of Virtues."

"Sister Rebecca?" Eve's knees threatened to give out as she read the message in Kyle's eyes. Something horrible had happened.

Kyle nodded. "That's the one. Anna Maria says it's all over the news. Guess she was killed last night."

CHAPTER 23

Bentz was walking with Montoya toward the cruiser when his cell phone rang. Caller ID showed that Eve Renner was on the other end of the line.

For the first time all morning, he picked up. "Bentz."

"This is Eve Renner. I just heard the news about Sister Rebecca. He's struck again, hasn't he?"

"I can't discuss the case, Ms. Renner, but I can confirm there's been a homicide."

"The news people have identified the victim as the Mother Superior," Eve went on, and Bentz wondered who had already leaked that information. "I know . . . you know it's the same guy. I want to help. I, uh, found something I think you need to see."

"What?"

"I think you'd better see for yourself."

Bentz didn't like the game-playing. "Okay, where?"

"At the hospital."

"What hospital?" he asked, but he felt a chill run through his blood as he understood.

"Our Lady of Virtues."

"I'm already at the campus."

"Then open the hospital main gate, and I'll be there in half an hour or so."

"Can't you just tell me what this is all about?" Bentz demanded testily.

"It's complicated, and you'll want to see it for yourself."

Her voice was firm, but there was a drip of fear in it. "Believe me, this is important. I also have something you'll want. Something I took from there," she said. "Faith Chastain's medical history."

"What!"

She hung up. Just like that.

"Son of a bitch!"

Montoya had stopped walking. "What the hell was that all about?"

"I don't know," Bentz said, "but I don't like it." He moved out of the way as a couple of guys from the coroner's office hauled a body bag out of the convent. The news crews still stood by, vans and trucks parked along the side of the lane leading toward the convent. Earlier, as he'd examined the cloister, he'd heard the distinctive whoosh of overhead rotors and looked up to spy a news helicopter hovering above, hoping to give the cameraman a better shot of the crime scene.

Bentz realized the newspeople had their place. Hell, sometimes the local stations were instrumental in investigations, posting pictures of wanted criminals or asking the public's help in finding a suspect or a victim. But today he wanted nothing to do with them.

"Give me a second. I need to get something. I'll meet you at the car."

"What?" Montoya called after him, but he didn't turn around, didn't understand why he felt compelled to do Eve Renner's bidding. Maybe it was the sound of desperation, of fear, in her voice. He chided himself as he made his way to the secretary's desk, where a shaken but priggish secretary by the name of Mrs. Miller manned the single telephone. There was a computer on her desk, though most of her notes seemed to have been scribed in perfect cursive by one of the three sharpened pencils that were arranged in a neat row at the edge of her desk blotter.

Wearing a gold cross and an expression that indicated she thought she was guardian to the sanctuary, she wasn't easily persuaded to find the keys to the old hospital, but when Bentz suggested she might be hampering a homicide investigation and that he could arrest her for it, she blanched and punched the buttons on her phone so quickly her fingers were a blur.

Within five minutes a caretaker arrived with the set of keys. Grudgingly, lips pursed, insisting Bentz return the "order's property" promptly, Mrs. Miller dropped the keys into Bentz's outstretched palm.

"Thanks," he said, then jogged back to the cruiser, only pausing long enough to ask one of the deputies to follow in his car. He didn't know what kind of show Eve Renner planned to put on at the hospital, but he figured he might need backup to guard the gates and keep the lookie-loos at bay.

"There's been a leak," he told Montoya as he settled behind the wheel of the cruiser and handed his partner the keys to the asylum. "The person who called was Eve Renner. From listening to the news, she knows that the victim was Rebecca Renault."

"Damn!" Montoya slipped out of his jacket and tossed it into the backseat. "So much for notifying next of kin."

"I think the sheriff's department is taking care of that. Sister Rebecca has a niece in Cambrai."

"I hope she found out before she saw it on the news."

"Me too." Bentz started the engine.

"The sheriff's gonna be pissed."

"He won't be the only one."

Bentz rammed the car into reverse and was about to back up when Montoya said, "Hey, wait. Something's going down."

Bentz hit the brakes as he saw Sister Odine, holding the huge skirts of her habit high, half running toward his car. Several of the officers standing near the door started to follow her, and a cameraman turned his head and caught the running nun on tape.

"Detective," she called, waving frantically, her cheeks flushed. "Please wait!"

Bentz rolled down the window as she approached. "I'm so glad I caught up with you," she said, breathing hard. From the corner of his eye, Bentz saw the camera crew hustling toward the cruiser.

"Get rid of them," he told one of the deputies who had followed Sister Odine to his car. With a nod, the deputy turned toward the news crew and ran interference.

Sister Odine said in a rush, "I just received a call from Sister Jeannette, the Mother Superior at All Saints." Bentz felt his back muscles tighten at the mention of the college Kristi had attended, where once she'd faced unspeakable terror. "She asked me if I'd heard from Sister Vivian . . . Vivian Harmon, who is part of their order?"

"What about her?"

"She's missing."

"For how long?" Bentz asked.

"Reverend Mother didn't say, but . . ." Sister Odine nodded, her head bobbing rapidly. "Her room is empty, and they found a rosary and prayer book in the garden. The Reverend Mother recognized them as both belonging to Sister Viv."

Bentz's gut twisted. He knew the campus well and was all too familiar with the dark terror associated with it. "Did the Reverend Mother call the police?"

"Not yet. They searched the grounds and thought maybe Sister Vivian had gone visiting and neglected to tell anyone, but that's unlike her." Sister Odine's face crumpled a little. "Someone from the college staff told one of the nuns about what happened here, about Sister Rebecca . . . Oh dear." Tears filled her eyes again. "Anyway . . . now the Mother Superior is worried that something . . . something horrible might have happened to Sister Vivian too."

Bentz wanted to reassure the nun, to tell her that Sister Vivian probably was taking a break from the order, that she was second-guessing her vows, that she would show up sometime soon, but he suspected that would be a crock. "Have her call nine-one-one, explain what's going on, and tell her that Detectives Montoya and Bentz will be out to talk to her in a few hours. In the meantime we'll call the Baton Rouge P.D."

"Thank you," she said fervently, far more relieved than she should have been as she made the sign of the cross over her chest. "Bless you, Detectives," she murmured as she bustled off.

Bentz turned the car around and headed down the drive where parked cruisers, vans, and trucks crowded the lane, scarcely allowing access between the tall live oaks and spreading magnolias.

"Hey," Montoya said as they fought through what appeared to bean ever-growing crowd. "Isn't that your kid?" He pointed a finger at the window and the slim girl in a Florida Marlins baseball cap. Again she turned away from the road, engaging another person in the crowd.

Bentz's lips tightened. Theirs had always been a difficult relationship, one that had probably been exacerbated by the lies he'd had to tell her while she was growing up. It had to have been tough on her when she'd finally realized the truth: Bentz wasn't her biological father. Yeah, well, that had been a helluva mess, and in the end, he'd been the one who had stuck by her, especially after Jennifer's death, then during those rough teenage years.

She hadn't had it easy, but that didn't give her the green light to put herself in danger. The fact of the matter was that he couldn't have loved her more had she been his natural child. End of story.

"What's she doing here?" Montoya was frowning darkly, his gaze following Kristi in the sideview mirror as they rolled down the length of the lane.

Bentz grunted. He knew damned well what she was thinking. Not that he'd confide it to anyone, much less Montoya.

A true-crime writer!

Of all the idiotic, half-assed ideas!

Why in God's name would she want to make herself more of a target than she already was as a homicide detective's child?

He didn't have time for it right now, but he planned to engage in another attitude-adjustment talk with her ASAP.

Montoya wisely let the matter drop. "What did Eve Renner want?"

"Us to meet with her. At the hospital."

"What hospital?"

"The one next door."

"Our Lady of Virtues? Why?" Montoya asked.

"She said she was there and found Faith Chastain's file. She wants to give it to us, but there's more. She hung up before she explained." Bentz reached the winding road, saw there was no traffic, gunned the engine.

"This just gets weirder and weirder," Montoya said, flipping down the visor to shield his eyes. "I told you about the picture Abby took of the place."

"Any luck with that?"

"The lab's still working on it."

Bentz turned off the main road and angled the cruiser toward the hospital. A fox squirrel ran onto the road, changed its mind, and darted back to the ditch. Bentz tapped on the brakes. "Idiot," he muttered at the long-disappeared rodent.

Montoya said, "I hope to hell this isn't a wild-goose chase."

Bentz found a pack of gum in his pocket and pulled out a stick as he watched an SUV from the sheriff's office pull up behind them. "Only one way to find out."

Montoya and Bentz were waiting.

Along with a deputy from the sheriff's department.

In front of the open gate to the hospital, the two detectives were leaning against the fender of a cruiser as Eve parked her Camry next to the cop's car. The deputy in the SUV was on the phone but hung up when Eve rolled up.

"This looks like it might turn out to be another gun-fight at the O.K. Corral," she murmured.

"They're just being cautious," Cole assured her.

"If you say so."

The deputy slid out of his SUV as Eve and Cole climbed from her Toyota. Both detectives visibly tensed, Montoya in black shirt, jeans, sunglasses, and his damned leather jacket, Bentz in T-shirt and faded jeans.

Oh great, another pissing match. Just what she needed. Slinging one strap of her backpack over her shoulder, Eve locked her car. The deputy hung a few steps back, eyes on the road.

"Wasn't there a restraining order?" Montoya asked, white teeth flashing as he zeroed in on Cole.

Eve held up one hand. "The restraining order was lifted."

Cole met his gaze squarely. "I'm escorting Ms. Renner."

A dark eyebrow cocked over the rims of Montoya's shades. "You her attorney now?"

One side of Cole's mouth lifted in that self-deprecating grin Eve had found alternately irritating and endearing.

"Last I heard, you were on the other side," Montoya said, his gaze focused on Cole.

"Water under the bridge, Detective," Cole said with a shrug.

"What about last night?" he asked, taking off his sunglasses so he could stare hard at Cole. "Where were you?"

Cole's smile widened. Dear God, he was *enjoying* this! At that moment, Eve wanted to strangle him, and Montoya for good measure. Before Cole could say more than she wanted, Eve said, "He was with me all night. We even spent some time at South General Hospital." She held up her sling. "I fell here, on the third floor in front of Faith Chastain's room."

"Here?" Montoya asked, but his eyes still challenged Cole.

"Yes."

Bentz stepped between the two other men, and the deputy looked back as if waiting for the word to come and assist. "Okay, we've had our fun. Now let's get down to it. So, where's the file?" Eve retrieved the thick folder from her backpack and Bentz took it gingerly, his forehead etching with new lines as he read the file tab. "Anyone else touch this?"

"Not since I found it yesterday. Just us. Both of us."

Annoyed, Montoya slipped on his shades and said, "That makes it easy. We've already got your prints on file."

Cole let that one slide while Bentz grabbed a flashlight and locked Faith Chastain's file in his cruiser.

Pocketing his keys, he asked, "So how did you come to find it in the first place? Where was it?" He glanced at the hospital as if he anticipated the answer.

She gestured toward the top floor as they crossed inside the grounds. "In the attic."

Montoya cocked his head. "Attic?"

"There's a small garret above the third floor. I used to play there as a kid. I came back yesterday because I felt compelled. Because of this whole 'Faith-Chastain-might-be-your-mother thing.' I needed to look around."

Bentz closed the gate behind them and locked it. "Make sure no one gets in," he ordered the deputy, then caught up with Montoya, Cole, and Eve. It was late morning, closing in on noon, and the sun was intense. Even so, Eve felt chilled inside, knowing what they would find inside the huge edifice that had originally been an orphanage and later a full-fledged hospital before eventually ending up as an asylum. The grounds and building had always been owned by the Archdiocese, and now, in its decrepit state, the hospital was slated to be razed.

All for the best, she thought as they walked up the buckled, cracked concrete drive and past an overgrown lawn gone to seed. The drive curved around a once-grand fountain directly in front of the front doors. As a child Eve had been enchanted by the three winged angels spouting water to the heavens. Now the fountain was bone dry and still, the angel statues chipped and stained, Eve's sense of wonder long dead.

"So, how did you get in?" Bentz asked as they walked the perimeter of the building. Her footsteps were still visible in the grass and dirt, but as they rounded a far corner, she noticed that the fire escape that had been lowered the day before was now unreachable, its ladder tucked near the landing on the second floor.

"This isn't the way it was," Eve said in surprise, explaining how she'd used the ladder to gain access to the building through a partially opened window.

"The ladder was down. I used it too," Cole continued as he stared upward to the window. "Now the window's closed too. We didn't shut it."

"You're certain?"

"Absolutely." Eve shaded her eyes as she looked upward at the red bricks and mortar. "Yesterday, when I was looking down from the attic through a hole in the floor, I saw a shadow in Faith's room, one I couldn't explain."

Montoya rubbed the back of his neck. "What hole? What shadow? I don't get it."

"You will," Cole said. "Let's go inside."

They circled the building but found no other open windows. They stopped at the marble steps at the front of the building while Bentz found a key that unlocked the dead bolts on the main doors.

He switched on his flashlight and Montoya and Eve followed suit with their own flashlights. Trepidation was Eve's companion as she once again stepped into the decay and gloom that was the abandoned asylum. Immediately her skin crinkled, raising goose bumps though the temperature inside had to be nearly eighty. The policemen, too, became more somber as they shined their beams over the reception area and hall-ways.

"Your father worked here," Bentz stated. "Did he have an office?"

She pointed in the general direction. "But there's nothing in it. I looked yesterday."

"Show us."

Eve led them to the small area her father had used for his counseling sessions and paperwork. Bentz searched the room while Montoya swept the beam of his flashlight around the small maze of rooms. "He was in office number one?"

"I think it was reserved for the chief psychiatrist."

She pointed out the other rooms: one for examinations, another for accounting, still another for the clergy, and then larger areas for the nursing and housekeeping staffs.

"What about the basement?"

"It was used for alternative treatments."

"Such as?"

"There were operating rooms and padded cells and rooms where electroshock therapy was administered." She met the questions in Bentz's eyes. "Some treatments seem barbaric and demeaning now, but they were widely accepted when the hospital was open." Eve heard a defensive note creep into her voice, but she didn't like even the least little intimation that her father, as head of the hospital psychiatric staff for years, had done anything the least bit inappropriate.

"You intimated there was something else," Bentz said. "A reason we had to come here?"

"In the attic," Eve confirmed, leading the way. She couldn't help glancing away as they passed the stained-glass window of the Madonna at the landing, an intricate piece of craftsmanship that for some reason had sustained no damage over the years.

They trooped silently upward, the steps creaking under their weight. On the third floor they paused briefly at the open door to room 307, illuminating the hideous discoloration on the floor with the beams of their flashlights.

Montoya took one look at the large bloodstain and said something harsh under his breath before turning to Eve. "So the attic? How do you get there?"

"This way." She showed them to the linen closet with its door hidden behind the chimney, unlocked the latch, explaining how she and Roy had played up in the attic as children, that they had a "fort" complete with books and toys.

They climbed the attic stairs single file. At the top she paused, took a deep breath, then told them about the doll.

Bentz couldn't believe his ears. "You pulled me off a murder investigation to look at a mutilated doll?" he said in disbelief.

"And Faith Chastain's file. There are also other patient files in the cabinet up here. I thought they might have information useful in your investigation."

"Legally they're off-limits," he reminded her. He

was irritated. None of this was good. Why had he let himself believe this trip had some merit?

"Where's this doll?" Montoya asked.

"Over in the corner by the window." Ducking under the overhanging rafters, Eve steeled herself as she turned her flashlight toward the spot where yesterday she'd discovered the sleeping bag and doll.

The beam crawled over the ancient floorboards, past an old bookshelf, to the sleeping bag.

But the doll was gone.

And in its place was the half-dressed, bloodied body of a nun.

"My God," Montoya breathed.

Eve stared then let out a keening scream. "No. Oh please God, no!" she wailed, her voice hoarse with desperation as it rose to the rafters of the dusty attic.

Cole was at her side in an instant, his arm around her, his gaze locked on the grisly, brutal scene before him. Clinging to him, Eve couldn't quit staring at the horror of this dark attic. Where once there had been a hideously mutilated doll, there was now a real woman lying in the same position she'd found the Charlotte doll. Facedown, knife wounds on her body, her habit bunched up around her waist, her panties pulled down.

Bentz and Montoya rushed to the woman then paused. Neither of them touched her, as she was clearly dead.

"That bastard knew we were here," Eve said shakily. "He was in Faith's room, I know it. . . . And . . . and he called me, right before you showed up," she said, pressing her cheek to Cole's chest.

"You got a call from him?" Montoya's head snapped her way.

"Yesterday, on my cell . . . yes." She was trembling now, partly out of fury, partly out of sheer terror. "He was taunting me, letting me know that he was watching." Her skin crawled to think he'd been so near.

Her knees threatened to turn to mush, but Cole supported her, holding her tight.

"That's the way the doll was positioned yesterday," Cole told Bentz. "Except that there were red slash marks in felt pen, just like the stab wounds on this woman's body. And the number . . . four hundred and forty-four was marked across the doll's belly. Eve's name was scratched in capital letters a little bit lower, across the doll's lower abdomen."

"Charlotte . . . my doll's hat had been taken off, and her hair had been cut too," Eve added, staring at the nun's nicked and tufted head. Nearby, stained red, lay her wimple, coif, and veil.

Bentz leaned closer to the corpse, his eyes examining the body before he shot a look back at Montoya. "Call this in and tell the guy at the front gate to let no one inside except the police. Shit." He rocked back on his heels, and his Adam's apple worked as he swallowed hard. "Looks like we just found the missing nun."

CHAPTER 24

Bentz stood outside the hospital, his stomach roiling, his thoughts black as night while the sweat rolled beneath the neck of his T-shirt. The sun was high in the sky, its heavy heat merciless, the humidity inching toward a hundred percent. A crime-scene crew had already started processing the scene, and yellow tape was strung around the hospital grounds.

Again.

Two nuns killed, their bodies tattooed and arranged in a posed position.

A signature killer?

Maybe, but some things didn't make sense.

Didn't follow the rules.

Serial killers usually stayed within the bounds of race. They usually chose a gender. There was usually time between the killings.

Usually, usually, usually.

"Our boy's upping his game," Montoya said as he lit the cigarette he'd bummed from one of the uniforms on the scene. "Escalating." He inhaled deeply then breathed out, twin jets of smoke curling from his nostrils.

"It's more than the usual thing, not just some creep getting his rocks off by killing a random woman," Bentz said. "This guy has specific victims."

"And he marks them with specific numbers. Tattoos them, for Christ's sake."

"We need to check all the local dealers of tattooing supplies."

"Already done. Zaroster's on it," Montoya said, hazarding a glance to the roped-off area in front of the gates where Eve Renner in her arm sling and Cole Dennis stood next to her Camry.

Bentz shielded his eyes. The press hadn't been ten minutes behind Montoya's call to the station, and all of the people who'd been fascinated with what had happened at the convent before were now parked outside the hospital. Sickos, every one of them.

Then there were the Feds. Taking charge. Which was fine with Bentz. Let the FBI use its resources and work with local crime enforcement. The Feds added a new perspective, and though a few of the agents rankled him, so what. There were cops in his own department that aggravated the crap out of him as well. "The videographer's taping the crowd, right?"

"Yeah."

"Good." Bentz wanted to make certain that anyone found hanging around every crime scene was identified and investigated. His eyes searched the crowd, looking for someone who just couldn't stay away, who felt compelled to be there. His gaze landed on Kristi. Oh hell! She was talking into a handheld tape player and had obviously blown off work for the day. Hadn't she told him this was the case she was going to use to write her ridiculous true-crime book?

As if she sensed him staring at her, she looked his way. This time she made eye contact and waved.

He tapped his watch, indicating that she should get her butt to work. She shrugged, ignoring his attempt at fatherly advice.

Crap.

Muttering under his breath, Bentz reached into his pocket, found one last antacid, tossed it into his mouth.

"So, what do you think about the missing doll? You buy it?" Montoya asked.

"Why lie?" Bentz countered. "Why take us up to the attic? I don't think they were bullshitting us."

"So where's the doll—Charlotte, isn't that what she called her?"

"Beats me."

"Could be a story, though."

Bentz gave him a look.

"The numbers didn't jibe," Montoya pointed out. "According to Dennis and Renner the doll was supposed to be scribbled on in red ink. 444. But our nun, Sister Viv, she's got 323 tattooed onto her forehead, same as the number written in blood on the wall with her finger. No 444 in sight." He sucked hard on his cigarette again, the tip glowing in the reflection of his sunglasses.

"The doll was supposed to have 'Eve' written on her as well."

"*If* the damned thing existed."

"The missing doll doesn't bother me as much as the missing files."

"Humph." Montoya took a final drag and tossed the

cigarette butt onto the concrete then crushed it with the toe of his boot. They'd discovered no other files in the attic. "Maybe they didn't exist either."

"We've got Faith Chastain's folder. It exists."

"That could have come from anywhere. Maybe Dennis stole it from Terrence Renner's house the night he was killed and just didn't bother to return it with the laptop. Or maybe it was at Eve's place all along. That house was owned by her grandparents, her father's family. Terrence Renner had lived and visited there, maybe not for a while, but the file's twenty years old. Who knows where Eve dug it up. We only know where she *says* she found it."

"Her key fit into the lock of the cabinet."

"The *empty* cabinet. Big deal." Montoya wasn't impressed.

"Dennis and Renner insist it was full the day before."

"So our guy, the doer, besides killing two people and hauling one from Baton Rouge to here, took the time to clean up. Not only did he swipe the doll, he took all the files from the file cabinet. Why? Cuz his name is in the cabinet?"

"Or something connecting the crimes to him."

"Maybe he was hoping to take Faith's file."

"Then why take the others?" Bentz asked.

"You tell me," Montoya said tensely.

"Maybe he couldn't find Faith's," Bentz allowed. "Panicked, figured it might be misfiled and didn't have time to search."

"So he takes everything inside? In what? Boxes? Bags? Who is this guy? Supermover? Where did he park? Close enough to haul those files to his vehicle? Then, after everything else, he takes the time to cover his tracks, close windows, and make sure the ladder's back up on the fire escape? I don't buy it." Montoya ran a hand through his glossy black hair and glared at Cole and Eve. "Besides, I still don't trust Cole Dennis. He may not be the doer this time, but he's holding back. I just know it."

"*She* seems to trust him now." Bentz was watching Cole and Eve. They were deep in a confab, talking, glancing up at the hospital then over at him, waiting for their cue to leave. "I called South General. They were there last night. Together."

"So what's that all about? After being a prime witness in Roy Kajak's death, now she sleeps with Dennis? After being convinced that the son of a bitch nearly killed her?"

Bentz shook his head, swatting at a horsefly that was buzzing near his head. "Don't know, but I think we should find out."

"No shit."

Eve slept for hours.

Cole had brought her back to her house and, over her protests, given her some of the pain medication the ER doctor at South General had prescribed then insisted that she rest. She'd been certain sleep would prove elusive, as her headache had returned and her shoulder had throbbed mercilessly. She was shaken to her core, her mind filled with spinning, disjointed, and terrifying images of a dark red bloodstain, the missing and mutilated doll, and Sister Vivian's posed, bloodied corpse with its hideous tattoo.

She and Cole had talked to the police, including an agent from the FBI, given statements at the station, and tried to come up with every bit of information they possessed. Eve had been asked about her father over and over again, the police intimating that he'd not only had a drinking problem but might have used self-prescribed drugs. They'd asked about her childhood, about Roy and her relationship with him. They'd wanted to know what names she'd seen on the missing files and if she remembered anyone from the list she'd pulled together. Then they'd zeroed in on her sex life, bringing up, once again, the man she couldn't name, the man whose sperm was found swimming in her vagina, a man she'd been with only a few hours after sleeping with Cole.

The interview had been exhausting. She'd been separated from Cole, and he too had been questioned relentlessly, to the point he'd even asked if he needed to call his lawyer.

She'd seen Van and Kyle at the station as well, though she hadn't spoken to them. They too had been questioned.

In the end, when the police had been convinced Eve and Cole had nothing more to tell, they'd been allowed to leave. Eve had taken Cole to pick up his

Jeep. Then they'd reconvened at the house, where Eve's energy had dissipated to zero.

By the time she'd lain down, it was midafternoon; now it was after eight in the evening, and her stomach growled from lack of food, which was a good sign.

She headed downstairs, where the lamps were lit and Cole was seated at the kitchen table, head bent over scads of yellow sheets from a legal pad he'd found somewhere. He glanced up at the sound of her footsteps, and a smile pulled at one corner of his mouth. "Ah, look, Sleeping Beauty has awakened," he said to Samson, the traitor, who was curled happily in his lap.

She caught sight of her reflection in the mirror and shuddered. "Maybe Sleeping Ugly is a better description."

He laughed and pushed back his chair, the cat scrambling to the floor. "Never."

"Close enough," she said ruefully, self-consciously touching her short hair. It was clumped and sticking up at odd angles, and what little mascara she'd once worn on her lashes was smudged beneath her eyes. Her lipstick had long faded, her clothes were wrinkled, and she was still wearing a sling. All in all, she was a mess.

He waved her over and patted his lap. "Sit and take a look. I've been busy while you've been catching up on your . . . *beauty* sleep."

She groaned as she settled onto his lap. One of his arms slipped around her waist.

"This could be dangerous," she said.

"That's the general idea." He pressed a kiss to the back of her neck then pointed to the papers strewn before him. "Just not now. So, here's what I did. . . ."

He explained that he'd made a sheet of information on all of the victims who'd been recently killed, trying to find a common link. Anytime he'd found something he could attribute to another of the victims, he starred the information then listed it on a separate piece of paper including all the victims' names to whom it pertained. "For example, both Sister Rebecca and Sister Vivian were nuns, so they're linked that way, but no one else—that I know of, anyway—is part of the order, so they're the only ones with this in common." He'd made a note on the information paper. "And these people worked at the mental hospital: your father and the two nuns. But not Roy. I know his father worked there, so I did put a question mark by his name, but the link to the hospital is broader, not about employment, or Roy wouldn't be included."

"But everyone's linked in one way or another to the hospital?" Eve asked.

"Yes, but not to Faith Chastain." He drummed his fingers on the edge of the table. "I thought everyone who'd been killed would have some major connection to her, but I can't find it. Roy didn't know her."

"Sure he did. . . . Well, at least peripherally. He wasn't just the son of the caretaker. Later, he spent time there as a patient."

"At the same time Faith was there?"

"I don't know," she admitted.

"For right now, the only total connection is the hospital," he said, tapping his pen on the page. "That's the key. . . . So, what do these numbers mean? 212, where Roy died, 101 at your dad's, 323 on the nun, and 444 on the doll."

"What about the Mother Superior, Sister Rebecca?"

"We don't know yet. We can assume there must have been something written in blood and tattooed on her, but the police have that information." He set his chin on her shoulder and stared at the pages scattered on the table. "Do you have any idea what the numbers mean? Are they part of a social security number? Or some other kind of ID? Or an address? Or maybe a date? February twelfth for 212? January first at your dad's house?"

"Well, that won't work. Look at 444. It's not a two-digit date. There is no forty-fourth month or day. . . . It would have to be years, April 4, 2004, but that won't work because of the 101. No month or day is zero. . . ." She stared at the notes, her head aching again, Cole's breath warm against the back of her neck.

"Maybe the 444 is the one that's off, because it was on a doll, not a real person? That whole thing: Charlotte posed and then the nun in the exact same manner, what's that all about?"

"I don't know." She was glad for the strength of his arm around her waist. "And why did he steal the files?"

404

"Because of something inside that cabinet? Patient records, right? Nothing else?"

"Nothing that I saw, but I didn't have time to go through every drawer or flip through all the files."

"So, what did you see?"

"Let me think. . . ." She remembered some of the names that had jumped out at her. "Enid . . . um, Enid Waller, I mean Walcott. And John Stokes, Ronnie Le Mars and Merlin . . . Oh God, what was his last name? Not Merlin, Mer*win* Anderson and Neva St. James. . . . There were others, but I can't remember."

He wrote down the names. "Do any of these connect with any of the victims?" he asked.

"Aside from being patients at the hospital and all treated by my father?"

"Were any of them close to Faith Chastain?"

She shook her head slowly. "I wouldn't know. I was just a kid for most of it. I wasn't paying much attention. It seems that they were all at the hospital at the same time, but then again, I can't be sure." She exhaled slowly. "I'm sorry. I just don't know."

He kissed her nape. "It's okay, but since we're getting nowhere, how about I take you to dinner?"

"Dinner?" she repeated. It sounded so normal. So welcome. "Yes, please." She glanced out the window and noticed that dusk was starting to creep across the backyard.

Cole pulled her to her feet. "Come on. I know this great little place that serves a mean bowl of dirty rice and mudbugs."

Eve smiled. "How romantic."

"Best I can do," he said, taking her hand. "Let's go."

"I'm just tellin' ya, it's not a smart move to quit your job and start poking around a homicide scene," Bentz said with forced patience, his cell phone plastered to his ear as Kristi tried to come up with every excuse under the sun why she should have "exclusive" access to the ongoing case. "Forget it."

"Dad, listen, please! I won't do anything to hinder the investigation. You have to trust me."

"The answer is 'no,' you got that? I'll call you later." He hung up, fuming. Why was she pushing him on this? Why mess up her job, a good job? Why complicate her life?

Montoya sauntered into the room. "You need to go home and get laid," he said, observing Bentz's utter frustration.

Bentz shot him a look. "Like that's gonna help."

"It always helps me."

"Fine."

"Look, you don't smoke, you don't drink, but you've got one helluva good-lookin' woman waiting for you at home."

Bentz stole a look at the picture of Olivia on his desk. Montoya was right. Petite, with gold curls falling down her shoulders, clear eyes, and a tight little butt . . . "I'm meeting her for dinner in half an hour," Bentz admitted then decided the less Montoya knew abut his love life the better. "You heard the information officer made a statement about the recent killings? He's asking for the public's help."

"Not much they can do. We don't even have a composite of the guy."

"Yeah, well, maybe someone saw something at Our Lady of Virtues or All Saints. Maybe we'll catch a break."

"Maybe," Montoya said, sounding unconvinced. Not that Bentz blamed him.

"What else is happening?"

"No DNA yet, but soon, I'm told."

"I'll believe that when I see it."

"Zaroster has a few leads with the tattoo ink and equipment, but nothing concrete yet. The plaster casts at the crime scene of footprints and tire marks haven't been analyzed completely, but the guess is we're looking for a guy who wears size twelve or twelve and a half."

"Big guy," Bentz said.

"So it would seem."

"What about Abby's picture?"

"Nothing yet, and again no one at either convent or the college noticed anything out of the ordinary."

"Two nuns killed and it's business as usual?" Bentz scowled and twisted a pencil in his fingers.

"We're not done yet," Montoya said, but he was irritated and anxious as well. "I'm still trying to put together a roster of the people who worked at the hospital when Faith was there, but the records, hell, they're obsolete."

"The state must know, or the Feds. Tax records."

"FBI's supposed to be on it. So, did you meet with Eve Renner's brothers?"

"Both of 'em."

"And?"

Bentz leaned back in his chair. "I think Eve's lucky she only has two. They were here to try and get the body released, so they can, let's see"—he found his notes—"'get on with our lives,' which I take as Renner-speak for they can't wait to get their hands on whatever Daddy left them."

"You think they could have killed him?" Montoya asked.

"Anything's possible. I'm waiting to see who inherits. There's got to be a will, and we're already checking into life insurance benefits. Neither brother has an alibi. Seems as if they were both out driving around about the time dead old dad had his throat slit. Kyle claims he was on his way here from Atlanta, and Van says he was driving from Arizona. I figure we might get credit-card receipts to bear their stories out."

"Or prove them wrong."

"Kyle, he's big. I'd guess the size twelve shoes would be about right, but the other guy is smaller in stature."

"So what reason would either of them have to kill the nuns?"

"What reason would anyone?" Bentz pushed himself closer to the desk again, studying his notes.

"What you got there?" Montoya asked, nodding at Bentz's desk.

"Just me trying to sort things out. Those are their tattoos."

Montoya spun the paper around and read Bentz's block letters.

FAITH CHASTAIN	LIVE
ROYAL KAJAK	212
TERRENCE RENNER	101
REBECCA RENAULT	111
VIVIAN HARMON	323
DOLL???	444

"So, what do you make of it?" Montoya said.

"First off, I'm not certain whoever tattooed Faith Chastain is our killer. Her tattoo was a word, not a number. And we can't really count the doll. We're not even certain it exists. But there's something weird about the numbers."

"Which is?"

"They read the same way backward as forward."

"So?" Montoya said, his forehead wrinkling.

"Well, it doesn't mean too much, but when you read the tattoo on Faith Chastain's head backward, what do you get?"

Montoya looked at the letters, and his cocky smile faded. "Evil."

Bentz dropped his notes on the desk as he stood.

"Jesus." Montoya's eyes narrowed. "Okay . . . but so

what? Maybe it's just a coincidence. I mean, Faith was tattooed over two decades ago."

"Thought you didn't believe in coincidence."

"I don't, but . . ."

"It's just a thought. Means nothing."

"It means enough for you to bring it up." Montoya rested a hip against Bentz's desk, apparently waiting for an explanation.

"It's just something to explore," Bentz said, but he felt that he was on the edge of something. Something that might be important. He just hadn't sorted it out, wasn't sure what it was quite yet. Throwing his pencil on the desk, he said, "I've got to run."

"I'm thinking you're gonna get lucky tonight." Montoya's grin was absolutely wicked.

"I'm always lucky."

"An old fat guy like you? Huh."

Bentz laughed despite himself. With Montoya in tow, he snapped out the lights and tried to shake off the feeling that he was missing something major about Faith Chastain. There was a reason she'd been tattooed twenty-odd years ago. He just had to figure out what it was.

CHAPTER 25

"This is where you live?" Eve looked around the small camelback house wedged tightly onto a poorly lit street. To say it needed work would be the understatement of the year, and when compared to the roomy Italianate home Cole had once owned, it was a dump. Pure and simple. Barely more than a roof over his head.

"I've really come up in the world," Cole said with a quick smile. He'd stopped by his place, grabbed a quick shower, a bag of clothes and personal items on the way to the restaurant. It was odd, really; in all the time that they'd talked about marriage, they'd never lived together, just stayed overnight at each other's places. But now, it seemed, Cole was moving in, at least for the time being, and it seemed like the right course of action.

Quite a turnaround from just a few days ago when you still thought him capable of murder.

"All set?" Cole walked out of the bedroom dressed in a pair of khakis and an open-collared dress shirt with the sleeves rolled up. "My wardrobe's pretty limited," he admitted when he noticed her eyeing him. "I think I have a ton of suits somewhere, but I'm not sure. Deeds could have sold them too. He certainly didn't leave me with a key to any storage unit, so . . ." He spread his arms wide and shrugged. "What you see is what you get."

"And I like," she admitted, walking into his open arms and kissing him soundly.

"Careful, darlin', you keep this up and we'll never get to those mudbugs."

"Can't miss that." She kissed him again, took his hand, and led him outside to the narrow little driveway where his Jeep was parked. There were kids hanging out, plugged into iPods and practicing jumps on their skateboards, an older man smoking on the stoop of an apartment building, and a couple of men in their twenties working on a car in a garage a couple of doors down the street.

On the corner of the next block, a sizzling sign for the local bar glowed neon green in the night. Farther south, past cross streets and old buildings, was the waterfront, where the Mississippi slowly moved toward the Gulf of Mexico. The night was clear, and somewhere above the streetlights there were stars, but Eve couldn't catch a glimpse of many as she climbed into Cole's Jeep and he drove her into the French Quarter. He located a parking spot three blocks from Chez Michelle then walked her inside, where the cozy wood-paneled interior was packed with patrons. The scents of tomato sauce, cayenne pepper, and sassafras made her mouth water the minute she walked through the door.

A thin, friendly waitress led them past an open kitchen where chefs in white coats worked their craft, braising meat, broiling fish and sausage, and creating sauces.

At a private table tucked in a back corner, Cole ordered the special mudbug appetizer and a pitcher of beer. "You'll love them, I promise," he said over the buzz of conversation and strains of jazz piped in from hidden speakers.

"You don't scare me, Counselor. I grew up on crawdads."

"Did you, now?" he said, a bit of the devil in his eyes. Oh, it was so easy to fall back into this routine with him, and despite the holes in her memory, she remembered clearly how much she'd loved him.

Frosty mugs of beer and a bucket of bright red, spicy mudbugs were served, and they both dug in, cracking the shells of the crayfish and dipping the tails into a succulent hot-pepper sauce. Eve ordered a spicy gumbo filled with seafood, sausage, and okra, while Cole chose the signature jambalaya.

For the first time all day, Eve relaxed, and the headache she'd been fighting for weeks retreated. She and Cole talked about inconsequential things, neither wanting to tread too close to the brutal murders, his life in prison, or the complicated layers of their relationship.

For now, they were able to push the rest of the world and the nightmare surrounding them into the darkest corners of the night. She wondered where they'd be now. What twists and turns would their love affair have taken if that one night had been different?

What if Roy hadn't called her?

What if she hadn't gone?

What if she hadn't been so certain that Cole had been there, pistol in hand?

Roy's throat had been slit, no bullet in his body, and yet she'd been shot from a handgun as yet unlocated.

". . . so I'm hoping to move out of the dive as soon as I get back on my feet again," he was saying, his blue eyes fixed on her in a way that made her shift in her chair.

"And move where?"

"Does it matter?"

"Maybe." She smiled up at him and knew she was flirting. *Don't do this, Eve. Don't be suckered in. . . . It's too soon. Too many horrible, unexplained things are still happening.*

He winked at her, and she melted inside. "We'll see."

They lingered over coffee and split a dessert of espresso-flavored crème brûlée and pralines.

He paid for the meal with cash. Then they walked into the balmy night. Cole linked his fingers with hers as they crossed the street. "So, what do ya think?" he asked, heading toward his Jeep.

"About what?"

"Everything that's going on."

"Do we have to think about it?" she asked, hating the lighthearted spirit of the night to end.

"We don't have much choice," he said, and the words were barely out of his mouth when her cell phone rang. She looked at the caller-ID screen and didn't bother answering it. "Television station," she said, groaning. "I don't want to talk to them."

"Then don't."

He unlocked the door, and, just before she slid into the passenger side, she felt a little tremor in the air, as if someone were staring at her, sending her bad vibes. She paused and glanced down the street.

"What?" Cole twisted his head, picking up her unease. "You see something?"

Shaking her head, she said, "No. Just a weird day. Too many awful things going on."

He slammed the door shut, and she kept her eyes on the sideview mirror, observing the sidewalk illuminated by streetlights.

She heard the clop-clop of hooves as a mule-drawn carriage creaked by.

A shadow appeared in the mirror.

Eve froze.

A tall, dark figure stepped out of the gloom for an instant.

She twisted in her seat, but as she stared at the circle of light from the streetlamp, a van rolled across the intersection, blocking her line of vision for second. In that heartbeat, the shadowy figure disappeared. She saw nothing.

"Something is wrong," Cole said tensely as he slid into the Jeep.

"I thought I saw someone staring at me, but I could be wrong."

"Let's check it out."

He pulled out of the parking lot, negotiated a U-turn, then drove through the narrow streets, where knots of people strolled amid slow-moving traffic. Eve's eyes scanned each intersection, alley, and street, but no one seemed out of place.

"I guess I was imagining it."

"I doubt it." Cole turned down a side street. "You're not prone to invention and paranoia."

"Except at Roy's cabin?" she asked.

He tensed as he nosed his Jeep around a corner. "You have to trust that I would never do anything to hurt you, Eve. Not that night. Not ever."

"So I just imagined you there." It was a statement of fact, not a question.

He slid her a glance and touched her leg as he shifted. "It was a strange night."

"Can't argue with that," she said, still unsettled.

Her cell phone rang again, and she checked the display. This time caller ID indicated only that the call was restricted. "Maybe the reporter's cell," she said and turned the phone off. "Whatever it is, I'm not dealing with it now."

But the damage was done.

Between the phone calls and Eve's thinking someone was watching them, they were back where they'd started. The few hours of breaking away from the nightmare were over, and the real world had intruded once again.

In silence, Cole headed to the Garden District, a place Eve had always loved. Tall, ornate houses and gardens were tended and well kept, the history of each building as lush as the surrounding grounds.

But tonight she noticed the vaults and headstones of a cemetery as they passed. In the dark the tombs seemed ominous, a reminder of the death that was stalking the city. As they turned onto St. Charles Avenue, even the castlelike universities of Loyola and Tulane appeared sinister and dark, malevolent fortresses that could surely house evil.

Stop it, she told herself. Hadn't Cole just said she wasn't prone to paranoia? Although she tried to tamp down the bad feeling that had crept over her, as Cole turned a final corner and Nana's house came into view, even the familiar sight of the broad front porch, tall, shuttered windows, and curved turret couldn't temper her unease.

Cole parked near the garage, and as Eve opened the Jeep's door she spied a shadow dart across the yard. "Samson?" she called as the cat climbed up the back steps and paced on the mat by the door. "How'd you get out?" She picked the cat up with her good hand and held him to her as Cole unlocked the door. "You're so much trouble, but I love you anyway."

"Nice to know," Cole said, opening the door and letting her step into the mudroom first.

"I was talking to the cat."

"Uh-huh."

As if he didn't like being in the middle of their discussion, Samson wriggled out of her arms, hopped to the floor, and shot through the open door to the kitchen.

"There was a time you said something like that to me," Cole reminded her.

Her heart clutched, and she had a fleeting memory of riding horses across a flat expanse of field at her father's house. It was after her father's trial, after he'd been acquitted of any wrongdoing. It was a glorious spring day, just before sunset. She and Cole had bet on whose horse was faster then raced back toward the barn. She'd been on the swifter little mare, but Cole had convinced his horse to jump a downed tree and somehow ended up at the barn a stride ahead of her. Still breathless, he'd claimed victory. She'd accused him of cheating, and he'd climbed off his horse, pulled her from the mare and, before her booted feet had hit the ground, kissed her so hard she'd scarcely been able to stand.

"It's time you paid up, Eve, or I might just have to take the winnings out of your hide."

"Promises, promises," she laughed, goading him.

"Is that a dare?" Eyes as blue as a west Texas sky had sparked, and beneath a day's worth of stubble, one side of his mouth had lifted a bit.

"Take it whatever way you want!"

"Dangerous talk, lady."

"Oh yeah, like you scare me."

"I should."

She'd laughed as he'd kissed her again. Hard. And when he'd finally lifted his head, she'd held his face in her hands. "You are *so* much trouble, Cole Dennis, but, damn it, I love you anyway. . . ."

Now he was staring at her with those same blue eyes, the same laser-sharp intensity that caused her stupid heart to pound. She tried to talk, but for a second her voice refused to work, and she had to clear her throat. "Let's just not go there, not tonight."

"When?"

"I don't know."

"I love you, Eve."

There it was. Hanging in the air between them, and all flirtatiousness, all signs of playfulness that had been with them through the night, were suddenly dispelled. Here, in this dimly lit room off the porch, Cole Dennis had bared his soul, and as she looked into his face, she saw that he was raw. Naked. His feelings exposed.

She swallowed back an impulse to blurt out her own feelings.

Cole's jaw was working, his hands at his sides. He was waiting for her to respond. To say what was lodged so deeply in her heart.

Tell him. Tell him you love him, that you've always loved him, that you've known all along that he couldn't have raised a gun at you. That you were wrong. That you are sorry for all the pain you caused him. Tell him, Eve.

The words stuck in her throat. How long had she ached to hear that he still loved her?

"We should be careful," she said, her own words

rushing through her head. *You love him. You do. Tell him. For God's sake, Eve, don't blow this!*

She had loved him. There was no use denying what was so patently obvious. There was a chance she still loved him, had never really stopped.

He touched her on the side of the face. "Take your time, Eve," he said, and she had to fight not to fall against him. "I'm not going anywhere."

His finger slid along the side of her throat then lower, hooking on the neckline of her blouse, his skin warm against hers. Leaning forward, his lips a hair's breadth over hers, he whispered, "I'll wait."

Oh dear God.

Tears, unbidden, touched the back of her eyes, but she refused to cry in front of him. Would not break down. Her skin tingled where he touched her, and she had thoughts of wrapping her arms around his neck and then stripping off his clothes. In her mind's eye, she saw them together, kissing, touching, sweat-soaked, naked bodies entangled in the sheets of her bed. Would it be so wrong? Would it?

Grabbing his hand, she wrapped her fingers around his. "I think we should take this slow," she said carefully.

"I'm not sure there's any 'slow' with you."

"Cole . . ."

"Stop fighting me," he said urgently.

Eve gazed at him. She wanted him. She tried hard to remember that she shouldn't have him, but all she could see was Cole, the man she loved. "Okay," she said on a shaky laugh.

Her sudden capitulation surprised and delighted him. He kissed her hard then grinned. "I'll go get my things. Meet you upstairs."

She turned and nearly ran through the kitchen, along the hall, and up the stairs, the cat following close behind. Was she crazy? Out of her mind? All she could think about was making love to him. Should she strip and lie naked in the bed?

Or put on a sexy piece of lingerie? Dear God, did she even own a teddy or flimsy nightgown? Surely she had something. . . . Not that he would care.

Samson shot ahead of her, bounding up the final flight to her turret room. Downstairs, she heard Cole reenter the house. She'd have to work fast if she wanted to surprise him with a sexy piece of lingerie.

This was nuts! But wonderful.

She was up the remaining flight in an instant. Heart pounding, gasping for breath, she pushed open the door to her bedroom, crossed the dark room, and snapped on the bedside lamp.

Then she saw the doll.

In the wash of warm light, Charlotte was posed in the same position as she had been at the old hospital: facedown, half dressed, red slashes marring her stuffed body, lying in the middle of Eve's bed.

But this time there was blood everywhere. And there was a message in blood on the wall. For her.

A strangled scream ripped from her throat. Loud and long, it echoed her terror through the house.

CHAPTER 26

The scream ricocheted down the stairs.
Eve!

Cole dropped his bag, bolted through the house, and took the steps two at a time, nearly tripping on the damned cat that was streaking down as he ran up. He reached the turret room just as Eve was backing out of it. Her hands covered her mouth. She turned to face him, her eyes round with terror. Without thinking, he grabbed her, held her tight, and peered into the room.

"Oh God, oh God, oh God," she moaned. Then he noticed it, the words scrawled in blood on the wall near the baseboard: DENNIS SINNED. In block letters, bold and dripping. His stomach clenched, and revulsion forced him to step back as he recognized the mutilated doll and what appeared to be blood drenching the bed and dripping onto the floor. Bile burned up his throat.

He couldn't pull Eve down the stairs fast enough.

"How?" she whispered. "Who?" She was trembling in his arms. "Why would anyone . . ."

"Someone who's seriously deranged," he said.
Dennis sinned.
Someone knew.

"Come on." He hustled her into the kitchen then handed her a butcher knife. "I don't think anyone's still here, but I'm going to check. Where's the gun, the one you pointed at me?"

"The revolver . . . Uh, I put it back in my grandfather's desk in the den," she said vaguely. Then, with more awareness, "But it's not loaded. I don't think we have any bullets."

"That's probably a good thing. What about a rifle or shotgun?"

"No. Nana sold them a long time ago."

So all he had to worry about was whatever weapon the psycho brought with him. If the madman was still around. "Okay. Now"—he grabbed the handheld receiver, quickly dialed 911, then handed the phone to Eve—"have them send someone out and have them locate either Montoya or Bentz. Can you do that?"

She nodded, but he wasn't convinced.

"You're sure?"

"Yes." She held the phone in one hand, still clutching the butcher knife in the other.

"I'll search this floor first then go upstairs."

"I'm coming with you," she said.

"No, Eve, stay here and—"

"This is Eve Renner," she said into the phone, then rattled off her address, begging Cole with her eyes to stay put until she was finished. "I'd like to report a . . . a break-in. . . . No, I don't know if anything was taken, but the person left me a sick message of some kind, a doll soaked in blood and . . . and . . ." She glanced up at Cole but couldn't force the words of the damning message over her tongue. "Please have Detective Montoya or Bentz call me. . . . Yes. . . . No, I'll wait here. . . . No, I'm not alone. I'll be safe." She hung up,

423

and, clutching Cole's hand in one of hers and the knife in the other, joined him in searching the main floor. Nothing was out of place. With trepidation they mounted the steps to the second floor, but it too was empty. Undisturbed. The unloaded revolver was where Eve had hidden it in the desk drawer.

Only the turret bedroom had been bloodied and scarred.

Cole's thoughts raced. What kind of fiend was hell-bent on frightening Eve? On using his name? With mind-chilling certainty, Cole realized these murders were more than a killer looking for prey. Whoever was behind this had a fixation with Eve. She was his ultimate target. Someone wanted to terrorize her. And they didn't like him being close to her. . . . Why else write his name in blood, for Christ's sake? All the murders, starting with Roy Kajak's, were because of this madman's fascination and ultimate need to control the woman Cole loved.

And that scared him to death.

Eve was still staring at the bed as he propelled her into the closet. "Pack a bag. We're not staying here tonight. There was no forced entry, Eve," he added as he found an overnight bag and handed it to her. "Someone has a key to your place."

"No one does," she argued, opening an overnight case.

"Wrong. I have a key, remember?" Cole pointed out. "You gave it to me when we were talking about marriage."

She nodded.

"Does one of your neighbors have one too? To check on the place when you're out of town? What about your brothers? You never changed the locks when you moved in, did you?"

"No, it was Nana's house."

"And who did Nana trust with her keys? A house-keeper? Maybe a gardener? Her best friend?" He pulled a couple of shirts off hangers and dropped them into the open overnight case.

"I don't know."

"Exactly. Come on. Pack. The police won't like it that we were messing around in here, but they can just deal."

She glanced at the bed one last time then tossed in underwear, a pair of jeans, and two pullovers. "This is insane," she whispered under her breath, and he agreed as they headed to the bathroom, where she scooped up a makeup kit.

Cole grabbed Eve's laptop on the way out, and they were heading out the door when they heard the first sirens screaming in the distance.

For the first time in a long, long while, Cole Dennis felt relief that the police were on their way.

Montoya snapped his cell phone shut then clicked off the television. "Gotta go," he told Abby as he found his wallet, sidearm, and badge.

"Where?"

"Trouble at Eve Renner's."

425

Abby's head jerked up. "Is she all right?"

"I think so, but I'm not sure." He scooped up his keys. "Doesn't sound like anyone's seriously hurt. I'll find out when I get there."

"I'm coming with you," she declared as she grabbed her purse.

"No way in hell. This is police business."

"And she might be my sister."

" 'Might' being the operative word." He was already halfway to the door. "I don't know what's going on over there, but you're *not* coming with me." He shot her a stern look, his dark eyes serious.

"You can't stop me."

"Sure I can. Don't interfere, Abs."

"I'm coming, damn it."

"Oh for the love of God, I don't have time for this. Stay. I'll call you."

She looked like she wanted to fight further but just gestured for him to go.

Montoya flew out the door, and Hershey whined after him.

"I know," Abby told the dog determinedly as she petted the animal's broad head. "Don't worry. We're going too, just not with him."

She waited until Montoya had roared off. Once his taillights had disappeared around the corner three blocks away, she whistled to Hershey and headed outside. As Hershey bounded onto the porch, she locked the door behind her and cut across the grass to her Honda. "Come on," she said, unlocking the hatchback.

The dog jumped into the backseat, and Abby sped away. She knew that Eve lived in the Garden District, and in a matter of minutes she was driving along St. Charles Avenue, then cutting past stately old manors until she saw the flashing lights of police cars in front of a grand Victorian complete with turret. Reuben's Mustang was double-parked nearby. This had to be it. Curious neighbors wearing pajamas, or shorts and T-shirts, had already wandered onto their porches or huddled together on the curb. Somewhere down the street a dog barked, and Hershey gave up an answering *woof.*

"Shh. Be good," Abby warned. "I'm gonna be in enough trouble as it is."

She parked a block away. Then, leaving the windows cracked, she locked the car and jogged to the Renner house. There were people clustered around outside. One officer was roping off the area, another taking names of anyone who tried to cross. A van with crime-scene techs had arrived, and just turning down the street was the first news van on the scene.

Abby approached from behind the garage, away from the porch, where Montoya was talking with Bentz, Cole Dennis, and Eve Renner, who stood surprisingly close to the man she'd once accused of trying to kill her. Abby had seen pictures of Eve, of course, and had even jokingly said to her sister, Zoey, that Eve could have been a member of their family, but it had been a passing thought. She'd also seen pictures of Eve in the newspapers and in sound bites on the television when Roy Kajak's murder had been front-page news, but not until now, seeing Eve in the glow of the porch light, watching her talk with Montoya, did she get it. In the semidark, Eve looked so much like Faith Chastain it was downright spooky.

She must've been blind not to see it earlier.

Before Montoya looked her way, she pulled her cell phone from a pocket of her purse and speed-dialed her sister in Seattle.

Zoey answered on the third ring. "Hey, hi!" she said, recognizing Abby's number. "What's up?"

"I'm at a crime scene, and I'm looking at her now."

"Crime scene?"

"I think everything's cool. I don't know what's happened yet, but I'll let you know when I find out."

"Like I would care? Wait a sec. *Who* are you looking at?"

"Eve Renner, and I gotta tell you, Zoey, if Eve isn't our sister, she should be. She's the spitting image of Mom."

"I thought that was your claim to fame. Everyone used to say you looked so much like her it was eerie. You were crowned with that particular honor."

Abby was still staring at Eve. "I think I just lost my tiara."

"Really?"

"A definite resemblance, Zoey. Definite."

"But no DNA test results back, right?"

"Not yet."

428

"If she is our sister, this is going to be really, really weird. Does Dad know yet?"

Abby thought of her father, Jacques, wasting away in an assisted-care facility, battling cancer and emphysema, and Charlene, his second wife, who was a basket case from trying and failing to care for her once-robust husband. "I don't think we should tell him until we know for sure. Same with Charlene. She'll spin out of control and could end up in the care facility with him."

Zoey snorted. "It'll never happen. But agreed. Let's keep this to ourselves until the DNA comes back." There was a pause. "So . . . does this woman—Eve?— does she look anything like Dad?"

Abby studied Eve's features—high cheekbones, small, straight nose, short, curly reddish hair. Then she imagined her father's face and build. "No," she said with a certainty that made her stomach twist. "Not a thing."

"Dear God," Zoey whispered. "You don't think . . . I mean, is there a chance that she could have been fathered by *him?*"

Abby shivered, her mind winding down a dark chasm of memories. Faith Chastain had not been faithful to their father, either by design, because of her frail mind, or because she was forced to do abominable acts while a patient at Our Lady of Virtues. No one knew for certain what abuse she had suffered.

"Let's not go there," Abby said into the phone.

"But what if she's our *half* sister and that sick, twisted psycho is her father. What then?"

"Zoey! Shhh! Let's not borrow trouble!"

"Okay, fine. Then you tell her she's the daughter of a psychotic killer."

"We don't know that for sure."

"Well, brace yourself. I have a feeling our odd little dysfunctional family is about to get a helluva lot odder and, if possible, even more dysfunctional."

"I think I'm going to talk to her."

"Go for it. And while you're there, give my love to Sis, would ya?"

Abby ignored Zoey's sarcasm as she hung up. It was now or never. Too bad it was a crime scene. She had to know. Had to. Steeling herself, she walked up boldly and found Montoya still talking to Eve and the man next to her, a man Abby had caught glimpses of on newscasts and in the local paper, the "scumbag" Montoya had tried like hell to convict for Royal Kajak's murder. Abby knew all about Cole Dennis. At least all the bad stuff.

Montoya must've seen her in his peripheral vision because he turned suddenly and, if looks could actually kill, Abby would have been six feet under from that one, black glare. "Excuse me," she said boldly and stuck out her hand. "You must be Eve Renner. I'm Abby Chastain."

The Reviver watched from the shadows.

As close as he dared.

The police were filming; he saw their cameras clicking off pictures of anyone who stepped a little too close to the crime scene. He had to be careful. There were still traces of blood on his clothes and in his truck. He couldn't risk getting caught. Not when there was more work to do.

He saw her in the porch light.

Small, beautiful, standing close to Cole Dennis as another woman approached, someone he couldn't recognize, as her back was to him. But it didn't matter. All he cared about was Eve.

Only Eve.

His back teeth ground together as he saw her shake the woman's hand then familiarly touch Dennis's arm and whisper in his ear. Dennis responded by placing a comforting arm over her shoulder and pulling her even closer against him.

His insides twisted at the display of affection.

In front of the cop.

In front of *him*.

In front of God.

He waited, half expecting the Voice to come to him, to note the blasphemy, to instruct the Reviver on how to deal with the situation. *Please*, he silently begged. *Let me kill him first and then Eve . . . when the time is right.*

He didn't dare pray for a few minutes alone with her, for the time to do what he wanted with her, to force her to kiss him, stroke him, lick him as he suspected she licked Cole Dennis. Oh, he'd known they were rutting, had seen the light in the tower room and *smelled* the scent of their dirty, vile sex. It had floated to him on a breeze, over the fragrances of freshly mown grass and magnolia blossoms. He imagined how it was between them and let his mind wander.

It was Dennis who tempted her.

Dennis who enticed her into sinning.

Dennis who tore off her clothes, exposing those perfect breasts with nipples that needed to be suckled. Dennis who brazenly poked and prodded her sex, burying his face in the dark curls at the juncture of her legs. Dennis who tasted her, nipped at her, bit her, then mounted her roughly, driving hard into her until she gasped in fear and revulsion, joining with her in a frenzied passion spawned by Lucifer, one that she no doubt regretted and feared.

The act was not only a rape of her body but a rape of her soul.

God would never have blessed so base a union.

Because of Dennis, Eve was a jezebel. A whore. A slut. There was no love in their sex act, only lust.

With the Reviver, the lovemaking would be pure. Ordained by God. A way of salvation for Eve before she paid the ultimate price for her sins and faced the Father herself.

Give her to me, he thought wildly, for the moment forgetting that he was close to the crime scene, that he was taking a chance by lingering. *Please, please, please, give her to me. Tonight. Oh, it had to be soon!* The Reviver ached for her so badly. His cock was rock hard as he just stared down the road and fantasized about her body. . . . If God would only talk to him now!

But the Voice only reached him when he was in his cabin, lying upon his bed, thinking of Eve. No other time did any of the voices fill his mind. Even the little nasty voices; they came to him only at night, interrupting his sleep, gnawing at his brain. So God wouldn't answer him now. And yet he prayed. *Please, Father,* he silently begged, making a quick sign of the cross over his chest. *Speak to me, tell me what You want. I am Your servant, and I want to do Your bidding, but I need to know what it is You want of me—*

"Hey, ya got a light?" a voice boomed beside him, and he jumped, looking up sharply to find a man standing next to him. So caught up in his fantasy and prayers, he hadn't heard anyone approach.

His heart pounded and instant sweat soaked his body as he tried to find his voice. He willed his cock to relax. The man, a Latino who looked to be in his midthirties, a cigarette stuck in the corner of his mouth, didn't appear to notice as he waited for a response.

The blood! This idiot of a neighbor will notice the blood! Leave, now!

Shaking his head, the Reviver backed away. He could not be seen. Did not want to use his voice.

"I wonder what went on down there?" the guy said, then turned to another man who was walking quickly toward them.

The Reviver nearly pissed his pants as he realized the person approaching was a cop. In full uniform. Staring straight at him and the Latino neighbor. Big, black, and bold, the policeman approached.

"Hey, gotta light, man?" the stupid neighbor asked the uniform.

Quick as lightning, before the cop could get a good look at his face, the Reviver ducked through a hedge then moved swiftly across a shadowed lawn. He didn't check to see if either man was following him, the cop or the would-be smoker. He just moved rapidly and quietly, circumventing the Renner house, cutting through yards and alleys, winding his way to the parking lot of a restaurant where he'd left his truck.

He was breathing hard as he reached the edge of the lot, nervous sweat nearly drowning him. He smelled the metallic odor of blood on his clothes and mentally chided himself for being so reckless.

He cast a glance over his shoulder and saw a movement in the shrubbery skirting the lot. The cop, athletic as hell, was on his tail.

No! He hadn't come this far to lose it all.

He sprinted to his truck and heard a sharp "Hey!" as he climbed behind the wheel and reached under the seat for his Glock.

It was too late to bluff his way out of this one; the cop would probably get his license plate if he tried. He rolled down the window, and, as the cop approached, he looked outside, his hand on his gun. Easily he clicked off the safety. "Is there a problem,

Officer?" he said through the open window.

"Just get out of the truck. Real slow." The cop's sidearm was drawn, barrel aimed at the open window. He had a microphone strapped to his shoulder, and his nametag read Officer L.J. Tiggs. It was only a matter of seconds before Tiggs would call for backup, if he hadn't already. "And show me your hands," the policeman ordered, his tone brooking no argument. "Keep 'em up. High."

The Reviver moved as if he planned to do as he was ordered. In a millisecond he raised his left hand then jerked up his right arm and fired point-blank at Tiggs.

Blam!

The cop went down in a heap.

CHAPTER 27

"Excuse me, you must be Eve Renner. I'm Abby Chastain."

Eve, standing next to Cole, turned her head to spy an athletic-looking woman somewhere in her thirties approaching, hand extended.

So this is the woman who might be my sister, the woman who's engaged to Detective Montoya, Eve thought, trying to shake off the absolute terror that wanted to keep her in its sharp talons.

"Nice to meet you," she said lamely, as nothing else came to mind. They shook hands, and the movement reminded her that her arm was still in a sling.

The woman, Abby, was beautiful, and yes, Eve

thought, there might be a resemblance. She couldn't help staring then quickly dropped her hand and forced her gaze back to Montoya, who was glaring at his fiancée as if he wanted to wring her neck.

"This is a crime scene," he said to her.

"I know, but I wanted to meet Eve." Abby managed a cool smile for Montoya. Then her gaze returned to Eve. "I know there's a chance that we might be related . . . sisters. I knew it would be awkward, so I wanted to break the ice."

"In the middle of an investigation," Montoya reminded her through lips that barely moved.

"I got it," she said. "You want me to leave." To Eve, she added, "I've got to go, but if you ever want to talk to me, have coffee or a glass of wine, just give me a call." She reached into her purse, grabbed her wallet, and slid out a card. "This has my business and cell number on it."

"Thanks," Eve said.

Montoya was seething, his jaw rigid as steel.

Abby blew him a kiss. "See ya later, honey." And then she was gone, walking swiftly up the street.

Muttering oaths about hardheaded women under his breath, Montoya watched her leave, his gaze lingering for half a beat on her butt. "Sorry," he said. "I guess we were about done anyway."

"So we can go now?" Cole, too, was watching Abby leave. But he drew his gaze back to Montoya. "Eve's not staying here another night. Not until the locks are changed."

436

"Good idea," Montoya said grudgingly. "Let me know if you can think of anyone who might have written that note, someone who's out to get you."

Cole didn't flinch.

Montoya guessed the jerk was thinking his biggest enemies were on the force. Well, truth to tell, Cole Dennis probably wasn't too far off base.

"I'll call if I think of anything."

Yeah, right, Montoya thought, checking his watch. Where the hell was Bentz? When the call to the Renner place came in, Montoya phoned him first, and Bentz said he was on his way. If that son of a bitch was taking time to get himself laid as Montoya had suggested, he'd wring the guy's thick neck himself. But then, that wasn't like Bentz. Reaching for his cell phone again—

Pop!

Montoya stiffened. He motioned to another officer standing by the porch. "Was that a gunshot?"

"I think so."

Cole, walking toward his Jeep, whipped around, facing the direction from which the sharp report had come.

Pop!

"Shit!" Montoya grabbed for his weapon, knowing that something bad had just gone down. He met the prick lawyer's gaze. "Yeah, go. You can leave. For now." And then he was on the move, reaching for his radio, talking in short bursts. "Detective Reuben Montoya," he said, giving his badge number. "Gunshots.

Somewhere off St. Charles." He rattled off Eve's address. "I don't know . . . checking now. Send backup!"

"Where's Tiggs?" one of the uniformed cops asked.

"He was going to talk to the neighbors. . . ." Montoya's eyes moved up the street, where he'd seen Tiggs heading less than ten minutes earlier. All of the neighbors were looking toward the sound of the gunshots, but there was no evidence of a uniform among them.

Fuck!

He jogged to his car. His radio crackled, and the dispatcher's voice confirmed what he'd already feared. "Officer down!"

Yelling at a patrolman to secure the scene, Montoya listened as the dispatcher spat out the address of the shooting.

Less than three blocks away in a restaurant parking lot.

Jesus Christ, this was getting worse by the second.

He was shaking inside.

Worried.

His guts twisting, mind in a panic, he drove out of the city limits, always checking his rearview mirror, never completely certain he wasn't being followed. He charged out in the wrong direction, doubled back, then did the same thing again, crossing the river four times before he finally headed in the right direction and the lights of New Orleans faded. On the outskirts of the city, the traffic thinned. But only when he was on the two-lane road, winding through the woods and swamps with no bright headlights glaring in his mirrors, did he draw a relieved breath. Twice he encountered the red glimmers of taillights ahead of him when the road straightened, but he slowed until they vanished from sight.

By the time he reached the lane to his private retreat, he was alone, his heart rate having slowed to normal. But the smell of blood reached his nostrils. He'd disobeyed.

Never had God told him to kill a cop.

Never.

He blinked rapidly, hoping all was not lost. Surely the Voice would come to him tonight, to reassure him he'd only done what was necessary; that still he would be deified.

I will do anything. ANYthing.

As he parked his truck, the series of pitfalls, of mistakes, came back in quicksilver images: Eve at the house with Cole Dennis; his own private fantasy that had clouded his judgment; the cop approaching and the ensuing chase through the neighborhood.

He'd had no choice. He'd had to shoot. Even though it was not part of the mission, even though the Voice had not told him to take the cop's life.

But it hadn't ended with that one shot.

As he'd gone down, somehow Tiggs had fired.

The Reviver had flinched.

The bullet had gone wild, ricocheting off the hood of his truck.

439

Adrenaline fueling him, the Reviver had rammed his pickup into gear and tromped on the accelerator. Burning rubber, his truck had screamed out of the lot.

Heart hammering, blood pumping, fear shooting through his veins, the Reviver had hazarded a quick glance in his rearview mirror.

Tiggs had lain still, not moving, bleeding onto the asphalt. Dying. People began streaming from the restaurant into the lot. Shouting. Pointing fingers. One son of a bitch had even run for his car to give chase. Someone else had fallen to Tiggs's side in a vain attempt to save him.

Too late, the Reviver had thought, driving out of sight, losing the would-be hero and knowing the cop's fate.

Tiggs was one victim who would never be revived.

Now he walked briskly through the surrounding woods, ignoring the taunt of an owl hooting from a nearby tree, taking no heed of the whir of bats' wings as he unlocked the cabin's door and entered the dark, welcoming interior.

He would shower.

Wash away the blood.

And then he would fall to his knees in front of the cold grate, and he would pray.

For guidance.

For strength.

And ultimately, for forgiveness.

Bentz stared at the woman sitting across from him in his office. Her name was Ellen Chaney. She was black, slightly plump, pushing fifty, and she'd come in because of what she'd heard on the news.

Dispatch had called him, ruining his dinner date with Olivia. He'd hated to cut the evening short, but fortunately his wife, who had been through her own share of terror, had understood.

So he'd met with Chaney at the station, where a few detectives were working at their desks. Compared to the noise of the day shift, the place was quiet.

"So you came in because of the press conference?"

"Yes." She nodded, her dark eyes troubled. "I was a nurse at Our Lady of Virtues," she said, twisting her wedding ring nervously. "For a while. It . . . well, it depressed me." She looked away from him into the middle distance. "Some of what went on was just plain wrong and . . . I should have reported it to someone. The medical board, the state, even the Archdiocese, but I didn't. I just did my job, and when an opportunity to move on came along, I was all over it."

Bentz listened, his small recorder taping the conversation.

"I thought it was all behind me. Especially during your investigation last fall, when that other serial killer was on the loose. So much came out, and I read about it, feeling as if I was finally free, but then"—she was working the ring so hard, it was nearly cutting into her flesh—"then all this started up again, and there's talk about Faith Chastain. I figured that when her body was exhumed, someone would notice that she'd had a C-section."

441

Bentz hid his sharpened interest, let the woman run with her story. The information about Faith Chastain's surgery had been kept away from the press for a reason. Only those close to her or to the hospital would know of another baby.

"And . . ."

"And she had a baby. I was there. The attending nurse. Dr. Renner delivered the baby himself."

"He was a surgeon?" Bentz asked, surprised.

"A psychiatrist. A medical doctor. He'd done surgical rounds in med school. At least that's what they told us."

"Why not call in an ob-gyn?"

Chaney looked at her hands. "They were worried about a scandal."

"Who was?"

"Hospital administration and the Reverend Mother. The baby, it wasn't Faith's husband's."

"How did they know?"

"Because there was over a year where they didn't see each other at all."

Bentz wasn't sure how much to buy, but the woman had enough facts to make her story believable. He just couldn't separate fact from fiction. She seemed truly rueful, her face tortured, the cross dangling from her neck testament to her faith. And yet . . .

"So, who was the father?"

"I don't know."

"Renner?"

"What?" She'd been staring at her ring finger, but

her gaze swept up quickly, offense evident on her face. "The doctor? No."

"What about Dr. Simon Heller?"

"Oh, no . . . I mean, I don't know. There was talk that he, um, was caught with a patient, but nothing ever bore out. But I really don't know whom it could have been. All I know is that the baby was stillborn. A boy. Faith named him Adam."

"Dead?" Bentz said, surprised.

"Yes."

"You saw him? This male child?"

She nodded gravely. "He wasn't breathing, and . . . and Faith was beside herself. The doctor sedated her, and then they shuffled me out of the room."

Bentz eyed the woman, watching as she avoided his eyes. Telling the truth? Maybe . . . just not all of it. And if what she was saying was true, then Eve Renner was not Faith Chastain's missing child. The acid in his stomach started to roil. He'd chosen to meet with her instead of joining Montoya at Eve Renner's house because he'd thought maybe they were going to catch a break with Ellen Chaney. Now he wasn't so sure.

"What happened to the baby?"

"I told you. He died."

"I mean the body."

"Buried in the cemetery. A grave with a blank headstone, as if he hadn't even existed. The only reason they marked it at all was for Faith, so she would have a place to go to visit. We were all sworn to secrecy."

"You and the doctor?" he surmised.

"As well as Faith, Sister Rebecca, and Father Paul."

"Sister Rebecca Renault?" he asked, noting the connection. "The Reverend Mother at Our Lady of Virtues?"

Ellen nodded and bit her lower lip. "I read about what happened to her. I wonder if she might still be alive if only I'd come forward earlier."

"What about this Father Paul? Is he still alive?"

"I don't know."

"How old is he?"

"Um, he was in his late fifties, I'd guess, at that time."

"What was his last name?"

"Oh . . . Gosh . . . I . . . can't remember. . . . A simple name, I think. There were a lot of priests who passed through, you know, and stayed for a few months or a year before they were assigned somewhere else, but Father Paul, he was there a long while." She massaged her temple, trying to think, like someone rubbing a lamp and hoping for a genie to appear. "It was a common name, I think. Like Smith or Johnson or Brown. . . . I really can't remember." She paused, lost in thought.

Bentz was trying to add her information into the total puzzle. Face grim, he didn't immediately ask another question, and after a silent stretch, Ellen reached for her purse.

"Well, I hope that helps you. I don't think there's anything else I can tell you," she said.

"Just a minute, Mrs. Chaney." He looked through

the pages of notes he'd taken over the course of the past few days. He'd seen the name Paul somewhere. Running a finger down one page, he located one of the names he'd found in Faith Chastain's file. "How about Father Paul Swanson?"

She hesitated, her hand in midair over her purse. "That's it, I think."

He made a mental note to find the priest with all the secrets. "Can you think back to the people who were employed by the hospital at the time of the birth of Faith's child? Anyone who was a patient? It could help."

"It's been nearly thirty years."

"I know," he said, offering a tight smile. He felt the clock ticking. He was running extremely late. Montoya was going to be really pissed. "Here's a partial list. Maybe these names will help jog your memory." He slid three pages across the desk. On it were the names of the patients whose files Eve claimed to have seen in the attic cabinet. Bentz had added a few more himself, names taken from the notes in Faith Chastain's folder, including Dr. Terrence Renner and Simon Heller, as well as others he hadn't recognized, such as Father Paul Swanson.

Ellen Chaney dutifully picked up the papers and skimmed the first page. "Oh. Enid Walcott. She was a sweet little woman, such a sad case, too nervous to sit and eat or do anything, and she was allergic to so many of the meds. Oh, and Neva. She was so lost, in her own world. A severely autistic child." She flipped over to the second page and stopped short, her expression turning to shock. "Oh no . . . Dear Lord . . ." She looked up sharply and dropped the paper onto his desk.

"What?"

She shivered and ran her hand through her hair. "I probably shouldn't say anything, but this person . . ." She pointed a long finger at the name of Ronnie Le Mars. "I've never in all my life met anyone I thought was born evil. I mean, I believe in Christ our Savior and redemption through prayer and that everyone can be saved, but . . . but that one, Ronnie, he'd sooner take a knife to your throat than look you in the eye."

"Whose blood was that?" Eve whispered once they were driving away from the house. "All over the bed. Whose blood was it?"

"I don't know." Cole squinted into the night. They'd loaded up his Jeep with the cat, some sleeping bags and pillows, and their personal belongings and left the police still finishing up. Though there was no body, no obvious homicide, the fact that there was so much blood in her room, and the sick message incriminating Cole, had left the police certain that this newest incident was linked to the crime scene at Our Lady of Virtues. They were treating her house as part of the overall homicide investigation.

"He wouldn't have collected blood from Sister Vivian and then poured it over the doll and the bed,

446

would he?" she asked, the idea so repulsive she could scarcely voice it.

"I don't know what he'd be capable of."

She glanced out the window, tried to gain strength in the lights of the city.

From the backseat, trapped in his carrier, Samson started howling.

"Wherever you're taking us, you'd better get there fast, before Samson drives us both crazy."

"It's not far," he said, and to Eve's surprise he didn't drive her to the little camelback bungalow where he'd picked up his clothes hours earlier. However, the apartment he ushered her into wasn't an improvement. If possible, he'd found a worse place, a one-room fleabag of a studio apartment, with no furniture, that seemed to trap all the heat of the day within its thin walls.

"What is this?" she asked as he threw the sleeping bags on the floor.

"I think of it as a safe house."

"Hmmm . . ." She looked around the room. "All it needs is a ten-gallon bucket of Lysol, some paint, new carpeting, appliances, and, oh yeah, furniture. Maybe a few throw pillows and pictures. Then it would be cozy."

He lifted a dark eyebrow. "Would you rather be back at your house?"

An image of the bloodied doll and bed flashed through her mind. "You have a point. This is just as good as a five-star hotel." She set the cat carrier on the

447

floor and opened the gate. Samson immediately streaked out and began exploring the room. "I guess we're lucky. We brought our own furry, four-legged pest control with us."

Cole walked to the window, left it shuttered but flipped a switch on the air-conditioning unit. It rattled to life; she hoped it would bring down the temperature and create some air movement. "The good news about this place is that no one knows about it."

"Except the landlord."

"Petrusky won't say anything," Cole told her. "He's got too much to lose."

"Ahhh. A client."

He shot her another look then organized the sleeping bags and pillows on the floor. She didn't want to think about what kind of creatures might have crawled across the stained carpet, nor who might have lived here before Cole took up residence.

"Now, Ms. Renner, if you can find a way to keep your hands off me, we could work."

"Meaning?"

"We need to find out who's behind all this, and I've decided to treat it like a case. Whenever I had to defend someone against the police department, I made it my business to know as much as they did."

"Oh yeah?"

He smiled. "There's always someone willing to talk. For a price."

"That's the most jaded piece of cynicism I've heard yet. Even from you."

He let the jab slide. "But it's true."

"Wait. Are you telling me you have a leak in the department?" she asked, astounded.

"Not just a leak, lady," he assured her, reaching into a cupboard and coming up with two legal pads and a box of pens. "A goddamned reservoir."

She was skeptical as she settled onto the makeshift bed and opened the box of Sharpies. "Why haven't you used this untapped reservoir before?"

He sat down beside her and took up a pen. "I have, but I had to be careful. I was a suspect. I was followed, dogged, tailed, whatever you want to call it. Maybe I was paranoid, but I was certain my phones were tapped, and I didn't even trust my cell phone. I couldn't risk getting any of my sources into major trouble, so I've laid low."

"And now?"

"Montoya and Bentz would love to nail my ass, but neither one of them is a moron, and now it's blatantly evident I'm not behind any of the murders. Including Roy's."

She was about to ask who this source was, but mention of Roy's name brought her up short. She felt a click inside her head, truly felt it, as if something had just unlocked in her brain.

Memories of that night suddenly flooded her mind. She recalled making love to Cole, the fight, her race down the stairs as he, behind her, was pulling on his clothes. He'd tried to stop her, but she wouldn't hear of it, and when she'd arrived at the cabin she found

Roy already dead, blood everywhere, the horrid number written in blood on the wall and, in the glass, pointing a gun at her . . . no . . . not at her . . . but close, as if he were aiming above her shoulder . . .

She blinked, and the image became sharper. Clearer. More defined.

"Cole," she whispered now, aloud.

Her heart raced as pieces of her memory forged and melded only to shatter again. But she had a glimpse, a very real glimpse, of what had happened that night.

"What?" he asked, but she was lost to the memory.

It was Cole's face showing in the darkness, the barrel of his gun steady. "Don't!" she'd yelled. But the weapon fired, a white flash as glass shattered and searing pain had exploded in her shoulder and head.

"Eve!" he'd screamed. The world had spun crazily. She'd fallen, her eyes fixed on him, her mind screaming, NO, NO, NO! He was so close and yet so far away. . . . And the knife . . . There'd been a wicked knife. Blood dripping onto the floor. Cole had been carrying a knife. . . . No! The knife wasn't in Cole's hand. . . . Someone else's. *Whose?*

The blackness had come at her from the outside in, eating at her consciousness. Within seconds she'd passed out.

Now she stared at Cole with new eyes. Shaking, her guts clenching painfully, she saw that he knew. His blue eyes registered pain and regret. He knew. And he'd known all along. For the past three months, and yet he'd kept his secrets. Lied to protect himself.

"You *were* there," she whispered in a low, rasping voice. "You lying son of a bitch, you were there!"

He didn't argue. Didn't have to.

"But we weren't alone. There was someone else in the room. Roy's killer." She swallowed hard, the events of the night coming into focus, sharpening, the fog dissipating. "You were trying to shoot him," she realized. "But you hit me. And then *lied* about it. Why, Cole? What is it you know? What are you hiding?"

CHAPTER 28

Cole gazed at the woman he loved. It was time to give up the fight. "I was there," he admitted for the first time to anyone. He hated the look of horrified betrayal on Eve's face, but he pressed on. "There was just something wrong about everything that happened that night. I knew where you were going, and, because I'd lived in the area, I figured I could beat you and find out what Kajak wanted, what this 'evidence' was. But Roy was already dead by the time I got there."

"You were there . . . ahead of me."

"I panicked. Okay, I admit it. I didn't have my cell, couldn't call the police, and then I saw you walking inside and I smelled a trap. I figured someone had coerced Roy into calling for you to come and meet him.

"Before I could call out to you, I saw him at the window. I fired, and you're right, I accidentally hit you. You saw everything I did in a mirror, not the window."

"And you left me there," she whispered.

"No, I stayed with you. That's why I didn't catch the guy. I called nine-one-one from your phone and stuck it out until they got there, but then, yeah, I took off. As the officer came in through the front door, I slipped out the back. It was a lone trooper, and by the time he called for backup, I was outside. I waited until the ambulance got there a couple of minutes later. Then I took off."

"I could have died. I—who *is he*?"

"I didn't get a good look. He was gone in an instant. I couldn't leave you." He tried to touch her, but she recoiled.

"You could have sent the police after the killer!"

"It wasn't going to work that way. They would never believe me. I was right there. I was jealous of Roy's relationship with you. Motive and opportunity."

"You should have stayed," she said, hysteria edging her voice. "Let justice run its course."

"And tell the police about the missing 'real' killer? The one I didn't get a good look at? Like Dr. Richard Kimble in *The Fugitive?* Always looking for the damned one-armed man." He grabbed her arm, and when she tried to pull away, he held on tighter. "Okay, maybe I should have stayed. Fought the charges like a man. Ignored the fact that the New Orleans PD had been gunning for me for years. But I thought I could figure it out for myself."

"Like Kimble," she said bitterly. "Now you're pleading both sides of the argument." She shook him off. "I told myself over and over, don't believe him, he's a liar, don't go with him, and for God's sake don't fall in love with him all over again!" She climbed to her feet, and when he tried to step forward and touch her again, she pointed a finger at his nose. "Don't! Just . . . don't! Not ever again! As soon as this is over, you and I will never speak again. Never!"

"Eve . . ."

"But we're stuck with each other for now," she said, her voice quivering.

He saw it in her eyes, the angry, disgusted resolve that stiffened her backbone and flushed her cheeks. God, she was beautiful. Enraged or sleeping soundly, scared out of her mind or teasingly playful, she was the only woman who had ever turned him inside out. And she was right. He'd failed her miserably.

"Think about the last few days—"

"You mean since you got out of prison? Those days?" she demanded.

"Everything I've done has been to prove to you how much you mean to me. I want to find out the truth as much as, maybe more than, you do."

"By making me look like a liar to the DA? By denying the truth and having people, even myself, suspect that I might be crazy? That's what you did to show me how much I mean to you. Everyone else was right about you, Cole, and I was wrong. You're just a slick attorney who will turn the truth around to make it serve his own purpose. Worse yet . . . worse yet, you're a lying bastard who only cares about his own damned hide, so just leave me the hell alone!"

She was so mad, she was seething, her breath coming in short gasps, her eyes filled with a dark fury that sliced right to his soul. He wanted to grab her, to hold her down, to promise that he would make things right, that he loved her and would do anything, even die for her, but he knew that she wouldn't believe a word he said. His fists opened and closed as he stared at her.

"Just think," he tried again.

"That's all I've done for the last three months. And all the while I was 'thinking,' trying to figure out if I was going out of my mind, you *knew* the truth. You didn't 'think' enough of me to confide in me. So don't even try to tell me what to do."

"I love you. That hasn't changed."

She looked at him coldly. "Go to hell, Cole. Don't talk to me about love or feelings or any sort of emotion. That's over."

He didn't call her a liar, though he wanted to, because it wouldn't change anything. Beneath her fury was pain. He didn't blame her for that. Maybe she'd never get over it. But for now he wasn't going to let her out of his sight.

Not until this nightmare was over.

"Now we've lost a cop!" Montoya raged when Bentz caught up with him at the station the next morning.

454

They were in the kitchen, each grabbing a cup of coffee.

"Last I heard, Tiggs was still hanging on."

"By a goddamned thread!" Montoya sputtered, running a hand through his hair and swearing again. "We've got to bring the bastard in. I was close last night, man, so close!"

"You know what they say—"

"Yeah, I do. Don't give me any crap about horseshoes and hand grenades!"

"Ouch." Lynn Zaroster walked in and winced at Montoya's outburst. "Wrong side of the bed?"

"Is there a good side?" he grumbled.

She shot Bentz an I'm-glad-he's-*your*-partner look, then picked through a box of muffins left on the table. "What's the occasion?"

"Brinkman's birthday."

"So who—?" she motioned to the box.

"Vera, in Missing Persons." Bentz took a sip, and the coffee nearly scalded his tongue. "Who knows why she does what she does, but help yourself."

"You think any of them are lite or no-fat?"

Montoya sent her a look that spoke volumes.

She held up one hand to ward off another verbal attack, grabbed a muffin that appeared to be liberally laced with chocolate chips, then hustled down the hallway.

Bentz chose poppy seed. "Don't blame anyone here. Everyone's working their asses off on this case."

"Yeah, tell that to Tiggs."

"I mean it, Montoya. Cool it."

"No way. Not until we catch this fucker."

"Let's get out of here." They'd already discussed why Bentz hadn't shown up at the crime scene and what had gone down at the Renner house.

"Where to?" Montoya poured coffee into a paper cup.

"Our favorite place. Our Lady of Virtues. Already got an excavation crew on call, just in case we need to dig up a grave or two."

"Great." Montoya picked up his cup and sloshed hot coffee onto his hand. "Damn it!"

"Looks like you could use a cigarette," Brinkman observed as he strolled in, reeking of smoke.

"I'm fine."

"Yeah, I can see that."

"You enjoy being a pain in the ass, man?" Montoya demanded.

"Rough night?" Brinkman asked.

"Fuck you."

"Not my fault that you haven't been able to catch the Three-Digit Slasher."

"The what?" Bentz asked.

"That's what they're calling him. I heard it on the radio on the way in today."

"No one knows about the numbers," Bentz said swiftly.

"They do now."

"Jesus Christ, what's with all the leaks!" Montoya was blistering now, as hot as Bentz had ever seen him.

"Your case," Brinkman pointed out as he strolled in the room. He took his time making his selection then finally picked up a fat muffin with thick chocolate icing. Licking frosting from his fingers, he added, "You might want to tell your people to put a lid on it."

Montoya tensed, and Bentz thought for a second he might throw a punch. Instead, he forced a frigid smile. "Thanks for the advice, Brinkman, and happy fuckin' birthday." To Bentz, he said, "Let's roll."

They walked through the department, and Bentz paused at Zaroster's desk. She was just picking up the phone but hesitated, lifting her brows at him in a question.

"You're working on tracking down Ronnie Le Mars?"

"Already got a call in to his parole officer. . . . Get this. Ronnie was released from prison about five months ago and kept his nose clean for a while then just disappeared, just quit checking in with the parole officer, and no one's seen or heard of him since."

"He can't just vanish into thin air," Montoya muttered.

"But he could've left the state."

"Has to work somewhere. There are records," Montoya argued.

Zaroster shrugged. "Fake ID or under the radar. Happens all the time."

Bentz took a bite of his muffin. "So, what about the priest? You workin' that too?"

"Yeah, but I just started. The Archdiocese is a little

touchy these days, but I think they'll come around. It'll just take time."

"Which we don't have," Montoya pointed out.

"I understand."

Bentz said, "Let me know the minute you get a location on either of them, Le Mars or Swanson."

"You'll be the first to know." Then she cast a glance at Montoya. "Or maybe the second. I'll flip a coin."

Bentz tapped on her desk. "Thanks." Montoya just headed down the stairs.

"I'll drive," Bentz said, taking another bite of his muffin before tossing the remains into the trash near the back steps. Because of the mood Montoya was in, Bentz didn't plan to get into a car with his partner at the wheel. There were times when Bentz had ridden white-knuckled while Montoya had lead-footed it down the city streets as if he were in the damned Daytona 500.

He was surprised that Montoya didn't fight him for the wheel but didn't mention it. One less argument. He drove, and Montoya cracked his window then slid a pack of cigarettes out of an interior pocket of his jacket, lit up, and offered his pack to Bentz.

He almost gave in but shook his head. He'd been known to break down and have a smoke when a case got tough, and maybe he would later, but for now he'd stick to gum. Montoya slipped his hard pack of Marlboro Reds into the inner pocket of his jacket. Finally he said, "That nurse claims Faith had a boy, born dead and buried somewhere at the convent's cemetery."

"Uh-huh."

"You believe her?"

"*She* believes her," Bentz said as he sped around a truck pulling a horse trailer. "I called the convent and talked to Sister Odine, but she was no help. She didn't like the thought of equipment up there, digging up graves, but I convinced her it was necessary if we were ever going to catch Sister Rebecca's killer."

"Eve looks like Faith. Abby's already bought into it after seeing her in person." Montoya shook his head. "Hell, she's nearly written Eve's name down in the family Bible."

"We should get DNA results soon. I put a rush on it. Then we'll know at least that part of the story."

Montoya took a pull on his cigarette. "So, where does that leave us with Eve Renner? If she's not Faith Chastain's daughter, why did she get that bundle of newspaper clippings all about Faith and the hospital?"

"Besides the fact that Eve grew up there? Beats me," Bentz admitted as he switched lanes again, maneuvering for the exit ramp.

"It makes ya wonder," Montoya said, blowing out a stream of smoke and crushing his cigarette in the ashtray. "Just who the hell is Eve Renner?"

Kristi walked out of the offices of Gulf Auto and Life and felt freer than she had since college. She'd known she wasn't the type for a sit-on-your-butt, eight-hours-a-day, forty-hours-a-week job, but she'd had to eat and pay rent, and there was no way she was ever going to move home again. No way. Especially now, when she suspected her stepmother might be trying to get pregnant. The last time Kristi had been over to their house, she'd spied the discarded package of a pregnancy test in a wastebasket in the bathroom. Which was just plain weird. To think that she might have a half brother or half sister that would be over twenty-five years younger? She couldn't imagine.

Besides, technically, the kid wouldn't be your half brother or half sister. At least not biologically.

She didn't want to think about it or deal with it, nor had she wanted to be under her father's thumb or watchful eye when she'd graduated from college, so she'd taken whatever jobs she could find: waitressing, clerking, just about anything steady. Finally, as luck would have it, insurance claims had become her way of life.

But now, thank God, she was done! Never again would she have to listen to someone whine about their deductible!

When Kristi had told her boss this morning that she was leaving, she'd been surprised at her response. "Well, you've accumulated nearly two weeks of vacation pay, so why don't you clean out your desk?" Her boss had smiled falsely, and Kristi guessed maybe Gulf Auto and Life was as glad to see her go as she was to leave.

It was perfect.

She took in a long, deep breath and actually saw this part of the city, the downtown area, with new eyes.

She could walk through the aquarium. Situated on the waterfront, it was supposed to be fabulous, and she'd never set foot inside. Now she could go put some money in the slot machines and have a free drink if she wanted, even though it was only ten in the morning. Maybe a mimosa or a Bloody Mary. Wouldn't her father, the teetotaler, have a hemorrhage if he knew? She smiled to herself. It wasn't that she didn't respect her old man. Good Lord, no. He'd done everything he could for her, raising her as a single parent, putting her needs above his. Most of the time. She hadn't been all that crazy about moving here from LA all those years ago but had finally blended in and now loved this city, couldn't imagine moving back to California.

She strolled along the sidewalk then up over the levee. The river, wide and dark, moved slowly. In one direction she saw an old paddle-wheeler docked at the Toulouse Street Wharf while tugboats were guiding a large cargo ship through the channel. The sun beat down on her head and glittered off the water while clouds piled on the horizon, moving steadily closer. Yeah, she liked it here, but she discarded any idea of wasting what was left of the day. The sharks and slots could wait. If she was going to make this true-crime-writer aspiration work, she had to get on it, follow this investigation.

She pulled her cell phone from her purse and speed-dialed her contact at the police department.

Today, she thought, the tables were turned.

She was the one checking up on dear old Dad, not the other way around.

Eve wasn't about to waste a single second. In the hour since she'd rolled up her sleeping bag, she'd cleaned out the cardboard box full of sand that she'd set up in the bathroom as a makeshift litter box, called a locksmith and made an appointment to have the locks changed, even found a maid service to do the cleanup, though she intended to scrub down her bedroom and any place else the creep had touched with gallons of disinfectant.

Last night she'd fallen asleep sometime around two in the morning, though Cole had still been awake, going over his notes, logging onto the Internet by way of her laptop with its wireless connection and some neighbor's unsecured server. While she'd been awake, he'd been animated, talking about theories of who and why and how they were going to crack the case. All the while Eve had seethed. How had she been so foolish as to trust him again? Hadn't she known better?

What a lying piece of dirt!

If it hadn't been for Samson, she would have checked into a hotel.

Or so she'd tried to convince herself.

She was conflicted; that was the problem. Mad as hell and conflicted to the nth degree!

He'd told her to think about the past few days; since then she'd thought of little else. True, Cole had been nothing but determined to figure out who was behind the murders, and he'd risked his own neck in trying to save hers and been her rock when she'd wanted to fall into a billion pieces, but that didn't change the fact that he was a liar, out to save his own hide.

He said he loved you, and that was before he admitted that he'd been at the cabin.

So what?

Talk was cheap.

Though he had seemed intent on protecting her, caring for her, loving her. . . .

She clenched her teeth and made a sound of frustration.

Has he done anything since being released from the jail that would make you think he isn't trustworthy?

Yes! He hadn't come clean from the get-go. It had been lie upon lie upon lie! Only when her memory was returning, and she began to piece together the night Roy had been killed, had he finally given it up and told the truth.

She couldn't trust him!

Wouldn't.

Worse yet, she couldn't trust *herself* when she was near him. She'd even woken up cuddled up next to him. Fully dressed but still surrounded by the warmth and feel and scent of him. She'd instantly scooted away from him and found her cell phone. While Cole, damn him, slept on top of the open sleeping bag, his dark hair falling over his closed eyes, his lips slightly parted, his tall body relaxed, she had made the calls.

463

She had to get on with her life, make her house clean and safe, go to the post office and make certain her address was changed from Anna and Kyle's house in Atlanta.

If she were even going to stay in the house she'd thought of as home ever since she was a child.

Which was a pretty big if, all things considered. At the thought of her bloodied bed, the doll, and the damned scrawled message, she considered moving. Nana's house or not, she couldn't imagine ever sleeping in the turret room again. Whoever was behind this nightmare, he was winning. She was a wreck. She didn't know up from sideways or what she was going to do for the next five minutes, let alone the rest of her life.

Cole stirred.

Her heart softened a little at the sight of him, but then she steadfastly shut down any vague romantic or sexual notions she might still possess. That part of her life, she was certain, was over.

He made some kind of growling noise that did strange things to her then rolled over and opened one eye. "Mornin'," he drawled, all west Texas again.

Oh sure.

He stretched, his arms reaching far over his head, lengthening him out, making his abdomen appear even flatter, almost concave. "So . . . where's the coffee?"

"Very funny."

"Still mad?"

She was aghast at his audacity. "What do you think?"

He sighed and rubbed his eyes. "Too bad. I thought maybe you and I could have a quickie this morning before—"

"Stop!" She threw a hand up, instantly incensed. "Do you remember what we're in the middle of?"

"Of course I do. I just thought we could lighten up a little. You know, they say it's not good to go to bed angry, and I figured once you'd had time to think about everything, sleep on it, come to—"

"If you were going to say, 'Come to my senses,' don't."

"Yesterday you—" he started to say.

"Yesterday I was a blind woman who didn't know the truth."

He didn't bother finishing what he'd been about to say. Instead, he stated flatly, "And today we don't have time for recriminations. Save 'em. We've got to figure this out. Fast."

She wanted to argue, to keep at it, but she knew he was right. Festering fury didn't get anyone anywhere. She still could not trust him, but she did need to deal with him.

"There must be some kind of method to this guy's madness," Cole said. "So, let's take the number that was written on the wall of Roy's cabin. 212, right?"

She nodded.

"And your father, 101?"

465

"Yes."

"And where the nun, Vivian, was found, up in the hospital . . . 323, while the doll was 444."

"I know what the numbers are," she said, still irritated. "So what?"

"And if you read them backward?" He held up his notes for her to see.

She looked the numbers over. "Okay . . . so . . . they're the same. Left to right or right to left."

"Now look at the message that was written last night. *Dennis sinned.* Read it backward."

"Dennis sinned. . . ." She looked at him in surprise. "I still don't get it."

"It can't be a coincidence, Eve. And there's more. The drug that your father was given?"

"Xanax." A pause. "Weird." She didn't understand this, not at all, but she was certain Cole was on to something.

"And your father's last name? Renner. A palindrome. A word that reads the same way backward or forward."

"Like Viv," she said. "But . . . Sister Rebecca . . . Becca . . . Renault or . . ."

"Let's go with 'nun.' "

"Okay. Nun." And then her eyes met his, and she felt a cold thrill rush down her spine as she realized where he was going with this. "Or," she said, drawing in a shaky breath, "like Kajak."

"Yeah, Kajak works, but that's just for starters." Cole was suddenly stone-cold sober, and before the words were out of his mouth, she understood what he was going to say.

"I hate to bring this up, darlin', but we can't ignore your first name. E-v-e. Same both ways. Eve and Renner both. I'd say whoever is behind this is definitely fixated on you."

CHAPTER 29

Bentz stared at the fresh grave, red brown earth turned and moist, a small cross marking its location between other, larger, engraved headstones. Cut into the grass and weeds, the earthy patch was impossible to miss.

"I don't understand it," Sister Odine said, worrying her hands as she walked with Bentz and Montoya around the machinery standing ready to chow into the ground. A driver was in the cab, another two workers standing by, the big backhoe idling noisily, smelling of diesel. "We've not had a burial here in six months." She blinked up at Bentz and shook her head. "I walked through here just three days ago, and this"—she pointed to the gravesite with its mound of fresh earth—"wasn't that way. There was a grave here, yes. The marker has been here for as long as I have, I think. But I swear, the grass was undisturbed."

"I believe you," Bentz said, then nodded to the excavation crew. He handed Sister Odine the necessary paperwork, though she wasn't the least bit concerned with legalities. Bentz assured her the Archdiocese might be. He motioned to the backhoe driver, and, with a grind of gears, the machine got to work, tearing through the soft soil, making short work of the grave.

"I don't like this." Montoya reached into his jacket pocket for his cigarettes then glanced at Sister Odine and thought better of it. "Digging up graves is . . . well, it's just creepy. I don't like messin' with the dead. Once in the ground, stay there, I say."

"Part of the job."

"Huh." He folded his arms over his chest, his leather jacket creaking as he did, then waited impatiently, shifting his weight from one foot to the other, glancing up at the heavens, where a jet cut across the sky, leaving a white plume in its wake before disappearing into the approaching clouds.

Noisily the backhoe kept working, extracting scoops of dark, earthy-smelling dirt, dropping each bucketful into an ever-growing pile.

It didn't take long for the backhoe to expose the coffin.

"Hey! Hold it!" one of the men on the ground said, raising a hand to keep the driver from lowering his scoop onto the coffin. "Detective?"

Steeling himself, Bentz walked to the gravesite's edge, and there, a few feet within the hole, still partially covered with dirt, was a small casket. A sense of sadness seeped through him. Unlike his partner, he wasn't creeped out by this part of his job, though he agreed that he never liked disturbing the dead or exhuming bodies.

"Jesus," Montoya said, edging nearer to the pit and glancing down at the small coffin. "Jesus."

"I assume that was a prayer," the sister said.

"Absolutely!" Montoya was emphatic.

Bentz actually believed his partner. He nodded at the graveside workers. "Bring it up," Bentz instructed, then stepped back as the men retrieved the box that was scarcely larger than the body of an infant.

Montoya's face tightened as the coffin was hoisted upward. Lips flat, skin drawn over his cheekbones, eyes glittering darkly, he waited while it was placed on the ground and, at a nod from Bentz, the lid pried open.

Bentz forced his eyes to the interior. In the simple wooden box lined with sheeting there was a body.

A fresh body.

Blood still lined the sheets.

But it wasn't a child. It was a baby pig, its throat slit.

"For the love of God!" Montoya said, repulsed, his skin almost visibly crawling. "What the hell is that?" He looked up at the nun and said, "Sorry, Sister" then turned his attention to the coffin again. "But man, what is that? A *pig*? A damned fresh pig?"

He stepped away from the coffin. No longer concerned about any kind of protocol or respect for the dead, he scrabbled for his pack of Marlboros and hastily lit up. "Jesus," he said under his breath again, and even the construction workers stopped their conversation.

The little nun frowned into the open casket and

hastily made the sign of the cross over her chest. She too was obviously shaken, her skin blanched, her eyes wide behind her glasses. "Why would anyone do this?"

"I don't know," Bentz said, "but we'll find out. I have to take this coffin back to the lab." Bending on one knee, he got a closer look. The pig was bloated, no sign of maggots but already starting to smell rank. Bentz pulled on a pair of gloves and gingerly lifted the carcass, then the sheet, so that he could peer beneath. "You got the flashlight?" he asked Montoya, who was already fishing it out of his pocket. He handed it to him, and Bentz clicked on the light, shining a beam along the inside of the box.

Partially hidden by the sheet, scrawled across the side of the coffin, was another message. He read aloud.

"Live not on evil."

"What?" Montoya stepped closer and read the words. " 'Live not on evil'? What's that supposed to mean?"

Bentz twisted his neck and squinted up at his partner. "Our guy wanted us to read it. He left the earth freshly turned, didn't try to hide it. He wanted us to find this grave and dig it up."

"So that we could find a dead pig?"

"So that we could find the message." Bentz dropped the sheet so that the pig rested as it had. Straightening, he yanked off his gloves. "Our boy is talking to us," he said. "What's he trying to tell us?"

・ ・ ・

God was angry with him.

The Reviver knew it. He'd lain awake all night, waiting for the Voice, hoping to hear that he was pardoned. But all that came to him were the scratchy voices making white noise in his head, and he'd fallen to his knees and prayed, begging absolution, tears streaming down his face, his pleas going unanswered in God's deathly cold silence.

"Please, forgive me. Father, I beg Thee, speak with me again and I will do Your bidding."

When there was no response, he took solace in his rosary and then laid out his tarp and candles and stripped bare. After carefully showering, protecting his new flesh engravings, cleansing his body and soul, he retrieved his tattoo machine, lit the candles, and checked the vials of ink. Soon he would have to buy more, but for now, all was as it should be.

Except that God was no longer speaking to him.

No longer instructing him.

No longer calling him the Reviver and hinting that he would soon be deified.

He needed to repent, to do a long penance to find favor with the Lord again.

Standing in front of the mirror, he turned on his machine then placed his hand on the inside of his leg, where the flesh was tight from all his exercise. He closed his eyes, said a prayer, and pushed the needle into his skin, deep, feeling the hot little bite, the sting of the first prick. He would write his name here, where

471

he could see it easily without the aid of a mirror. Though it might rub, and he would have to be careful with it for the next few days, it would be a reminder.

Concentrating, revived by the pain, he started to ink the word "Reviver" onto his flesh. And as he did, he turned his mind to God, away from Eve, where it often strayed whenever he touched himself. To want her was a sin. He knew it, and yet he hoped that the Voice would speak to him again and tell him that his patience, his waiting, his obedience had bought him a little time with her.

Just enough . . . Not much . . . but enough that he could do all the things he'd dreamed about. Touch her. Taste her. Nip her flesh.

The needle cut deep, and he quickly banished Eve from his thoughts.

For now, he would concentrate on God.

Cole had gone to the store for donuts, juice, and coffee, and the remains were strewn around the sleeping bags that had become their bedroom, kitchen, and den. The air conditioner wheezed but brought some kind of movement to the stale air. They'd cracked the blinds, and pale morning light striated the dirty floor as it passed through the slats.

Eve felt a little sick with the rush of sugar and caffeine, but she'd managed to concentrate on the pages of notes they'd taken. She was certain he was on to something with this pattern of palindromes.

And it scared her.

Not just for herself.

But what about Anna Maria? Her first name was the same backward and forward. She knew no one close named Bob or Lil or Ava or Gig, or any other name that could be construed as reading both backward and forward. But what about someone called dad or mom? Cole and she had worked on a list of potential victims, and Cole had even thought that Sam Deeds—if you used just his first initial, as 'S. Deeds'—could be another person in the killer's sights.

It was twisted. Made no sense. But it must mean something, and it was somehow connected to Our Lady of Virtues and Faith Chastain.

Eve had called Anna's cell phone, but her message had been instantly sent to voice mail. Desperately wanting to know that her sister-in-law was alive and well, she'd next phoned Kyle, only to get a terse greetings, "Leave a message."

Great.

She was already sick with tension. Not being able to reach Anna Maria only ratcheted up her level of anxiety.

Cole sat cross-legged on his sleeping bag, leaning over his papers, T-shirt stretched tight over his shoulders, the waistband of his jeans pulling low enough to show a slice of his bare back. He glanced up and caught her eye on him. "Quit ogling me and get back to work."

"I'm not ogling."

He smiled infuriatingly. Eve looked away. She found herself shocked to realize her anger was dissipating. Damn it. She was way, way too susceptible to this man. And she was infuriated with herself for caring.

"Look at all these numbers and words backward and forward," he said, bringing her back from her self-flagellation. "I put the numbers by the names, the way I think the killer has them . . . see?

"I've seen this before," she said but sat down beside him, careful not to let her and his skin touch anywhere. She stared at the sheet again. Samson wandered over to her and settled into her lap. Idly, she petted his head and back, stroking his long fur as she read Cole's bold block letters.

KAJAK	212
RENNER	101
NUN or SIS	111
VIV or NUN or SIS	323
??? (doll) EVE	444

"Just look more closely. I think the doll represents you. It was found up in the attic, in a place that hadn't been disturbed since you were a child, and then again in your bed."

"Oh great," she muttered.

"I know," he said, the muscles in the back of his neck tightening. "But he didn't go after you. Just did things to scare the hell out of you."

"Mission accomplished," she whispered.

"Sick son of a bitch," Cole muttered harshly as he pointed at the numbers. "Do these mean anything to you?"

She stared at the list and shook her head. Samson rolled onto his back, purring. "I've thought about this a hundred times over, and the only thing that comes to me is the floors of the hospital."

"Meaning?"

"Well, both my dad and Sister Rebecca had offices on the first floor, and then, I think, when Roy was back at the hospital as a patient, he was on the second floor. The attic would be the fourth floor."

"What about Sister Vivian?"

Eve lifted her palms. "But she could have been a patient at one time."

He ran a finger down the numbers. "Okay . . . let's take it a step further. Did your father's office have a room number?"

"Yes. Number one. He liked that. I remember because he'd whisper to me, 'I'm number one.' You know, like every football team heading for a bowl game."

"And Sister Rebecca?"

"Not sure. Her office was down the hall from Dad's."

"Could it be room eleven?" he asked, reopening the cap of a half-drunk bottle of cranberry juice and talking a long swallow.

"Yesss . . ." Samson batted at her hands, as, lost in

thought, she'd quit petting him. She absently began to stroke him again.

"Do you think it's possible that these are room numbers of the hospital?"

"Maybe. But what about the attic? There were no numbers up there."

He screwed on the cap and dropped the bottle onto the floor next to the open box of donuts. "Maybe I'm all wet . . . but, okay, think about it. If the attic were sectioned off into rooms like the floors below, what numbers would they be?"

"You're taxing my brain." Examining this so closely brought her fear bubbling to the surface.

"Come on, Eve," he urged. "The rooms on the second and third floor were stacked directly above each other, the composition the same, so imagine the floor beneath the spot where you made your little fort or whatever you want to call it. What room was that? Three forty-four?"

"Could be . . ." She fought back her urge to push this away and tried to remember the configuration of the halls.

"Maybe your little attic nest would be where room four forty-four would be if there were a set of rooms up there."

"That's a pretty big leap, isn't it?"

Cole inclined his head in agreement. "But it's something. The only thing we've really got."

"Which isn't much," she said, disheartened, then reached for her phone to call Anna Maria again.

476

"Please answer," she whispered, but once again the call was sent directly to voice mail.

It was nearly five when the call came in from the lab. "I think it would be best if you all come on down here," Bonita Washington told Bentz. "See for yourself what we've got."

"I'm on my way." He turned to Montoya, who was cradling a phone to his ear while scribbling notes.

"Yeah . . . yeah . . . Okay . . . Got it!" He hung up and explained. "Another case . . . The knifing down at the waterfront. Got a snitch who's coming in later to say what went down. What's up?"

"Washington called. Wants us to come down to the lab ASAP."

Montoya grabbed his jacket. "Serious stuff."

"Sounds like it."

On their way past Lynn Zaroster's desk, Montoya dropped off his jotted notes. "I'll be gone for a while. If this guy calls in"—he tapped the note—"get the info, and I'll call him back. I'm not sure he knows anything, but he's making noise like he knows what went down the other night near the park."

"Got it," she nodded and placed his note near her phone. "I think I've got a lead on the priest, Father Paul, who used to work at Our Lady. Paul Swanson. He's retired. Might be in a nursing home or assisted-care facility. I'll let you know if and when I locate him."

"Good. And Le Mars?"

"No luck yet." She twirled a pen in her fingers. "I'm checking with all his known contacts, friends, family, old girlfriends. So far, zilch. But I'm still working on it."

As they all were. Bentz and Montoya each had spent hours running down leads on Ronnie Le Mars. They'd all ended up going nowhere. Zaroster's phone started ringing again. "This might be it," she teased. "The call that breaks the case."

Montoya snorted. "From your lips to God's ears."

"Yeah, that's right. God and I are real tight. He answers all my prayers pronto." She reached for the phone. As they headed downstairs, they heard her answer, "Homicide. Detective Zaroster . . ."

They found Bonita Washington in the photo lab, talking with Inez Santiago. "Montoya . . . glad you came along. Come over here and take a look at this." She guided them to a long counter and switched on undercabinet lights. "Here's the original photo that Abby Chastain took of the hospital. There's definitely a shadow of a man in the window. Now, I could give you the long and boring speech about how we enlarged, sharpened, and enhanced the image, but it doesn't matter. What does is this." She pointed to the last in a series of about twenty prints. "It's the clearest image we have."

"Pretty good," Bentz observed. The image was definitely a man, a big man, his features a little muddy but distinct enough to be recognizable.

"Not pretty good, Detective. It's damned good. Got it? Damned good. Now . . . take a look at this."

She handed him a mug shot of Ronnie Le Mars, the same picture Bentz had already viewed when he'd checked the computer records. "I'd say this could very well be your guy."

Montoya, who had been silent so far, nodded. "It's him."

"Maybe." Bentz wasn't completely convinced.

"Good chance," Santiago piped up. In a lab coat, her red hair twisted onto her head, she added, "We've got more good news."

"That we do," Washington agreed. "Blood work." She led them around a corner and along a well-lit corridor to an area dedicated to examining bodies and body parts. "We've got company," she announced to A.J. Tennet, who was seated on a rolling stool and staring into a microscope.

He looked up. "Good." Sliding his chair along a counter, he stopped sharply and picked out some papers from a basket. "First of all, the blood found at the Eve Renner house was porcine, not human."

Bentz felt a wave of relief. "I think we found the pig."

Tennet nodded. "We're double-checking that now and looking for any other stains or epithelials in the coffin."

"The coffin's old," Washington explained. "We figure it might have been used before. We're taking soil samples from the area around Our Lady of Virtues, from the pig's hooves, and from the coffin, just to see that they match. Any other trace evidence, including the sheet, will be analyzed."

"Good."

"Montoya, why don't you go over the lab work here with A.J. in more detail," Washington suggested. "Detective Bentz, I'd like to show you something else. In private."

Montoya lifted a dark eyebrow, obviously curious, but didn't follow as Washington led Bentz into her office.

"What's going on?" he asked as she closed the door behind them.

"Something I thought you should find out about alone. Then you can handle it any way you see fit."

"Okay." Bentz felt more than a little apprehension. Bonita Washington had always been a straight shooter. Never pulled any punches. Not into high drama in the least. "So what's up?"

"The DNA report came in on Eve Renner."

"She's not related to Faith Chastain," Bentz guessed. "We already know that Faith had a son who died at birth, the baby who was supposed to be in that coffin."

"Then you got your information wrong." She handed him the report. "Not only does Eve have enough identical genetic markers to make it clear that she is Faith's daughter, she also has markers that match another person."

"Who is that?" Bentz asked. "Ronnie Le Mars?"

"No."

"Not Roy Kajak?"

"No." She was staring at him as if he'd lost his mind.

"Then I don't know. Who else?"

Washington looked him squarely in the eye. "You, Detective," she said, watching his reaction. "According to our tests, and I ran them three times to make certain of the data, you're related to Eve Renner."

CHAPTER 30

"There's got to be a mistake," Bentz declared, disbelieving. He was holding his hands up and shaking his head emphatically as the wheels whirled in his mind. "I never met Faith Chastain. Never."

"Well, someone related to you did. And it was a whole lot more than just meeting her."

"Wait." There had to be something wrong! But the first dark worm of understanding was boring through his brain. "Jacques Chastain was her husband. He could have . . . There's a mistake," he repeated.

"You're not listening to me, Detective," she said determinedly. "This is Bonita. I don't do anything half-assed. I checked your daughter's DNA as well. We still had a sample on file from that case a few years back, you remember, with that psychopath who called himself the Chosen One?"

Bentz nodded. Both Kristi and Olivia had nearly lost their lives because of that twisted maniac.

"So I ran the sample . . . and sure enough, bingo, Kristi's an instant winner too. Related to Eve Renner."

"Through Eve's biological father." Bentz felt the need

to sit down, but he stayed on his feet by sheer will.

"I knew there was a reason you were promoted so quickly." She slapped the reports into his hand and let him scan them for himself. Some of her bad-ass attitude fell away, and her intense green eyes appeared surprisingly compassionate. Pushing a hank of kinky hair from those eyes, she said, "Look, Bentz, I don't know what this means, other than you and Eve are related, but I figured you might want to process this yourself and decide how you're going to tell the rest of the department. Anyone working on this case will be privy to this information."

He shook his head to clear it. How could this be? Who in his family had even met Faith Chastain. For a second, he questioned his own legitimacy.

With a kindness he hadn't thought her capable of, she added lightly, "I figure you owe me big-time."

"Diamonds. I know."

"You got that right." She patted his shoulder. "Remember: big ones."

Report in hand, Bentz connected with Montoya, who was on his phone pacing through the labyrinth of hallways, deep in conversation. "Uh-huh . . . I'll check it out. Yeah, that's fine. . . . We're done here now. Okay, we'll meet you there. Thanks." Montoya fell into step with Bentz. Together they headed out of the building. "That was Eve Renner," he explained. "She and Cole Dennis have cooked up this theory. Kind of out there, and I wouldn't buy into it all, but it's a lot like yours."

"How so?"

He explained about the names or titles of the victims being palindromes, how the numbers at the crime scenes read both left to right and right to left, how they also might represent room numbers for the hospital. "Terrence Renner's office was room 101, and Sister Rebecca's was 111. They're not sure about all of the victims, but it's worth looking into." Montoya tugged at his goatee. "Seems kinda far-fetched to me, but we've walked down that road before."

Bentz grunted in agreement. "Far-fetched" sometimes felt like it was the norm.

They continued single file as two officers came through, hurrying the opposite way. Montoya added, "Eve's really freaked because she can't get hold of her sister-in-law, Anna, who has one of those backward-forward type of names."

"Does this Anna have any connection to the hospital?"

"None we've found. Yet. Hell. But Eve does, and she's obviously already in the killer's sights."

"Maybe they're on to something." Bentz fell into thought as his shoes clicked on the polished floor. "The whole palindrome thing is too much of a coincidence."

"I told Eve we'd meet at her house. She's already got a cleaning crew and locksmith lined up. We're done there, right? We can release the house to her. All the evidence and photographs have been taken. We've got the sheets, blood samples, prints. No reason to keep her out of the house."

"If she wants to go back there."

"I wouldn't," Montoya admitted as they walked outside.

Heavy clouds had rolled in, blocking what was left of the afternoon sun, and the temperature had dropped a few degrees. Traffic, full in the throes of rush hour, sluggishly snarled its way through the streets as, cars, buses, and trucks moved out of the city.

"So, what was it Washington wanted to talk to you about?"

"DNA." Bentz handed the pages to Montoya, who scanned the information quickly.

"So . . . wait a minute. Ellen Chaney swears Faith Chastain had one baby, a boy, who was stillborn. How do we get from that to a dead pig in a coffin and a *woman* who is very much alive and Faith's daughter?"

"Read on."

"There's more?"

"Oh yeah." Bentz flexed his hands, still trying to process the information Bonita Washington had handed him. The story wasn't hanging together—the dead baby, Eve's DNA matching Faith's . . . Something was wrong somewhere. Ellen Chaney was either lying or hadn't gotten her facts straight. That bothered him. He could usually sense bullshit, but Chaney had seemed sincere. Now, running a hand through his hair, he felt his stomach begin to roil and thought the hell with it. To Montoya, he said, "I'll take that smoke now, if you've got one."

"Sure." Montoya found his cigarettes and handed the pack and his lighter to Bentz.

Bentz lit up, drawing deep, sensing smoke curl into his lungs as his partner flipped through all the pages slowly, his eyes narrowing as he read.

Montoya stopped dead in his tracks and looked up at Bentz. "What the hell does this mean?"

Bentz handed over the rest of the pack and the lighter, enjoying the first buzz of nicotine. "Don't know. I never met Faith Chastain."

"But—"

"I can't explain it," Bentz said, but his mind was taking a trip of its own, running down a long, dark corridor with doors to rooms that he'd hoped would never be opened again. No matter how hard he wanted to lock the truth away, it always fought to get out, to be known. His gut gnawed, and he reached into his pocket for his antacids.

Montoya's dark eyebrows slammed together as he read the information for the second time. "For Christ's sake, you must know something. This is your damned family."

"Yours too, if you marry Abby." He plopped a pill into his mouth and chewed. "We might all be related."

"Jesus, Mary, and Joseph. Related?" Montoya shook out a cigarette for himself, jabbed the Marlboro into his mouth. He flicked his lighter to the tip of the cigarette, inhaling as if the smoke were life giving.

"That's sick," he said as he exhaled a cloud of smoke.

You don't know the half of it, Bentz thought as he considered all the possibilities of who in his family could be Eve Renner's father. He didn't like where his logic took him and couldn't imagine how to tell Eve or Kristi. Montoya was right. It was sick. "Looks like Abby can start adding Eve's name to the family Bible after all."

"And yours too? Man, what a mess."

Amen, brother, Bentz thought, crushing out his cigarette on the sidewalk. *A-damned-men.*

Eve couldn't believe her ears. Stunned, she stood next to Cole in the backyard of her grandmother's house. The wind was sighing through the branches of the magnolia tree, dusk was slowly creeping across the land, and Bentz's shocking statement still hung in the air as if it were a living being.

"The DNA tests prove that you're Faith Chastain's daughter. And I'm afraid there's more. It looks like you're related to me as well."

She stared at Detective Rick Bentz, and he stared back. "How . . . I mean . . ." She held up her good hand and processed the unlikely information all over again. *She was related to Bentz. And she also was Abby Chastain's half sister. And Faith's daughter. But not Jacques Chastain's child.* "I don't believe it."

Cole, too, was skeptical, but then he'd never trusted the police. "You're sure?" he asked Bentz, his gaze moving from Montoya, who was resting a hip against the fender of his car, to Bentz, who was standing closer, delivering the unlikely news.

"I understand this is difficult."

"Difficult?" Cole laughed silently at the understatement.

"I have the reports. The tests were run three times. I had trouble believing this too. Believe me. But the DNA markers are clear," Bentz said.

Eve regarded him with new eyes, trying to decipher if there was any resemblance between them. The answer to that question was a firm no. Eve had a slim build, curly reddish hair, a short nose, and blue eyes tinged with green. Bentz was stocky, with brown hair showing hints of gray, a square jaw, and flinty, deep-set eyes. "Related how?" she asked suspiciously. She needed more specifics before she could swallow this story. She saw no reason for him to lie, but . . . this just couldn't be true! What was he saying? That he was her *father*, her *brother?*

He must've read the questions in her eyes. "I'm not exactly certain how we're related, but no, I'm not your father. I never met Faith Chastain."

Eve was more than a little relieved. She'd suffered too many blows in the father department as it was. Terrence Renner had just been brutally murdered, not even as yet buried, and she couldn't come to grips thinking this rugged detective with whom she'd been so combative could be the man who had sired her. Bentz, along with Montoya, had doubted her word from the moment they'd met, and both men had been dogged in their quest to see Cole put behind bars.

Nonetheless, she was convinced by his expression that he believed the news he was delivering was the truth.

"Could you be my half brother?" she asked, rubbing the arm that was still in a sling. "Could we have the same father?"

Montoya found his cigarettes and fired one up.

Bentz responded, "I don't see how. My dad was shot in the line of duty, long before you could have been conceived."

"An uncle, then?"

"I don't have the answers yet. But believe me, I'll get 'em." His jaw set determinedly.

"But Abby's my half sister?"

"Yes."

Montoya, leaning against his car, gave Eve a searching look. "I was going to tell her tonight, unless you want to."

She didn't have to think twice. "I'll leave that to you, Detective. But ask her to call me when she wants to."

Montoya nodded. "Knowing her, it'll probably be as soon as she hears the news."

"Anytime would be fine." She felt strange. At sea. If it were true . . . if . . . then Abby and Zoey Chastain were both her half sisters, and somehow Rick Bentz was part of her family as well.

"You should also know that we found a grave, the one that was supposed to have held Faith's child, her boy child," Bentz said.

"A grave?" Eve froze, felt Cole step closer to her. "With a baby?"

"There was no baby, at least none that we could find."

She pressed the heel of her palm to her head and closed her eyes. "You found an empty grave for Faith's baby, for *me*, is that what you're saying?"

"We think it was originally for Faith's child, but it had been tampered with, the earth fresh, and when we opened the casket we found a dead pig inside."

Repulsed, she wrapped her good arm around her middle and turned into the safety of Cole's arms.

Montoya added, "Not just a dead pig. There was a message inside as well, written in blood. 'Live not on evil.'"

Cole said, " 'Live not on evil.' Another palindrome." His expression grew darker. "The hits just keep on coming."

"The blood we found in your bedroom—it was the pig's."

"Oh for the love of God, why?" she whispered, digesting the news. Though she was relieved that the blood splashed all over her room hadn't been human, she was still sickened by the idea of the horrible, gruesome mess, that someone was perverted enough to mutilate a doll, pour blood onto her bed, then take the time to write a cryptic message in that blood. It was sick and psychotic and chilled her to the bone.

"What kind of a pervert are we dealing with?" Cole asked as a thick, starless twilight stole over the city.

Montoya pushed away from the car. "This guy's a psychopath. Sick. Deranged. And yeah, if you're asking, for some reason he's focused on Eve. We're just not certain why."

She knew about psychoses, had witnessed for herself the results of such severe mental disorders, and yet, faced with an unknown killer who somehow drew great satisfaction, perhaps even sexual excitement, in gruesomely terrorizing her, she felt sick inside.

"Police protection is available," Montoya offered.

"You think I'm in serious danger."

"Don't you?"

"I think that if he had wanted to kill me, he would have by now. I'm sure he's had opportunities."

"But he's stringing it out, getting off on scaring the hell out of you," Cole said. "I think you should accept."

She was astounded. Cole never trusted the police. Never. His eyes met hers, and she saw that he was wrestling with his own conscience, that he was really worried.

"It couldn't hurt. Might deter the maniac," he said.

Bentz added chillingly, "He's going to escalate. He's already taken lives."

She quivered inside. But police protection? Someone watching her around the clock? Having zero privacy?

"I'll be with her," Cole said when she hesitated.

"Well, that's all fine and good, but as far as I know, you don't own a gun. At least none that you admitted to during the Kajak investigation. So how're you going to protect her?" Montoya's gaze slid from Cole to Eve. "If I were you, I'd take my chances with the professionals."

"How would that work?"

"We'd stake out the place. Have someone watching the house."

"Do it, Eve," Cole said.

"I'll think about it. Tonight I'll be at a hotel, so it won't be an issue. But after I get the place cleaned up and move back in, then I'll let you know."

"You're sure?" Bentz asked.

"I'll be okay," she said, thinking of Cole. She didn't doubt that he would protect her. Gun or no gun. That much she trusted.

"And we do have a revolver, still registered to my grandfather. It's just a matter of buying bullets."

"I'd feel better if you had an officer trained with a weapon right now," Bentz said tightly.

"I'll call you if I change my mind."

"Do it. In the meantime, we'll look this over," Bentz said, holding up Cole's notes about the numbers and names. "I'll also keep trying to reach your sister-in-law. So far, she hasn't shown up, hasn't called."

"Please do," Eve said, worried sick. She'd left Anna three voice mails on her cell phone during the course of the day and had even called her house in Atlanta. It was just odd that Anna had been so desperate to get in touch with her after Terrence's death then had gone ghostly silent, completely incommunicado.

While people all around Eve were being slaughtered.

Montoya's cell phone rang. He glanced at the screen. Then, turning a shoulder to Eve, Cole, and Bentz, he wandered off to take the call.

Eve said to Bentz, "Would you please let me know if you hear from either of my brothers?" After demanding to meet with her and the police, both Kyle and Van seemed to have disappeared. Neither was answering his damned cell phone. True, it had only been a few days, but as eager as they'd been to divvy up Terrence Renner's estate, it was strange that they had gone completely and inexplicably silent.

Bentz nodded as Montoya hung up, shoved his phone into the pocket of his jacket, and turned back their way. He looked at his partner and said curtly, "We gotta roll."

"I think we're done here anyway." To Eve, he added, "I'll be in touch."

"Thanks."

Bentz jogged back to the Mustang. Montoya was already inside, behind the wheel. Bentz opened the passenger-side door, and the car's engine roared to life. A second later the tires chirped, and Montoya pulled away from the curb.

Eve watched them leave. "How strange was that?" she murmured, still trying to digest everything Bentz had told her.

"Too strange," Cole said as the taillights of the Mustang disappeared around the corner. "Dead pigs, new

492

siblings. You being related to Bentz himself *and* Montoya's fiancée? It's out there. Waaay out there. It's almost like a setup of some kind."

"A conspiracy? What do you mean?"

"To tell you the truth, I don't know what to think," he admitted, glancing back at the house, which was still surrounded by pieces of crime-scene tape that flapped and caught in the breeze. "But I do think you should take them up on their offer."

"Not tonight. Okay? I just want . . . to shut it all down for one night."

"You think you can?"

"I'm going to give it my best effort," she said, hoping she could manage to get a night's sleep without this horrible nightmare encroaching. She needed to sort things out and get a new perspective on her life.

"You said something about staying in a hotel tonight?"

"I can't stay here, and though your place is . . . well, safe, I suppose, I need a real bed. Maybe we could leave Samson there for a few hours then in the morning meet the locksmith and the house cleaners back here."

"So, we're together?"

She felt that same old rush whenever she was around him. It would be just so damned much easier if she didn't care about him. "Yes." She glanced at the old house with its smooth siding, paned windows, and dark shutters. In her mind's eye she saw

493

her grandfather at his desk, her grandmother in the kitchen, wiping down the tile or baking a custard. This house, more than anything, represented family to her. More than the older brothers who'd never cared much for her, or her sickly mother, or her psychiatrist father who had been cool and distant one minute, overtly affectionate the next. This three-story Victorian with its memories of her grandparents was home and hearth, her bedroom a sanctuary. She gazed upward to the turret room, where she'd once found such solace.

All that had changed in the flash of a killer's blade.

An evening breeze, fragrant with magnolia, shivered against the back of her neck. She felt a deep, abiding sadness with the realization that her home was forever violated. Biting her lip, she admitted, "I don't know if I can ever stay here again."

CHAPTER 31

"Son of a bitch."

Kristi sat at her desk in her apartment and fumed. Damn Detective Rick Bentz! Oh, how she'd like to pick up the phone and taunt him with what she knew! Her lighthearted I'm-free-free-free attitude had flown out the window when she'd learned what her father was doing. Not from him, of course, no way, but from some guy she barely knew in the department. *He* was the one who was her confidant, the one she could phone any hour of the day or night to get information. Not dear old, sealed-lips Dad. Never him.

She drummed her fingers on her desk, glaring at her computer monitor, where she was researching every article that had been written on this new spate of murders. Just recently, according to a local station's website, there had been vandalism at Eve Renner's house, and it had to have been something pretty bizarre and gruesome for so many police officers to have been called in. One policeman had even been shot while chasing a suspect.

Just minutes ago, over the phone, her new friend in the department told her that Detective Rick Bentz had been at the grounds of the old mental hospital again, digging up a grave no less. Her father was looking into DNA on Eve Renner *and* Faith Chastain.

Her source didn't know exactly what had transpired at Eve Renner's house. Either that or he was keeping it to himself—he liked to mete out the facts a little at a time—but she knew she would eventually weasel it out of him. One way or another.

The case that apparently had started with Royal Kajak's murder was growing more fascinating and weirder by the minute. And of course her dad had completely shut her out of it.

"I shouldn't tell you any of this," her contact had warned in that low, sexy tone of his. Kristi always ignored the tenor of his voice. The guy was interested in getting into her pants, so she let him think he could have a chance, just to get the information she needed.

"Oh come on," she said, playing along, matching his sexy tone with her own low voice. "It's all going to come out in the papers anyway."

"Yeah, but . . . I could lose my job."

"I won't use anything you tell me, promise, not until the press has gotten hold of it somewhere else. I'm not trying to beat someone to a byline for the next edition. This is going to be a book. A great book!"

"And when you publish that book?" he said suggestively.

"You'll get plenty of credit, trust me."

"Like what?"

"More than a one-line acknowledgment."

"Promise?"

"Promise." She almost gagged on the word. It wasn't that the guy wasn't cute enough. He was just a little too smooth, too proud of being a part of the whole cop thing, which Kristi was over. Big-time.

"You know, there's something else that might sway me into letting you in on this," he added in the suggestive tone that, the more she heard it, was starting to nauseate her.

"Nuh-uh. Business, remember."

"Someday you'll break down and go out with me."

"I suppose. If you play your cards right." Her words were an out-and-out lie. She'd made a personal vow never to seriously date anyone in law enforcement. No exceptions. She'd seen firsthand how a being a cop could ruin a relationship. Then there was the matter of Jay. The boy she'd left behind. Who, right out of high school, had wanted to marry her. Whom she'd dumped and now worked in the forensics lab.

She sure didn't want to run into *him*. She'd heard he was engaged, and that was good, or at least she told herself so, remembering at one time she'd accepted a "promise" ring from him. A lifetime ago.

So no, she wasn't about to date anyone where there was a chance, however remote, that she'd run across Jay's path.

She made a note to herself to check out the grave soon, during the day, and poke around the old hospital too. At that thought she felt a few qualms but tamped them down. This was her new career, and it wasn't for sissies. She was athletic, had taken a ton of martial arts, and wasn't stupid. She always carried pepper spray. She could handle a visit to a crumbling-down old building.

Kristi surfed the Internet for a while then returned to the story she'd started. She needed a title. Something that would catch the eye of an editor and a reader. Something explosive. Hot. Sexy. Something that had to do with the crime. A double entendre would be nice.

Unfortunately nothing came to mind, probably because she was inwardly seething, still burned that her father hadn't confided in her.

It's his job. He can't talk about the crime with you, can't compromise the case. You'll have to find another source, not just the one you've got in the department but someone on the outside. Maybe one of the nuns at the convent, or someone who worked at the hospital.

Someone who is close to the case but won't be in jeopardy of losing his or her job if they discuss it.

She started making lists of things to do.

She thought about interviewing the killer.

After the arrest, of course.

But wouldn't that be something?

Not only an exclusive discussion about the case from her father as lead detective but also with the psycho who was committing the crimes.

Yep, she thought, leaning back in her chair and stretching her arms high into the air. This was going to make a great book. Maybe even a best seller.

Put that in your pipe and smoke it, Rick Bentz.

The inn was over a hundred years old, renovated, situated in the middle of the French Quarter, and, compared to the Petrusky apartment, pure heaven.

Eve and Cole checked in, and she tried to tell herself that it was no big deal, that she was here with Cole because she needed his strength, his eyes, his mind. Oh for the love of God, did she really and truly *need* him?

A part of her screamed a loud and vibrant *No.* She wasn't the kind of woman who was dependent upon a man, especially not a manipulative, bald-faced liar.

The other part of her said, *Hell, yes, you need him! He gives you strength and a deeper insight. He's smart, clever, maybe even wily. Yes, he did lie to save himself, but he's proven himself over and over since he's been back. You don't have to marry the guy. All you have to do is trust him a little. You do need him.*

She was still angry with Cole, no doubt about it, but she decided to be pragmatic. The truth of the matter was that she just felt safer when he was nearby. For the night, they were together, and she would try to ignore the romantic overtones to the charming room complete with gas fireplace, four-poster bed, and French doors that opened to a veranda flanking the second story.

She realized ruefully that she should have picked a clean, tidy, and sterile motel on the freeway. It would have been cheaper and definitely less conducive to eliciting any romantic or sexual fantasies.

"Hungry?" Cole asked once he dropped their bags near the bed.

"Starved."

"Let's find something."

He knew of an Italian restaurant one block off Bourbon Street, and during the meal they somehow managed to keep the conversation light, away from the death and gore of the last few days. Cole bought a bottle of wine for the room, and though Eve thought sipping Riesling near a fire with Cole sounded like a recipe for disaster, she didn't complain.

Just keep your head, she told herself. A feat that seemed near impossible with Cole sometimes.

When they were back in their room, Eve kicked off her shoes. Cole uncorked the bottle and had just poured them each a glass when Eve's cell phone rang.

"Don't answer it," he suggested.

She glanced at caller ID and saw her sister-in-law's name on the screen. Relief flooded through her. She flipped her phone open. "Anna Maria! Where are you? Are you okay?" she said, making eye contact with Cole.

"I'm . . . I'm fine. I'm driving." Anna Maria's voice was thick, belying her words. "But how about you? Geez, Eve, I just read about what happened. Are *you* all right?"

"I guess that depends, but yes, for the most part," Eve said. The papers and news reports had been sketchy about the vandalism at her house, as the police had kept some of the evidence from the press. Eve couldn't fill her sister-in-law in on the full story, but, as she settled into a chair near the hissing fire and tucked her bare feet beneath her, she explained where she was and that she wasn't moving back to the house until it was cleaned and secured.

"I don't blame you," Anna said quietly.

Cole, to give her privacy, walked onto the veranda and closed the French doors behind him. From her vantage point, Eve watched him place his hands on the wrought-iron rail and look down at the street below. Her gaze skimmed over his backside, lingering for a second on the back of his jean-clad thighs and tight butt.

Aware of what she was doing, she readjusted her gaze, staring instead into the fire, where yellow flames licked at charred ceramic logs that would never burn.

"Well, where are you? I was out of my mind with worry!"

"I . . . I mean we, Kyle and I, were at a motel. Well, he was there some of the time," her sister-in-law explained. "I haven't called because I have bad news." She paused for a second. Eve could hear her inhale deeply, probably on a cigarette. Eve scarcely dared breathe. More bad news? She braced herself. Then Anna said heavily, "Kyle and I are separating."

"Oh . . ." Eve hardly knew what to feel. It was a let-down of sorts. A welcome letdown, but she could sense how much Anna was hurting.

"I know it's a shock. For me too, but it's what he wants. He needs his space, whatever that means. We've spent the last couple of days fighting. Like cats and dogs. All of this old, repressed anger. . . . It's just been awful." Her voice was hoarse with unshed tears. "We'll be together for a few hours trying to sort things out. Then the fight escalates, and one of us walks out. It's been an emotional yo-yo, and I finally realized, accepted, I guess, that it's just not working. I'm not sure we even like each other, much less love each other." Her voice caught as she finally admitted some-thing she'd feared. Sniffing, she added, "I don't like it, but there's nothing I can do. I . . . Oh God . . . I wouldn't be surprised if there's another woman. He swears there isn't, but what's he going to say?"

"I'm sorry, Anna."

"He won't admit it, won't tell me her name."

In her heart, Eve thought divorce might not be a bad

thing and that Anna might find someone so much better than Eve's dumb-ass brother. However, that's not what Anna wanted to hear. "I wish there was something I could do."

"Nothing to do." She was crying now, sobbing.

"I didn't help things by staying with you forever."

"It wasn't forever, and besides, that's what family's for."

"Look, Anna, where are you? I don't think you should be driving. I'm at an inn downtown. Either drive here or we'll"—she glanced at Cole again—"I'll come and get you."

"I'm . . . I'm fine."

"It doesn't sound like it. Come on, you can stay with me here for the night. We can talk things over or not, but I don't like you being alone."

"I'm fine." She sniffed loudly. "I don't need babysitting. I'm depressed, yeah, but not suicidal or anything."

"Anna—"

"I'm on my way home. My wonderful husband has decided he's going to 'bunk in,' that's what he called it, with Van for a while. He's talking about moving his business down to New Orleans, but he'll lose so many of his established customers. Jesus God, what's he thinking?"

"Why don't you turn around? You can live with me until you sort it out."

"After you move back to the house? Thanks, but with all that's happened, you may as well sell that thing. I don't know why you'd ever want to go back there again." She laughed shortly. "I gotta go. I'll call you tomorrow, once I've had time to think. I might need a damned lawyer. So much for love ever after, huh?"

Eve murmured a response and replaced the receiver. She looked through the watery glass panes to the veranda, where Cole was standing.

Love ever after.

She didn't really believe there was such a thing.

Maybe tonight she'd find out. Maybe tonight she'd let Cole into her heart. She glanced at the bed. They'd spent so much time arguing and fighting and not trusting. Tonight, she thought, would be different. She would let down some of her barriers. Cinching her robe around her more tightly, she walked through the glass doors and slipped her arms around his waist.

"Hey, what's this?" He turned and looked down at her.

She grinned and arched an eyebrow. "Well, if you play your cards right, 'this' might just be your lucky night."

Late at night he lay in his bed and closed his eyes.

He was tired. Needed sleep. But he was jangled. Anxious. He bit at his fingernails. Spit them into a waste basket next to his bed. There was so much to do. And little time. He trembled inside, and his head was filled with thoughts of Eve.

Always Eve.

He found other women attractive, but none were Eve.

Eve the beautiful.

Eve the princess.

Eve the loved.

It was time to find his ultimate absolution.

It was time for him and Eve to finally meet.

No more teasing. No more games. No more dolls. And no more waiting. Everything was in place. Finally, finally, she would be his. To the death.

Their destiny entwined.

As it had been from the beginning.

EVIL LIVE.

LIVE NOT ON EVIL.

Isn't that what Mother had always said? Hadn't she always talked in palindromes? Hadn't she told him they were the secret ways to communicate? Forward *and* backward?

He listened to the sound of the night seeping through his windows, the warm breath of spring slipping through the slight crack between glass and casing.

He visualized her surprise. Soon he would see it on her face. He'd drawn out the anticipation as long as possible, and now, oh God, now it was time. His lips were dry in anticipation, and he moistened them with his tongue then closed his eyes and imagined what he would do to her. At long last.

"She's the princess, you know," his mother always said, taunting him, telling him little details of Eve's perfect life as she'd sat at her sewing machine, clipping threads with her sharp teeth or cutting fine lines of cloth with her shiny pinking shears. They too had teeth. Many steel teeth.

"Oh yes, that Eve!" Mother had clucked her tongue. "She's always had the best, you know, never wanted for a thing, her father being a doctor and all." Mother's brows arched emphatically over her reading glasses as she sat on her stool at her sewing machine, brightly colored fabric spilling onto the floor. "Fancy house, shiny cars, frilly dresses, the little princess. And she's pretty too—oh, my, how pretty. Her mother loves her, her father adores her, and she's pampered by that grandmother of hers! Nothing's too good for little Eve."

He'd tried to close his ears to her poison, but his mother, the poor, hard-working seamstress with her arthritic knuckles and ever-growing envy, had never let him forget. She always brought up Eve. Especially at night, when the entire house was asleep, his father snoring soundly in the room far down the hall, his younger siblings already long dreaming in their bunk beds.

Then she would come to him. In the early hours of the morning, creeping down the hallway, padding barefoot into his bedroom, clicking the lock behind her and bringing with her the smell of gin and smoke and sick desperation. It had always been just to "tuck him in" or "kiss him good night."

But the soft little brush of lips against his cheek had

been far from chaste, and the tucking of his bedsheets with her smooth hands had led to exploration of his body. "You're a good boy, such a good, good boy," she'd cooed, as if he were a dog who had just performed a difficult trick. "So much better than that nasty little Eve. She's a whore, you know, in her designer dresses and expensive panties. Doesn't matter how much they cost, the truth is, Eve's underpants are always at her ankles. She's a dirty little girl, believe me. Lying and panting and spreading her legs for anyone."

He would lie upon his mattress, frozen, unmoving, sweating and nauseous, silently praying to God that she'd stop, that she wouldn't lick away his tears and tell him everything was all right, that she wouldn't slide under the covers and press her naked, bony body up to his. She'd told him displaying affection between a mother and a son was only natural.

But he'd known better.

Even then.

During those awful, debasing nights, he had called up Eve's image. Bringing her, not Mother, to his bed. Eve the princess, Eve the beautiful, Eve the loved . . .

He'd tried to close his brain to the things that were happening to him, attempted to take himself to a faraway place safe from his mother's sweaty, trembling hands as they caressed and fondled him. All the while he'd thought about Eve . . . How much better it would have been if she, the nasty little whore, had been in his bed.

And now, as he lay in bed, nervously biting his nails even though Mother no longer came to him, even though his nightmare of an adolescence was long over, he still thought about Eve. Constantly.

Eve the beautiful.

Eve the princess.

Eve the loved.

Eve the bitch.

CHAPTER 32

The Voice had come to him early in the night, while he'd been sleeping dreamlessly. It had been clear. Concise. Reverberated without interruption from the tinny little voices of white noise that often preceded Its arrival. As he'd lain in the bed, the Voice had told him precisely what he was to do.

God had forgiven him!

But there was a price to pay.

An atonement.

And this was it.

The Reviver wouldn't blow it again. His nerves jangled. He realized he was being tested.

He'd driven for nearly eight hours and arrived in the predawn, the neighborhood not yet waking, the streetlights glowing as he'd found the address.

She was inside.

Only her car was parked in the driveway, as the Voice had told him.

Boldly, he backed his truck into the driveway, confident that the Florida license plate he'd ripped off at an all-night dinner outside of Mobile wouldn't be missed for a while. The tags were current, and that was all that had mattered. The owners of the Dodge sedan might notice the missing front plate in the morning light, but by then it would be too late to identify him. His mission would be accomplished.

He drew his gun, complete with silencer, and slipped into the backyard. The sliding door to the patio was unlocked.

With a smooth whoosh, the door opened.

He braced himself.

No dog barked.

No alarm system began bleating.

But he heard voices . . . soft and low. Every muscle tensed, but he couldn't give up, couldn't flee. He looked down a dark hallway and saw the flickering blue light of a television showing through an open door.

Carefully he inched toward the master bedroom. A floorboard in the hallway creaked. He froze, expecting to hear someone shout or feet hit the floor, but there was no disturbance, just the voices from the television, dialogue from a movie. Cautiously he peered inside and saw the bed in the reflection of a mirror mounted on a wall.

She was lying on the mussed covers, her dark hair tangled over the pillow, her eyes closed, her mouth open. Soft little snoring sounds were nearly muted by the television. He pushed the door open a bit, slid inside. There were pill bottles on the table, next to a bottle of Vodka and a box of tissues. Wadded-up used Kleenex littered the floor and night table. Two of the pill bottles were open.

For an instant, he panicked.

What if she'd already tried to kill herself?

Oh no, that wouldn't work, wasn't part of the plan.

He couldn't mess up again. God had been specific.

She had to be alive! Had to!

He stepped forward anxiously, and he nearly tripped over a shoe she'd kicked off at the end of the bed. His knee slammed into the footboard, and he bit back the urge to curse.

On the bed, she stirred. Lifted her head, pushed back her tangle of hair, and blinked. "Kyle?" she said, already reaching for the phone or bedside light. "Is that you, baby?"

He sprang.

His body landed over hers.

"Ooof!" The air blasted out of her lungs.

In an instant she was fully awake, writhing, wrestling, trying to throw him off her as she opened her mouth to scream. One gloved hand covered her mouth. With the other he shoved his Glock to her temple, the barrel pressing into the flesh next to her eye. "No, honey," he rasped, enjoying the fear that he saw in her wide eyes, the terror he felt in her stiff body, the pure, wonderful horror that was evident in the rapid rise and fall of her chest, "I'm not Kyle."

"Found him," Zaroster said. She stepped into Bentz's office holding a memo pad. A triumphant smile creased her pixielike face.

"Ronnie Le Mars?" Bentz asked.

"Father Paul Lavender Swanson."

"Lavender?"

"No wonder he became a priest," she said dryly. "If anyone in high school ever found out, the poor kid would have been laughed out of school."

"Or become the toughest guy on the football squad."

"Maybe so. He's in a nursing facility not far from here. Just across Lake Pontchartrain, in Covington." She flashed him another grin and stripped a piece of paper off the memo pad. "Here's the address. Still working on Ronnie Le Mars."

Bentz was out of his seat in a second. "Tell Montoya where I am. He can call me or catch up with me there."

"You got it."

She returned to her desk. Bentz grabbed his jacket then headed through the maze of cubicles where other detectives were talking on phones, staring at computer screens, taking statements, and shuffling papers. He nearly plowed into Arvin Noon, a junior detective hauling in a suspect who reeked of whiskey and vomit. The guy's hair was stringy, his clothes filthy, and his wrists were cuffed behind his back.

"This is Herman Tessler. Got caught trying to rip off a convenience store."

"And?" Bentz asked. There had to be a reason for Noon to haul the suspect's ass up to the homicide department, though sometimes the big detective's methods weren't conventional. "Tessler claims he was at the Black Bird Restaurant the other night, combing through the dumpster, and he saw what went down between Officer Tiggs and a guy in a dark blue pickup. Says a bullet ricocheted off the truck, and that's consistent with the shell casing found at the scene. Officer Tiggs's gun had been fired."

"But the bullet missed Tiggs's attacker?" Bentz asked.

Tessler, the drunk, was nodding.

Too bad.

"I'm taking his statement then letting him sober up before I talk to him again. Show him some pictures, see if he can pick our guy out of one of our albums."

"Why bother having him make a statement now?"

Tessler was obviously drunk.

The younger cop's blue eyes flashed with a bit of defiance. "I just want to compare what he has to say. Sometimes inebriation helps bring out true feelings."

"Sometimes it just brings out bullshit."

"I'll do this my way. All right with you?"

Bentz gave the younger man a long look. "Handle it however you want. Just let me know the outcome." He didn't have time to get into a pissing match with the junior detective. Let him work it out with Tessler. The drunk would sober up, make his statement, and that would be that. So Noon was a bully, so what?

He grabbed his sidearm, jacket, and keys, then patted his pockets to make certain he had his wallet as he hurried downstairs.

Once in the department parking lot, he unlocked the door of his assigned Crown Vic and was getting inside when he spied Montoya's Mustang wheeling into the lot. Bentz flagged him down.

Montoya, his mood obviously as black as his goatee, jogged up to the cruiser. "Somethin' up?"

"Father Paul's in the St. Agnes Nursing Home in Covington."

"Let's go." Montoya slid into the passenger side, and Bentz nosed the Crown Vic toward the freeway. Though the day was overcast, the interior of the car was warm. Bentz hit the AC as he blended into the thick of afternoon traffic. He headed north toward Metairie and the Lake Pontchartrain Causeway, a twenty-four-mile bridge that spanned the vast estuary and ended up not far from Covington.

"I just came back from the hospital," Montoya said, slouching down in his seat. "Tiggs has been upgraded from critical to serious."

"That's good."

"Well, maybe. Part of his face is missing, and there could be brain damage. He's lookin' at tons of plastic surgery, physical therapy, and God knows what else." Montoya glowered out the window, staring at the endless stretch of water as Bentz drove onto the causeway.

Pelicans skimmed the lake's surface, and gulls,

calling noisily, floated higher in the air. The sky had taken on the ominous hue of an approaching storm.

"Shit, man, Tiggs has a wife and two-month-old little girl. Two months! She's so little, she probably doesn't even recognize him. Now he'll never be the same. Lose his job. Be on disability. Who knows if he'll ever . . . Oh hell! It's all just bullshit, I'm telling ya. Bullshit!"

Bentz didn't say anything, just let him rant. Everyone on the force had been in the grim spot Montoya was now occupying. It was part of the job. But it never set well. Never. From the console, the police radio crackled and sputtered, officers talking back and forth, cutting out over the static while the cruiser's engine rumbled smoothly. Neither of them spoke for a while. Then finally Bentz said, "Sometimes this job can be a real bitch."

"Yeah," Montoya agreed. "And that's on a good day."

On the north side of the causeway, Bentz drove through Mandeville and along Highway 190 until they reached the outskirts of Covington. Once inside the city limits, it was only a matter of a few blocks before they found the parklike setting of the care facility, a newer two-story building that housed individual apartments and could only be entered by means of a code punched into a keypad or a buzzer that called an attendant.

They buzzed, showed their badges to a woman who appeared on the other side of the glass door, and were allowed inside the cheery edifice. She took them to meet the on-duty manager, Alyce Smith, a robust African-American woman with neatly cropped hair and half-glasses perched on her nose. She occupied a meticulous office filled with bookshelves, cabinets, and a huge desk. A Bible lay open on a stand, a crucifix dominated one wall, and windows overlooking a courtyard allowed some natural light to filter through the blinds and diaphanous panels. The room smelled of jasmine, compliments of an air freshener plugged into a wall socket.

Again, upon Mrs. Smith's insistence, they showed their IDs and explained that they wanted to see Father Paul Swanson on police business.

"Just be cognizant that Father Paul is frail and tires easily. He also suffers from dementia, so I'm not certain how much he can help you."

"We need to talk to him," Bentz insisted.

"Please don't upset him," she said, flashing a smile that showed off a tiny gap between her teeth but did nothing to reveal any real warmth. She meant business. She hit a buzzer, and a girl of about eighteen appeared. "Sherry, please show Detective Bentz and Detective Montoya to Father Paul's room."

They followed Sherry along a hallway, trying not to notice the stares from the nursing staff and patients, some in wheelchairs, others with walkers or canes, as they approached an elevator. They silently ascended to the second floor then turned down a short hallway, passing a single window that overlooked the same

514

courtyard they'd viewed from Alyce Smith's office.

"He's not always clear," Sherry said. "It kind of depends on what kind of day he's having."

Montoya was accepting no excuses. "We still need to talk to him."

"Of course."

The studio apartment was furnished sparsely with a twin bed, dresser, television, and recliner. A large crucifix, identical to Alyce Smith's, decorated one wall; a calendar with pictures of the saints, another. And again, the air freshener, to help disguise the smells of a body slowly dying.

The occupant, a tall, excruciatingly gaunt man with sunken features, was sprawled upon the recliner. He was dressed in a plaid shirt and cardigan sweater, slacks and slippers, no sign of a clerical collar. His eyes were closed, his mouth agape, and he was snoring softly over the muted tones of an announcer for a golf match playing on the televison. "Father Paul?" Sherry said loudly.

The priest snorted and opened one eye.

"Father Paul? You have visitors."

"What?"

"Visitors. These men are with the police," she nearly shouted as he fumbled with his hearing aid.

"I don't know any policemen."

"No, they're here to ask you some questions."

"Questions?" he repeated. Blinking from behind glasses that made his eyes appear owlish, he scrabbled with one hand for the handle of his recliner, pushing the footrest down with some difficulty in order to force the chair and himself into a sitting position.

"Detectives Montoya and Bentz," the aide said, pointing to each of the cops in turn.

"We need to talk to you about Faith Chastain," Bentz said loudly. When Father Paul didn't respond, didn't seem to understand, he added, "She was a patient at Our Lady of Virtues when you were the priest there."

"Faith," he repeated dully. Something clicked, and his eyes cleared a bit. "Oh, Faith. Yes. Lovely but confused, very . . . Ah, well, she died. Fell from a window . . . I think. A pity."

"Yes."

"It was a long while ago, wasn't it?" He blinked up at Bentz as if he really didn't know. Then he swiped at the corner of his mouth with the back of his hand.

"Yes."

"Sad . . . Faith? Yes . . . yes . . ."

"But she had a baby while she was at Our Lady of Virtues, by a Cesarean section."

"And Sister Rebecca, she died too," he said, his face twisting with sudden agony. "Someone killed her. I read about it. A terrible thing, that. A pity."

"Yes."

"But she is with God now," Father Paul went on, running a hand over his head and smoothing some wayward gray hairs over his bald pate.

"What can you tell us about Faith Chastain and the baby she gave birth to about twenty-eight years ago?"

Bentz decided it best not to bring up the name "Adam," the still-birth issue, or the fact that Eve Renner's DNA said she was Faith Chastain's daughter. Even though Sherry had warned them that Father Paul was in and out of lucidity, and that much was evident, Bentz wanted to see what the priest could remember without being given every prompt.

"The child," Father Paul said softly and gazed so long at the floor Bentz thought he was memorizing the pattern of the carpet. Finally he said with more clarity than Bentz would have expected, "I suppose it's time someone knew the truth. Before anyone else is hurt."

"Or killed," Montoya put in. "Who was the baby's father? And what happened to it? We found the coffin in the cemetery. Someone had dug it up, put a pig's carcass inside."

Father Paul winced. "So it's come to this." He rubbed his large hands on his knees. Guilt settled on his narrow shoulders, stooping them even more. "Faith was confused and active. . . . She had men to whom she bestowed favors."

"She was abused by members of your staff and other patients," Bentz corrected.

"But she wanted the attention." He glanced out the window, where a wren was flying toward the roof.

Bentz and Montoya waited for more, but minutes passed with no further response. They exchanged glances.

The priest seemed fascinated by, even fixated on,

the bird outside the window. The sky was dark and menacing. Raindrops began to pepper the glass.

"She wanted attention from whom?"

He started, as if he hadn't remembered anyone was in the room with him.

"Faith Chastain. You said she wanted attention?"

"Father James. He counseled her."

"James McClaren?" Bentz supplied, his gut twisting. The familiar name sent his mind down pathways he'd rather not travel. But it was imperative that he did.

"Oh, I don't know . . . McCafferty?"

"McClaren."

"Oh . . . Father James . . . yes."

"He was assigned to the parish."

Bentz felt Montoya's gaze on him.

"Yes. No . . . Oh, for a while." Father Paul was obviously troubled, his forehead wrinkling as he tried to call up the memories. "I think he and the woman, the patient . . ."

"Faith Chastain."

"Yes, yes. That's the one. She had a baby. No." He shook his head, and one long, gnarled finger moved in the air as he thought. "She had two babies. I was there. They thought the boy child died."

"He didn't?"

"Oh no." He shook his head thoughtfully. "It was just after the nurse left the room that the doctor . . . Dr. . . ."

"Renner."

"Yes, Renner. That's it. He realized the baby was

alive, and then the other one . . . The woman was in so much pain. There was nothing to do." He looked up pleadingly then sat back hard in his chair. "I, we, vowed . . . never to tell. Never. I prayed about it."

"Can you tell us about it?" Bentz asked, pulling up a chair.

He folded his hands and bent his head. "Yes . . ."

In fits and starts, with Father Paul moving from periods of clarity and guilt to cloudiness and what seemed total loss of memory, he told them of the more dark secrets within Our Lady of Virtues. It took nearly an hour to pull out the story, and they were left in silence, absorbing what the old priest had told them.

Father Paul revealed that when Faith delivered, two babies were born. The first was a boy, who was originally thought to have not survived the birth. He was born vaginally, the cord wrapped around his neck, and he was blue . . . but, "Miracles of miracles from the Holy Father, the boy child began to breathe."

The discovery that the boy was alive had apparently happened after Nurse Chaney was excused from the birthing area. Then there were complications. Father Paul wasn't clear, but it seemed from what he said that Faith had started to have more contractions, and the doctor had realized she had another baby to deliver. For another unclear reason, the delivery had been performed by C-section, though the nurse was not called back into the room. The hospital was ill equipped for that kind of procedure. The priest wasn't sure if Faith knew she had delivered twins, only that she was not "thinking clearly" and very "confused," possibly "delusional." All he knew for sure was that Faith thought she had one baby, a boy named Adam, who died at birth. For her, nothing else registered except shame and fear and desperation. "She confessed to me often and was always in tears, but I'm not sure she knew why she felt such overpowering guilt."

Nor, it seemed, did Father Paul any longer. He could provide no information about the people who had adopted the boy, only that both babies were put with "people of strong faith." The girl had ended up with Renner, but the boy's parents and identity were a mystery. Father Paul recalled nothing of them, not even if they were parishioners, though he did mention that Dr. Renner took care of all the paperwork, whatever that meant. That was also how Renner adopted Faith's daughter with no questions asked.

When the priest was asked about the grave where Faith's child was supposed to be entombed, he sighed. "Another lie," he muttered unhappily, rubbing his hands nervously. "To protect her from the truth."

"Protect who?" Montoya asked.

The priest opened his mouth and closed it again. He seemed to drift into a place far away but finally whispered, "Everyone."

They asked a few more questions. Bentz even brought up Ronnie Le Mars's name, but they got nothing further, not the least flicker of recognition in his eyes. The old man seemed to have shut down.

When the nurse came in with his medication, they

left. They took the stairs down and exited through the main entrance. Bentz wondered if the boy Faith bore might still be named Adam. His adoptive parents may have changed his name to make his adoption all the more anonymous.

At least now they had something to go on. Renner probably had fabricated some of the information, but hopefully he hadn't switched dates or times of birth. There still should be some kind of record for them to find.

As they drove off, Montoya said, "Half of what the old guy said could be fantasy. Just in his mind."

"Possibly, but enough of the facts agreed with Chaney's."

"Can you believe that crap? Hidden babies, falsified records, illegal adoptions? Who are these people who think they're God and can just bend or break the rules to suit their needs because a kid, a damned human being, was inconvenient or even an embarrassment? Jesus H. Christ! All in the name of religion."

"This has nothing to do with the Church. It's people abusing power, thinking they were doing the right thing."

"All to avoid a scandal. Unbelievable!"

Bentz glanced back in the direction they'd come. "Do you think Father Paul is safe? Sister Rebecca was at the birth. So was Terrence Renner. Both of them were murdered. So is there a connection, and, if so, what about Ellen Chaney and Father Paul? Are their lives in danger?"

Montoya pulled his cell phone from his pocket. "I'll tell the FBI and the local authorities for Covington and in Ellen Chaney's hometown."

"Call Zaroster too and have her check vital records. Get a copy of Eve Renner's birth certificate and see if there are any other birth records for boys who were born on the same day, in the same area. Anyone named Adam. That might have changed, but maybe not."

"And about Father James . . . You going to tell Eve Renner you're her uncle?" Montoya asked.

"Right after I tell Kristi she's got a sister," Bentz said flatly.

"There's no way I'm going to be able to keep this from Abby so, let me know, will ya?"

Bentz nodded and flipped on the wipers.

The house was clean, the locks changed, and yet when Eve walked through the familiar rooms and hallways, she could feel her skin lift into gooseflesh. This, the home she'd loved, the place she and Nana had baked pies and cookies, the house where she'd felt on the top of the world in the turret room.

She glanced at Cole but didn't say anything as she dropped Samson to the floor. The cat skittered up the stairs ahead of her, and Eve trudged up dutifully, steeling herself. She was glad for the sound of Cole's footsteps behind her.

On the second floor, everything was the same as she'd remembered it. Nothing had changed, but in the turret room, when she pushed open the door and the clean and

522

gleaming room greeted her, she still cringed. She'd bought new bedding, including a new mattress pad. Even so, in her mind's eye, she still saw the bloodstains on the mattress, quicksilver images of her doll lying facedown on the coverlet, along with images of Sister Vivian's body in the attic of the old hospital.

The doorbell rang, and she nearly jumped from her skin.

"I'll see who it is," Cole volunteered. He was down the stairs before she could protest. She hurried to follow him, and as she reached the first floor she spied Detective Bentz in the foyer. He was grim as ever, and Cole was still holding on to the edge of the door as if he intended to slam it closed the minute the cop left.

Bentz looked up at her, and she saw that whatever he had to say, it wasn't good news. He barreled right in. "I met with Father Paul, who was the priest who worked at Our Lady of Virtues the night you were born. He confirmed what I'd already guessed: a priest by the name of James McClaren is your biological father. He's also my half brother, so technically, you're my niece."

She stopped short. "Your niece?" He nodded, and she saw that what was about to come next was difficult. "There's more."

He sighed. "It's a complicated story, but the long and short of it is that James McClaren also happens to be my daughter, Kristi's, natural father."

"What?"

"My first wife had an affair with my half brother,

who also happened to be a priest."

"Why the hell is that guy a priest?" Cole asked, his own disbelief evident.

"Good question. But too late. He's dead."

A dull roar started deep in Eve's ears. "So I'm related to you and to Kristi on . . . on my father's side and to Abby and Zoey Chastain on my mother's?" She couldn't believe it. She'd gone from being an only, adoptive child to a woman with three sisters and an uncle in one fell swoop.

"Are you kidding me?" Cole demanded as if he smelled some kind of trick. "What are the chances that Eve would be related to both you and Montoya?"

"Technically not Montoya. Only by marriage, if he and Abby tie the knot."

They were all still standing in the foyer, the door open, the wind and rain slapping onto the front porch.

"Close the door, please," she said to Cole.

"So, what does this have to do with the investigation?" he asked. "It's interesting history, but so what?"

"We think Eve has a twin."

"A twin?" Eve repeated, lips parting.

"A boy, now a man. A boy called Adam, who was thought to be stillborn. It was his grave we dug up at Our Lady of Virtues, but it was a fake."

"Wait, you're going much too fast," she said, her head spinning.

Bentz said by way of apology, "It's a lot of information. We don't know how, but we think he might be a part of this. I thought you might want to know about it."

"Yes . . . I do. Come in, Detective," she said. They walked into the parlor, a room rarely used, and she waved Bentz into one of her grandmother's Queen Anne chairs. She settled on a corner of the sofa. "Go on, please."

Bentz launched into his tale while Eve listened and Cole, standing in the archway from the foyer, crossed his arms and stared at Bentz as if there was some kind of trap lurking in Bentz's words.

Eve listened quietly. It was a wild tale. With her father right in the center of it. Was it really possible? Did her father and the staff at Our Lady of Virtues hide two births for twenty-eight years? She glanced over at Cole, who was glowering.

"So," Bentz finished, "we're trying to find your brother, see what he has to say."

"And you're linking him to the crimes somehow? As a killer or a victim?" Cole finally asked, the defense lawyer in him coming to life.

"That's a question I'd really like to ask him."

Bentz's phone rang, and he looked at the screen, saw it was Montoya, and picked up. "Bentz."

"Thought you'd want to know. The suspect that Noon brought in, Tessler, he picked Ronnie Le Mars out of the photo lineup."

"I'll be right there."

"That's not all, Bentz," Montoya said, his voice dark with anger.

"What?"

"Tiggs just died."

CHAPTER 33

Eve was going stir-crazy. For the past three hours they had been working with a security expert from a local company. Cole wasn't satisfied with the locksmith who had come and done his job. He was insistent that Eve have the entire house rewired for a security system. As soon as Bentz had left, he'd called the same company he'd used on the house he'd had to sell.

"I don't even know if I'm going to stay here," she'd argued, but he wouldn't hear a word of it.

"Even if you sell, where are you going to live in the meantime? A hotel? For how long?"

"Maybe your friend Petrusky could find me a place," she'd teased but had given in. And so here they were on the back porch discussing how much it would cost for the system. She heard her cell phone ring in the kitchen, where it was charging, while Cole told the guy exactly what kind of high-tech security he envisioned for a house that had, in all its history, survived without the aid of security cameras and laser beams and access codes. From Cole's description of what he wanted, Eve was certain this old Victorian would rival the White House for a high-tech alarm system. "Seems a little over the top to me," she'd confided in Samson three hours earlier when this had all started.

"I'll be right back," she said and hurried inside. By the time she reached the phone, it had stopped ringing.

She saw that the last caller was Anna Maria. She pressed return call but was thrown to her sister-in-law's voice mail. She waited then called her own voice mail and heard the message from Anna, who, upon Eve's advice, had returned to New Orleans and wanted to meet. Anna suggested a bar downtown and said she'd be there in fifteen minutes. Eve called her back immediately but again Anna didn't pick up.

Sometimes high tech was nothing but frustrating.

She walked back to the porch, where Cole and the security guy were still hashing out the details of the new system, going over pages of several different models. "That was Anna Maria. She wants to meet me for a drink down at Gallagher's."

"Give me half an hour and I'll come with you," Cole said. "We'll have this figured out then, won't we?"

The security tech nodded. "Sure. Piece of cake."

"Mmmm. Why don't I go on down, and you meet me later. I'll scope out how she's feeling, you know, about everything, and once I see that she's okay, I'll call and give you the green light."

He hesitated. "I don't like you going out alone."

"Oh for Pete's sake, it's just downtown."

"Give us a minute, would you," he said to the security guy as he shepherded Eve into the kitchen.

"No problem." The man was flipping through pages of diagrams for a variety of systems.

"I don't think this is a good idea," Cole said, shutting the door behind him.

"Obviously, but I think I should see her. She needs a

friend, and my brother is being a real jerk. She drove all the way back here because I asked her to."

"She'll wait a few minutes."

"Maybe she doesn't want you there. You're not her favorite person, and this is probably just some kind of girl talk. I'll call you the minute I get there and then again when it's okay for you to join us."

He shook his head.

"Look, Cole, you can't keep me on this tight of a rein, no matter what the reasons. I get it that you're worried. Really. And no, I haven't forgotten what happened right upstairs or that there's a nutcase on the loose, but I can't live my life inside a cave."

"I'm just asking you to be smart."

She let out a huff of air. "So . . . how about this, and let me tell you, I don't like it. You follow me down there, just see that I get inside safely, then vamoose before Anna spies you." She heard her own words and rolled her eyes. "Oh God, that sounds so ridiculous. Like I'm some pathetic little woman who can't handle her own life."

"You're just being cautious."

"Yeah, and I'm letting some kook determine how I'm going to run my life!"

"Not a 'kook,' Eve, a killer. A sadistic, deranged serial killer who's focused on you."

She let out a long breath and met his gaze. "Sorry, Cole, I can't live this way. I've got things to do. As soon as I know that Anna Maria's all right, I'm going to call Abby Chastain and meet with her to discuss all this business about being sisters. After that, I'll need to talk to Kristi Bentz. So you can handle the security system, okay? I'm pretty booked up today."

He wasn't buying her light and breezy mood. "This is serious, Eve."

"I know, but I think I've got a couple of policemen watching over me. Even though I told Montoya and Bentz I didn't want the extra security, I don't think they listened."

"Oh? Not that I wouldn't think they might do something behind your back, but why do you think you've got your own personal bodyguards?"

She took his hand and led him upstairs to the turret room and ignored the eerie feeling that stole through her blood whenever she crossed the threshold. She guided Cole to a window that overlooked the neighboring street. "See that red Pontiac?"

He nodded.

"It's been there for a couple of hours. Two people inside. Before that, there was a blue Blazer parked about two spaces down. It was there when Bentz was here."

"How do you know it's the police?"

"I don't, but I'm willing to put fifty bucks on it. You watch, when I leave, if they follow."

"It could be the killer."

"Nah . . . not with two people." She turned and pecked him on the cheek. "Face it, Counselor, the cops are watching our every move. So go figure out the alarm system, and I'll keep in touch with you via cell phone."

A muscle worked in his jaw. He obviously wanted to argue with her, but she was hearing none of it. She felt stronger today, ready to take on the world. Though the room still bothered her, she might eventually get over it.

Might.

She tore off her sling and tossed it onto the bed; her arm had quit hurting, and she was tired of having her movements restricted. After rotating her shoulder a couple of times and deciding it was working without too much pain, she changed into clean jeans and a red cotton sweater while Cole stood, arms crossed over his chest, eyeing her with disapproval. "I'll call, promise," she said and kissed him again. Then, before he could argue, she was down the stairs and out the door.

As she drove through the rain, she saw Cole still standing in the turret window, staring down at the street. The guys in the red Pontiac came to life. She turned the corner, passed them, and, in her rearview mirror, saw the Pontiac pull away from the curb and do a quick one-eighty.

Poor Anna Maria.

She had no idea Eve was coming with her own personal posse.

Anna Maria could barely move. Whatever the whack job had given her was taking effect, and her legs felt like rubber. Scared out of her mind, she was lying in the back of his truck, trying to keep her wits about her, alternately praying and trying to find a way to escape.

The prick had held a knife at her eye and forced her to make the call to Eve. Now she was lying in the truck, listening as rain pounded on the canopy and wondering if she'd ever see Kyle again. That bastard. Oh God, how she wished he'd come and save her . . . that someone would. And now she'd dragged Eve into this madman's sickness.

She hadn't seen his face. He'd worn some kind of neoprene mask, but he was big and strong and had attacked her in the bedroom, gagged her, bound her, and hauled her out to his truck, where she'd ridden for hours, her body aching, her bladder stretched to the breaking point.

He must've figured out that she'd have to pee because he'd pulled off into the woods somewhere, yanked down her pants, and watched as she'd relieved herself. She'd been so mortified, she'd almost been unable to go, but then nature had finally taken its course.

She'd been forced into the back of the truck again, onto the stained mattress, her arms once again bound behind her, but, as he'd pushed her inside, she'd caught a glimpse, beneath her blindfold, of the license plate mounted on the truck's bumper. She'd immediately pressed those letters and numbers into memory just in case she somehow got the upper hand and escaped. Then he'd driven away again, and she'd listened hard, hearing the sing of the tires on the pavement, the rumble of the truck's engine, and his voice droning as if he were chanting or praying, the words unclear.

She'd felt an increase of speed when he'd reached the freeway again and tried to remember how to make the vehicle noticed by other cars, how to communicate to the other drivers on the road that she was being abducted.

By a madman.

But bound as she was, she couldn't move, could communicate with no one.

In her heart she knew the psycho who had captured her was the same killer who'd taken the lives of her father-in-law, Royal Kajak, and those nuns. Dear God, what could she do?

And she'd been weak.

She'd spent the next, long stretch of hours crying and praying. Then she'd felt the truck's speed slow down, and the sounds of the traffic had changed. She knew that he'd driven her into a large city, most likely New Orleans. The truck stopped and started at several lights. Then he'd parked, and her heart had been a wild drum.

Was this it?

Where he planned to kill her?

Oh dear God, no!

Her mouth was dry as sand, her fear palpitating as she heard him climb into the back of the truck with her. It was so dark. So damned dark. He'd touched her, and she'd recoiled. Then she'd felt something cold and hard as steel, the barrel of a gun, now pushed against the underside of her chin. He'd told her what to do. And promised to kill her should she make one slipup. Too terrified to do anything but what he'd demanded, she'd made the call to Eve.

And so she'd lured her best friend into the psycho's trap.

She'd thought he would kill her right then and there once Eve had agreed, but he'd lowered the gun and said, "Good girl" in a soothing voice that made her want to scream.

Then he'd slithered out of the canopy like the snake he was and locked her inside again. She'd yanked on the ropes that bound her, tried to bang and get someone's attention, but the sounds were muffled by the mattress, the gag stopping her screams.

Dear Lord, forgive me, she prayed, fighting tears and mind-numbing terror. Desperately, she tried to concentrate. There had to be a way.

She had to save Eve.

Save herself.

Oh God, please help me. Please!

So he hadn't lied.

Kristi stood in the cemetery and stared at the open pit where once there had been a casket. Just like her source had told her. She peered inside then pulled her digital camera from her backpack. The day was dreary and overcast, threatening rain, but it was light enough

533

to click off a few pictures for the book. She imagined a section with photographs of the crime scene.

Which led her to believe she should really get some shots of the hospital. Before it was torn down. She knew there were a lot of pictures available; the place had been photographed hundreds of times. But she'd like a picture of Faith Chastain's bedroom, and the stairs leading to the attic, where Sister Vivian Harmon's body had been found. The attic itself, of course, Eve Renner's house, and, if she could swing it, pictures of the cloister of the Our Lady of Virtues convent. That might be a tough sell because there were nuns living in the convent, people working there. She doubted anyone would just let her enter without some kind of viable excuse.

This is why it would be nice if her father would open some doors for her, use his influence.

She stared through the trees and the thickening shadows toward the convent and figured it would be a dead end. But the hospital, if she could scale the walls, shouldn't be a problem.

She glanced to the menacing sky just as the first few drops of rain started to fall. It was dark as twilight already, so she'd have to work fast. She'd come prepared, not only with her camera but with a few tools, a strong flashlight, and, of course, her pepper spray.

She felt the slap of wind against the back of her neck as she looked through the gloom at the crumbling headstones, some of which had toppled, and the few family tombs that rose above the ground or cut into it.

534

If she let herself, she could be creeped out by all this, but that would serve no purpose. She took a few more pictures of the graveyard then climbed into her car and drove to the convent, searching for the access road she'd heard about from her father the last time there was a serial killer on the prowl near the old hospital. Supposedly there was a driveway that led to the garages and working sheds of the convent and a walking path that cut through a hedgerow of arborvitae and led to a gate in the fence surrounding the hospital. This path had been used by the nuns of the convent and some of the gardeners and other staff as a shortcut.

Or so Kristi had heard.

Well, it was time to test the theory.

The rain was starting to come down hard enough that she flipped up the hood of her jacket as she reached the garage area, where a pickup was parked and a dumpster rusted in the rain. A hedge grew beside the fence line, and she walked next to the dripping evergreen shrubs until she spied a flagstone and an overgrown path that sliced between two of the tall bushes. As she stepped along the stones, wet branches slapped at her shoulders.

On the other side, she found a rusted gate hanging open. She stepped through, onto the campus of the hospital. Through a canopy of limbs just starting to leaf, she spied the dark roofline of the asylum.

Ridiculously, a chill swept through her, but she ignored any trepidation as she found her camera and started clicking off shots. She couldn't let unfounded fears stop her. The rain was really coming down now, and she ducked her head and followed what had once been a trail through the thicket of pine and live oak. Her heart was pounding, and she felt a little as if she'd stepped into another world, a dark and forbidden path that wound through the pain and misery of the past. Closer to the hospital, she clicked off a few more pictures and considered the people who had lived here, who had been misdiagnosed, mistreated, or trapped in this monolith of an institution.

Her cell phone jangled, and she jumped, saw that her father was calling again and decided to keep ignoring him. He'd ask what she was doing, and then she'd either have to lie, which he always seemed to sense, or she'd have to tell him the truth, in which case he would come unglued and start in on his routine, discouraging her from writing the true-crime book.

She didn't want to hear it.

For God's sake, she was an adult.

She switched the phone to vibrate and continued. Once she had finished her business, she'd call him back. She'd heard the earlier messages about dinner, but she wasn't all that interested, wasn't going to change her plans to suit him. Nah, she was done with that.

So what if he's had a change of heart, what if he finally wants to talk to you?

It could wait.

At least a few more hours.

Frowning, she kept walking through the wet puddles and damp leaves that had never been raked from the fall.

Closer to the asylum, she saw the decay. The crumbling mortar, the falling bricks, the broken windows, the encroaching weeds and vines. Once grand and imposing, the structure was now forbidding and bleak. Again she found her camera and trained her lens on the rusted-down spouts, freakish gargoyles, and black windows. What a creepy, almost hellish place.

It was great!

And the pictures were turning out better than she'd anticipated. There were still a few hours of daylight, though the damned rainstorm was turning day to night. She had to hurry.

So, how to break into this fortress?

She saw the windows near the back door had been boarded, and she knew she was probably wasting her time, but she walked up the back service entry steps, twisted on the knob, and, with only the slightest creak of old hinges, the door swung inward.

Kristi hesitated.

An unlocked door just didn't seem right.

But maybe the nuns left it open, or maybe because of the last murder someone had forgotten to check the latch. It didn't matter. As far as she was concerned, it was a godsend.

She stepped inside.

• • •

The rain was spitting as Eve parked in a spot as close to Gallagher's as she could get. She made a mad dash through the drops and walked inside, where the after-work crowd was taking advantage of the happy hour and the dark ambience of the bar. Blue smoke hung near the ceiling, and the jazz combo, despite their heavy-duty speakers, was nearly drowned with the sound of conversation and laughter. People clogged the dance floor and waitresses bustled past while bus-boys cleared the tables. Not a great place to have a quiet conversation, but then maybe Anna needed noise and people and a singles scene.

A hostess was mapping out tables.

"I'm looking for a woman named Anna," she said, nearly yelling. "I'm Eve."

"What?"

"Never mind. I'll find her." Eve wended her way through the tables and booths, jostling dancers as she searched the smoky interior. Nowhere did she see Anna. She made another pass and then saw a drink, a cigarette in an ashtray, and a scarf and wet coat that she recognized as belonging to her sister-in-law. Even her purse was on the bench. What was she thinking? Anyone could pick it up. She searched the dance floor, didn't see Anna, then decided she was probably in the restroom, which was just down a short hallway.

Scooping up Anna's purse, she walked toward the restroom and was jostled by a big man heading in the opposite direction. The contents of the purse scattered.

"Excuse me," he said as she reached down to pick up the pieces and he did the same. "Let me help."

"No, I can—" His hand was over her mouth so fast she couldn't scream, and something sweet and sickly smelling filled her nose and mouth. Too late she tried to scream, to fight, but her arms and limbs were already not obeying her, and the punches she threw glanced off him as he quickly dragged her past a janitor's closet and through an open door to the back alley.

The rain was coming down in sheets, blown by a crosswind.

She tried to fight but could barely stand, her legs wobbly, her mind beginning to fog. She blinked. Tried to clear the cobwebs and stumbled a bit, just like she'd had too much to drink. She knew then that no one would stop and help her. No one even knew there was a problem. She looked like a drunken woman whose caring husband was guiding her to their car.

No! She tried to articulate, to yell at someone, but her words came out in a slur.

Then she saw it.

The dark pickup; the one she'd seen following her from Atlanta. She fought the effects of the ether and the urge to throw up, but it was no use.

She blacked out.

CHAPTER 34

The room numbers lined up. Bentz had spent most of the day running down friends and relatives of Ronnie Le Mars and drawing a rough sketch of the hospital, adding layers, lining up the floors, then doing research. Vivian Harmon, before joining the order, had been a patient at Our Lady of Virtues. Her room number had been 323, the same as tattooed on her forehead. And the area where her body had been found, the nook that Eve Renner had claimed as a child, was positioned right above 344, so, conceivably, to a twisted mind, Eve's childhood play area could be considered room 444. Roy Kajak had occupied room 212 when he'd been a patient at the hospital. He'd known Ronnie Le Mars, as had Vivian Harmon.

His shoulders ached from too many hours leaning over the desk. Rotating his neck and listening to a series of worrisome pops, he thought it was time to call it off for the day. He'd planned to meet with Kristi and tell her about Eve Renner being her half sister, but he wasn't looking forward to it. He needed something to bond him more closely to his kid, not drive a wedge further between them.

"It is what it is," he told himself, stretching his arms upward.

"Hey!" Montoya shouted, then burst into the room. "I think we got the son of a bitch!" Montoya's dark eyes glittered. "Le Mars," he said, unable to keep from grinning. "We found him!"

Bentz was already reaching for his coat and sidearm. "Where? How?"

"Anonymous call to 911 from a pay phone in town. Someone claimed to know Ronnie, heard him bragging, says he's staying in a bayou cabin about twenty miles outside of the city—get this—about fifteen minutes as the crow flies to Our Lady of Virtues. The place is owned by someone named Lester Grabel, deceased. Lester's son Raymond just happened to be a cellmate of Ronnie's in prison. We've already sent an officer to check it out, and the FBI will be there, but I'd like to see the look on this guy's face when we nail him."

"You think this is legit?"

"Good as anything we've got."

"Let's go." Bentz was already around his desk. They hurried down the stairs together, and for once Bentz didn't argue when Montoya said he'd drive.

They were in a department-issued Crown Vic, lights flashing, when a call came over the radio. The first unit from the state police was closing in and would secure the access road to the cabin. Within two minutes, a second unit would back them up. No one was entering until they received word from higher up.

Montoya sped onto the freeway like a bat out of hell. Lights flashing, siren screaming, he cleared traffic in front of him and never took his eyes off the road.

"Can it really be this easy?" Bentz asked. "An anonymous tip out of the blue?"

"Not exactly out of the blue. We've been beating the bushes on this one, contacting anyone who ever knew any of the victims and Le Mars. Someone finally decided to give him up."

"Maybe." Bentz was skeptical. But then, that was his nature. Always had been. He didn't trust in coincidence or happenstance or just plain good luck. In fact, he lumped all of the above in with the Tooth Fairy and the Easter Bunny.

The sky was darkening, getting black as night, and what was at first just a drizzle started pouring, coming down in sheets, aided by the wind. Montoya didn't slow. The cruiser's tires splashed through the puddles and standing water, spraying up against the undercarriage and any vehicle he passed. Bentz popped a couple of Tums then dialed Kristi again. He'd been trying to reach her all day. He wanted to take her to dinner, talk things out, but now, he figured, dinner was out. He left another message, telling her there might be a change of plan, then hung up, not wanting to think how many times he'd had to cancel or postpone because of work.

Well, damn it, tonight it was important.

The first unit had reached the location; the second would be there in minutes.

"I can feel it," Montoya said, his hands tight over the wheel, his eyes narrowing as he stared through the windshield as the wipers slapped away the rain. "This is it. We're gonna get the bastard!"

Bentz hoped to hell he was right.

Cole checked his watch as the security guy drove off. Eve had been gone an hour and a half.

So what?

She said she would call.

He walked from the kitchen to the front room, glanced out the windows, and then headed back to the kitchen. She and her sister-in-law were probably deep into some kind of conversation. No big deal.

Nonetheless, he called.

She didn't pick up.

Should he go down there?

His phone rang in his hand, and he felt a second's relief, then read the screen and realized it was his attorney calling him. "Hello?"

"Hey, good news," Sam Deeds said.

"Great. I could use some."

"The DA's dropping the marijuana charge."

"I expected that. I was set up. We all know it."

"Baby steps, my friend. Baby steps. But I'm working on all of the charges that have ever been filed against you, going to see if there's a way we can get everything off your record. The partners are on board. They're taking you on, pro bono."

Cole wanted to say, "Big of them," but held his tongue. True, the firm hadn't stood behind him during the Royal Kajak mess, but he wasn't going to look a gift horse in the mouth. If the partners at O'Black, Sullivan and Kravitz were finally going to do something for him, he'd take it. For now. "Great."

"That's all you can say? Hell, Cole, I've stuck my neck out for you, pushed these guys. And all you can say is 'Great'?"

"If you've been reading the papers, you know I've got bigger issues."

"I told you to stay away from Eve. And what was that nonsense of siccing her brothers down here to check on the will?"

"Doesn't the firm have it?"

"Yeah, and they got the information they wanted, though they weren't happy with it."

"Cut out of Daddy's will?"

"Essentially. But you didn't hear it from me."

Cole imagined that pissed Eve's brothers off big-time. He glanced at the clock and couldn't tamp down the worry that dogged him. He and Deeds talked a little longer, and then he hung up, tried to call Eve again, and decided enough was enough. Grabbing his keys, he walked outside, turned his collar against the rain, and headed for his Jeep.

He couldn't sit around and wait.

He had to find out that she was all right. If that bothered her, it was just too damned bad.

Eve was in and out of consciousness, unable to keep her eyes open. Everything that had happened seemed as if it were a dream. She remembered being shepherded into a dark truck . . . and she hadn't been alone. Anna Maria. She'd been there. Or had she? And after driving for a while, the big man had stopped and forced her to drink something, and then she passed out again. . . .

Right?

She wasn't sure.

Where was she now?

On a bed?

Where were her clothes? . . . No, this wasn't right.

A blindfold covered her eyes, but it had worked its way up her forehead and she could peek beneath it. . . . Wherever she was, it was nearly dark, with spots of light . . . candles . . . Yes, candles . . . and someone was crying. No, chanting. No, praying. She tried to concentrate, to hear the murmured words of the rosary—yes, that was it—but someone was definitely crying. Who? Why? Where? Or was this all just a dream?

Cole.

She needed Cole.

But . . .

From beneath the edge of her blindfold, she saw him. A big, muscular man. Naked. His skin gleaming in the firelight. She couldn't see his face, but his body was covered with scars, all kinds of scars. . . . No . . . not scars. Tattoos. Some had healed; many had not. . . . Numbers and names . . . Her name in large letters: EVE . . .

She knew she should be afraid.

She sensed the situation was dire.

A woman was crying, for God's sake.

She tried to focus and started to drift again but caught a glimpse of his face in the mirror, a face she thought she recognized. Those eyes. Oh Lord, they were the same as they had been so many years before, looking down at her with a lust that was as raw as it was evil. Fear sliced through her, but even that deep, visceral emotion wasn't enough to stave off whatever drug it was that held her in its grip. She couldn't keep her eyes open, couldn't think.

Somewhere, far away, she heard a door open, but she was fading. The chanting stopped abruptly. The muffled crying ended with a long, tortured, muted scream. . . .

And then there was nothing but the blackness that consumed her.

The hospital was getting darker by the minute. Kristi had spent a lot of time on the first floor taking pictures, walking the hallways and trying to imagine what the asylum would have been like twenty years earlier, filled with patients, uniformed staff, and the ever-present vigilance of the nuns in their habits.

It was time to leave, but she felt compelled to at least visit the floor where Faith Chastain had lived and died. The stairs creaked as she raced up them, and she felt more than a little creeped out by the stained-glass window of the Madonna on the landing, her beatific features seeming sinister in the dim light. The round window was unharmed, each colored panel intact, unlike so many of the other panes. She clicked off a couple of shots of the window then headed upstairs to room 307, Faith Chastain's room.

The door opened with a soft whisper, and she stepped inside to an empty room with a huge dark stain on the floor. She pulled out her camera and clicked off several shots. Not all of them would be used, of course, but she'd rather have a ton to choose from, and she wasn't certain when she'd be able to return. This was her chance.

Her phone vibrated, but she ignored it and headed for the end of the hall and the stairway leading to the fourth floor, where the dead nun's body had been found. She tried not to let her imagination run away with her as she kept her flashlight's beam steady on the dirty wood floor and found the linen-closet door ajar.

Inside, behind a wall of shelving, was another door. She unlatched it and shined her light up the stairs that wrapped around a chimney. Dozens of footprints from the crime-scene investigators, the detectives, and all kinds of law enforcement were visible.

Kristi felt more than a little apprehension, but she told herself it was now or never and started mounting the steps. It wasn't until she was in the attic, sweeping the beam of her flashlight over the floor and rafters, that she spied the blood, a dark stain and smaller drips.

Her stomach turned over.

And there was something else . . . marks on the floor, probably made by the investigators. Every so often. Circles around what appeared to be holes in the flooring. Kristi leaned closer to one and peered through, to see one of the rooms below.

How odd.

And interesting!

She'd have to remember this.

She looked through a second hole and realized from the dark stain spread upon the floor that she was looking into room 307. Faith Chastain's room. She felt a thrill. It was too dark to take any pictures now. She could barely see the rooms below. She'd just have to come back when it was light.

Tomorrow morning.

Hopefully the rain would quit.

She turned to head down the stairs when she heard a noise. The soft, distinct click of a lock being turned.

Her heart jumped to her throat.

Who would be coming to the hospital now?

She swallowed back fear and told herself not to jump to conclusions. Maybe one of the nuns had stopped by. Or a maintenance man or gardener might have the key.

Or the killer. For God's sake, he's obviously been here before!

No, no . . . Don't go there. Don't let your imagination run away with you. Maybe you didn't really hear anything. A lock turning? Could you hear that clear up here? No way. The hospital is quiet, yeah, but you're letting your fears get the better of you.

A few floors down, a door creaked open.

Kristi froze.

She listened hard, over the thundering beat of her heart.

And then she heard footsteps.

Heavy and steady.

Inside the hospital.

The city was far behind when Montoya cut the siren
and lights then peeled off the freeway and flew down
the two-lane road that sliced through the parish. Farm-
houses were sparse, fields stretching into forest and
lowland, the smell of the swamp reaching into the car
as the rain pounded. Bentz's phone rang, and, seeing
that it was the station, he answered. "Detective
Bentz."

"Hi, it's Lynn," Zaroster said. "I thought you'd like
to know that Cole Dennis called in. Apparently Eve
Renner is missing."

"What?" Bentz said. "We had guys on her."

"Yeah, I know. I talked to them, and their story
dovetails into Dennis's."

"Which is?" he asked. The road narrowed, winding
through stands of live oak, pine, and willow. Even
Montoya had to slow a bit.

"That she went to meet her sister-in-law at a bar
named Gallagher's. She was supposed to check in
with Dennis, and he never heard from her again. He
got worried, so he went down to the place, and a
hostess remembers seeing her but doesn't recall anything else. No one at the restaurant remembers serving
her or her leaving. This is confirmed by the officers
who were assigned to watch her."

"And where the hell were they?"

"Keeping a low profile, as the 'subject,' that would be the now-missing Ms. Renner," Zaroster said with a bit of a bite, "didn't want any kind of police protection."

"Did she meet anyone? Leave with someone?"

"We don't know."

Bentz tried to keep the anger out of his words, but he was furious. "What the hell do our guys say?"

"They knew she was in the bar. Watched her walk in. Then they staked out her car and the front door. They didn't realize she'd ducked out the back."

"Son of a bitch. Son of a goddamned bitch! Look, put out a BLOF for her. See if Gallagher's has a security camera and get the tape if you can."

"This could be just a matter of Eve Renner wanting some privacy."

"I know, but I doubt it."

"Yeah, me too."

His stomach burned as he hung up.

"Trouble?" Montoya asked.

"Maybe. Maybe not. Eve Renner gave Cole Dennis and our boys the slip." He ran a hand over his jaw. He didn't like this, not at all.

Montoya missed a turn, hit the brakes, backed up, spewing gravel, then turned down the road and stepped on it again. Bentz's phone rang again, and he saw the caller ID. "Hell. It's Cole Dennis." He felt compelled to answer. "Bentz."

Dennis didn't bother identifying himself, just said, "Eve's missing. I just called 911. I thought you and Montoya should know."

"I heard. We're looking for her."

"Wasn't someone watching her back?"

"She didn't want protection."

"But you gave it to her anyway," Cole accused. "We saw the cops parked just down the street."

Bentz frowned as the gloom of the day seemed to seep into the interior of the cruiser.

"We thought it would be a good idea."

"Well, it sure as hell wasn't very effective. She left to meet her sister-in-law and then disappeared."

"Where is Anna Maria Renner now?"

"I don't know, Bentz, but you guys have to find Eve. You have to!"

"We will," Bentz promised, but he had a bad feeling.

Obviously Dennis was angry. And scared. And probably riddled with guilt.

A few miles down the road, they spied a state trooper's rig parked at the end of a long drive that was partially obscured by brush.

Montoya slammed on the brakes and the Crown Victoria shuddered to a stop. He was out of the car in an instant, with Bentz at his heels. The troopers had already sealed both the front and the back entrances to the place, which was little more than a shack hidden from the road by a long, weed-choked lane.

Bentz knew they should wait for more backup, or the FBI, or a damned SWAT team, but he was too hungry. This was way too personal. He didn't want to chance Le Mars somehow slipping into the coming night because protocol wasn't observed.

Through the storm, two state troopers ran to the back of the building and took up positions at the rear door. Bentz flattened his back against the cheap siding by the front door, while Montoya pressed against the wall on the opposite side of the door. Troopers covered the windows.

He waited.

Gathered himself.

"No signs of life," Bentz said.

No light shined from any of the windows.

No smoke rose from the chimney.

"Nice and quiet," Montoya observed. "Kind of spooky."

Weapons drawn, Bentz nodded at Montoya through the dripping rain, then banged on the door. "Ronald Le Mars! Police! Open up!"

No response. Just the steady beat of the rain.

Bentz didn't wait. He twisted on the door handle, certain it would have to be forced, and was shocked when the door swung open to a room as dark as death.

"Le Mars!" he yelled again as Montoya shot a look inside. "Ronnie! Give it up!"

"Police!" Montoya shouted.

Taking a deep breath, Bentz whirled through the doorway, hitting the floor, his weapon drawn. There was no light inside, so Bentz lay still, hardly daring to breathe, trying to get his bearings. He didn't dare use his flashlight in case Le Mars was hiding and lying in wait, searching for a target.

"Le Mars!" Montoya shouted as Bentz's eyes

adjusted to the gloom and he saw the bodies. Naked and shadowy, lying faceup in front of the fire. His stomach lurched, and he felt something wet on the floor. Too thick to be run off from a leaky roof. He rubbed a thumb and finger together then lifted the substance to his nose.

Blood.

He was half lying in a pool of blood.

He climbed to his feet and, using his flashlight, exposed the bodies. "Oh sweet Jesus," Montoya whispered as, with his weapon drawn, he stepped into the room. "It's Le Mars."

"Yeah," Bentz agreed, staring at the woman. "And Anna Maria Renner."

"So where's her sister-in-law?"

Bentz was already reaching for his cell phone. "Nowhere good," he said, sick inside. "That's for damned sure."

Kristi hardly dared breathe.

She heard the footsteps climbing the stairs. Slowly. With a heavy tread. But never faltering. Over the sound of the rain peppering the roof and gurgling down the gutters. She swallowed back her fear and strained to listen, all the while trying to figure out what to do.

She had her cell phone. . . . She could call someone.

And say what? That you're hiding up in the attic of the old hospital? That you're trespassing and someone else is here? Grow some damned balls,

Kristi, and think, damn it. You don't want to sound the alert until there's a reason to.

So she'd play it safe. Quietly she extracted her cell phone. It was still on mute and vibrate, so she didn't have to worry about anyone calling her and the phone ringing. Biting her lip, she typed out a text message: *I'm at OLOV asylum. Not alone. Send help. K.* Then she picked two people to send it to. She just wouldn't press the send button until she was certain she was in a dangerous situation.

The footsteps paused.

Kristi's heart nearly stopped.

Had he heard her?

How?

She strained to listen, thought she heard a moan, and clenched her jaw so that she wouldn't scream.

She doused her flashlight and wondered if someone outside had seen the moving beam through the few small windows that allowed natural light into this garret. That was ridiculous, right? No one ever came onto the property.

The footsteps started up again, climbing upward until she was certain he'd stepped onto the third-floor landing.

God help me, she thought and made the sign of the cross over her chest.

Send the message. Send it now. It will take a long time before anyone can come here anyway. Send it!

He walked slowly down the hallway, and her eyes followed the sound, her gaze traveling over the floorboards that lay directly beneath the center of the attic. He slowed, and she heard the moan again as he switched direction, entering one of the rooms.

She crept silently to a spot directly above and knew that he'd entered Faith Chastain's room. Without making a sound, she got to her knees and looked through the hole. Oh Lord, it was so dark, but she saw a shadow pass beneath the peep hole. More than a shadow: a large man, and he was carrying something. Oh dear God. She watched as he dropped a woman onto the floor.

Kristi pushed the send button on her phone.

Help would soon be on its way. She just had to wait for a few minutes, keep her head and—

She heard a trill, loud and sharp.

Somewhere a cell phone was ringing.

Echoing through the empty hallways of this hospital!

Oh dear God.

No, oh please, NO! It couldn't be!

The footsteps stopped completely.

And the trilling ceased.

Kristi knew her message had been received.

By the man in Room 307.

By her contact in the police department.

A.J. Tennet would know she was on the floor above him.

All her hope died.

CHAPTER 35

Bentz wanted to throw up.

Once they'd found the light switches and illuminated the cabin, he'd been sick as a dog.

Fortunately the FBI was now on the scene, securing it, waiting for the crime techs, who were on their way.

Bentz looked over the cabin one last time. The naked bodies were still stretched in front of the dying fire, posed together. Anna Maria's corpse was unmarked aside from a single bullet hole in the back of her head. Along with his matching head wound, Ronnie Le Mars also sported tattoos that were repeated over and over, inked into his body as well as scribbled across the walls of the room:

Eve, 323, Renner, 444, Nun, Viv, Xanax, 101, evil, Kajak, 212, Deified, Reviver, Dennis sinned, Live not on evil. Never even. Evil live.

The tattoos were all recent; no mention of them were in the file on Ronnie Le Mars.

"A real nutcase," Montoya said, shaking his head. They were waiting for the crime-scene specialists, but time was slipping away.

As far as they knew, the killer might already have Eve Renner.

"Look at this place, it's all wrong," Bentz said, eyeing the cabin. Though parts of it were neat and organized, the rest was filthy, as if all that really mattered was the fireplace, a kind of shrine. He eyed the rosary hanging from the mirror and the blackened windows. He'd been at enough crime scenes to sense when something didn't quite fit. "This place doesn't match our mastermind. Do you think Ronnie Le Mars was capable of pulling off all the killings? Getting away clean? The guy was a maniac."

Montoya tensed. "What're you saying? He's our killer. The tattoos are evidence . . ." He stepped closer to the fireplace. "You think he had a partner."

"I think he had someone calling the shots."

"That's a helluva leap."

"I've read Ronnie's file, talked to his parole officer and yeah, he was our killer, but something's just not right."

"Hey!" an officer shouted from outside. "We found the truck. Got a scratch on it consistent with a round."

"Shootout with Tiggs," Montoya muttered. "This is our guy."

Bentz swallowed hard as he searched the room, carefully examining the mantel, mirror, and desk. He found tattoo supplies and patterns and again, a notebook with pages of pages of palindromes, as if the guy lived for them.

It still seemed wrong. A bad feeling ate at him, roiling his stomach. He eyed the bed. Carefully made. Obviously the man spent all of his time either at the fire doing God knew what or here in the bed. "Hey, hand me a flashlight."

"Looking for bedbugs?" Montoya asked, grabbing a flashlight from a uniform.

"Maybe."

On his knees he shined the harsh beam over the sheets, pillows, and quilt. When he peered under the springs, he saw it. "Jesus H. Christ," he whispered. Hidden deep inside the springs and mattress, he found tiny speakers, some kind of receiver and electronic gadgets he didn't recognize.

"What is it?" Montoya asked.

"I don't know." He glanced around, searching for a radio or stereo that would transmit to the speakers and found none. "I don't get it," he said, but the bad feeling that had been gnawing at him just got worse.

"So who killed them?" Montoya said, motioning to the victims. "Obviously not Ronnie as he's now a vic. So who's left? The son? Eve's twin? The guy we can't find?" He shook his head. "Why would he off Ronnie Le Mars?"

"Good question." Bentz popped a couple of antacids and walked outside, where the rain was a welcome relief from the stuffy, hideous cabin. "Somehow he knew Le Mars was here. No one else did."

"Except the anonymous caller," Montoya pointed out, scratching at his goatee. They walked toward the cruiser, wending their way through the other vehicles that had arrived, including a news van.

Bentz was not in the mood. Fortunately a spokesperson for the Feds was fielding the questions of two reporters.

As they reached their car, Bentz's cell phone rang. Caller ID told him the call originated at Our Lady of Virtues.

"This is Detective Bentz."

"Oh, hello, Detective. This is Sister Odine, with the convent."

She got right to the point. "Remember, you asked me to let you know if anyone showed up here? Well, I thought you should know there's a car parked at the cemetery. A red Volkswagen Jetta, I believe. I have the license plate."

"What is it?" Bentz asked, but he could barely hear the nun's words over the crashing of blood pounding through his brain. She rattled off the letters and numbers of the plate, confirming his suspicions. The Jetta belonged to his daughter.

"We're on our way. I'll meet you at the front gate of the convent. We'll need the keys to the hospital." He climbed into the passenger side of the cruiser. "How fast can you drive to Our Lady of Virtues?" he asked Montoya.

"Twenty minutes," Montoya said, firing up the engine. "Give or take."

"Make it ten."

"Why?" Montoya was already cranking the wheel and hitting the gas. "What's up?"

The cruiser shot forward.

"Kristi's there." Bentz hit the speed-dial button for his daughter and waited. No doubt she wouldn't pick up. For the first time in a long while, he sent up a quick, short prayer. *Please keep her safe!*

The phone connected.

"Kristi!" he said. "Kristi!"

But she didn't answer.

The phone indicated he'd just received a new text message.

I'm at OLOV asylum attic. Not alone. Send help. K.

Cole drove his Jeep as if he were fleeing Satan himself. As the wipers tossed off sheets of rain, he mentally kicked himself up one side and down the other. Why had he let Eve go to the bar alone? He'd known it wasn't safe. He shouldn't have allowed her to bully him, and now she might be lost to him forever! Now, after they'd just crossed so many hurdles, when they'd finally come together. He thought of their last night of lovemaking, in the hotel, and his jaw clenched so hard it ached.

He had nothing to go on but gut instinct.

He had no weapon, just the tools in the back of his rig.

He didn't doubt that she was with the madman, though he had no idea where he'd taken her or what he'd done to her. In sharp, jagged pieces, he remembered Royal Kajak's mutilated body, then Sister Vivian's naked corpse, and the doll propped on the bloody bed.

His only hope was to piece together the messages that the killer had given them, the clues. Palindromes and numbers, backward and forward.

560

Through the slap of the wipers, in quick tempo, he thought *101; 212; 111; 444; 323; Eve; Renner; Kajak; Viv; Nun; Dad.*

He was certain the numbers referred to rooms at Our Lady of Virtues, and he intended to walk those rooms and decipher their meaning. Somehow he would piece together the clues. He had no other options, and time, he felt with every breath he drew, was running out.

Eve opened an eye.

Where the hell was she, and why was the darkened room spinning?

Lying on her back, staring upward at a high ceiling, she heard the beat of rain, steady and hard. Her headache was back, pounding in her skull, and as she fought it, images came back. Fuzzy bits of memory. She'd been abducted. At the bar. And Anna . . . Oh, God, was she dead?

She blinked hard, remembering the cabin and Ronnie Le Mars and a woman weeping. . . . then . . . oh, God! Someone had come in and shot them both then hauled her away. She'd passed out again, only to wake up here.

In the hospital.

He'd brought her to the mental asylum.

She realized now that she was in Faith Chastain's room, lying on the stained floor.

For the love of God, why?

And where was he?

She tried to sit up, but her arms and legs were still uncooperative and useless.

Try again, Eve.

It's a situation of mind over matter!

Concentrating, she willed her right arm to move. Nothing.

Come on, come on, don't give up!

She tried again, focusing and straining, and her arm slid a bit, though in no controlled fashion.

Again! Hurry! Who knows how long he'll be gone?

This time she was able to get her finger to twitch, but that was it. No great show of strength, no ability to push herself upright, no chance of running.

Then find a weapon.

She looked around frantically, but the room was empty.

Don't give up. Be creative, damn it!

She looked frantically again, her gaze scraping every corner of the room. Nothing . . . Oh God . . . And then a little glitter near the hearth. Glass?

She started to try and move closer to the fireplace, but she heard something and froze.

Footsteps?

Overhead?

In the attic. What was he doing up there? Spying down on her? Using the peep holes in the attic, the ones she'd used as a child. How ironic that someone now might be spying on her. No, that didn't make any sense. What the hell was he doing up there?

She was going to die. She knew it. There was so much

she had planned for her life, so many things she still wanted to do. Cole's image came to mind, and she nearly wept as she realized how much she loved him and that, recently, she hadn't had the nerve to tell him how she felt. She remembered making love to him, feeling his body entwined intimately with hers and how he'd whispered words of love as he'd pushed her hair from her face. But never had she told him how she'd felt.

Fear of being hurt again had paralyzed her.

How foolish she'd been.

Now, she might never get the chance.

A lump filled her throat, but she ignored it. She had no time for "could have beens" or "should have beens." She had no time for anything.

She looked again at the little bit of glitter near the fireplace. A piece of glass? Not much of a weapon.

But better than nothing.

He was coming for her.

Kristi's only hope of escape was down the very stairs he would ascend into the attic.

His footsteps thudded as he ran down the length of the hallway. Hers were silent. While every instinct told her to run in the opposite direction, she quickly tiptoed to the chimney and melted against its far side, the rough bricks pressed hard against her back.

How could she have been so foolish? So stupid as to trust him?

She reached into her backpack and fumbled until she found the pepper spray. Then she waited.

And felt sick when she saw the beam of a flashlight. So much for hiding. So much for surprising him.

Not daring to breathe, she waited.

"I know you're up here," he said, standing in the doorway, sweeping his flashlight to the farthest reaches of the garret. In the illumination, she saw a rat scamper into a hole in the roof, and she bit back a gasp.

"You know, Kristi, you are such a tease. After everything I've done for you, now you're going to hide?" There it was again, that sexy, cocksure tone that she found nauseating. "You know I've got Eve, don't you? Your half sister."

What? Half sister?

"Funny thing about that. She's my sister too. Did you know that? My twin. She and I have the same mother, you two share the same father. How incestuous is that? We're all just one, big, happy, sick family."

Don't listen to him. He's talking crazy.

"Now wouldn't that make one helluva story?" he asked nibbling on a pinky nail.

She was sweating, waiting for him to step deeper into the attic.

"I guess your dad never got around to calling and telling you the news. Maybe that's because he's not really your dad, now, is he? Old Rick is really, what? Your uncle? Isn't that how it works? Your mother fucked around with a priest, right? Good old Father James. If only he could have kept his pants on."

How does he know all this? Her heart was pounding, her muscles strung tight. *Don't let him bait you. That's what he's counting on. Do not listen.*

"So the story is that your mother wasn't the first woman that let the good priest into her panties. Oh, no. Father James was nothing if not persuasive and charming. Faith Chastain, a woman of . . . well, less than high moral standards, went for him too. Of course, it didn't hurt that she was mentally disturbed. Did that stop the good priest? Hell, no! And bingo, she got pregnant. My mother, oh, make that my *adoptive* mother, she saw them, you know. Told me how Faith screwed the priest, really shook my mama's faith." He snorted as if the idea were absurd. "She considered herself a good, God-fearing Catholic, but it didn't stop her from coming into my room at night now, did it?" he said, his voice rising with emotion.

Kristi felt her stomach lurch. She had to fight to keep from throwing up, to stay still and quiet. "So what's really interesting," he continued, his voice causing her to shrink against the rough bricks, "is that somehow Faith managed to hide her pregnancy from just about everyone."

The guy was nuts! Insane! Kristi swallowed back her fear. Tried to keep a clear head.

"So you see . . . You and I, we're blood, little sister. I can call Father James 'Daddy' too!"

No. This was unbelievable. No friggin' way!

He swept the beam across the floor again and stepped into the room. "Come on, Kristi. Where are you? Believe me, you do *not* want to make me mad."

You are mad. Crazy. Insane! But there was a grain of truth in his words, enough fact woven into his fiction to give her pause and make the skin on the back of her skull tighten in revulsion.

He turned the flashlight toward the ceiling, as if he thought she might be in the rafters. She clenched the pepper spray in a death grip.

He took one more step, and she sprang.

Just as he turned and shined the light right in her eyes. Blinding her.

"Stupid girl," he muttered, and she blasted him with the spray, shooting a stream straight into his eyes.

He dropped the flashlight. It rolled onto the floor, shining in a wide arc.

For the first time, she saw the gun.

Pointed straight at her heart.

He was coughing. Tears streamed from his handsome face, but he didn't seem to mind. He grabbed hold of her arm and forced her down the stairs, the gun pressed into her back.

She thought he was taking her to the third floor, but he pushed her farther and farther down the stairs, through the foyer on the first floor, past the dining room, and into a horrible place that was once the kitchen. Near the back door, he prodded her around the corner, where he yanked open a door to the basement.

Her heart sank, and she nearly stumbled on the stairs and half fell into a long hallway. Kerosene lamps had already been lit along the tiled corridor. They passed by darkened rooms that looked more like cells, and Kristi's imagination ran wild as she thought of the patients who had been isolated here, below ground.

"Stop," he said and nudged her into a room where a lantern burned and ancient tools and equipment hung from hooks screwed into the molding tile. She spied an electrical prod, a straitjacket, and a tray of time-dulled surgical instruments. Lights protruded from the ceiling, and she imagined the room had been one where surgical procedures had been performed. Her stomach churned.

A.J. plucked a grimy straitjacket from the wall. While pointing the gun at her head, he held the jacket out to her with his other hand and said, "Slip your arms through."

"No." She shook her head, her skin crawling at the thought. "I can't."

"Do it, Kristi, or I promise you, I'll shoot you. Not in the heart to begin with. I'll start with your femur, shatter the bone. Then I'll shoot you in the hand." He smiled through his tears and running nose. "Consider yourself lucky. That's as sadistic as I get. If you would have run into my buddy, Ronnie Le Mars, he would have brought his knife. Done exactly what I told him to do. He thought I was God, did you know that? I had to look long and hard to find someone with ties to the hospital, someone who remembered Eve, someone who was psycho enough to play into my hands. And along came Ronnie. Released from prison. Someone I knew about from my mother who worked in the laundry at Our Lady of Virtues. I kept track of him, because he was perfect, and when he was released, everything I worked for could happen." His eyes, still red and glistening with tears, actually gleamed, and he smirked with satisfaction. "But you won't have to worry about Ronnie or his weapon of choice, because I put him out of his self-inflicted misery." His face suddenly hardened again and he sniffed loudly. "I won't hesitate to put you out of yours, so do as I say. Got it?"

Ronnie Le Mars was dead? Killed by A.J.? Stunned, she had to keep trying to make sense of this, find a way to best him. Desperate, she tried another tack. "I thought you were my friend."

"Brother, Kristi, get it right," he said, angrier than ever, his nose still running. "No, we were never friends. You were using me, that was all, and I saw through it from the beginning. But it worked for me, so I went with it."

"And used me," she said.

"Yeah, how's that for irony?" He shook the strait-jacket. "Put this damned thing on. Now!"

She didn't move fast enough, so he took the gun and fired it point blank at the wall.

BLAM!

The shot cracked in her eardrums and split the tile.

"Watch out! The bullet could ricochet!" she yelled, jumping backward. He caught her with the hand holding the gun, wrapping one strong arm around her and forcing the sleeve of the straitjacket on her with his other hand.

She started to struggle until the gun barrel pointed at her, cool against her cheek. He was a cold-blooded killer. She believed that.

Once her arms were inside the sleeves, he set down the gun and tightened the straps, forcing her to hug herself, rendering her hands and legs useless. Dear God, what did he plan for her? She felt helpless and knew if she didn't do something, she would die.

But your legs are still free. . . . Don't give up. Remember. Never give up.

Crack!

A gun blasted.

Eve screamed. Sweet Jesus, what was happening? She shuddered to think.

She could only assume the monster had murdered someone. Possibly someone she knew.

Her stomach quivered and her head pounded. Trembling, she tried to somehow hold onto her thoughts. *Think, Eve, think! Save yourself. Before he kills again!*

One. Two. Three . . .

She had no idea why he hadn't killed her yet, but she knew that it was only a matter of time, probably minutes rather than hours, until he'd end her life as well.

Unless she did something . . . took action.

Heart racing, she tried to swallow back her dread and think.

Four. Five . . .

She'd heard two sets of footsteps walk down the stairs. Whoever had been hiding in the attic had been caught. And killed. Holy Mother Mary, she couldn't imagine who would have been in the garret or why. One of the nuns? Someone hiding, seeking shelter, a homeless person? Or someone she knew?

But now, she was certain, it was her turn.

Dear God, help me. . . . Please, please, help me!

Pull yourself together, Eve. You're not dead yet!

Six. Seven. Eight . . .

Slowly her limbs began to tingle and ache. She could flex her fingers, straighten her toes. . . . She gritted her teeth, forced her arms and legs to drag her. Slowly. Inching. Her muscles rebelled, not listening to her brain. *Come on, come on! You can do this! You have to!*

With supreme effort, she started to move. Muscles straining, screaming in protest, she pushed herself ever so slowly across the grimy, dusty, blood-stained floor. Closer and closer. Toward the fireplace where she'd seen the glittering piece of glass.

Let me get there, please. . . . Please . . .

Her hand closed around the sharp-edged fragment.

CHAPTER 36

Cole parked at the front of the hospital, pulled out a pair of bolt cutters from his toolbox, and went to work on the chain that held the wrought iron gates together. Rain poured down his neck and the wind slapped at him as he worked.

"Come on, come on, you bastard," he said, his jaw set, his shoulders and arms pushing, straining. "Come on!"

Crack!

He heard the muffled report of a gun and then, faintly, a woman's scream.

Eve!

Adrenaline fired his blood.

Don't go there!

He couldn't think that she'd been shot. Wouldn't. He pressed hard again, his arms shaking, and the metal link snapped. The chain gave way, slithering like a dying snake to the ground. Cole shoved hard on the gates, and, with a horrific groan, they opened. In an instant he was through and running up the drive.

He couldn't lose Eve.

Wouldn't!

Oh, God!

Once before he'd seen her lying in a pool of blood, a gunshot wound at her temple. But not this time. Oh God, not this time!

The monster returned.

Holding a flashlight in one hand, he pointed a gun at Eve and grabbed her by the shoulder she'd injured earlier. "Come on, let's go. You should be able to walk now." He yanked her to her feet, and pain screamed down her arm. Still, she held on to the shard of glass, hoping beyond hope that he wouldn't notice her fist was clenched. Dozens of questions raced through her mind, but she asked none, instead pretending to be duller than she was, a zombie.

Face red, eyes gleaming with evil malice, he was sniffing, snorting, and coughing as he prodded her with the gun to the stairs.

"Move it!" he yelled.

Her legs were still unsteady, and she had to catch herself on the railing, cutting her hand in the process. Still, in the darkness, blinking as if he'd been crying, he didn't notice, not even when blood began to drizzle down her fingertips and onto the stairs.

Give me strength, oh, Lord, please, give me strength.

Down to the first floor and then around the corner and through the kitchen to the basement steps where he unlocked the door. She cringed inside, her blood running cold as death. Oh, how she hated dark, dank places. The hairs on the back of her neck stood on end as he pushed her down the creaking, filthy steps.

Don't let your fears get to you. . . .

One, two . . .

With the gun at her kidneys, he locked the door

behind him. His flashlight aimed over her shoulders, illuminating the cobwebs and filth as he shepherded her to the basement. Quivering, her skin pimpling in fear, she walked along a long corridor lit by kerosene lanterns, their golden light glowing, dark smoke curling to the low ceilings and the smudged tile walls.

Eve could barely breathe. Her heart thundered in her ears and the glass cut her hand, but still she stumbled forward past rooms where unspeakable operations had taken place. If she listened, she thought she could hear the desperate, raw whispers of ghostly patients.

She swallowed hard, closing her mind to the horrors that had occurred here. "Stop," he ordered halfway down the shadowy corridor, and she froze.

He unlocked a door and as it creaked open, he nudged her inside with the nose of his gun. But he didn't lock the door, she noticed, as the lock was only on the outside, in the hallway, used to keep people inside.

Another woman was waiting, standing, wearing a filthy straitjacket where a single lantern illuminated the room.

"Isn't this cozy," the maniac said, sounding pleased with himself over the drip of rusting, ancient pipes. "I assume you two have met. . . . No? Oh, that's right. Kristi, meet your half sister, Eve. And Eve, have we met? Do you know who I am?"

She didn't respond.

"Oh, come on, now, Sis," he said, obviously enjoying her confusion. "Tell her, Kristi." Then before the girl could say a thing, he added, "I'm A.J. Tennet, actually Adam Tennet. Get it? Adam and Eve? Like some kind of great cosmic joke, the gods, or really your father played on us."

In the semi-dark she stared into eyes that were as cruel and cold as they were like her own.

Her twin! The brother she hadn't known existed!

"That's right. You've got it. We came into the world, right here, in this hospital. Together. Trouble was, Dr. Renner adopted you, and he tossed me out in the garbage, handed me over to a couple who didn't give a crap about me, especially once they suddenly got fertile and had kids of their own. So you were the lucky one, weren't you, princess?"

He was psychotic. No telling what he planned to do, but no doubt it was demented and evil. Death lurked around the corner. *Don't give up. Fight him! He thinks he has the advantage.* Her fingers tightened over the shard of glass.

He reached for another straitjacket, but as he pulled it down it fell apart in his hands, the ancient cloth disintegrating. "Fuck!" he said. Then, to Eve and Kristi, "Sit the fuck down!"

He's unraveling, right before my eyes, like the straight jacket. If things don't go exactly as he plans, he falls apart. . . .

Both women slid slowly to the floor.

He wasn't through raving, and though Kristi tried to meet Eve's eyes, Eve stared straight at this abomination who was her twin.

"Yeah, my mother, Lara Tennet, she was a piece of work. A real sweetheart. She taught me everything I know about women." He said it with disgust as if it brought a bad taste to his mouth. "Whoring cunt. If you knew what she did to me. Her own damned son." He was furious now and something more. . . . Beneath the anger there was another emotion visible . . . Self-loathing?

"And you, Eve," he snarled. "The princess. Good old Mom told me all about you. Couldn't give it up. She was fascinated." He came closer then, bending down, staring at her with a lust and envy that scared her to her soul.

Pretend. Act like you're not with him. Maybe he will let his guard down.

"You don't know how many times I heard about you. I'd love to fuck the hell out of you. But I don't think that's possible and besides. . . ." He was shaking now, his gun trembling in his hands.

Oh God, it could go off at any second!

"I–I don' unnerstand," she said, as if she were still more woozy than she felt. She wanted to keep him talking, hoping that he would slip up, his attention diverted, if only for a split second. Then she'd attack.

"Of course you don't," he said, nibbling a fingernail. "You didn't have to join the army to get away from your mother, did you? You didn't have to depend on the government to buy your education for you. You didn't have to fudge on your application and hope to hell that it would get through. You didn't sweat that the police wouldn't accept you into their ranks." He tore off a nail in his teeth and sank to the floor, his gun still trained on her. "I've been planning this a long time, you know, but I had to wait until the time was right, until Ronnie got out of prison." Adam grinned then and whispered in a raspy voice, "Heeee's freeee . . ."

Eve's skin crawled, and he saw the reaction.

"Oh, I know you thought I was talking about Cole Dennis. . . . Nope. It was Ronnie. I needed someone who would do my dirty work, and who better than nutcase Ronnie? You may not know this, but he had a real hard-on for you, Eve. Um-hmmm. Planned to fuck the hell out of you and then kill you. You won't have to worry about that now." He leered at her as if he imagined what it would be like to rape her, but something held him back, something ridiculously tied to sanity. "Ronnie thought we were doing God's will."

"How do you know that?" Kristi demanded.

"Because I'm God," Adam said, still staring at Eve. "The Voice, I think he called me. I had it wired so that I could talk to him at night, tell him what I wanted him to do. He heard other voices as well, whispery conversations that made him think he was insane. It was sick how he begged and prayed for me to come to him. He was the Reviver, that's the name I gave him. Told him he would be deified and because I'd planted the seed, another gift from Mom and her sick palindromes, he was convinced that he was doing God's work, God who thought backward and forward. 'Reviver' is a word that goes both ways, same with 'deified' and 'Eve,'" he said, looking straight at her. "And the numbers tattooed onto the victims? Room numbers from the hospital. Even Sister Viv stayed here."

Eve swallowed hard. He was sicker than she imagined.

Kristi said, "You told him who you wanted killed?"

"Yeah, and as I said, I worked palindromes into the equation and that started with Mom, too. Ronnie saw her tattoo Faith's head with 'live' all those years ago. She knew Faith had been screwing around, and so she upped Faith's meds, made her woozy and tattooed her. 'Live,' but really 'evil.' And then, on top of it all, Mom and Dad adopted me, all under the table. She told me this, you know, right before she overdosed on her own meds, poor woman. That's why I had to steal all the files that were hidden here, in the attic, so you wouldn't guess Mom's death was connected to Our Lady of Virtues."

He grinned as she realized he'd started the killing with his own mother.

He's proud of himself. Bragging, Eve realized, sick at his story and filled with a colder fear. He'd accomplished whatever it was he thought was his mission, so now he had no goal, no reason to live, no reason to keep either Kristi or her alive.

The hand holding the gun was more relaxed, but he still gnawed on the fingernails of the other hand, nervously chewing. He was volatile, liable to snap at any minute.

"Don't you want to know how you ended up with two sets of sperm in your vagina, Eve?" he asked, and she forced herself to roll her eyes at him, her head lolling. "That was my idea. Ronnie actually did the honors. He had no problem getting off on you."

She nearly threw up at the thought of the maniac with the needle.

Sensing her revulsion, he grinned. "Don't fret, princess. The Reviver didn't touch you. I did the lab work myself, added his sperm to the rape kit." His watering eyes gleamed as he leaned close, adding, "So they'd all know you're a whore, just like our mother."

She fought the urge to attack, to leap across the room and pummel him with her fists and slice his face with her measly weapon. But it was no match for a gun. She glanced at Kristi, who was watching his every movement. If only she could convey her thoughts to Kristi.

Not yet. . . . Wait. . . . He's letting down his guard. Maybe we can somehow get the upper hand and if not kill him, lock him inside his own prison!

"So you see, sisters, I think we should all go out in a blaze of glory. As much as I'd love to fuck you both, we don't have time, and that would be the ultimate sin, wouldn't it? In another lifetime," he whispered, and Eve felt as if the grim reaper had just slid his fingertips down her spine.

Adam glanced over at Kristi. "You know, you weren't a part of this until you came snooping. I really was going to let you write your damned book, but once you tried to call the cops on me, well, I figured you deserve the same fate as the princess. Especially since you called in the cavalry. So . . . we all die. Become martyrs. We, the illicit spawn of Father James. Fitting, don't you think? Listen . . ."

He cocked a head as if to focus on sounds, and Eve heard it then, the sound of footsteps, running overhead.

Where was she?

Oh God, where was she?

Heart pounding, pulse thundering, his hand bleeding from the window he'd broken to get in, Cole raced through the old hallways and stairs of the hospital. Up, up, up to the attic. Surely that's where the son of a bitch would take them. To Eve's retreat as a child, where the doll and Sister Vivian had been found. Frantic, he eased around the chimney, his heart in his throat, his gut churning.

Eve! Hang on, darlin'! I'm coming. Oh please, please hang on!

Around the corner and into the attic, a desolate garret where the rain pounded on the roof and the interior was still as death.

Where are you, you bastard? Cole thought, frantic as his gaze scraped the deep umbra and every cranny. *Where!*

His mouth dry as the Sahara, he stepped across the floorboards and heard the rush of the wind and scream of sirens.

No one leapt at him.

No one shouted.

He didn't stumble over any bodies.

No one was here. . . . So where, damn it, where in God's name was she?

Back down the stairs and, quickly, silently, searching every room. His heart hammered and fear tore through him as he ran, feeling every second of Eve's life tick away as if it were her last.

Montoya stood on the brakes, and the Crown Vic screeched to a stop right beside Cole Dennis's Jeep and the worried form of Sister Odine, who was huddled under an umbrella. Rain pelted from the sky, dark and ominous as a curse.

"I just got here," she said, eyeing the Jeep as the officers sprang from their vehicle. "I have no idea who this belongs to or who opened the gates."

"Don't worry about it," Bentz said, eyeing the bolt cutters and clipped chain. "You've got the keys to the building?"

"Yes." She singled out one key and handed the ring to him then saw the blood covering his shirt. "Oh, my."

"Not mine," he assured her, snagging the key ring.

"Thanks. Now, please, Sister, go back to the convent and stay there. I've called for backup, but please leave. Now."

"God be with you," she whispered then made the sign of the cross. Holding her umbrella against the wind, her skirts billowing, she started back to the convent just as sirens screamed from a distance.

Bentz didn't wait. Weapon drawn, he ran up the cracked, wet driveway and heard Montoya's footsteps as the younger cop kept pace. Past the overgrown lawn and empty fountain, through the sheeting rain, they raced toward the behemoth of a hospital that rose sinister and dark, a malevolent brick beast where only evil resided.

Bentz's heart nearly froze.

Kristi was inside.

In the attic.

And not alone.

With the killer!

God help her, he thought, reaching the doors and jamming the key into the lock. His fingers were wet and the metal was slick, but the latch gave way. With a groan, the huge doors swung open.

"Hear that? Didn't I tell you? We have company," Adam said as the sound of footsteps echoed from above. "Time to end it." He was agitated. Edgy.

He glanced toward the ceiling as he stood up, and in that instant Eve nodded sharply at Kristi then sprang, her arm raised high, the piece of glass cutting into her palm.

She struck.

Hard.

Blood spurted from his neck.

Rained on her.

Adam bellowed, shocked. Twirling, he fired. The gunshot echoed like thunder in the small room, a bullet zinging past her head.

Kristi rolled, using her entire body to whip his legs out from under him. A. J. fell hard, landing on his back. He shot again, wildly.

Hot pain sizzled through Eve's thigh.

Kristi kicked hard, landing a blow to the side of his face.

He screamed. Rage and agony reverberated through the room. Footsteps thundered on the stairs.

Hurry, hurry, hurry!

He bobbled the gun, but somehow held on, blood streaming down his neck and staining his shirt. His eyes were wild, his rage palpable. He turned the muzzle on Kristi.

"Bitch!"

Kristi kicked again, trying to knock the weapon from his hand and knocked over the lantern. Kerosene and fire crawled across the room.

Blam!

The pistol went off again, the noise like thunder.

Kristi crumpled.

Voices shouted from outside in the hallway.

"NO!" Eve screamed, staring in shock as she realized the bastard had killed her sister. The sister she'd never gotten to know. Eve whirled on him, her gaze locked with his as flames began to spread. "You bastard!"

"Like you," he gasped, winded from the blow, but

still hanging onto his weapon. "Like you, princess!"

Someone pounded on the door. "Police, open up!"

Slowly, deliberately, unafraid, he raised the gun again. Staring down the barrel, Eve knew this was what he'd planned all along. In the puddled kerosene, fire crackled around them.

"You and me, Eve. We came into the world and we go out together!"

"Open the damn door! Now!" Bentz's shouted urgently.

Crack!

Wood splintered. The door to the cell burst open the same moment the gunshot echoed.

Bentz fired.

Point blank.

A second later he rushed into the room, Montoya on his heels, Cole a step behind. In time to see the killer slump over and drop his gun.

"Get them out of here. Shit! Fire! For Christ's sake, get extinguishers! There's a fire here, damn it!" Montoya yelled. "Jesus Christ! It's Tennet!"

Eve nearly fainted.

But Cole was suddenly beside her, pulling her into his arms, kissing her hair, cradling her protectively. "I thought I'd lost you," he said, holding her as if he'd never let go. "I thought . . . Oh God."

Tears sprang to her eyes and she broke down, clinging to him as EMTs and cops streamed into the small room. "I love you," she sobbed against his ear. "Damn it, Cole Dennis, I love you."

"Move it . . . Sir, please," an EMT said. "I need to get in here!"

"Over here! She's bleeding out!" another voice said. "Call Life Flight. Where the hell is the fire department!"

"Life Flight? Wait," Rick Bentz said at Kristi's side. "This is my daughter! She's going to be all right!"

"Move, sir. Get out!"

"But she has to be all right," Bentz insisted. "Kristi!"

"Out of the way, Detective." The EMT was all business. "And get the damned chopper!"

Hours later, Olivia met Bentz at the hospital. "Oh God, Rick," she whispered. "I'm so sorry."

He crushed his wife to him, drank in the smell of her and wanted to break down and bawl like a baby. "She'll be okay," he said and realized it was his mantra, that if he said it over and over long enough, he'd believe it.

Kristi had been in surgery for three hours . . . and he hadn't heard word one. He didn't know the extent of her injuries, just understood that it was bad. Real bad.

Images of her life floated through his brain, and he couldn't even consider what his life would be without her. They'd been through so much together, good times and bad. Sometimes it had been them against the world, other times it had been them against each other.

He knew now that Adam Tennet had been hired by

the department and never should have been. That the guy had sailed through all the tests given him and somehow made it in, literally falling through the cracks in the system to gain employment with Bonita Washington's crime scientists. He was a whiz kid who had fooled everyone. He'd been with the department less than a year and had managed to set his sick, twisted plan into motion.

Was it over now? All the sickness that had come out of Our Lady of Virtues Hospital? Was it truly and finally over?

Only if Kristi survives, because if she doesn't this will be your curse for the rest of your life.

He squeezed Olivia hard and fought the tears as he twined his hands in his wife's lustrous hair.

"Have faith," she whispered as the doors to the operating rooms swung open and a woman not much older than Kristi walked through. Wearing surgical scrubs and a grim expression, she approached.

"You're Rick Bentz?" she asked, and Bentz felt his insides shatter into a million pieces.

"Yes."

"Your daughter's had a tough time of it but she's a fighter. We lost her twice during surgery, but we were able to get her heart started again."

He felt the blood drain from his face as the doctor rattled off the injuries Kristi had sustained and the procedures she'd suffered through. Essentially what it all came down to was that one bullet had hit her in the gut, rupturing several organs, all of which had to be surgically repaired. Another bullet had ricocheted and scraped across her temple, and there was a possibility of brain damage.

"But she'll live?" Rick said.

"We're doing our best."

The doctor left, and Rick slid into a chair. He cradled his head in his hands. "This is my fault. My being a cop, that's the cause."

"You can't blame yourself."

"Like hell."

"Bentz!" Olivia's tone brooked no argument, and when he looked into her eyes, he felt a kind of solace. "She needs you to be strong now. Believe in her. Believe in yourself."

He looked away and cleared his throat. "Okay," he said huskily, though he wasn't certain he could do everything she told him. "So, when did you get so smart?"

One side of her mouth lifted in a tiny smile. "I think it was around the day I agreed to marry you. Yeah, that's when it was. Come on, Detective, let me buy you a cup of coffee. You look like hell!"

"I love you too."

"I know it." She laughed, and damned if he didn't feel better. Somehow they'd get through this. And the doc was right. Kristi was a fighter.

"I don't want to spend a night here," Eve protested from her hospital bed, but Cole wasn't listening. He stood at the window, the night backdropping him. It was late, the hospital was hushed and comfortable, but she'd had enough of being a patient to last her a lifetime.

"It's just for observation. You were lucky the bullet didn't hit any arteries or veins or bones."

"Just a helluva lot of muscle." She was going to be sore for a long time and it looked like a lot more physical therapy was in her future. But she really couldn't complain, not with Kristi Bentz battling for her life.

"So it's really over?" she asked.

He nodded. "It looks like Adam had been gunning for you for a long time. He just needed a psycho who knew you to do most of his dirty work. There was electronic equipment hidden in the mattress of Ronnie's bed, little speakers and a small receiver. I'll bet they find the transmitter at Adam's place."

"I don't want to think about him."

"Good idea." He leaned over the railing and placed a kiss on her forehead. "Why don't you concentrate on me?"

"You know, Counselor, I might just do that," she said and reached upward to wrap her arms around his neck. "I wasn't kidding back at the asylum. I do love you."

"Well, then, darlin', as soon as they release you from this place, you can show me just how much."

"You're on, Counselor," she said around a yawn. "You are definitely on."

EPILOGUE

Three months later

Limping, still using a stupid cane, Eve walked into the hospital room where Kristi Bentz lay comatose. She was breathing on her own, and the doctors expected her to awaken. But so far it hadn't happened.

Rick Bentz sat at his daughter's side, reading aloud to her as he had every day since the incident. He looked up over the tops of his reading glasses but didn't smile.

"I thought I'd spell you," Eve said. "How is she today?"

"Better, I think."

"Good. That's good." She managed a smile and didn't say aloud that she didn't believe him. Kristi looked the same to her, lying on the bed, barely moving.

As Bentz made his way down to the cafeteria for a cup of coffee, Eve took Kristi's hand. "Now tell me," she said, feeling a lump in her throat as she stared at the beautiful, serene woman who was her sister, "How are you really doing?" She linked her fingers with Kristi's, though there was no response. "Well, let me fill you in on what's happened. You know I met Abby, and we get along great. I haven't connected with Zoey yet, but that will probably happen in a few months because Abby and Montoya have set a date. Do you hear me? They're getting married this June. You have to come to the wedding. They're counting on it.

"And, uh, what else? Oh, well . . . I guess we made it official, too. Cole moved in. So far, fingers crossed, we're getting along. . . . Even your dad and Montoya have decided he's an okay guy; at least that's what they tell me. . . . Well, speak of the devil."

Cole appeared in the doorway only a few steps in front of Abby. They talked for a while, including Kristi in the conversation, but of course, she didn't respond.

It seemed so wrong.

But then there had been a lot of wrong in the last few months. They didn't see her eyes flutter beneath her lids and missed the fact that one of her fingers twitched. They had no idea Kristi was dreaming.

But Kristi saw the images, weird, distorted pictures of people she knew going about their daily lives, running errands, walking dogs, shuffling paperwork, mowing lawns, cooking, or whatever. All in vibrant, incredible color.

The image today was of her father. He was riding with Montoya in a cop car. The sirens were shrieking, the lights flashing bright, the radio crackling. They screeched to a halt in front of a Gothic-looking house and jumped out of the vehicle.

Crack!

A bolt of lightning sizzled from the sky, splitting the lone tree in the yard. Both men ducked instinctively, and, when it was over, they straightened. Montoya looked the same, but Bentz's color had faded to black and white. Though he still climbed into the car with Montoya, his color didn't return and he fell over, bleeding black blood onto the street.

Rick Bentz was dead.

"Kristi? Can you hear me?"

Who was that? Olivia?

"Kristi?"

She tried to talk, but only a tiny croak escaped her lips. God, her mouth tasted terrible. And every muscle in her body ached.

"Did you hear that? She's responding! Call the nurse!" Olivia's voice pierced Kristi's thick brain. It was as if she were thinking in a bog, her brain mired in quicksand.

She blinked. Her eyelids felt as if they were cracking.

"Oh my God, she's waking up! Kristi!" Olivia's voice broke with emotion. "Kristi!"

Kristi forced one eye open then squeezed it shut against the bright light. She felt a pain in her gut and her head and heard footsteps walking quickly toward her.

She tried to open her eyes, and this time, wincing and blinking, she was able to fixate, though the images were a little blurry.

Slowly her eyes came into focus.

She was in a hospital, lying half propped up and Olivia was standing over the bed, tears shimmering in her eyes. On a table were several baskets of brightly hued flowers: gold black-eyed Susans, blue bachelor's buttons, pink carnations, and yellow roses.

"Oh honey!" Olivia cried, her blond hair falling over her shoulder. "Bentz! Look who's awake!"

Kristi turned her head to the doorway where her father stood. She gasped. Her blood turned to ice water as fear shot through her.

Backdropped against the smooth green hospital walls, Rick Bentz had no color. His skin and hair and clothing were in shades of black, white and gray. Just like in her dream.

"Thank God," he said, his eyes filling with tears. But as his gaze dropped to her bed sheets they reflected no light. He ran to her and held her tight. "Kristi," he whispered, his voice cracking. "Oh, honey." Tears rained from his eyes, dampening the bedsheets, but Kristi couldn't feel them. And the arms that held her so tightly felt weird, almost weak. The side of her father's face was gray as death.

It was an omen, she was certain of it.

Kristi felt like she might throw up. She'd had the dreams and realized now that they weren't dreams at all; they were glimpses into the future.

In a heartbeat she knew that Rick Bentz was doomed.

Her father was going to die, and he was going to die soon.

Center Point Publishing
600 Brooks Road ● PO Box 1
Thorndike ME 04986-0001 USA

(207) 568-3717

US & Canada:
1 800 929-9108
www.centerpointlargeprint.com